Silly SEASIDE STORIES:

for the fogbound or becalmed or
hopelessly off course

Twisted tidewater tales by Perry A. Hood

Goose River Press
Waldoboro, Maine

Library of Congress Card Number: 2023932524

ISBN: 978-1-59713-257-2

First Printing, 2023

Published by
Goose River Press
3400 Friendship Road
Waldoboro ME 04572
email: gooseriverpress@gmail.com
www.gooseriverpress.com

Dedication

In great appreciation of my brother, Brian,
and his steadfast logistical and moral support,
and of my capable sister-in-law, Carol,
who gamely laughed her way through the typing
(whether at me or at the stories) and offered
many well-conceived suggestions.

Contents

The Launching//1

The Rescue//13

The First Arnold Expedition//27

The Pixilated Pirate//40

The Happening in Gobbler Holler//50

Letters from Woodrow//89

Everyone Loves a Parade//103

Some Days . . .//114

Dulcinea's First (and worst) Cruise//119

Them Things //134

Rails to the Island//158

Spies Among Us: The Possibly Nearly True Story//172

Telemess//188

The Birds and the Bees//193

Harbormaster//212

The Old Man and the *C*//223

The Great Chowdah Bowl//234

Coffin Corner//249

It's in the Mail//266

His Last Boat//286

The *Tortoise* and the Hair//296

Stock Sail//317

The Outcome//330

Silly Seaside Stories

Foreword

These little stories have but two purposes in common: to entertain and amuse. They contain no morals, no attempts to teach lessons or edify in any way, no hidden meanings or universal truths, no allegories, no cryptic messages from beyond the veil, no subliminal suggestions or advertisements, no trans fats (except maybe for one or two of the stories), no communications with or between lurking extraterrestrial forces or prospective invaders. College fiction professors may not like them for any of the above disclaimers that encourage resistance to deeper interpretation.

I do feel obligated, however, to assure readers that no animals were seriously mistreated, injured, or humiliated during the writing of these stories. I cannot in good conscience make the same claim for the humans involved!

Perry Hood
2018

The Launching

A gloriously red sunset this Thursday evening was viewed by Orville Hobson, Mooseport's 78-year-old last remaining boatbuilder, to be a good omen for this coming Saturday's launching.

The object in his thoughts was Orville's final project, the epitome of his 61-year career working with wood. The 58-foot schooner hull gleamed with fresh paint and bright hardware, even in the soft light infiltrating the ancient two-story building shed. Orville was the last of his breed—five generations of boatbuilders of the Hobson clan who slid over 100 fine vessels into the Mooseport harbor on the edge of Passawassatumkeag Bay— just familiarly known as "The Bay" by Mooseporters, and as "Pass By" by most coastal mariners.

Mooseport, Maine, had a stellar history as a ship-building town, reveling in its heyday on The Bay during the late 1800's. It's early Native American appellation had been interpreted as "Moss Landing," but over time that name was corrupted and Anglicized into its current Mooseport, despite the apparent lack of moose in the immediate area. The village once had nearly 2,500 souls; now it had just 129, give or take a few.

Orville, despite his advancing age, had lofted, framed, planked, caulked, and painted the new schooner nearly alone. He'd recruited a local

The Launching

part-time lobsterman, Elroy McCoy, to help when brute force was needed, and he'd arranged for several more helpers for the launching—the first in Mooseport for nearly 30 years. In fact, few folks remaining in town could clearly remember the previous one, and most of that launching crew were deceased or had moved away. Orville was certain that he could organize and supervise the task despite a foggy recollection of the necessary details. He expected the collective memories of his current volunteers to be of assistance; later experience demonstrated that thought to be a bit optimistic...

Orvillle's building shed, a family heirloom, was just about 80 feet from the water's edge. The building and launching ways were built entirely of wood—massive timbers of oak, hemlock, and pine separated from their native forest during generations before and no longer in the peak of repair. Underpinnings of pilings were mostly buried in soil, mud, and/or water and were virtually uninspectable. Orville thought that they would suffice for this last launching. After all, they had seen much larger, heavier vessels slide down their ways. What could possibly go wrong?

The next day (it had to be a Friday the 13th) dawned gray and fogbound as was common along The Bay this time of year. Like a typical summer day, the fog would lift as the sun warmed the air, and the southwest breeze would push the remaining fogbank a few miles out into the Gulf of Maine. Orville had a lot to do this day to get ready for tomorrow's festivities.

On his mentally preserved chore list were rounding up his volunteer crew, greasing the ways, moving the schooner out of the shed and into the open air, arranging for Homer Gastineau's tugboat to stand by at the town dock, checking on the town band and refreshment committee preparations, assembling the necessary tools, confirming the presence of the obligatory bottle of champagne, reassuring himself that the vessel owner and daughter (the 15-year-old nearsighted pitcher on Mooseport's coed softball team) would be on time, etc. There was much to do, too much to accomplish without delegating some responsibilities.

With that in mind, Orville had appointed Harvey Harmon to grease the skids—the ways upon which the new schooner would soon glide gracefully into the harbor. To do so, he had to go up into the shed's loft and retrieve the sealed buckets of lard-like lubricant that last saw the light of day at least 30 years before. The loft's sole light source was a waterside round window, and there were many buckets, boards, barrels, molds, odd hardware and fastenings, several irritated bats, and the dust of several decades.

Harvey waded through the murk and rubble, selected what appeared to be a few likely buckets, and carefully descended the loft staircase with one in each hand. No labels identified the contents; he depended upon Orville's description to make his selection—not the best strategy as it turned out.

The pig in the poke, so to speak, was Orville's great-grandfather's experimentation with laminating timbers well before Orville's entry into the world. Those early efforts resulted in several semi-successful glue concoctions, most of which were eventually ferreted away for posterity, out of sight, out of mind…in buckets in the shed loft.

With the greasing project delegated, Orville turned his now-fragmented attention to Neville Carter's assignments: setting up a temporary stand for the christening dignitaries, another for the band, and then checking the long-standing docks that flanked the launching ways. Resting upon pilings of uncertain vintage, they would be covered with townsfolk tomorrow and deserved a cursory inspection…which Neville happily would forget to do.

Next came the procurement of the bottle of christening fluid. Trouble was, Mooseport had remained a "dry" town long after the ending of prohibition. Like many a Maine coastal settlement, however, it had a fine tradition of importing spirits and ignoring the temperance movement despite the official words on the books—which the local constabulary was reluctant to enforce.

Ol' Pete Cabella was designated to be the specialist to obtain the necessary bottle, given his lengthy history of knowledge and expertise on the subject. Orville was relieved to see the green bottle in Pete's shaky hand, totally unaware that Pete had managed to drain the bottle and replace the cork, "just in case" the bubbly might "go bad" before taking its critical role in the christening.

Orville next sought out the owner, who would convey the name of his new schooner, and then the owner's girl, Cassie, who was to fasten the champagne bottle to the red ribbon firmly attached to the boat's bowsprit and swing it into the bow to formally bestow the vessel's name. Pete would see that Cassie was provided with said bottle.

The conversation about the schooner's name took place outdoors, on the dock by the ways. Orville was just trying to finish up a hastily assembled sandwich, which fell apart as he turned to face the owner.

"The name I wish for my new boat is *Magic Moose*," the owner intoned as a raucous flock of seagulls fought over the remains of Orville's lunch. The new vessel was to be named after a then-popular children's story, *The Magic Moose*. Against the gulls' squawkings, however, Orville heard *Manic Moose*, and so dutifully recorded that nomen on the launching invitations and carved it into the fancy nameboard affixed to the schooner's transom…and thus *Manic Moose* she regretfully remained.

Those details duly checked off, Orville then moved on to Homer, whose bay tugboat was to be close at hand during the launching for at least two reasons. First, once the schooner was afloat, it would not be ready to move under its own power. The tug, appropriately called *Beast*, would catch up with the schooner, take her lines, and guide her to the spectator-filled wharf adjacent to the ways.

The second possible function for the *Beast* was to provide some pull if the schooner should hesitate on her way to the briny, a not uncommon occurrence during launchings. Some vessels did seem to balk at times on their short journey into as-yet untested waters, and the *Beast* would be ready to act quickly should Orville signal with a predetermined seaward wave that Homer's charge should take a strain on the discreetly placed hawser.

His various contacts and chores nearly done, Orville then went to visit Nettie and Lettie Ferguson, spinster twin sisters who reportedly were descendants of the town's founding fathers. Nettie was the chairwoman of Mooseport's official Celebrations & Festivals Refreshment Committee, while Lettie's role was as prime mover and leader of the Mooseport Community Band. Both were heavily involved in preparations for the big day—or any big day—and were expecting to check in with Orville on that Friday. All was going well—the pieces were falling into place.

A few words about the band might be in order. Lettie's recruits ranged in age from 16 to 92, and the composition of the group was totally dependent upon each member's questionable skills and instrument of choice. Hence the band of 11 included Horace Halpern on the bass drum, Charlie Strong on the fife, Sarah Caldwell on the bagpipes, portly Beulah Smith on the sousaphone, Teena Moss on the trombone, and six others with violin, oboe, bugle, kazoo, accordion, and ocarina among them. What the assemblage lacked in technique it made up for with reckless enthusiasm!

The Fergusons now checked off on Orville's mental list, he ran out of ideas and energy simultaneously, and figured that he was due for a nightcap before ending his productive day. He didn't bother to check on Harvey's greasing work, nor on Neville's efforts with the viewing stand, christening scaffold, and dock inspections. He assumed that all were in order.

Orville's imbibing buddy was his cousin, Kincaid Hobsen; Orville usually identified him as his "next of kin." Kincaid had a steady connection with Ol' Pete and was undoubtedly Pete's most reliable customer. Kincaid also was the local game warden, a part-time position of dubious distinction, given Mooseport's native wildlife: seagulls, cormorants, a few harbor seals, and sundry sometimes-pet dogs and cats. In his more lucid moments, however, Kincaid enjoyed the notoriety and responsibility that came with the title. The nearest "real" game warden, Jasper Ste. Amand, was based in the county seat of sparsely populated Harrison County, Forreston. He supposedly supervised Kincaid's position, but he was best known for his accepting gratuities for being at the wrong end of the county when poachers were afoot.

Taking into consideration his perceived self-importance, Kincaid was miffed that he wasn't included in the planning or execution of the launching celebration. While he and Orville sipped and chatted that early Friday evening, he devised a clever (he thought) scheme to make a contribution to the next day's festivities. What Mooseport's launching of the proud schooner *Manic Moose* needed was the presence of a genuine moose! In the classic annals of understatements, Kincaid's thought, "I bet Orville will be surprised!" would be unsurpassed.

Kincaid excused himself from drowsy Orville and hastily hit the road for Forreston and Jasper Ste. Amand's humble homestead on the Mooseport side of town. Jasper was at home, suitably lubricated for a Friday night, and agreed to round up his tranquilizer gun and darts and set off into the woods to try to bag a moose, figuratively speaking. Jasper knew his woods and had seen many moose by a certain stream near a certain saltlick—Jasper did not share his knowledge with many people, and *especially* not with strangers or writers!

The 1200-pound bull moose never knew what hit him—sleepy time came on too quickly. A great struggle ensued, however, to position the somnolent creature on the bed of Kincaid's half-ton flatbed truck—good thing the bed had no side railings. Neither Kincaid nor Jasper had any clear idea of how long the moose would be in dreamland, but Jasper was almost sure that the moose would regain consciousness in time for the launching at Saturday's 11:30 a.m. high tide. Both Orville and Kincaid (and the recumbent moose) slept well for the rest of that night.

Part II

Dawn again made its appearance at the expected hour on Saturday the 14th. The fog was light and fleeting, the breeze a mere zephyr, and the tide past its ebb, slowly creeping up the waiting shoreline to play its part in the day's events.

Orville dragged himself out of bed and the clanging of his wind-up alarm clock, checked the time (6:30 a.m.), and headed downstairs for a double dose of caffeine to quiet his nagging headache. While he shook off the hangover and anxieties of the previous day, Harvey was also up to do his part: grease the ways and use the ways-side winch to ease the schooner out of the building shed. It needed to be in the open to participate in its own christening. Orville was to help, along with his other pre-launch volunteers.

Down at the boatyard, preparations proceeded apace. Bunting was hung, docks swept, refuse picked up, parking space cleared (with a VIP spot for the owner and his guests), and some of the shores removed from under soon-to-be *Manic Moose* so that she could slide down the ways out of her natal home.

Having a vague hypothesis about the function of the grease, Harvey

The Launching

pried off the long-encrusted lids, grabbed an old brush from the workbench, and went to work to slop the syrupy liquid onto the heavy skid timbers. "More is better," Harvey speculated, so he was very generous with his application. By 8:30 a.m., his diligence was rewarded with two shiny wooden rails on which *Manic Moose* would soon glide, albeit grudgingly.

By 10 a.m. the heavy schooner had been eased out of its birthplace, although the force required seemed to belie the liberal spread of the necessary grease. All involved in the move noticed, and some remarked on, the unusual texture and odor of the presumed lubricant, but it was universally attributed to the long hibernation in the sealed buckets stored in the loft.

As the thin mist cleared and the warming sun began to heat the day, Orville noticed with some concern that the erstwhile grease appeared to be losing its gloss and becoming firmer. "Perhaps Harvey should put on a second coat between the boat and the water," crossed Orville's mind, but then other distractions pushed that thought aside—there were other developments underway.

By 9:30 a.m. the spectators were starting to trickle in, the refreshment tables were collecting their potluck dishes and platters, and the band was just leaving its practice quarters after a brief and spirited warmup session.

Homer fueled up the *Beast* and navigated across the harbor to position the tug just offshore of Orville's launching ways. Homer picked up the buoyed hawser and made ready to haul away, in case his assistance should become necessary. He was certain that he soon would be rafting up with the freshly baptized *Manic Moose*.

By 11:15 a.m. the tidal rise had reached its apogee, and all seemed ready. The owner's out-of-town guests had not yet arrived, however. When they finally showed up hours later, they recounted blowing a tire and bending a wheel as a result of an encounter with one of the many potholes in the one state highway leading into Mooseport.

Their absence at the launching left a significant void in the VIP parking area, a void that reassured Kincaid that he was welcome when he pulled into the emptiness with his flatbed and its still-snoozing load. His arrival went unnoticed for at least two reasons: attention was directed toward the christening platform which Cassie was about to ascend, and Kincaid had pulled in cab-first, which essentially shielded his cargo from easy view.

Cassie was nervous. With shaky hands she had tied the bottle earlier to the red ribbon, noticing that it seemed lighter in weight than she had expected. She mentally observed, "I'll remember this day for the rest of my life," a thought that would prove to be profoundly prophetic.

Now she was making her way through the crowd, then starting up the five steps. A stray hair caught her attention as she reached the first step. She quickly tried to brush it away, knocking off her glasses in the process. Not wanting to delay the show, she bravely put a foot forward onto the second step and heard the telltale crunch of her glasses underfoot.

"So much for those," crossed her mind as she carried on to the top of the platform and grasped the hanging bottle firmly. She had expected her dad to be close by on the platform as well, but he instead had elected to be aboard his new vessel as the proud owner (not uncommon for ship launchings), along with several of the village's dignitaries. Bare seconds after Cassie's ascent the mayor delivered a few appropriate remarks to the attentive (barely) crowd, followed by a short statement from the owner to introduce Cassie and echo the historic nature of this event.

When 20 years hence the long out-of-print *History of Shipbuilding in Mooseport, Maine* is revised and updated, the tale concerning the building and launching of the schooner *Manic Moose* will have garnered an entire chapter unto itself. Many details below will not have been entered into that text, but the historic, and hysteric, nature of the launching will have been dryly summarized.

As noted above, Cassie had the christening bottle firmly in hand. As she solemnly intoned the requisite phrase, "I christen thee *Manic Moose!*" the band swung into a lusty and barely recognizable rendition of "The Star-Spangled Banner," and Cassie swung the bottle mightily toward the bow of the schooner…and missed.

Amidst the cheers of the audience and the cacophony of the National Anthem, three things seemed to happen almost simultaneously. The moose, apparently easing out of its tranquil(ized) state, and apparently roused by the din, staggered to its feet, leaped clear of the truck cab and made a beeline for the refreshment table.

The moose's charge not yet fully registering, the assembled mass fixated on the swing of the bottle as it described approximately 190° of a circle and then parted company with its red tether. Vertically airborne now, it reached its zenith and resumed its course in a downward plunge, headed straight for the cluster of personages on *Manic Moose*'s foredeck, owner included, all of whom dove for cover from the unexpected air raid.

At virtually the same time, the launching crew members were trying to drive out the last of the vessel-restraining wedges to get the show on the road, so to speak. The lack of progress was clearly noticeable—thanks to great-grandfather's heat-curing glue, the *Manic Moose*'s wedges were firmly glued to the cradling shores, which, in turn, were cemented to the timbers of the launching ways. *Manic Moose* was not going to budge, unlike the berserk bull moose who was now scattering all in his path of destruction, refreshment tables and serving ladies included.

Orville, seeing the rampaging animal barreling his way, waved his arms frantically to try to head off further disaster.

Homer, out on the *Beast* and unaware of landbound events, understood Orville's arm waving to be his signal for engaging the *Beast*'s power to facilitate the launch. "Big boat, big power," flitted across Homer's consciousness as he signaled for full throttle from her 1,500-horsepower diesel and six-foot propeller.

The hawser tightened and took up the slack and strain, but the *Manic Moose* did not budge...at first. While the *Beast* churned the harbor waters to a murky froth, two other things resulted: the violent stream of water undercut the shoreline under the piers, the supporting, rotten pilings gave way, and about 80 unsuspecting witnesses were unceremoniously dumped into the frigid harbor. Meanwhile, the crowd nearest the ways and building shed became aware of a nearly imperceptible (at first) movement of said ways, boat, and shed toward the harbor—movement which shortly became obvious enough to excite those present not currently swimming for their lives. Shed and ways had parted company with their decayed underpinnings.

As the wooden mass gained some momentum, Homer glimpsed only the shoreward movement of the schooner and continued to apply *Beast*'s energy to the task, pleased with the presumed results. The bulk of the crowd who were not swimming became instantly engaged in moving away from the ways and shed—running for safety might be a more accurate assessment.

There is little safety near an agitated bull moose, however, and only Lettie's pummeling the critter with frosted cupcakes made it pause for a few moments, enough time for nearby persons to steer clear. The moose then apparently halted long enough to retrieve some of the cupcakes for a morning snack (does a moose have a sweet tooth?), allowing more spectators time to retreat.

Meanwhile, the movement of boat/ways/shed, still well glued together, was going swimmingly! The *Manic Moose* reached the harbor edge just as the dignitary party aboard was recovering its wits and dignity after the bottle-bombing, resuming their vertical orientation just long enough to be dumped overboard as the heavy schooner settled some, broke the grip of the not-grease, slewed sideways from the current, and being largely unballasted as yet, gracefully capsized before eventually righting herself.

The *Beast* wasn't done yet, though. Homer experienced one of his coughing fits just as the *Manic Moose* took her roll. The *Beast* continued on, temporarily oblivious to the shed creeping up to the shoreline and collapsing into the harbor right astern of a rocking *Manic Moose*...at which time Homer became acutely aware of the situation and managed to cut the *Beast*'s power.

Part III

The launch of the *Manic Moose* made the national news that Saturday night, right after the extensive coverage of Hurricane Homer (coincidence?).

Amazingly, no one was killed, and resultant injuries were few and minor. The moose eventually extricated itself from the scene when the cupcakes ran out. Homer and Orville made up after a time, but Kincaid remained *persona non grata* in town for several months. Cassie got new glasses and never did forget the christening—she got a kick, though, out of seeing her father tossed into the harbor by his own blasted boat.

Manic Moose suffered minor scrapes and bruises, and after suitable repairs and commissioning, was sold by the owner to become part of Maine's "dude schooner" fleet—and a legend in her own time. Orville was never the same—not that he ever was anyway!

The Rescue

"It's an Outrage!" quipped the salesman as he slapped the side of the shiny Boston Whaler's topsides. "And it's unsinkable!"

"So was the *Titanic*," Chauncey Franklin DeWart III (hereafter referred to as CFD III) wryly observed with an obvious air of disdain. "Do you really want a tender like this?"

"I'm not sure, son," Chauncey Franklin DeWart II (CFD II) replied, "But I do want another one for the *Sovereign Seas* (the family's 158-foot yacht). "Right now, I'm just looking."

"Well, you need to get me a new boat, too. *Dollar Dinghy* (a 26-foot Riva speedboat) is too small," CFD III whined.

"We'll talk about it after your birthday this weekend. You're going to like your surprise," CFD II assured his only son.

"I'd better, after that dismal year at Moulton Academy, Father."

Father and son coldly exited the showroom and drove back to the summer "cottage" in stony silence. "Edgewater," the historic family summer compound, was comprised of 15 rooms, three stories high, a gate house, boat house, guest house, and a five-car garage, all situated on 8.6 acres of shorefront on Clam Cove, Maine. The cove was too small and shallow to accommodate *Sovereign Seas*, so the yacht was berthed in Portland, and the family commuted to it by one of its three tenders.

CFD II was a self-made man, if you count inheriting 300 million dollars and parlaying it to over two billion during the previous 30 years. CFD III was the only heir; CFD II's wife reluctantly became pregnant, but later commented about sex: "Tried it once. Didn't like it." She also said the same about being pregnant, giving birth, and raising a child. The fact is, though, that the family governess did most of the raising, abetted by occasional stabs at fatherhood by CFD II, not all of which were appreciated by CFD III.

CFD III, on his part, was 12 years old, arrogant, inquisitive, bright, and independent (strong-willed)...and did I mention spoiled? In some ways he was a chip off the old block, matching the chip on his shoulder.

Around the corner coastwise was the village of Stonarbor, a contraction of sorts of its original appellation of "Stone Harbor." Stonarbor was a working port, dependent for its meager existence on fishing, lobstering, and clamming. Among its inhabitants were triplet lobstermen of the Davis clan. When first brought into the world, these babies were the only triplets ever born in the vicinity, quite a sensation at the time. Their mother, Frances, when asked for the names to be entered on the birth certificates, displayed her total lack of imagination and ancestral regard; Tom, Dick, and Harry they became. Much later they agreed that their mom could have done worse: Moe, Larry, and Curly were thankfully avoided.

The brothers grew into strapping young men of the sea—athletic, strong, successful in their work, and fiercely competitive...with each other in particular. Also, they became diehard pranksters, not disguising their exploits from public view. In fact, they often relished their notoriety.

A few examples may suffice: Tom once fastened a 30-foot line from the midpoint of the keel of Dick's skiff to one chain holding the floating dinghy dock, then watched with mock concern as Dick tried to row out to his moored lobster boat and couldn't get beyond a certain point no matter how hard he rowed. All three brothers participated in the lobster boat races held at various harbors during the summer months. Harry once dove under Tom's boat and wrapped a large plastic bag filled with popcorn around its propeller. When Tom put his engine in forward gear, the bag slowed its motion and all of the popcorn came loose to the surface, attracting a huge flock of seagulls that descended upon unsuspecting Tom and his boat.

Another time, Dick put a dab of superglue inside each of Harry's sea boots, then drew a small crowd to watch Harry try to remove them at the end of his working day. Most pranks resulted in little serious damage, except maybe to a brother's dignity at the time.

The townsfolk rarely mingled with the wealthy summer folks who occupied seasonal properties along the coast. There usually was little reason to do so—it was the hired help who made occasional forays into the village to purchase lobsters, or some necessary article of hardware or food item. Neither CFD II nor CFD III had ever set foot in Stonarbor.

At Edgewater, CFD II was checking on the weather forecast for the coming Sunday, CFD III's birthday. The son became intensely curious and began to pester his father for an explanation. After being badgered by his son nearly nonstop for two days, CFD II finally yielded in self-defense.

"For your birthday I have arranged a hot-air balloon flight for us for the day. We can't go, though, if the weather is not cooperative. We may have to postpone the flight for a day or two," CFD II timidly explained.

"The weather *better* cooperate," the son huffed. "We're the DeWarts!"

Despite CFD III's protestations, the weather did *not* settle sufficiently until that next Tuesday, at which time father and son had baskets of food items (healthy snacks, lunches, and drinks), jackets, etc., loaded into the limo and then set off for New Chesney where the hot-air balloon business called home.

Upon their arrival in New Chesney, at the field which until recently doubled as a cow pasture, they were greeted profusely by Farley Foghorn (honest, that's his name), the balloonist/businessman and former carny (carnival entrepreneur and promoter). Farley fully expected his current endeavor to "reach new heights," he was fond of boasting.

Ever curious, CFD III had a flood of questions about the balloon, its mechanisms, functioning, durability, range, and so on. In response, he found out some valuable information: the gondola (basketlike box) under the balloon could carry up to six people (today there would be only three—father, son, and Farley); the various items the DeWarts had brought would add the equivalent weight of a fourth person; the burner mechanism's controls and fuel supply; miscellaneous tools and the gear that anchored the balloon once fully inflated (which would happen momentarily), and—Farley's own invention—the quick-release mechanism, which would free the balloon from its four ground tethers and allow it to ascend.

While father and Farley were at Farley's office trailer, son wandered over to check out the balloon and oversee the chauffeur's loading of the food and clothing items into the gondola.

Farley was on his ham radio, checking the weather conditions with his regular spotters all along the coast and up to 20 miles inland. The normal summer wind pattern for this part of Maine tends to start with a calm early morning, followed by a slowly building southwest breeze. Since the coast of Maine roughly runs southwest to northeast, not considering its hundreds of rivers, bays, coves, peninsulas, and islands, both Farley and CFD II anticipated a leisurely drift northeastward...but the son had other ideas.

CFD III checked surreptitiously to see his father and Farley in deep discussion around the radio, probably talking weather or money, CFD III guessed. He silently slid over the side of the gondola, opened two of the food baskets, then simultaneously triggered the burner and the quick-release mechanism. The response wasn't as dramatic as he had hoped, but it was predictable: the balloon slowly started to rise.

Farley must have detected the movement out of the corner of his eye. His reaction was instantaneous—a deeply blue curse, followed by a lumbering dash in the direction of his ascending aircraft. Close on his heels came CFD II, puffing mightily from the uncommon (and undignified) exertion. Both men were greeted by a barrage of apples, bananas, and walnuts wielded by a whooping and exhilarated and, fortunately inaccurate, CFD III!

"Up, up, and away!" CFD III crowed. "Master of my own fate! Pilot of my own aircraft!" CFD III was elated to be free of his father and gave no thought whatsoever about how the day might end.

Back on the ground, however, his father was frantically pacing and mumbling, while Farley seemed far more concerned about the fate of his balloon...and business. Both agreed that quick action was needed. Farley picked up his radio mike and put out the word to his many contacts downwind. CFD II abruptly grabbed the mike out of Farley's hand and blurted into it, "Ten thousand dollars for the safe return of my son! No, make that $50,000! Catch that balloon!"

The radio waves crackled with the news of the reward, and quickly carried over to marine VHF channel 16, the emergency channel that all vessels at sea are required to monitor. Listening in were several hundred commercial fishermen and lobstermen, as well as dozens of pleasure boaters and a few ships on coastal voyages. Tom, Dick, and Harry were no exception and, unlike many others, they were willing to set aside their daily routines to keep a lookout and perhaps join the hunt. Tom was busy pulling one of Dick's trawls (string of lobster traps) to place rubber chickens in each trap. Individually, each of the brothers reasoned, "Fifty thousand dollars is more than I make during most years. I'm gonna go for it!"

CFD III was enjoying the ride immensely. He could see the ocean to the east once the balloon cleared the trees and inland hills. His course would bring him over shoreside villages and occasional rivers, coves, or islands. While ascending, he toyed with the burner controls and had some success controlling his altitude. He also took inventory of the gondola's contents. Besides the food containers, CFD III located more gas cylinders, several lengths of rope, a four-pronged grappling hook, and a flask that Farley had secreted away for special occasions (like whenever he felt thirsty).

CFD III had never tasted whiskey. After a couple of sips, he decided that he hated the taste, but liked the warm feeling that came over him shortly afterward. He'd save the rest for later.

The colorful balloon was not hard to spot. Messages came in to Farley frequently, but as yet no one had come up with a concrete plan to retrieve it and its human cargo. Suggestions, though, ranged from "shoot it down" to "let it run out of gas," ignoring the fact that it could eventually set down at sea. CFD II was confident that his money would provide a solution. Maybe he was right.

People were climbing steeples in churches en route, hoping to snag the passing gondola. Kites were tried with the idea of entangling and retrieving the wayward balloon. No one on the ground realized that the pirate captain aboard was prepared to repel all boarders—he was having too much fun! One RC airplane with a mounted camera came close but met with a fusillade of apples and Brazil nuts, and ultimately was shot down. "Take no prisoners" became CFD III's new motto. The offer by an enthusiastic archer to snag the balloon with a tethered arrow was instantly declined as being a bit risky. Law enforcement refused to get involved, because CFD III technically was not lost—everyone knew where he was— and he did not seem to be in imminent jeopardy. CFD II hesitantly agreed with that assessment but boosted the proffered reward to $75,000.

Tracking the balloon's flight was not a problem; the chaos caused on the ground, though, definitely was. As the reward amount escalated, so did the frenzied efforts to keep up with CFD III's freedom flight and devise ways to bring same to ground. Even winter storms hadn't resulted in so many auto accidents; many intersections became impassable. Fortunately, the balloon drifted slowly, as did the pursuing traffic.

After three hours of overland pursuit, a complication presented itself. Parts of Maine's coastline consist of lengthy peninsulas, the ends of which could be miles from the primary coastal track, U.S. Route 1. CFD III's flight was now along the coast, leapfrogging many of those headlands and frustrating those chasing the balloon's flight by road. The game now seemed to be up to those on the water, and there were dozens with the desire, including the triplets from downwind Stonarbor. It didn't hurt either that CFD II recently had upped the ante to 100,000 Simoleans.

Downeast in Stonarbor, the three brothers set to work, each determined to beat the competition, including his brothers, to the prize. Tom set aside the rubber chickens and thrust the throttle to the max as he pointed his boat southwestward to try to pick up the trail. Both Dick and Harry hurriedly made port to drop off their respective catches and then turn southwest also, along with dozens of others. This was a time when having a fast lobster boat might pay off bigtime!

It's been suggested that "great minds think alike." The same may be true for mediocre minds as the triplets were shortly to demonstrate. From the radio chatter related to the balloon's recent trajectory, it seemed likely that it would pass over the tip of Kennisett Point. Located there was a rocky promontory about 150 feet above the abutting ocean. Each of the brothers reached the same conclusion. While other boat traffic continued beyond, each of the brothers dodged the outlying ledges to tie up at any available pier, all but the Kennisett town dock being privately owned.

All three vaguely noticed the nearby presence of the other two, but

The Rescue

haste ruled Tom and Dick, while Harry tiptoed along the shore with a wrench in hand and quietly removed the sparkplugs from his brothers' engines—then he ran up the hill. Tom took up a position to the west of the crest, Dick to the east, and Harry to the northeast, each sure that he held the best interception position. Eventually, the balloon floated into view, the gondola no more than ten feet above the peak of the Point, but 50 feet seaward of it.

Tom was the first to realize that the balloon would be out of reach. He immediately headed for the opposite shore where all three boats were docked. Quick work at Dick's and Harry's boats resulted in loops of heavy line around each rudder, securely tied to a piling closer to shore.

The other two brothers made tracks for their respective boats, Dick intercepted and chased by an incensed dock/landowner with a broom and sundry colorful epithets.

Upon reaching their respective vessels, it became abundantly clear that none of the three would be going anywhere soon, furious landowner notwithstanding. Despite their competitive propensities, each man had to admit reluctantly that some cooperative teamwork might be necessary. If successful, they would split the reward money in thirds...and draw straws for the odd penny.

Their plan focused on using only one boat—Dick's, since it often was the fastest. They would shadow the errant balloon, try to identify a high point downwind, and attempt to intercept the balloon there somehow if it drifted low enough. The other two boats were rafted together and left anchored in Kennisett Cove.

Dick weaved his way around the ledges, then put the throttle down to flash his way through the thinning throng of boats still trailing the balloon. Tom and Harry, meanwhile, were poring over the coastline charts to try to determine the next likely interception point. Given current wind speed and direction, and the balloon's apparent course, a clear possibility presented itself.

The earliest charts of that part of the coast, from the 1700's, identified the spot as "Wreck on It." Later charts had perhaps distorted the name into "Reckoning Rock," and locals now referred to the ledge as "The Reckoning." The islet was all stone, about 120 by 60 yards, and by itself stood about 40 feet above the normal high tides. Most significant, though, was the 85-foot tower of the now-automated lighthouse, once a manned coast guard station. The light was a flashing white, visible as far as 15 miles at sea under ideal conditions. If Tom's and Harry's calculations were correct, the balloon might pass right over that structure.

While Tom and Harry were engaged in their computations, CFD III had begun to do some of his own. He was enjoying his observations of cars, people, and boats appearing to follow his progress, surmising his father's involvement somehow. Frankly, he was getting a kick out of all the frantic activity! He took stock of his current situation, though: plenty of food and clothing, a dwindling fuel supply, a nearly empty flask ("darn!"), and a drift that seemed closer and closer to the cold and unwelcoming Gulf of Maine. "No need to panic yet," he reasoned, but clearly some action on his part might be necessary soon.

Up ahead at some distance CFD III could see what appeared to be a vertical stick in the sea. Unsure of its nature, CFD III thought that if he came close enough, he could perhaps snag it with the grapnel tied to the end of one of the pieces of rope at his disposal—chancy, but worth a try.

Below, the triplets were making time toward that same stick in the sea—the lighthouse on The Reckoning. Dick would stay with the boat to fend off other rivals, while Tom and Harry would take a fishing pole, usually rigged for catching bluefin tuna, and climb the lighthouse tower to try to hook bigger game—the $100,000 balloon. All three agreed (readers:

underline the *greed* part) that this strategy would provide their best chance for success.

CFD III rigged his grappling line and hung it over the side of the gondola, the grapnel dangling about 60 feet below his perch. Dick and his brothers were closing fast on the prominent rock, outdistancing the other vessels still in the hunt.

Serendipity smiled as CFD III's grapnel anchor found its mark on the railing surrounding the light at the top of the tower. Noticing the pursuit craft below, CFD III decided to wait out whatever might happen next, have a sandwich, and drain the flask. The balloon seemed to be in no hurry to continue on.

Landing along The Reckoning was tricky at best. The old Coast Guard float on the landward side was long gone, as were the pilings that fixed the dock in place. What did remain was the concrete abutment that used to support the float's gangway. Dick eased his lobster boat in as close as he dared, at which time Tom and Harry each made a successful leap for safety. Dick then stood off and positioned his craft so that no other vessel could come near.

As expected, the door to the tower was padlocked, but battering by a sizeable rock eliminated that impediment to progress; no lock was worth $100,000! Tom threw open the door and started up the stairs, but was tackled immediately by Harry, who darted ahead and tried to bound up the staircase. The struggle continued up to the first landing.

"Get out of my way!"

"No! You get out of *my* way!"

"That money is *mine*! I don't care what we said!"

"Well, if *you* don't care, then *I* don't care. I'll get to him first!"

"You won't give any of the money to Dick if you win."

"You won't either. You'll keep it all for yourself!"

The words flew, tempers raged, and wrestling continued up to the second landing and beyond. At the top of the staircase it was Tom who tackled the lunging Harry and clambered past to gain footing on the narrow walkway surrounding the light itself. He spun around to avoid Harry's outstretched arm and dove for the grapnel embracing the railing.

"Got it!" Tom exclaimed as a sudden puff jostled the balloon and freed the hook, which Tom was not about to release. Both Dick and Harry watched in horror and, to be honest, some amusement, as Tom sailed off the walkway looking like a two-legged fish at the end of a line. With rocks and 55-degree ocean below, Tom wasn't inclined to let go, at least not yet. The best he could do was hitch himself up the rope a bit to rest a foot in the curve of the grapnel. He was too exhausted from his struggle with Harry, and from fear, to do much else.

CFD III soon realized that he was on the loose again and that Nova Scotia might be his next stop—if he could make it that far. Also, the balloon seemed heavier somehow, and he'd never reach land again with extra weight aboard. His attempt to retrieve the grapnel and line was met with firm resistance. A look over the side confirmed his worst fear; he had gained a passenger somehow who was now unwelcome ballast that had to go.

With no thought to Tom's predicament or safety, CFD III rained down a deluge of fruit and nuts to try to dislodge his unwitting guest. Tom, on the receiving end, was totally taken aback and did his best to dodge the descending missiles; he was not about to let go, being at least 100 feet above the waves. Dick was in hot pursuit, having watched Tom's take-off, and having left Harry abandoned for the time being on The Reckoning.

CFD III's cruise could not last forever. Tom, despite his pummeling from above, was not about to release his grasp of the rope, and CFD III eventually ran out of ammunition, the empty flask being the last missile to see action. An uneasy truce ensued.

The balloon's altitude crept lower and lower as the late day cooled, to a level at which Tom imagined hungry sharks watching with eager anticipation, eyes upward. Dick had had to give up the chase temporarily to refuel, as had the last of the other opportunists. All poor Harry could do was sit on The Reckoning and wait, with an occasional futile beckoning wave toward a passing vessel.

CFD III stared ahead toward the downwind horizon—or what used to be that. The ocean seemed to disappear into a cotton haze. Tom, too, noticed the change, but recognized it immediately for what it was: a thick bank of fog. Looking down, the waves seemed ever closer, maybe now 30 feet below his boots.

Unbeknownst to both parties aloft, in that bank of obscurity was the racing fleet of the Mudstuc Ocean Racing And Sailing Society (M.O.R.A.S.S.), the lead boats about to turn the marks protecting vessels from the perils of Goode Reef.

That ocean hazard was named after a little-known Anglo-Hispanic sailor, Juan Juno Goode, the man who in 1610 recorded the first grounding there—and the second, third, and fourth. That honor gained him the coveted Persistence Award presented by the Windsor Royal Expedition Club (W.R.E.C.)—mostly because all four groundings occurred within a one-week span.

The M.O.R.A.S.S. regatta was held one weekend every four years, allowing one year to prepare for the upcoming races and three to repair damages from the previous ones. It seems that the organization, located not far from Lubec, Maine, was named for a small native people, the Mudstuc Nation. Back in the early 1600's, the Mudstucs sent out a raiding party to attack the recent settlement at Popham on the Kennebec River. The party eventually made landfall at what is now Yarmouth, Nova Scotia, leading to their first recognizing their rare, indigenous form of dyslexia.

In honor of the intrepid Mudstucs, the race requirements included the provision that each racing boat's navigator must be blindfolded throughout the race.

Goode Reef was marked by two buoys, both of which had to be kept to starboard. Nun "RU1" guarded the eastern, seaward side of the shoal, while can "UC" was located south and a bit to the west of the reef.

Among the racing craft, 17 of them on this day, were an additional number of vessels of the M.O.R.A.S.S. simply along for a day sail. Several years before, the club had recognized its two distinct factions: the diehard racers (dubbed the Mores) and the cruisers (the Asses). All were out in force in the fog.

Tom thought he was catching glimpses of shadows moving through the mist, but his tearing eyes could have been playing tricks on him. CFD III, meanwhile, had decided to lighten his load by jettisoning the empty gas cylinders if his balloon should sink much lower.

Hot air balloon met chilly fog just south of Goode Reef, and just as the M.O.R.A.S.S. was beginning to round the treacherous reef—not a for-tuitous coincidence. Loud voices of protest penetrated the fog as empty gas cylinders rained down on unsuspecting crews who were trying to change sails and watch for obscured buoys.

Tom watched with quickly mounting terror as his body soared past one sailboat after another to finally fetch up face first on the mast of the sloop *Charmed*. The grappling hook held fast on the spreaders, resulting in a sudden dive by the CFD III-carrying gondola onto the deck of the 60-foot *Welcome*. The balloon itself carried on a few yards further to collapse over the entire yawl, *Serendipity*, virtually guaranteeing the resultant collision between that vessel and the close-aboard sloop, *Tipsy*, illustrating the old mariner's maxim: "a collision at sea can ruin your whole day."

The Rescue

The resultant confusion drew attention away from the nearby rocks, onto which all four above-named vessels now found their way, emulating Juan's much earlier exploit. Dick cautiously caught up with the splintered M.O.R.A.S.S. and rescued his bruised and beaten brother.

The $100,000 reward money, you ask? It ultimately provided a down payment on the boat repairs, insurance claims, and lawyers' fees—the balances of which were deducted from CFD III's inheritance!

The First Arnold Expedition

*The story below is a work of fiction. Only the names, dates, locations, events, and situations have been changed to prevent (that should read **present**—Ed.) historical inaccuracies. History sometimes misses things.*

Benedict Arnold's ill-starred march up the Kennebec River of now Maine during 1775 was actually the second Arnold Expedition, as you will soon see. Neither Amazon nor Walmart had made inroads into the territory as yet, and Benedict Arnold's troops required plenty of provisions and equipment.

***

Reuben Arnold, Benedict's second cousin and withered branch on the family tree, was in shallow conversation with his second (and last) in command, Ethan Barstow. The exchange reportedly went something like this:

Reuben: "Ben(edict) plans to go on a scouting trip upriver soon. He said he needs a bunch of cows."

Ethan: "Herd of cows."

Reuben: "Sure, I've heard of cows. Ain't you?"

Ethan: Sigh...

Reuben: "He also wants a cow skin to have a coat made."

Ethan: "Hide."

The First Arnold Expedition

Reuben: "Huh?'

Ethan: "Hide…hide…is the cow outside."

Reuben: "I dunno. I haven't looked. I'm not afraid of a cow anyways."

Ethan: "Also, he ordered a bateau."

Reuben: "What does he want a bat for? They're hard to catch."

Ethan: "A bateau is a boat. He wants a boat."

Reuben: "Why didn't you just say so? Tyler's got a tippy canoe that Ben could borrow."

Reuben took pride in knowing a little bit about watercraft, having served for a short time on HMS *Indubitable*, nicknamed *Old Papersides*, after her third ignominious defeat in combat. According to official records, Reuben was soon discharged, however, for "gross incompetence and conduct unbecoming a galley slave."

History regretfully (better read **thankfully**—Ed.) has never made mention of a little known and poorly understood clan of the Maliseet tribe, of whom only three male members remained at that time. Known by the French as the Paraqueets, the three were recruited by Reuben to be scouts, game trackers, and guides for his various forays away from the river, into the surrounding forest. The native men experienced an uneasy interrelationship with the pale foreigners, who they viewed with disdain as incompetent interlopers, especially the one they called, "Reuben." The three Paraqueets were well aware of the animosity between the British and French and often craftily conspired to play one against the other.

After a thorough search as well as a grilling of the native peoples, it became apparent to Reuben that there were no cows to be had in that vicinity. A hunt would be needed to provide meat for the upstream journey ahead. The Paraqueets would guide and track…hopefully.

[From here on in this account, all conversation in the Maliseet tongue

is rendered in English as nearly as is possible to facilitate the reader's comprehension. Maliseet speakers may request an untranslated copy. — Ed.]

Reuben strode into the Maliseet village to seek out his trusty guides [Anglicized names—Ed.]: Running Turtle, Broken Wing, and Crying Wolf. Upon understanding Reuben's request, the offer was made that Running Turtle would lead Reuben's hunting party, Broken Wing would go with Ethan's troops, while Crying Wolf would remain behind to watch the deer trails near the river. To Reuben it seemed like a reasonable and potentially time-saving plan, so he readily agreed.

The Paraqueets had had their share of troubles with the haughty French; they suffered the later British presence with resigned indifference at times, barely disguised amusement or hostility at others. They had no great affection for either.

Hunting

Reuben's party of eight set off with Running Turtle in the lead, signaling the Europeans to keep very quiet. Ethan's group of seven, with Broken Wing several yards ahead, also had been warned to tread stealthily. Although they had entered the woods in essentially opposite directions, their guides slowly worked their courses into converging semicircular trajectories. Once the two groups were within about 50 yards of each other, their two guides melted into the forest at the same time that Crying Wolf, stationed nearby, yelled in his best pseudo-French, "Vive la France!" and fired two shots into the air.

That action garnered an immediate and wildly erratic response from both hunting parties, each of whom assumed that they were under attack by a French raiding party!

29

"Let's get at them, lads!" bellowed Reuben to his troops.

"Don't hold back, chaps. Let them feel the might of British guns!" Ethan encouraged.

Given the misperceptions concerning their adversaries, and the sporadic and greatly inaccurate discharges of their muskets, the battle might have continued on for days. Thankfully, darkness and paucity of ammunition intervened. Each group joyfully returned to camp in the utterly firm belief that it had warded off an ambush by those dastardly French...but with no game.

Hunting II

The meat shortage still unresolved, another forest foray was arranged for the next day. This time only Reuben would go while Ethan would be consulting with Ben about the design and construction of the bateau in which the river expedition would later embark. The box score for this hunt would be Colonists 2, Deer 1...to whit:

Crying Wolf was still chuckling to himself about the previous day's gambit but agreed to lead the unsuspecting ex-Brits on their second romp among the trees. This time it was Running Turtle and Broken Wing who provided the entertainment for the occasion.

The Maliseets often obtained salt by placing ocean water in cavities in the shoreline ledges, and allowing it to evaporate, leaving the salts behind. They then placed small piles of salt along known deer trails, creating salt licks that attracted attention from the salt-seeking deer. It was relatively easy then to either bag them or drive them toward possible captivity—no hunting license required.

Crying Wolf led the party down a well-beaten game path while his two clanmates crept down the trail from the opposite direction. Luck was with them: twelve deer were clustered in the small meadow surrounding one of the salt licks. It didn't take much to start the stampede—two Paraqueets leaping abruptly out of the trees was sufficient. Deer scattered in all directions, five bursting directly down the trail toward the oncoming group. Reuben managed to get a shot off, as did one of his companions. Two critters fell, but the biggest buck drove straight into and over a startled Reuben, who had no time to reload or even react. Crying Wolf entered the tally on his imagined scorecard while trying to suppress an insistent grin.

With some venison now ready to be salted away or smoked, the expedition provision-providers turned their attention to the waters nearby—river and sea. Salted fish could provide additional sustenance for the long journey to come.

Neither Reuben nor Ethan professed to be experienced or capable fishermen, but they knew who might be—their Maliseet compadres. All three clansmen readily agreed to guide the fishing effort, the twinkles in their eyes going unnoticed.

Crying Wolf delivered the Maliseets' alleged fishing technique with all of the solemnity of a professional poker player. He explained that tribal fishing best took place at the mouth of the river during an incoming tide. At least six canoes are required, with the leader in one canoe and ten tribesmen or more distributed between the other canoes. The lead canoe lies upstream of the other craft, broadside to the current. The five down-river canoe occupants watch carefully for the fish, usually salmon, to buck the river current as they move with the rising tide. Once enough fish have passed under the canoes, one of the tribesmen signals the leader, whose responsibility it is to leap up and wave his arms rapidly while yelling loud-ly. The terrified fish will turn quickly and dart back toward the waiting men, who will scoop them up in large, loosely woven wicker baskets.

Anyone with a mariner's knowledge of the Maine coast will readily perceive the potential flaw in this purported strategy. Not so Reuben, however, whose most salient small-craft experience was gained while handcuffed and inebriated, being rowed ashore in HMS *Indubitable*'s longboat. The Kennebec River is one of Maine's largest, and an incoming tide stirs the river mouth into nearly vertical billows. The Maliseets were excellent canoeists. Reuben was not. Ethan visualized the likely scenario, but out of respect for his superior, he stifled his reservations and tactfully kept silent...as did the other smiling Maliseet's present.

Fishing

The weather and spirits (religious and liquid) were fishing-favorable the next morning. While the morning fog slowly lifted and drifted seaward, the Maliseets loaded the requisite canoes and demonstrated for Reuben and Ethan the safe way to enter and stabilize their canoe. Poor Ethan quickly professed a sudden attack of palsy, gastro intestinal distress, and/or lumbago, and had to beg off at the last moment—discretion is the better part of valor, or as Ethan more specifically opined, "He who learns to run away lives to fish another day".

Per plan, Reuben occupied the lead canoe alone, however, while the three Paraqueets and other tribesmen manned the others. After laughing hysterically at Reuben's thrashing attempts to paddle his vessel in a straight line, the Maliseets offered to take Reuben in tow; Crying Wolf suppressed a smirk while reminding Reuben of the signal and the importance of his role.

Six canoes danced upon the Kennebec waters as the flooding tide sought to fill the Popham basin at the river's outlet. The fish purportedly swarmed in (Reuben didn't see any), and the critical signal was flashed. An already green and woozy Reuben bolted to his unsteady feet, arms flailing madly, not to scare any fish present, but in response to the imminent capsize of the formerly underfoot canoe. The water was cold—very cold—while the reaction of the rest of the fishing party was spontaneous and, in hindsight, amazingly predictable! A sputtering and thoroughly chilled Reuben turned out to be the only fish retrieved that day!

Bearies and Bugs

The ever-helpful Paraqueets suggested that berries might provide an enjoyable gustatory treat during the northward journey. Early summer brings tasty wild strawberries, followed later by red raspberries, blackberries, and blueberries—all flavorful and nutritious. Gathering berries does involve some risks, however: thorns, mosquitoes, and bears. Thorns could be worked around, bears watched out for, and mosquitoes repelled. The Paraqueets had a tribal anti-mosquito concoction that they would be happy to share.

Running Turtle took the lead for this escapade. Crying Wolf and Broken Wing would produce the mosquito repellent and keep a lookout for bears. Ethan was beginning to sense a pattern here but held out hope for a positive outcome. Reuben forged blindly ahead as usual, intent on redeeming his cousin Ben's faith in his provisioning capabilities.

Running Turtle assured Reuben that timing was critical to try to minimize possible contacts with bears. In actuality, he was waiting for a cool, damp day when mosquitoes would be unlikely to be about—they were voracious during hot spells. Broken Wing procured the bug repellent, the ingredients supposedly known only to tribal elders, and encouraged Reuben and Ethan to spread the sticky potion liberally over any exposed skin. Sadly, Ethan experienced an immediate allergic reaction to the smell and felt obligated to remain at camp while hardier Reuben carried on. The fact is, Ethan detected the faint odor and consistency of honey in the mixture and drew a hasty, tentative conclusion about its real purpose.

The early part of berrying went well. No cold water to fall into, no shots ringing out, no deer to run him down and, even more gratifying, no pesky mosquitoes about—the repellent concoction seemed to be working. Reuben even was able to avoid for the most part being shredded by the thorny thickets of the raspberries and blackberries.

"Shhh," Running Turtle cautioned. "Bear coming. If she come close, lie down, curl up in a ball. Don't move. Don't make sound. I try to scare off."

Reuben ducked down and assumed the recommended position as Running Turtle slunk off to "scare" the bear away. In actuality, Crying Wolf and Broken Wing laid a trail of honeyed sweetness directly toward the berry patch, downwind of Reuben's position.

Soon enough, a black bear waddled onto the scene, as if on cue. In a sense, it was. That particular bear was not exactly wild, nor was it particularly tame. It was known to the Maliseets, though, and had had some benign human contact in the recent past.

The bear sniffed the air while erect on its hind legs, then ambled on, straight for the terrified Reuben, who was hoping and praying mightily that he was in the "correct" position. Despite his trying desperately to remain still, he trembled all over as the bear trundled up to him and began licking his hands, then his face. Reuben began quaking even more—he was ticklish! The more the bear licked, the more Reuben shook. Finally, he could stand the bear's gentle tongue-lashing no longer. As the bear sat back on its haunches for a moment, Reuben made the instant decision to exit stage left as fast as his feet would carry him. The bear studied Reuben's strategic retreat for a few seconds, then turned its attention to the basket of berries that Reuben had left behind. At the same time, off in the bushes, the three Paraqueet clansmen were gasping for breath with unrestrained laughter.

Le Bateau

Reuben had had enough, and Ethan had seen enough, that both men needed a break to regroup. Building a boat that could be rowed or poled upstream while carrying a load of supplies was an essential part of the scouting expedition. Reuben also had experienced enough to know that a canoe would not be a good choice—a more substantial craft was required. The common river vessel of the early French trappers was flat-bottomed and somewhat slab-sided—easy to build, stable, cheap, and able to carry a fair load. Reuben seemed especially enamored of the "stable" descriptor, Ethan noted.

Ascertaining that no suitable lumber was readily available nearby, Benedict was told that there might be an experienced boatbuilder a few miles up the coast. That craftsman also ran his own high-speed sawmill— he had *four* sawyers working pit saws instead of just two!

[An early pit saw required two men, one standing on the log on the upper end of the two-man saw, the other down in the pit below, the saw being nearly vertical. The pit man usually looked like a walking pile of sawdust by the end of the day. – Ed.]

Crying wolf volunteered to guide Reuben to the spot; Reuben accepted the offer, albeit a bit warily. The short journey took place the next day.

After several miles of climbing boulders and ledges along the shore, Reuben's small party reached a stream tumbling into a cove, at which point Crying Wolf turned inland for perhaps 100 yards, coming to a fairly large clearing surrounding a large log building and sawpit, with four men clearly hard at work.

The First Arnold Expedition

Crying Wolf banged on the large door of the log structure, and out stepped a wiry apparition of a man covered in sawdust with a bottle in hand—Pierre Gastón Giroux, boatbuilder extraordinaire, and the last remaining vestige of a large French community that had vacated the area some years before when the British arrived. Pierre missed the boat, so to speak, being "indisposed" at the time of the strategic retreat, a diplomatic way of saying that he was passed out under a table in the community's makeshift tavern.

Pierre greeted his guests with obvious enthusiasm and inquired as to the reason for their visit to his "humble shop."

"We would like to have a bateau built, sir," opened Reuben.

"Oui, monsieur. I build zee best bateau evair," Pierre responded. "How beeg zis bateau?"

"Big enough to carry six people, equipment, and provisions at least 50 miles up the Kennebec River on a scouting trip," Reuben explained.

"Why you scouting up zee rivair, monsieur? Zis rivair, she beeg for miles and miles," asserted Pierre.

"My cousin, Benedict Arnold, is going to take a large number of troops up the river to attack the French there in Quebec," Reuben patiently (and naïvely) explained.

"Oui? Mon Dieu! A dangerous thing, no?" Pierre seemed agitated… and suddenly cagey. "I have un bateau almost done. She only need zee bottom. I make le bateau special for you, zee best bateau for the British or my name is not Pierre Gastón Giroux! Come back in two days, monsieur." "I feex zis bateau trés bon," Pierre thought to himself. "C'est la guerre."

Behind his shop at the edge of the woods, Pierre had a pile of drying boards that he had rejected for boat use; they contained borers. Some softwood trees are infested with bugs that tunnel throughout the wood, rendering it unsuitable for many applications, including boats.

Pierre was very selective for this boat. He chose only the boards that showed the living borers' holes on one side; that side went toward the underside of the new bateau. The apparently "good" side showed inside the boat. The holes showing on the underside were filled lightly with a mixture of sawdust and pitch.

As promised, two days later the bateau was waiting for Reuben upon his return. It took four men to drag it to the stream, on which Reuben was able to tow the craft to the coast by rope, wading along the shallows and forested banks.

"Le bateau, she need time to swell her planks," explained Pierre. "She take some water for a few days, then non. She's a bon bateau or my name is not Pierre Gastón Giroux! Bon voyage, mon amis!"

A beaming Reuben arrived back in camp after a somewhat perilous trek along the shore and riverbanks. Yes, the bateau did take in some water, but the seepage seemed minimal. Reuben was sure that his vessel would be enough for the upriver scouting expedition by the end of the next week.

Scouting

Benedict had made it very clear to Reuben and Ethan that this exploratory foray upriver would be of the utmost importance. Reports from trappers and early settlers had varied widely about tidal effects, rocks, rapids, navigability, etc. Natives' descriptions of the river's conditions seemed to be the most accurate, but not all of the tribes along the watercourse were friendly.

The day arrived that found the scouting party ready. The bateau was loaded with surveying tools, camping equipment, provisions, arms, oars, paddles, poles, and various trinkets for the natives, if needed. Six people would man the bateau: Benedict Arnold, Reuben, Ethan, and three other troops. All would be required for the exertions of moving the laden bateau against the current and whatever else lay ahead.

Progress was slow. Two days out, Ethan noticed some dampness on a few items in the bottom of the boat. Three days out, Reuben was chagrined to find soggy biscuits among the food stores. Four days out, Benedict noticed small pools of water sloshing back and forth, wetting his boots. Five days out, most of the extra clothing and bread items were displaying signs of mold, and some were dripping wet. By the sixth day, it was necessary to bail "le bateau" every few hours. On the seventh day, mid-morning, before the party could reach shore, they sighted rapids ahead, at the same time their "bon bateau" rapidly sank from under them in five feet of water…very cold water! The borers had accomplished their unwitting mission. Vive la France…

"Reuben, I'm wet!" bellowed cousin Benedict. Not a strong swimmer, he quickly excelled at wading, the other scouting party members not far behind. Few of the items in the boat survived their dousing, but apparently enough did to allow the soggy group to work its way back downstream and reach its base camp and waiting troops ten days later, much the worse for wear.

A follow-up raid on Pierre's encampment two days later found an empty clearing and cabin, and over 100 empty bottles. No full ones were located. The Paraqueets commiserated with Benedict and Reuben while in their presence but could hardly contain their merriment when back at their village.

Written history picks up the story from here, starting with the preparation for Benedict Arnold's actual *second* expedition up the Kennebec. No mention is made of cousin Reuben, banned from the undertaking, and purged by Benedict's edict from any and all accounts of the fiasco. Ethan did go along, preferring to do so anonymously. Despite his hurt feelings, after learning about the disastrous outcome, Reuben was just as glad that he was not present.

The Pixilated Pirate

It has been suggested that truth is stranger than fiction. That may be true. I will let you, the reader, decide for yourself after reading this story within a story, within a story.

My Story

I went down to the city to visit my close friends, Stacy and Jack Demers, who were running a very successful seafood restaurant there. It was well established in a replica 18th century sailing ship docked along-side a commercial wharf on the busy waterfront, less than 75 yards from the municipal park that projected somewhat into the harbor.

The couple and I had grown up together in the little Maine coastal vil-lage of Northeast Southwestport. Ever since their teens it had been their dream to operate a first-class seafood restaurant, but our town was too small—they needed the big city. Given their commercial fishing connec-tions at home, they could be assured of a steady supply of fresh lobster, fish, clams, scallops, and shrimp.

They had sailed down to the city on their 30-foot fiberglass sloop, grandiosely named *Corsair*, on which they had lived aboard while trying to establish their business. They soon managed to get a business loan, using their sloop as collateral.

This particular night we were sitting at a table in the dining area after the bar had closed at midnight (food was served until 11 p.m.). We were sipping a fine Sangria and chatting, while sporadic muttering and puttering sounds were emanating from the kitchen. At first, I tried to ignore the clatter, but as the conversation turned to their recent success with their culinary business, a crash of pots and pans interrupted the flow, followed by a string of oaths the likes of which I had never heard before.

"That's just Greybeard," Jack explained. "We just humor him as much as we can this late at night, when he's had his tot of rum."

The bewildered look on my face surely tipped off Stacy and Jack that some further explanation would be helpful. Jack was the first to pick up the cue.

Jack and Stacy's Story

"It all started on a quiet night on the *Corsair*, after closing up the restaurant for the night," Jack began. "Before opening the restaurant, we had been attending nautical antique auctions to try to pick up some items for decorating the dining room—to enhance the nautical theme. When we first opened, we were located across the street from the harbor in a dingy former warehouse space, kind of dark and gloomy..."

"And creepy, actually," Stacy chimed in, "but it was all we could afford at the time. We had good food, but we barely made ends meet. The prime location, this wharf slip, was occupied by an old wooden ferry boat restaurant that had mediocre food but was doing a booming business because of the location—lots of publicity, tourists and regulars. We couldn't compete well with that."

Jack continued, "The wharf slip was the only one that the city would allow for a floating restaurant. We put our business on a waiting list for the

41

slip and gradually moved up to number one in line. There we sat for two years, watching the ferry restaurant make a haul while we barely eked along.

"One night we were sitting in the cockpit of *Corsair*, as I started to say earlier, and I was starting to polish a cabin lamp that we recently had acquired at an auction. As I began to rub it there was a tremendous concussion, almost like an explosion, and there was a blinding flash of light and thick mist or dust in the air. Neither Stacy nor I could see or hear for a minute or two, and when the fogginess cleared, there was a man standing on the bridge deck of our boat."

"Not exactly *any* man," Stacy continued, "but a pirate—at least he looked like one. He stood at least six feet four, had on a white ruffled shirt and baggy black pants, a red sash around his waist, a dirk stuffed in the waistband, a cutlass at his side, and an eye patch over one eye. His hat was kind of nondescript, cocked to one side, and he wore gold earrings. His long hair seemed straggly, and he sported a longish gray beard. His countenance seemed to be a combination of irritation and confusion. Jack and I were stunned."

Both Jack and Stacy took long sips of their wine, and then Jack picked up the thread:

"The man stared at us for a few moments, and we stared at him, shocked beyond telling. He then looked around, bent down and tapped on the deck of the boat."

"What wood is this?" he queried.

"Wood?" I stammered in reply. "That's not wood—it's fiberglass," was all I could come up with.

"What kind of tree is that?" the man then asked. "I don't know that one."

"Who *are* you?" Stacy asked as she began to get her wits about her.

"And what are you doing on our boat? And where did you come from? And why are you dressed like that?" Stacy blurted out in a nervous rush.

Jack continued, "His demeanor seemed to change immediately. One minute he seemed distant and threatening; the next minute he spoke softly with a twinkle in his eye."

"Ye are wondering about me, are ye, lass? Well, I 'spect you didn't figure to see me here, and I weren't sure where I was bound when I set sail," the man replied. "I'm known to my friends and foes alike as Greybeard, but you can call me Greybeard."

"Are you a pirate?" Stacy blurted out.

"Aye, lass, some calls me such, but I think that's a bit harsh—a hasty judgment perhaps. I prefer the terms 'buccaneer' or 'picaroon' meself, although I've cottoned to 'freebooter' and 'cutthroat' of late. Anything but 'late for dinner'. As for where I'm from and why I'm here on this foin vessel, aye, now that's a tale to tell!"

Greybeard's Tale

[Editor's Note: Greybeard's account, delivered with 18th century language, has been rephrased into modern English, with some colorful vocabulary sanitized so as to not offend the refined sensibilities of our readers.]

"So's ye can unnerstand the whole of the picture, I will begin at the beginning to start. I was born at a very young age. My paternal father was Edward Teach. Some folks knew him as Blackbeard before he turned gray.

"Me and me twin brother were both named Beach—Beach Teach. Pop liked sea names. To tell us apart, we had different middle names. Mine is Peach, 'cause I was born in Georgia; my brother is Leech. So, I'm Beach

The Pixilated Pirate

Peach Teach, 'n' he's Beach Leech Teach.

"All of us Teaches are illegitimate. Pop took a woman in each port. Me 'n' Beach are the oldest. The other boys is Frigate, Raider, Hurry-Caine, Gunner, and the youngest was born without any legs. We call him Bob. The girls are Sandy, Dunea, Gale, Stormy, 'n' Rummy.

"I had no schoolin', but I tried several jobs; the idea of being a pirate scared me, at least the way Pop went about it. I took up crocheting and knitting after getting me first ship, a captured prize that Pop passed on to me along with my first mate, Smirch. I think Pop wanted to get rid of him.

"Anyway, I knitted a sweater for Smirch. When I got done, the sweater had three arms; Smirch only had one. I decided then that I weren' cut out for knitting, and I had a bonny ship. I named her the *Jolly Robber,* figgerin' that might scare pirates away. So's I got the idea of sellin' ice for cold drinks in the Caribbean.

"We sailed her up to Greenland and hitched onto an iceberg off Labrador, with the idea of towing it to Dominica. All was going good, a bit slow, until we reached the Gulf Stream. It was flowing north; we was goin' south. We fought; it won. The iceberg had melted by the time we got to Hatteras.

"We tried again—bigger iceberg this time. We sailed mightily for three days. Turns out that iceberg was hard aground. It had been a titanic struggle."

At this point Greybeard pulled out a flask and took a couple of generous gulps before continuing. He seemed to pause to reflect, and then rambled on after switching his eye patch to his other eye.

"I gave up on the iceberg notion and thought I'd start a store, selling ice cubes to Eskimos. Didn't work out. I made a go of selling counterfeit doubloons to the Spanish but got chased out of Hispaniola after a while. I tried one more store idea: selling cannons and powder to Corsairs, but that idea blew up in my face. My career as an animal doctor for Caribbean crocodiles proved to have some toothy repercussions.

"Well, Skipper, I still had hopes of makin' an honest livin'. Smirch 'n' me started building skiffs for fisher folk and such. Some of 'um didn't sink, too. But one day Smirch took an order for five 20-foot skiffs. He don't write so good, an' I don't read so good, so we built 20 five-foot skiffs—they weren't worth a darn. The owner weren't too happy, neither. Sold five for kiddie cribs after puttin' rockers under 'um, ten for rat coffins wit' lids, 'n' the rest for flower planters.

"My gunpowder business ended unexpectedly, y' might say, 'n' then I went into used cannon sales, until I found out that most available cannons were at the bottom of the sea. I was stumped."

Greybeard shrugged his shoulders at that moment, let out a long sigh, took another swig from his flask, and launched into a continuation:

"Gots to have me grog, y' know. Tradition, ain't it. So's I come to a conclusion—pirating was in me blood, aye, and it was all I would be good at. I had the ship, me trustworthy mate be Smirch, an' I was willin' to sail the seven seas...or is it eight? That always confuddled me.

"Well, to make a long voyage a bit shorter, I needed an intimidating pirate moniker—Beach wouldn't scare anyone. We, Smirch 'n' me, tried out a few: Pinkbeard (too effeminate), Bluebeard (too much like bluebird), Blondbeard (it were more reddish than yellowish)...we settled on Greybeard as I might be grey someday 'n' some waves are called 'greybeards.'

"So now I had a name, and I set about to piratin'. We took a few small vessels—well, truth be told, a rowboat with two lads and load of watermelons, an island trading sloop with an old lady skipper, 'n' a schooner carryin' the plague—we let that one go in a hurry!

"I was set on chasing bigger game, though, to build my reputation—

very 'portant to a buccaneer, y' know. O'er the next three years we took several prizes [captured vessels—Ed.] and got ourselves a reputation as equal opportunity pirates: we were sunk by the English, Spanish, French, Dutch, Portuguese, Swiss, an' Mongolians…an' Inuits, I forgot.

"We got into a skirmish with a Spaniard off'n Haiti once. Somehow a cannon come off'n its carriage 'n' swung sideways when I give the 'fire' order. We blew off the stern of the ship. Embarrassing, it were."

Another draught to grease his skids, so to speak, and Greybeard forged on.

"Smirch was to row me ashore once, 'n' when I dropped down into the gig, the thing lurched, I fell hard, and me cutlass tore through the bottom. We sank that time, too. Embarrassing. Again.

"Wit' no luck against vessels, we charted another course: sacking and plundering port cities. Pirates did it, some very nicely. Over the next five years we attacked, and were repelled by Porto Alegre, Port Arthur, Port-au-Prince, Port Huron, Portland (Oregon *and* Maine), Port Louis, Port Moresby, Port Orange, Port Said, Port of Spain, Port Stanley, 'n' had a major setback with Port wine. We also got chased off by the ladies of a brothel in St. Augustine. Embarrassing."

At this point Greybeard sat back and seemed to drift into a profound reverie. After another deep breath and sigh, he wrapped up his monologue:

"I know I were a failure as a pirate when I had to print my own wanted posters to try to boost my notoriety. The posters read: 'Wanted: Dead or Alive—preferably alive, Nasty rogue Greybeard, $500 reward for capture.' At Port-au-Prince somebody wrote over the poster: 'Wouldn't bother for twice that—he'd have to hire someone to do it.' I thought about it. Embarrassing. The British offered five pence for me, to turn myself in; the Spanish offered a chicken. Embarrassing."

Greybeard paused again in apparent contemplation.

Stacy and Jack Pick up the Thread

"As Greybeard's recitation—almost a soliloquy—drifted to a halt, Stacy and I sat there speechless," Jack recounted. "We actually felt sorry for the guy, completely losing sight of the fact that he was saying that he was actually here from the 1700's. By his account, he was a failure at everything he'd tried."

"Jack knows I'm a softie. I spoke up and offered Beach/Greybeard a job at the restaurant," Stacy added. "I figured he could wash dishes or at least sweep floors."

"We had to explain to a glum Greybeard what a restaurant is. He brightened up considerably, though, when we told him that we had a bar. He thought at first of a reef or sand spit but clearly had the concept of *tavern*," Jack explained. "The upshot was that Greybeard came to work with us for the next day but never made it to the kitchen. Customers saw him and immediately seemed attracted to him. Greybeard stayed in the dining room just as he was and became our official greeter. We had no ship then, and still no slip for one. Greybeard slept in the back storeroom."

Stacy continued on: "The patrons loved him. He turned out to be quite popular. Kids and women especially seemed drawn to him, but the men, too, seemed intrigued. On his part, Greybeard could best be described as indefatigable, flamboyant, and amiable. He was there for breakfast, luncheon, and dinner meals. We actually never saw him sleep or eat a full meal. We would be exhausted, and Greybeard would be going strong. He did like his rum, though—he closed the bar every night at midnight. We didn't need a bouncer; Greybeard's stare could be intimidating when he wanted it to be."

"We kept the restaurant's name as 'Stacey & Jack's' during that time. Meanwhile, the ferry restaurant, *The Landing*, seemed to be losing a few customers to us. Then one night everything changed."

Jack re-entered the tale: "The park down the street is called Buccaneer Park, oddly enough. As you might have noticed, it juts out into the harbor and parallels the wharf where *The Landing* was docked, and we are now. There are four antique cannons on the green.

"To this day, no one has been able to explain what happened that night. It must have happened between about 2:00 and 4:00 a.m. All four cannons were mysteriously repositioned to point toward *The Landing*. Each must weigh at least 800 pounds. They are civil war relics—they hadn't been fired since 1865. No one saw the cannons move. No one saw any powder or balls or shells. There were none in the park." Jack took another sip after speaking. More clatter and mumbling floated from the kitchen.

Stacy waded in: "Two hotel maids on their ways home that night swore they heard a deep, male voice yell 'fire!' at which point those silent cannons let loose with a broadside that would have made Lord Nelson at Trafalgar proud! The roar was heard all over the city, and the shock wave shattered many windows along the waterfront. The effect on *The Landing*, just down range, was immediate and dramatic—the ferry disintegrated into millions of flying fragments. She was no *Old Ironsides*! The remaining hulk promptly sank.

"The insurance adjusters and civic officials were on site later that day, but there were no solid clues: no fingerprints, no eye witnesses, no dropped candy wrappers or cigarette butts--and the cannons were fixed where they fired from—no tracks on the ground; no signs of moving equipment. *The Landing* was out of business, and we were told that the berth could now be available if we still wanted it, but we had no vessel to put there."

"Greybeard appeared to be unusually upbeat that night—almost euphoric, I would say," observed Jack. "And if the cannons' firing was a mystery, what happened the next week was utterly inexplicable: the city woke up to find a sailing vessel—this very ship—in that vacated slip! And even more incredible, an elaborate sign on the pier read *The Pixilated Pirate—fine dining, fine grog!* A lot of questions were raised, and an investigation ensued, but we all had alibis and no direct connection could be made between our new facility and the recent event. From the day the ship appeared, though, we prospered. People were intrigued by the coincidences and the ship—she's technically a caravel—and they loved the food and ambience. Greybeard seemed to glow—he was very charismatic—and he denied any knowledge of the park's cannonade or ship's abrupt appearance."

"'She's a foin vessel, Skipper,' is all he would allow," added Stacy. "Nautical archeologists examined her construction; very typical 18th century, they concluded. We're a success, I guess, but I still don't know how it all happened."

More clatter from the kitchen, then another resounding crash. More oaths, more muttering, then a loud guffaw.

Me Again

I never did get to lay eyes on Greybeard that night, but Stacy and Jack eventually excused themselves to head for the sack, giving me free rein to explore the ship top to bottom.

While moving barrels aside to examine the keelson structure in the bilge more closely, I found a fragment of very yellowed, water-stained paper. All I could make out on it was, "Want...Dead or...Nast..." Honest!

The Happening in Gobbler Holler

Prologue

I swear that this whole story is true, mostly. I ain't smart enough to make this up.

Buzz Werdly helped me with the spellings and words and sentences—"vocabulary" he calls it. I surely don't even know what some of the words mean. Buzz is the part-time editor slash writer slash sole proprietor of the *Gobbler Holler Herald*, our local weekly. I don't know what a "sole proprietor" is, but I think it might have something to do with fish, or maybe boots, since Gobbler Holler is on a swamp. Buzz said the story needed a Prologue, but I never considered myself to be anti-log. Buzz says that some folks, called "historians," debate (debait—more about fish, maybe taking back the worm?) about where the name of "Gobbler Holler" came from ("originated," Buzz says). Some say it relates to an early settler family named Cobble who still have kin in town. Part of the family has always had trouble hearing ("congenital deafness," Buzz calls it), and Cobble Hollow came out to be written down as "Gobbler Holler." Others say the name came from the wild turkeys in the area—not that they could talk, y'see. Still others make mention of a shoemaker who set up shop for a short time in what was then the newest village in this corner of Munrow County. I guess he was called a "cobbler," and considering the town clerk was one of the hardly hearing Cobbles, it's no surprise that the name "Gobbler Holler" got stuck.

Before I launch into what really happened that week, I'm supposed to tell you that some of the names have been changed to protect the innocent, as if some of them were. I also need to tell you more about the town—that's Buzz's idea. He calls it a "suggestion," but he wouldn't help me with the story if I didn't take his advice.

Gobbler Holler is not very big—about 193 "souls," as the sisters call us, give or take a few. We don't have industries as such, but we do have some businesses, a paper, a convent, a community church, a seasonal distillery (Buzz says that they really just make moonshine), a part-time garage slash funeral parlor, and just outside of town in the woods, an "adult entertainment emporium" (a "brothel," Buzz calls it, though it seems that just "sisters" work there). Oh, we do have a school for grades 1-8; the two high schoolers get bused to somewhere, but they rarely come back. Mert Cobble dropped out of our "alimentary school," as he calls it, when they dropped the occasional lunch program. He still can't read or write and can barely hear most of the time.

The Convent is run by the Sisters of Innocence, all five of them. Mert calls the sisters "numbs" and refers to the Convent folks as the "Sisters of Inner Sins," but he really don't know, or hear, any better. Some think he may be close to the truth—you decide after reading the story.

Gobbler Holler used to have a drive-in food place until Herb Gardner made it a one-time drive-through in his pick-up after a night of shining the moon. It ain't been open since.

The "pleasure palace," as some call it, at the edge of town is really called the *Passion Pit*. It's run by a guy named Ferguson Foxx, but he goes by "Sly" to most folks in these parts. Several local girls work there—I'll introduce them to you when they fit in the story. Sly comes and goes. No one seems to know where he really lives, but he drives a white Cadillac sometimes, though most people find a 4-wheeler to be best for reaching the *Passion Pit.*

Sly usually seems to be on good terms with the county sheriff, Dewey Kaire, and the county attorney, Conway Kruuk (maybe because he's Dutch they pronounce Kruuk as "Crook"). We hardly ever see either one in this part of the county, but Dewey has a part in the whole story, too.

The story actually starts with one of Sly's girls, who I will call "Cherry-Anne" (Sherryanne said she'd never speak to me again if I used her real name in the story). So this is the way it was, using some of what Buzz says is "artistic license," though I don't ever remember buying one of those.

Chapter One—How It All Started

Cherry-Anne looked in the mirror, checking for those telltale signs of getting older: wrinkles around the eyes, drooping skin, sagging body parts. Hard as she looked, though, she could find none, despite her advanced age of 24. She figured her historic profession demanded perfection, kind of. She was not the brightest bulb on the Cobble tree, but she could hear, and sometimes she thought she heard too much.

Like the time when she heard Sly talk with Kitty (that's not Katherine's real name, either), the *Passion Pit's* hostess, about some kind of seafood deal between the sheriff and some up-north businessman—she heard Sly say that it seemed "fishy." Or the time she heard her nearly deaf brother, Charlie (that's not Carl's real name, either), talking with Kitty about buying out Sly if he could raise the money somehow. It would cost at least $10,000, he thought, to interest Sly in the deal. Charlie weren't too smart, either, though. He once asked Buzz how to spell "KKK." Kitty had said that Sly might not sell; Charlie heard, "I might not tell," which got Charlie a bit nervous.

Anyway, Cherry-Anne felt that she already knew too much, which made her a lot nervous. Although she was a bit chubby and not too tall, she was Sly's favorite and "a good earner," he said. I guess them guys who went to the *Pit* often liked their women a bit fleshy, maybe. My own favorite was…well, she comes later in the story.

Cherry-Anne turned from the mirror at the sound of the doorbell. That meant she had to join the girls down the hall to see who the customer might choose for his entertainment that night. She was hoping that it was not one of the shiner boys, as they usually were drunk and smelled like a startled skunk, as she liked to say.

Sure enough, it was Mert Cobble and one of his shiner cousins, Grady.

Neither one could hear a lick, and both were tighter than a size small corset on a hefty hog. Kitty met them as they reeled though the front door.

"Sly don't want you boys here while you're drunk," Kitty opened.

"We ain't shot no skunk tonight, Kitty," countered Mert.

"You got no bunk for us, Kitty?" came Grady.

"Grady is quite a hunk, but we don't want no girls tonight. We got news for you," offered Mert.

"I can't sing blues tonight, Mert—I'm too stiffed," Grady.

Mert: "We won't need a lift. I can still drive."

Grady: "Of course we're still alive. We're not *that* drunk."

Mert: "I already told her we ain't shot no skunk tonight."

Cherry-Anne didn't pay no attention to the rest of the conversation with Kitty and the Cobble cousins until they got to the news—then her ears tuned in.

"Sly says he wants to buy the Convent. Cousin Clapper overheard him talking with the sheriff while Clapper was with Herb in the county seat getting his pick-up fixed." [Buzz—Clapper was so-called because he usually clapped to get the attention of his nearly-deaf family members before speaking, which he rarely did.]

Now Kitty weren't exactly enamored (Buzz's word) with Sly and perceived (also Buzz's word) an opportunity—that's a good chance—to gain some advantage over Sly, if she could get to the sisters first. She had a proposition in mind. (Buzz says that may be "a bit of an oxymoron," but I only know about a normal moron.)

Chapter Two—Kitty's Visit

Kitty is tall—she's six foot, if over a foot, and scary. Buzz says she's "imposing," but I never knew her to pose for anything. But she was about to pose an offer.

You see, the Convent only had the five sisters and one product—elderberry wine. The shiners didn't see theirselfs in competition with the sisters as the shiners only sold in town, while the sisters had a truck come a few times during the season to take the sisters' output who knows where. It seemed that their income was enough to keep them comfortable. We really didn't know for sure 'cause they kept to themselves with their prayers and such most of the time. It turned out, though, that we really didn't know the sisters well at all.

For all her "posing" nature, Kitty weren't sure how to approach the sisters about her idea. After all, the leader of the sisters (senior sister?), Sister Mary Miracle, could be pretty stern herself—she was not to be taken lightly as she came to at least 300 pounds dry. Kitty said later that she wanted to make a cash offer, but she wasn't wanting to insult the sisters with a lowball offer, but she also wanted to outdo any deal Sly might have in mind. The trick (no pun intended—Buzz) was to undercut her boss without his finding out. To do so meant using some of what Buzz called "diplomacy," but I wasn't sure what diplomas had to do with it.

Anyhow, Kitty couldn't wait in case Sly made his move soon, so she hitched herself up and strode over to the Convent, doing so after dark, in case anyone might see a lady of her profession at the door of the Convent place (since Kitty was not usually known for making house calls?).

Kitty's knock was not answered right away, and she said later that she thought about backing out, but greed spurred her on (as Buzz put it), and she knocked again, louder.

The Happening in Gobbler Holler

She expected Sister M&M, as some locals referred to her, to be at the door, but it wasn't—it was Mert.

"Now what's he doing here?" Kitty thought.

"Now what's *she* doing here?" popped into Mert's mind. Neither spoke up at first.

"Who is it, Mert?" as Sister M&M's voice broke the silent standoff.

"I can't say, Sister...I won't say," stammered Mert.

"You don't know who it is?" Sister M&M asked.

"I know, but she's not supposed to be here, I think." Mert gradually turned redder and redder, Kitty said later...much later.

"I'm coming, Mert. Let her in, whoever she is."

"Yes, ma'am, but she's a whorer," Mert weakly protested.

"Mert! I'm sure our guest is not a horror!" passed Sister M&M's lips as she wallowed into the foyer. Buzz said I should use "descriptive" terms, whatever that means. Like, what's a *foyer*? I've heard of the Foys, and I know that pigs sometimes *wallow*, but I never thought of Sister M&M that way before. Buzz liked that *image*, though, he said. I don't think he liked Sister M&M much, maybe.

Howsomever, Mert allowed Kitty in as Sister M&M appeared. Mert said later that the sister seemed speechless at first, but he also allowed that she might just have been talking too quietly for him to hear. He didn't catch much of the conversation between the two women, but he noticed that Kitty seemed very "intense" as he saw it, and Sister M&M became quite upset ("agitated," as Buzz put it).

Kitty only found out later that Mert was there to carry an offer from the shiners for the convent property—Mert said they'd taken a shine to the property (I thought of that one!) and maybe wanted to partner with the sisters to produce some "first-class shine wine," as Mert put it. Sister M&M had just heard Mert's speech when Kitty knocked at the door.

Now Sister M&M hadn't become a sister for nothing; she could be pretty shrewd herself (Buzz described Sister M&M that way, but I'm not sure she's really a shrew.) As the story unfolded, she got to figuring that something was up if people were suddenly interested in taking over her convent's property one way or another. She was not really interested in selling out—the five sisters would have nowhere to go—and their combined incomes would be "severely curtailed," as the *Gobbler Holler Herald* told it when it was all over.

Besides the income from the elderberry wine, the sisters did have some other ways to make money. Turned out that Sister Sally Forth, I'll call her, was not a nun at all. In fact, she moonlighted ("literally," Buzz said) at the *Passion Pit*—would that be a bad habit? No one would recognize her there, out of uniform and with skimpy outfits, make-up, and wigs. So she thought, as did Sister M&M, who as it turned out, was not a real nun, either. No one afterward seemed to recall when the sisters came to town, or when the old Cobble place had become a convent (Buzz says it could be called a *nunnery*, too, but the only -ery I know of is a piggery).

So Sister Sally brought in some cash, and as it turned out, so did the sisters' basement printing press. Ten-dollar bills were their specialty it seems, but I might be getting ahead of the story.

Kitty made her pitch, not knowing about the sisters' combined incomes. She made a cash offer that she hoped would outshine, so to speak, Sly's intentions and the offer by the shiners. Sister M&M said she'd talk with her sister sisters, but she weren't very excited about the prospect (as Buzz put it). She pretended to be sincere but knew that no offer would be good enough. Sly would not do well, either, but he might never know why.

Chapter Three—Sly's Foray (Buzz's term, even though I told him that this would only be Chapter Three)

Sly stopped by the *Pit* before heading over to the convent. Kitty played it cool, pretending to be pleased to see her boss (not!) and making small talk about the girls and the condition of the *Pit* (an overgrown mobile home of uncertain vintage—Buzz's words again). Sly listened with barely contained impatience—he was anxious to see Sister M&M, and nervous, too. As sleazy as Sly could be, Sister M&M could be "formidable" (Buzz said) as a business woman herself. The shiners had already seen how set she could be.

Sly had washed and polished his Caddy, not that it would stay that way after navigating the road to the *Pit*—a dirt track along the edge of the swamp. He was out to impress "those numbs," as Mert called them, and was ready to flash some cash in the donation plate if he had to. Little did he know that Sister M&M had more cash available than Sly could ever muster.

Sly decided ahead of time that he had to appear smooth, confident, and sincere, at least on the face of it. The truth was that he never was confident with women in uniform, going back to his days in parochial school in Munrow's county seat. A classmate there, in fact, was Dewey Kaire, later to be elected sheriff on a law-and-order ticket (imagine a sheriff having a ticket!). Sly still shuddered at hearing "Ferguson!" in a stern voice. He much preferred "Sly" now.

Now one of his failings—and there were many—was that Sly considered hisself to be a bit of a lady's man. After all, he did manage the Passion Pit's women quite well, didn't he? And so his leading lines with Sister M&M should put his charm to good use.

Sly's knock on the convent door brought Sister Dorothy in answer.

"Yes?" was all the sister could muster at beholding Sly on the threshold (Buzz told me to "vary" my "vocabulary"—I think he meant that I should use lots of words that he told me, even if I weren't sure what they mean).

"Good day, my dear sister," Sly was heard to say. "Would the good Sister Mary be present today?"

Sister Dorothy later told me that her first thought was, "She would be if she was here," and her second thought was, "She really ain't that good," or something like that. Sister Dorothy also had a third thought: "Why do you want to know?"

What she actually said, though, was, "Do come in, Mr. Foxx."

Sly stepped through the front door and quickly looked around, expecting "Ferguson!" to come bellowing out from some hidden corner at any moment (*moment* is a fancy word for *minute*, Buzz says).

"Good morning, Mr. Foxx," is what he actually heard when Sister M&M came into the foyer, but her voice startled him anyway.

"Good morning, Sister Mary. My, you're looking sparkling today!" led Sly.

That bit of attempted Foxx flattery fell famously flat (Buzz says that that is called *alliteration*, and that poets use it sometimes, but I don't see how it rhymes).

"What brings you to the convent this morning, Mr. Foxx?"

Sister Dorothy witnessed Sister M&M's reply, along with an "icy stare," as she later put it.

"May I have a word with you alone, in confidence?" Sly then asked. Sister Dorothy then had to leave, so I never did learn what exactly was said, but it supposedly weren't all "sweetness and light." (Buzz's words. I don't know for sure what he meant, but it sounds like a good dieter's dessert to me.)

The Happening in Gobbler Holler

I guess Sly made an offer that was not well received, but that got Sister M&M to wondering why there was so much sudden interest in a property that had been pretty well ignored for so many years. After all, the convent had been there a long time and had very few visitors—truth be told, none actually. So she paid a visit to Buzz at the paper, but I don't see why she had to pay when everyone else who goes there gets in for free. Some things I will never understand, I guess.

Chapter Four—Buzz's Research

I always thought of Buzz as a friend and a good helper who really cared about Gobbler Holler and its folks. He told me later about the sister's visit and told me that I should "summarize" his research for my story, though I didn't see what summer had to do with it.

To make a long story shorter so I don't have to use so many words, Buzz went up to the county seat, to the records office, to do some research on the convent property (but never told me why it was *re*search, since he hadn't searched it ever before). What he found out really was kind of interesting, though.

Turns out that Gobbler Holler was first settled in the late 1700's, around 1780. Some guys ran away from fighting in the Revolution (when was the first volution?) and settled in the woods at the edge of the swamp in southern Munrow County, but it weren't the county back then. Their last names were Cobble, oddly enough (they're still odd), and they were all cousins.

For whatever reasons (not good ones, I expect), the families prospered (Buzz says that means they made money) and eventually built the big house that now is the convent—it was donated sometime in the late 1800's; the Deed of Gift, Buzz says, was recorded Oct. 31, 1898, and made out to the Sisters of Innocence. Buzz later said that that name is a "misnomer," but I'm not sure if there's a *misternomer* somewhere, too. Some things I'll never know, I guess.

Buzz also went to the museum archives while at the county seat (why do counties have places to sit—seats—but states or cities or towns don't?), whatever *archives* are (like beehives?). He found out that some of the early Cobbles were pirates—"buccaneers," I think he said, though that's awful expensive for corn—and that a famous pirate, Jean Lafitte, was seen in the area of Gobbler Holler from time to time.

To Buzz, though, it was still a mystery why there was such sudden interest in the convent property. He published a nice history of the town and convent in the *Herald* that week, then only later found out about the sudden interest.

Chapter Five—Mert's Message

As I think I said before, Mert and his cousin, Grady, are both hard of hearing (not stone deaf enough, Buzz "opined"—his word). They also tended to imbibe (Lord knows where Buzz got *that* word from, but the cousins did drink a lot, and often), and they were regular customers of the shiners.

I should tell you a bit about the moonshine boys now, as they have a part to play as this story unfolds, too (but I don't remember ever folding it earlier—the pile of pages was too thick. More Buzz words I borrowed at his suggestion).

The main shiner I'll call "Gaston LeBuze." Hubie Grant said he liked that story name for him since it sounded French, and he always liked French dressing, French fries, French pastries, and French kissing!

Anyway, Gaston was always looking to make a penny (usually a lot more), and was always alert (I asked Buzz if there ever was more than one *lert*) for an opportunity.

Seems as how Mert tagged along when Gaston and company went to visit Sister M&M with their proposal (turns out it didn't have nothing to do with marriage, though) to either buy the convent outright (is there an *inright?*) or merge their interests in alcohol production (Buzz says it was probably a "spirited conversation," but I don't get it). As usual, Mert was a bit under the weather (when was he ever *over* the weather or even even with it?), and with his diminished hearing (*dim* I can understand!), he only caught bits and pieces of the conversation.

As we all found out much later, Mert only picked up on a few key words: "*merger*" he heard as "murder," *cold* or *mold* (both were said) he heard as "gold," *team up* became "steam up," *hurried* as "buried," *tie up* to Mert was "pirate," *tap* was "map," and *shine* became "find." I've heard

63

that folks tend to fill in gaps to have things make more sense to them, and Mert was a master at that. His sworn conclusion was that there was pirate gold to be had somewhere in or under or around the convent...period.

Now I don't know if you've ever played that talking game called, "Telephone." Folks sit in a circle, and the leader starts a detailed story by whispering it into the ear of the person to the left. That person whispers the story to the next person and so on until the story goes around the circle. The last person then says the story out loud, and usually the story is very different from what was said at the start. Gobbler Holler had its own version of that game.

Buzz later said that the "gossip train" (we had no railroad and no station, so I'm not sure about the train part, but there was lots of gossip) started with Mert. Mert, of course, told Grady, who was sweet on Cherry-Anne and visited her often, who told Sally soon afterword, who told Sister M&M, who didn't tell anybody. But Cherry-Anne also told Kitty, who didn't tell anyone, and told Sly, who didn't tell anyone...at first. So a lot of people eventually heard versions of Mert's story, and you can imagine the many "embellishments" (another Buzz word). The upshot was a kind of "gold fever" in Gobbler Holler, with Sly being the main spreader of the infection beyond the Holler...all the way to the county seat and sheriff, Dewey Kaire...sort of.

Chapter Six—Sly's Ploy Play

Truth be told, Sly and Dewey have had an off-and-on love slash hate, hot and cold kind of relationship ever since they were in grammar school. Folks say that Dewey used to pick on Sly when he could get away with it, just to hear the teacher sister yell "Ferguson!" Buzz calls their relationship "ambivalent" and "opportunistic." I have no idea what that means, unless "tunistic" has something to do with music.

Anyway, Sly had a plan to get hisself into the convent to do some looking around, but he needed Dewey's help. Dewey, being the voice of law and order for the county, had ignored Sly's illegal business, the *Passion Pit*, figuring that it was so far on the edge of the county that most proper folks wouldn't know (or care) that it was there. Besides, he knew of men who took advantage of its services from time to time and didn't need anyone else to know. Dewey avoided Sly most of the time, and Sly usually stayed away from him, so Dewey was surprised when Sly went looking for him the day after the *Herald*'s article, and the day after Mert's story hit the rumor mill (Buzz's term. Most mills I know of grind something). Sly's approach was to get Dewey's help without letting on his real reason, if he could.

I heard later that the talk between them went something like this, at Dewey's office:

Sly: "Mornin', Sheriff."

Dewey: "'Tis. What do *you* want?"

Sly: "Now, Dewey, I was just stoppin' by for a neighborly visit with my favorite public servant."

Dewey: "Uh huh. So, what do you *want*, Ferguson?"

Sly: "What makes you think I'm after something?"

Dewey: "You wouldn't be here otherwise. So…"

The Happening in Gobbler Holler

Sly: "I'm deeply concerned for the safety of our dear sisters of Innocence, who are living in that rundown Cobble homestead in Gobbler Holler that they now use for their convent. I really think the building inspector should take a look-see."

Dewey: "What makes you think the nuns might be at risk?"

Sly: "Well, I hear that the roof leaks, and the foundation has shifted, and the toilets may not be up to code, and rats are in the cellar, and..."

Dewey: "Okay, enough, Ferguson. What are you *really* after?"

Sly: "Well, I think you should move the sisters until we can be sure the building is safe. Say for a few days or maybe weeks..."

Dewey: "And where would you suggest that they go in the meantime?"

Sly: "With my connections in the Holler, I'm sure I could find them a safe and suitable place."

Dewey: "You really think the place is that risky?"

Sly: "Oh, indeed I do. It'd be a shame if one of them dear ladies got hurt, don't you think?"

Dewey: "Okay, Ferguson. I'll speak to the inspector, but I'm still wondering what you're up to. It better not be trouble."

Sly: "Why, sheriff—I'm just trying to be a concerned citizen."

That was the gist (Buzz's term) of the talk between Sly and Dewey as best I can tell. In any case, the building inspector showed up at the door of the convent the next day to make an inspection appointment for later, much to Sister M&M's chagrin (another Buzz word). I'm guessing the sisters weren't too happy about the visit, but Sly weren't done at that—he played another card (as Buzz said) during his day at the county seat.

I already told you about the sisters' elderberry wine business. Sly decided to up his ante (Buzz says that means he wanted to put more pressure on the sisters) by getting the county's health inspector to check out the convent's wine-making operation. Of course, Sly volunteered to introduce the health inspector to the sisters and accompany him on his inspection (I don't know how that makes him "a company," but Sly definitely wanted to be there).

So Sly's plot was set in motion, but his was not the only plan afoot. (Buzz confuses me a lot. How can a plan be "a foot"?)

Chapter Seven—Kitty and the Shiners

Buzz suggested the word *attack* for the next part—says it adds "drama" to the story. I weren't writing no play, though, just telling the story as best folks can recollect it (though most didn't *collect* it all in the first place).

The same day Sly was making his visits at the county seat, Kitty was taking matters into her own hands, so to speak. Sister Sally never knew it (until later), but Kitty had suspicioned that Sister Sally and one of her working girls were one and the same (seems like *the same* would be enough to make the point, I think). Kitty decided to approach Sister Sally "obliquely" while at the *Pit* (Buzz seems to know something about trigger-nometry, but we all know he's not a very good shot).

Sister Sally's working name at the *Pit* was "Sweetpea," but Kitty sup-posedly slipped and started talking by saying "Sally" instead. She must've caught Sister Sally off guard (is that the opposite of *en garde* like in sword fighting?), 'cause Sweetpea turned toward Kitty and right away turned beet red (I always thought beets were more like purple).

"Were you talking to me?" Sally slash Sweetpea quickly stammered.

"I must have startled you, Sweetpea. I'm sorry. But I've suspected who you were for quite some time now. I won't tell, and won't stop you from working for Sly, though I'm not sure why you'd want to." Kitty tried to sound kind and sympathetic (when Buzz first told me that word I thought he said, "sin pathetic").

"It's complicated, Kitty," Sweetpea slash Sally supposedly said. "If you only knew…"

"That's okay. I probably don't *want* to know, but I do need your help—I have some questions that aren't personal." Kitty needed informa-tion, and a way to get into the convent without letting on about her real reason. The easiest way might be to get the sisters out of the convent for a time. Vacation? Scare? Pretext? She wasn't sure yet how to work it (Buzz added the *pretext*; am I supposed to follow up with a "posttext"?).

At the same time Kitty was pondering her attack (*pondering* must be kind of like fishing of some sort?), Mert and Grady were being set up by Gaston to be his "confederates" (I figure Buzz needed to use a southern word, since we're in that part of the county) to help carry out his plan to find the gold, without letting on that that was his idea. Mert and Grady couldn't hear too well, though, so Gaston had to be careful about his choice and loudness of his words, in case someone might overhear (better that they *underhear*). Gaston decided he had to be *deceptive* (don't you have to be *ceptive* first before you *de* it? Buzz really loses me at times. Good thing he does the spelling for me when I ask for help!)

The talking went something like this:

Gaston started by telling Mert and Grady that he'd pay them for their help, but they had to be discreet. Mert heard that last word as "greet," and Grady heard it as "cheat."

So Mert says, "When are we going to meet, and who with?"

"You want to pay me to cheat?" Grady asks.

"I won't eat no gray meat for any amount of money, Gaston," Mert protested.

"No, Mert! I need help to get some stuff into the convent some night," Gaston tried to explain.

Mert came back with, "I don't usually like it rough, but some say Daena might."

That's all Grady needed to (mis)hear—dynamite was his forte (Buzz says that means that Grady was good at it—explosives, that is. I should explain...).

69

Chapter Eight—Fortes

My momma used to say that everyone of God's children has something they're good at— "strengths" she called them—but some folks seem awfully weak to me. Buzz uses the word *fortes*—I think that's from *forts*, since they are usually *strong*holds I read once.

Mert has a special strength—he's really good with animals. I once saw him put a wild hog to sleep just by singing to it and hitting it with a hammer, but I'm not sure he really needed the hammer.

Grady is a really good fisherman. The swamp drains into the Howe's Bayou, and that leads into the bay, which is part of the gulf. Grady gets in his skiff and goes out into the bay, drops a stick of dynamite over the side, and then scoops up all of the floating fish.

Kitty is a great hostess, and her three best entertainers are Cherry-Anne, Sweetpea, and Daena (Dyna said I shouldn't use her real name for my story, so I made up a different one for her). Cherry-Anne is soft and smells good, Sweetpea is "mysterious" (Buzz's word), and Daena is really smart and fun, I guess—she said she used to be a playmate.

Buzz is really good with words. Besides running the *Gobbler Holler Herald*, he said he does crossword puzzles (I didn't know words could get mad) and likes history things.

Sly is a good businessman, I think. Some say he's "slippery,"—and I've heard others say he's "sleazy" or "seedy," but I've never known him to be a farmer. I've wondered if all those "s" words mean that he's crooked somehow.

Anyway, Gaston is really good at making moonshine, but his wife says he's not good for much else.

Mert and Grady set off on their "quest" (Buzz word) to aid Gaston in his mission—to "gain access to the convent and explore its nether regions"

(Buzz told me all that; I couldn't make it up) to look for the gold. Mert was thinking animal, Grady something more dramatic.

Chapter Nine—The Quest

Mert headed out with the single-minded goal (gee, Buzz. Everyone here knows that Mert only has one brain, if that) to carry out his part of the plan, with four-legged help.

"Here, kitty kitty," could be heard throughout the woods near the swamp and the "extensive town repository of excess items" (Buzz's fancy term for the town dump). Mert was armed with a blanket, bottle of shine, some shallow tins, and spring clothespins—and a lot of nerve or stupidity, depending on your point of view.

Most folks livin' in the country know that skunks like to eat, and they'll eat most anything, anytime. For that reason they tend to hang out around trash cans and dumps, sometimes keeping company with the local raccoons. Mert discovered something else about skunks years ago—they also like shine. In fact, like Mert hisself, they'll get downright tipsy to the point of passing out sometimes. Mert was depending on that.

Mert picked a few likely skunking spots and set out some pans of shine, one swig for hisself, one for the skunks…well maybe two for hisself, "just in case" (I have no idea what that case was).

After a few hours of patient waiting—and let's face it, drinking and dozing—Mert visited his makeshift "skunk taverns" (as Buzz later called them) and found two willing customers, neither of whom was able to "navigate independently." (Buzz came up with that one—I never knew skunks were sailors, too. You learn something new every day, I guess.)

"Just in case," as Mert said, the purpose of the clothespins became clear—nose protection "in case" a skunk should come to "in transit" (Buzz's term. I knew a surveyor feller once with a transit, but it weren't big enough to hold a skunk. Buzz can be confusing sometimes!).

Mert gently wrapped his "quarry" (not the stone kind, Buzz said) in the blanket, being very sure to keep their tails down "just in case." As soon as he could, he snuck over to the convent, "under cover of darkness" (as Buzz put it) and found an open basement window. He then ever so gently lowered the blanket to the stone floor of the cellar and rolled the skunks off'n the blanket so he could take it back home. There they lay until sometime later.

On his part, Grady was busy, too. He'd understood his part of Gaston's plan to require dynamite, so he laid aside "a store" (Buzz's words. I never knew Grady to own a store) from his fishing supplies, tucking several sticks into a wooden box that used to hold wine bottles before it got soaked in shine. He figured that Gaston planned to move some stones while looking for the gold, which he was sure was hidden in the convent's cellar.

Chapter Ten—The Inspection

While Buzz was researching the convent property, he found out that the main part of the Cobble House went back to 1810—it was very old and had some additions over the years. The house had no near neighbors for a long time, neither. The early Cobbles were decent folks, I guess, but they wanted to be helpful to their pirate ("buccaneer," Buzz said) visitors; I suspect they were really afraid of them, though.

Howsomever, they had hiding places built into the stone walls of the cellar, both as places to hide themselves and to hide other things.

From his research, Buzz "surmised" (his word) that many Cobbles took advantage of those many "nooks and crannies" in the cellar over the years. The house had lots of visitors during the war of 1812, the war over the south, and from others from time to time. Buzz guessed that kegs of powder (not the lady kind but the gun and cannon kind) must've been "cached" (Buzz says that's not money) in many places in the cellar. He also said that a lot of it could have become "unstable" over all those years (I've been in stables, but I don't know if any of them ever were turned into an *unstable*). So there they sat without anyone knowing.

Soon after Sly's meeting with the sheriff, the sheriff had an unexpected visit from the FBI, and I'm going to let Buzz tell the rest of this part of the story 'cause it gets too tricky for me. I had to talk him into it since it's really my story—he just wanted to "consult," he said.

Buzz: Sheriff Kaire told me that the FBI agent sought him out to follow up on some leads about a counterfeiting ring that apparently had been moving its operations from state to state over a period of years. The FBI's informants had reported the presence of bogus 10-dollar bills in the Munrow County area, unusual as most counterfeiters produced larger denominations—100-dollar bills especially. The agent also described some possible suspects, a family of five women, who may be involved. Something rang a bell in the sheriff's mind when the FBI agent mentioned "five sisters" ("rang a bell" may explain why some folks call Dewey a "bit dingy"—I added that).

The upshot was that the sheriff invited the FBI agent along on his upcoming expedition to Gobbler Holler, along with the building and health inspectors.

The four of them arrived on the convent's doorstep around 10 a.m. after their hour's drive from the county seat. As luck would have it, Sister Mary responded to their knock and after introductions and comprehending the possible reasons for their visit, explained that the sisters were at prayers and could not be interrupted for the next 20 minutes.

The sheriff said he understood and did not mean to interrupt the sisters' routine—they would "wait outside on this lovely day."

While the wait went on, the sisters were frantically busy implementing a pre-arranged plan. Their cellar winery, such as it was, was quite primitive, but one large vat down there was always kept nearly full of elderberry juice, "just in case." The sisters quickly disassembled their old iron counterfeiting press and placed the pieces in the juice vat, where they would not be visible to casual view. In their haste, they never noticed two black and white balls of fur among the cellar's litter.

When all was ready, Sister Mary went upstairs to retrieve the inspection crew. The other sisters prepared tea and treats for their visitors as a way to keep busy and conceal their nervousness.

The sheriff had prepped the building inspector to look for mold, rusty pipes, insects, or rats in the basement—anything that might force the sisters out for a while.

Dewey made a point of his concern for the health and safety of "those dear nuns". The sisters couldn't be allowed to inhabit an unsafe dwelling

(I put in the *inhabit* word, figuring that's how nuns usually were dressed).

The inspection team found few concerns during their tour of the upstairs rooms, and as the sheriff's ploy for both the building and health inspectors included the basement, they headed down there next—about the time that the two skunks were coming to, and all hell broke loose!

Those two skunks were clearly not pleased to be awakened in a confined, dark dungeon of a space, and I imagine they were in foul humor. Just as the inspection party spread out to examine the visible basement, two striped fur balls raised their tails and punctuated their displeasure with two well-aimed sprays delivered with great enthusiasm.

The initial reaction by the two-legged interlopers was one of shocked disbelief, followed immediately by a stampede to the narrow stairway as *eau de skunk* permeated the air, causing tearing eyes and many signs of nasal distress.

It was a situation demanding survival of the fittest, which happened to be the FBI agent. Sheriff Kaire was at a strategic disadvantage, given his bulk and location farthest from the stairs. In his headlong rush, however, he shoved past the health inspector, who was forced into an unexpected plunge into the vat of elderberry juice. The building inspector, nearest the stairs at the time, was run down in turn by the FBI agent first and the sheriff second. The building inspector's broken arm became the least of his problems as the skunks moved closer for a parting shot, which the history of the occasion suggests was convincingly redundant. (I don't think it was necessary neither, but it sure was effective!)

The FBI agent reached the top of the stairs just as Sister Mary came to the spot to see what the commotion was all about. The odor reaching her nostrils might have convinced her to retreat, but before she could, she essentially was flattened by the sprinting FBI agent. The next in line, sheriff Kaire, tripped over the prone sister and mimicked a walrus performing a flying tackle.

Meanwhile, the health inspector did his best to extricate himself from the vat, grabbing at whatever was handy, which happened to be hunks of metal at the bottom of the juice cistern. Once back in the open, fragrant air, though, he dropped the press pieces to grab at his nose. He then staggered toward the stairway, where he managed to trip over the building inspector and receive the benefit of the skunks' final salvo before propelling himself up the steps and directly into the slowly rising Sister Mary and Sheriff Kaire.

Lacking a completed report, all concerned agreed that the convent would be temporarily uninhabitable, given the strength of the odor and the continued presence of the black and white defenders. The sheriff was delighted for the most part—he would find a way to deal with the skunk issue—and both Gaston and Kitty were equally happy when they learned that the convent would be vacated for a time, with the windows and doors left wide open, while the building was left to defumigate itself.

Chapter Eleven—Temporary Home Sweet Home

Mert was mighty pleased with hisself that his part of Gaston's scheme had gone so well, but without his knowing, he'd made some other folks happy, too: Kitty because it would leave the convent wide open for her to explore, Sly for the same reason, and Dewey because it would make it easy for him to look for evidence about his hunch about the sisters that was stirred up ("aroused," Buzz said) by the FBI agent's "inquiry." (Buzz said, Is there an *outquiry*, too?)

For the time being, the five sisters needed a place to stay. Sly approached Kitty with an idea, and she readily agreed (as Buzz noted later). Both saw a good chance to keep an eye on the whereabouts of the sisters while taking advantage of their absence from the convent premises. (Buzz sure uses a lot of 25-cent words to mean a nickel's worth of idea!)

Kitty was pretty sure by now of Sweetpea's other identity as Sister Sally, but she decided to approach the move-in subject "tentatively," as Buzz put it, (even though the *Pit* was not a tent), by just talking out loud about Sly's housing idea where Sweetpea could hear. Kitty hoped that Sweetpea would cotton to the idea and maybe pass it on to Sister M&M, which, it turns out, she did. So, Sister M&M was ready with her answer when Sly got up the moxie to ask her hisself—she said, "Yes," fast to avoid any discussion and doubts about turning the *Passion Pit* into a temporary convent.

"It'll only be for a few days," she hoped when she saw Kitty later. Sly meantimes was slapping hisself on his back (not sure how—Buzz's description) at his cleverness in performing his "civic duty," as he told Buzz for the *Herald*.

Since skunk smell was everywhere ("essence of mephitis," the *Herald* had it), the sisters moved quickly with only the clothes on their backs (and

78

fronts and sides, to tell the whole truth for their sakes), and those clothes weren't smelling so good neither!

The upshot was that the good ladies of the *Pit* offered other things to wear so the sisters' clothes, "habits" they called them, could be washed. Took all the cans of tomato juice in town to do it, they said.

Sister Sally slash Sweetpea was used to wearing whorehouse clothes, and truth be told, she looked right good that way. I can't say the same for Sister M&M, though—she kind of stuck out all over, being built more cow than pole-like. (Buzz said she is "statuesque." She really is more like fat.)

The *Pit* crew (nothing to do with racing cars here) were really kind to the sisters, but the sisters being at the *Pit* played hell, so to speak, with the regular customers, as it turned out—as if that were a surprise! Sly and Kitty didn't care, though—the regulars would get over it—as they each had their "sights set on bigger (that is, golder) game" (Buzz's way of saying they were greedy).

For a time, no one had a clue what to do about the skunks in the convent cellar, but finally Gaston "remembered" that Mert was good with critters and "maybe" could come up with some way to get them skunks out of there. He could. Lowering a tin of 'shine through the same window, waiting a few hours, and then making "judicious use" of the clothespins for his nose while he "extricated" (you guessed it—Buzz words) the sleeping skunks via blanket did the trick. It weren't really a *trick*, though—the ladies at the *Pit* did those, I think.

Chapter Twelve—Grady and Mert's "Uh oh"!

It took me and Buzz some days to piece together this next part of the story, but here's what we come up with to explain the happening.

The convent's wine-making produced about 40 cases a year during its three years. The bottles were shipped out in wooden boxes labeled "Taste of Heaven Winery," 12 bottles to a case. For the holidays the sisters had special gift boxes made up that held four bottles each, also labeled like the bigger cases. Sly got a gift box, Buzz at the paper did, Gaston begged one, the sheriff got one, etc. (Buzz says *etc.* saves me writing some names of people I don't know anyways.)

Gaston's gift box got emptied quickly (no surprise there!), as did Sly's box at the *Pit*. The empties sat around as the sisters could collect the bottles to clean and reuse. The empty boxes did, too. You need to know this to make sense of what happened after the sisters moved into the *Pit*.

Mert took care of the skunks as he said he would, but the convent still stunk to high heaven, not meaning the wine. Grady was still focused on Gaston's maybe needing to move some foundation rocks to make some holes, figuring his fishing technique might need to be employed (as Buzz suspected later).

Supposedly, Mert and Grady had a conversation something like this:

Mert: "You takin' yer boat 'n' goin' fishin'?"

Grady: "Ain't nothin' missin'. I put the sticks in that empty wine box Gaston give me."

Mert: "Keep 'er off'n the rocks. You might want to sell 'er someday."

Grady: "Yup. That cellar's all rocks. Gaston said we might need to blow some, so I'm ready."

Mert: "Nope. I ain't seen Freddy for some time. He fishin' with you? For fishin' he's got some real know-how."

Grady: "Go now? Okay, I'll get the box and head over to the convent. I hope no one's there."

Mert: "Yup. Today's mighty fair. Good luck!"

Grady: "Right—tough way to make a buck."

Chapter Thirteen—Timing

Buzz says that timing is as important in life events as is location for a business or real estate sale. (Is there "fake estate," too? I suppose it'd be hard to sell a phony estate. Gobbler Holler don't have any estates anyhow.)

Turns out that Sister M&M was getting restless at the *Passion Pit*. She was nervous about the convent being left wide open, the condition of the press hid away in the vat of elderberry juice, and the chance of the FBI or sheriff finding it there. The wine press was okay, but the bill press not so much. She also was not happy about being mistaken for a "lady of the night" by the *Pit*'s customers (Buzz's term, but I don't see how it fits as the ladies work during the day, too).

As things turned out, Grady got to the convent first that day. He'd borrowed a clothespin from Mert, which he still needed even though the odor in the convent was not eye-watering anymore. It did still stink some, though—enough so Grady didn't want to stay for long. He saw lots of empty wine bottles and crates around the basement, and hid his box of "boomsticks" (Grady's word for his dynamite) in among them, then left in a hurry.

We figure that Sister M&M must've got there about a half hour later. She'd had an idea for how to speed up the destinking process—incense. The convent had a good bunch of incense sticks she could spread around in hopes of overcoming the skunks' spraying. She was ready for the smell with a scarf soaked in borrowed perfume wrapped over her nose. She told Buzz afterwards that she found the incense sticks, went down into the basement, and spread them around on the stone floor as she lit each one, being careful to keep them away from anything else that could burn. She then left and headed back to the *Pit*, figuring to report back to her sister sisters and Kitty.

As luck would have it, the sheriff came down alone from the county seat, hoping that the smell wouldn't keep him from investigating the convent for any funny business the sisters might have been up to—like printing "funny money," for example. He, too, was ready for the smell with a clothespin of his own. He also brought a swim mask and can of air spray, "just in case." No one was at the convent ("Good," Dewey thought), so he checked out the upstairs rooms again before heading down to the cellar. He was sure that something important would be hid there.

As he came down the stairs, he could see that bottles, boxes, and burning incense sticks were everywhere. It would be hard to find a place to walk, never mind look into all the corners of the whole cellar, and there were lots of these because of the additions over the many years.

Now Dewey weren't known for his genius or his patience. "Sizing up the logistics of the setting" (Buzz's description), the sheriff started moving boxes around into a pile—a neat stack, he later insisted—and then gathered up the incense sticks and set them in a bunch on top of one of the boxes. He "gave no thought to the possible consequences" (as Buzz put it)—he was in a hurry and too set on his investigation to bother thinking, I think.

Dewey stayed at the convent for over two hours, but he never did think to look into the vat of elderberry juice. He did manage to move some stones around and discovered some of the casks of gunpowder that got stuck away long ago.

When he left, Dewey weren't happy, though. He didn't find any evidence, and he had to rush back to the county seat to be on time for his meeting with the FBI agent. He didn't give another thought to the convent basement, the boxes, the powder, or the burning incense sticks.

No one knows for sure which box the incense was perched on, but I suspect that you might figure by now where this story is headed. Grady guessed that his box might've caught fire first, but it don't really matter now—the deed's been done, with spectacular results.

Chapter Fourteen—Having a Blast in Gobbler Holler

My words could never do it justice, so I will use as many words as I can from Buzz's front-page story in the *Gobbler Holler Herald* after that day:

"The results of the tremendous explosion at the Convent of the Sisters of Innocence this Monday past were truly a wonder to behold.

"The horrific concussion rendered the old Cobble place into particles of dust, and the sound was heard as far away as the county seat, where the Munrow Institute's seismograph registered a 4.8 possible geologic event.

"Nearly every window within a mile of the blast was shattered, and even the stone-deaf Cobble family members swore they heard it.

"Many consequences of the event were instantaneous and unpredictable:

"The walls of Miller Composte's outhouse were thrown a half-mile away while Miller remained perched over the open hole to try to complete his morning's business.

"Down at the *Passion Pit*, Cherry-Anne was sent airborne off her bed while Bobbie Conway was summarily tossed off of her.

"Boys down at the swamp reported that all of the water seemed to drain out of the bog at once, leaving LeRoi Finster high and dry over the side of his fishing boat until the water came rushing back.

"Charlie McCoy, the local paper boy for the *Munrow Daily Bugle*, had just flipped a paper toward Carl Cobble's front porch. He watched in awe as the shock wave sent the paper clean over the house to land who knows where. He said that he was not able to find it afterwards.

"Hillary Hendel told the *Herald* that at the moment of the blast, her toast had just popped up, but it went out her kitchen window along with the glass and the family cat, who usually lay in the sun on the windowsill.

"Other damage reported included the *Pit*'s being knocked off its pilings; two cars nearest to the convent being rolled over; Jeb Cornfeld's cow barn being flattened and his cows refusing to give milk later that day; the steeple on the Community Church & Gambling Hall being toppled, and Caroline Calloway's hairpiece blown clear of her head to land a mile away on the head of Chester Buereaux's pregnant sow. Chester was heard to remark on the improvement to both creatures.

"Long-term consequences of the explosion are yet to be seen, but the crater left by the event has been measured at 18 feet deep and 120 feet across at its widest girth. Fragments of the structure itself are said to be unrecognizable and widespread. The building inspector can rest easy that his unfavorable verdict about the convent's condition is now moot—or perhaps more accurate?

"Law enforcement has yet to issue a preliminary investigation report, but Sheriff Kaire was reported to have been overheard muttering, "Good riddance to bad rubbish," or something to that effect. (Mert Cobble was the informant for that quote. Supposedly the blast caught him sober, but he quickly rectified that oversight.)

"The detonation also had other unintended, but apparently fortunate, sequelae. The FBI's investigation of the convent came to an abrupt halt, some say to Sheriff Kaire's and Ferguson Foxx's respective relief due to pulverization of the likely evidence.

"Some constructive use may yet come of the convent's property, considering that it is still "holey ground," as one local wag observed. Possible uses suggested have included a municipal swimming hole or a new site for the town dump, or both."

Epilogue

When Buzz suggested I write down this story, with his help, I didn't know what *epilogue* meant. I knew what a *log* is, of course, but I had to look up the *epi* part. The dictionary says that *epi* is a prefix meaning "over, on, upon, above, around, near, close to, besides, or after."

Since a *pre*fix must come before the actual *fix*, I don't know why Buzz said to put this part at the end of the story and what it has to do with a log. I'm told that paper's made somehow from logs—maybe that's what made the idea of a log book?

Anyhow, here's what happened after the happening:

It took some days and hard work by many volunteers, but the *Pit* was put right back on its pilings, and Sly's business continued as usual. Sally slash Sweetpea soon disappeared, though, as did her four sisters, who really were sisters but not sisters. No one took over the elderberry wine business, but the shiners did try an elderberry flavoring that was not well received.

Sly held the window glass concession for a time, and he tried to promote the blast site as a tourist attraction; the guest book last I look had three names—all Cobbles.

The church steeple was rebuilt from the gambling proceeds, but it took a year or so. Sly started a fund-raising effort to buy a traffic light to help handle all of the expected tourist traffic. He found one second hand, but it's still in its crate. He's now trying to raise money to build a cross street for Main Street, so there'll be a place to put the light. So far that fund has collected $11.47.

The hole is still there a year after the blast, still unused, but some water has collected, reeds have started to grow, and a family of snapping turtles has set up housekeeping. Maybe it'll become a "wildlife sanctuary," as Buzz suggested, but I've seen more wild life at the *Passion Pit*, especially at New Year's.

Mert and Grady ain't heard any better since the explosion, but they both said they did hear the blast quite well. Cherry-Anne recovered but says she hasn't seen Bobbie Conway since, and he was a regular. Some say his mother found out about his visits to the *Pit* because of that night. He 'posedly fessed up to her what he had been doing, thinking that Cherry-Anne's leaping off the bed somehow was his fault.

I'm done with my writing this story, too. I don't know any more words, and the story's pretty much over. You can just call me "Golley" when you see me, 'cause that's my name. Buzz says some writers use "pen names," but I usually write with a pencil.

Golley Klimbo

Letters from Woodrow

"What a mess!" Sadie exclaimed to no one in particular, except perhaps to the moths, spiders, and flies that inhabited the old attic. The last of the Sochs had died, and the 22-room family mansion was to be razed in favor of a waterfront condo development. Sadie, grandniece by marriage, was saddled with the responsibility—the onerous chore—of clearing out and disposing of the accumulated heirlooms, most of which could properly be described as junk, first-class.

A few items might have lawn-sale value: the wood-framed rawhide snowshoes, the dust-filled bearskin robe, the stuffed deer head with shaky antlers, some early 20th century dresses, a few trinkets from trips to the Orient and Africa, and maybe those old shoe and hat racks.

"What about that old steamer trunk?" crossed Sadie's tiring mind. "Someone might pay a few dollars for it."

Sadie crept into the corner under the eaves, brushed aside a cobweb for the ages, and slowly dragged the dusty chest into better light. It was latched, but not locked, and upon further inspection seemed to be lined with colorful paper or cloth. Its contents consisted only of two bundles of envelopes tied neatly around with blue ribbons.

"We won't get anything for those," sighed Sadie to herself. She needed a break, though, and was near to choking on the clouds of dust raised by her morning's efforts. She retreated downstairs, bundles in hand.

Sadie set the bundles on the kitchen table and heated some water for tea. It was too early in the day for stronger libations, although she was tempted. While the water heated, she sat down and untied the ribbon from one bundle. The pile of envelopes fell over and spread across the corner of the table. As she started to reassemble the pile, Sadie noticed postmarks from all across the country, as well as a few from overseas. Intrigued, she examined the postmarks more closely. They ranged from September of 1910 through December of 1916. Undoing the second bundle's ribbon revealed postmarks from January 1917 into December 1920. All of the writing on the envelopes seemed to have been by the same hand.

While sipping her green tea, Sadie opened the first letter from the first bundle and proceeded to step back a century into the world of her Sochs ancestors. The letter, dated September 2, 1910, was addressed to Mr. and Mrs. Argyle Sochs, and signed, "Your Son, Woodrow." Sadie started to read:

Dear Mother and Father,

I arrived at Mouldie Academy two days ago, but I did not have time to write before the dormitory fire, sorry. The fire inspector said it was Arson, but Arson was down at the gymnasium at the time.

The Headmaster seems stern. At his welcoming address he said that he expected to mold us new students into "Mouldie men." With the dampness here, he might succeed. I think I will enjoy 8th grade. One of my dormmates said that he is starting his fourth year in 8th grade, he liked it so much.

The trip here went well, at least after the train was rerailed. The steamboat crew lost my luggage, but that was a good thing, as they had to burn up the other passengers' luggage to keep steam up while bucking the 70-mile-per-hour headwinds.

Oh, all the buildings here at the Academy now have indoor plumbing. They kind of had to install it after the outhouse building blew up. Someone apparently lit up their pipe after someone else had discarded dirty gasoline down one of the holes. The sitter survived; he attributed the explosion to the bean dinner the night before.

I will write again after classes start. Please be sure to attend graduation ceremonies on June 20. Maybe you can be here for my 12th birthday on the 26th. Love to the family.

Your Son,
Woodrow

***

After reading this first letter, Sadie became curious and sought a slim volume from the study's book shelves that contained a chart depicting the family tree.

"There you are," Sadie brightly observed. "Woodrow Sochs, b. June 26, 1899, son of Argyle and Nida Paira Sochs." She returned to the kitchen table, book in hand, determined to continue her reading and set aside her attic work for a time. Her perusing the letters carried her far into the night, however, skipping over many letters along the way.

July 22, 1911
Camp Watsituya

Dear Mother and Father,

I arrived here on July 20 in time for the rededication of the rebuilt lodge building, the old one having been consumed by the

91

Fourth of July celebration. We were told that it was quite a specta-cle...patriotic, though.

Please let Calvin's parents know that he will write to them as soon as his poison ivy allows him to use his hands again.

I received a short note from Uncle Sean about Uncle Frederick's new law firm, Dewey, Trye & Beatim. I didn't know that he had been cleared and reinstated. It's too bad that his previous firm, Stiphem & Paioph, went out of business.

This camp really does live up to its promise as a "wilderness experience." We are going on a 10-mile hike tomorrow to try to find our camp guide who, we think, got lost yesterday. The Director said that we could use an empty wine bottle as a clue.

I'm looking forward to canoeing and sailing. The 21-foot war canoe is being repaired after being defeated in a mock battle with the girls' camp down the lake. We are to make our own paddles in the craft shop, after we make the new mast for the sailboat and refloat the swimming raft.

I've got to go. They're choosing up teams for a baseball game. Since he can't play yet, they're using Calvin for second base.

Love to you all!
Your Son,
Woodrow

August 18, 1911
Camp Watsituya

Dear Mother and Father,

I wanted to write to you immediately to correct any misconcep-tions that you might have because of the erroneous newspaper

92

accounts of last week's unfortunate occurrences here at camp.

The forest fires were not solely the result of our candle boats regatta. We might be correctly blamed for the conflagration on the lake's east shore, but we are certain that the west shore blaze was ignited by the same lightning storm that struck the cookshack and burned it to the ground.

The good news is that our unanticipated barbecue fed us handsomely the next day, with some left over. The bad news is that the bears the leftovers attracted tore up the camp—it wasn't marauding natives as the newspaper accounts have suggested.

*One other supposed fact needs to be corrected: the strong winds did **not** overturn the camp's boats. We think that the meteor that hit the south end of the lake did it; it wasn't the tornado's doing.*

I hope that this puts your minds at ease.

Love you all,
Your son,
Woodrow

p.s. The other campers gave me the nickname "Woodie," but I prefer Woodrow, as I think the word "Woodie" could be misconstrued.

August 19, 1911
Camp Watsituya

Dear Mater and Pater,

Last night's mixer with the girls' camp down the lake, Camp Itchiglumi, went well after the bee swarm left.

One girl, Bertha, invited me to go canoodle with her after someone called me "Woodie." It turns out that I didn't need my life vest or paddle, or a canoe. Who knew?

She thinks our children may be smart. I think she's kidding, maybe.

Your wiser Son,
Woodrow

***

Sadie took a couple of sips of her cooling tea and opened the next letter in the pile.

March 8, 1912
Mouldie Academy
Upper Cutt, Maine

Dear Uncle Sean,

I recently received a letter from your brother, my Uncle Frederick, postmarked London, England. He asked me to write to you to save on overseas delivery.

Uncle Frederick has booked passage on a new ship, the **Titanic**—*first class, he said. You remember when he bent his canoe around a rock in the Chilly River rapids. Who could forget the day that he jumped down from the dock into his rowboat and went right through the bottom?*

The rescue service people were very kind when Uncle drove his cabin cruiser onto that ledge. Capsizing a sailboat could have happened to anyone.

Uncle Frederick noted that he hasn't had much good luck with boats, so he is really glad to be sailing on an unsinkable ship!

Love to you and cousin Lusitania,
Yours Truly,
Woodrow

***

Sadie looked over the pile of letters and finally realized that she would not be able to read them all at one sitting. One did stand out, though, for its star next to the postmark. She shook off the dust, opened it and read:

June 21, 1915
Mouldie Academy
Upper Cutt, Maine

Dear Aunt Eloise and Uncle Sean,

First, I want to thank you for the lovely fountain pen with high-capacity reservoir. It truly is elegant! Before I read the copious instructions, though, I sprayed the front of my graduation gown with ink. Our gowns were black, so the stain barely showed. Not so for my white dress shirt.

Mother and father came to the ceremony, which was held last night under the new gas lights. The lights attracted bugs. The bugs attracted bats. The bats were generally unobtrusive until the part of the ceremony when we graduates tossed our caps into the air, at which time pandemonium let loose. One could not readily tell flying hat from bat.

Calvin, Teddy, and I plan to attend Sterndoin College in Bunswick next year to study Finance Management and Tax Law, in case there may be a recession or federal income tax someday. Father says that that will be a waste of my time and his money—he assured me that neither could possibly happen.

Thank you again!
Your Grateful Nephew,
Woodrow

***

Sadie skipped through a few more letters, then drew one out random-
ly:

May 25, 1919
Washington D.C.

Dear Mother and Father,

*We started on our cross-country trip last Saturday when we
loaded the new Oldsmobile on a train flatcar in New Jersey. Teddy,
Calvin and I are very excited! This transcontinental journey is a
wonderful college graduation present. I'm glad that you didn't
believe all those rumors about final exam cheating.*

*Loading the automobile went well for the most part, except
when Calvin confused the accelerator with the clutch. The car shot
off the train faster than when it was embarked, but with minimal
damage to the car, popcorn wagon that it hit, and the newsstand
behind it. Not so for Calvin's ego, I'm afraid.*

*The train portion of the trip was marred by only one minor set-
back—you probably read in the newspaper about the open draw-
bridge. Only the locomotive and first two cars took the plunge.*

*We arrived in the nation's capital late at night and promptly
sought inexpensive lodging. Teddy thought that a big white building
on Pennsylvania Avenue might serve, but we were summarily eject-
ed. We camped in a park next to a large rectangular pond that
night. Early the next morning we were rudely awakened by bicker-
ing congressmen, followed by the capital police.*

Silly Seaside Stories

Calvin asked to tour the Treasury Department, hoping that they would be passing out free samples. I wanted to visit the Lincoln Memorial, but our tour map took us several miles away. Teddy had bought it from a street vendor. Close inspection revealed that it was actually a map of Washington, Maine.

Tomorrow we plan to leave as early as we can to drive south toward Florida, after we replace the two wheels stolen off the Reo overnight.

Thank you both again for a magnificent present!

Love to the family,
Your Grateful Son,
Woodrow

***

The next letter she chose was postmarked July 2, 1919, from Appalachicola, Florida:

July 1, 1919

Dear Mother and Father,

Today we reached Florida, crossing into the state after getting lost in the swamps of Georgia. We practiced shooting mosquitoes, lacking proper skeets. Our 12-gauges proved only moderately effective—there were more of them than we had shells.

I had the opportunity to eat rattlesnake for supper last night. It tasted like chicken. Come to think of it, so did alligator tail; and frog legs tasted like chicken, too. The chicken here tastes like ham.

The doctor said that Calvin's rattlesnake bite would not be lethal. He should recover fully within a week or two.

We went swimming in a murky pond, the ocean being too salty.

Teddy was nearly bitten by a large snapping turtle, but an alligator beat the turtle to him. Teddy and Calvin are sharing a lovely hospital room for the week.

While they rested, I got to go deep sea fishing in the Gulf. I did not know that a swordfish could sink a boat. I do now. Thank you for my swimming lessons at camp.

I will write again once our trip resumes. Please give my love to the family.

> *Your Son,*
> *Woodrow*

July 18, 1919
Swinglo, Mississippi

Dear Mother and Father,

We have had a bit of a glitch in our travel plans of late. It seems that Teddy turned 21 last Friday and wanted to celebrate with his first legal drink. He apparently uttered some audible slur against the Confederacy. Big mistake.

The ensuing brawl involved dozens of the tavern's patrons, while Teddy crawled free of the melee and into the arms of the local constabulary. He was charged with "disturbing the memory of the Confederacy." His father posted the $2.00 bail, so we should be on the road soon, if the folks in the white robes and hoods are willing to move out of our way. I may have to mail this from a post office farther along in our travels, perhaps out of state.

Much love to all at home.

Your Son,
Woodrow

Sadie leaned back in her chair, then decided to refresh her tea. That done, she lifted up another envelope and dove in:

August 9, 1919
Port Flatlands, South Dakota

Dear Mother and Father,

I am sick of corn—eating corn, seeing corn, hearing corn, smelling corn. Nebraska is one big cornfield! Where is there room in Nebraska for people? I did meet a friendly farmer, though.

In a burst of patriotic fervor, I tried to enlist in the Army to go to the war. I've never been to Europe. The draft physician said that I couldn't go—I had flat feet. The farmer had to run over them twice with his tractor to be sure. That impulse passed quickly. The war was over anyway.

So far, all three of us have dodged the flu epidemic. Dodge, Kansas, effect?

Much love,
Your Son,
Woodrow

September 12, 1919
Somewhere in western South Dakota

Dear Aunt Eloise,

Thank you for sending us money after Father refused to do so. His new job as General Manager of a railroad must be keeping him preoccupied. The masthead of his latest letter read: "Versus & Khorus Railway—The Khorus Line." I've never heard of it.

Letters from Woodrow

Today we drove into the hills of western South Dakota. We camped near Mt. Rushmore, quite a pile of rock! Teddy swore that he could see faces up on the cliffs. I attribute it to some bad mushrooms. No way that faces could ever be that big or as up high...as Teddy.

We also got to see the Badlands. Teddy hallucinated dinosaurs walking about. It took him two hours to catch one. The buffalo was not amused. Teddy got a kick out of it, though.

I will write again when time and my broken wrist permit. Love to you and the family!

Your Nephew,
Woodrow

***

October 1, 1919
Mediocre Junction, Colorado

Dear Mother and Father,

We have worked our way south into the mountains of Colorado. We were tired after the long drive and set up our tent in the dark over an ant hill. Red ants are not good bedmates.

We have met a man, native to the area, who said that he would take us fly fishing in the Rockies. The hooks look awfully big to be catching flies, and I'm not sure if we are to mount them or eat them after catching them. Maybe they taste like chicken?

The fishing guide said that we would have to ford a stream on the way, but we are driving an Oldsmobile. The trip should be very illuminating; he said that we would be starting out before sunrise.

There is lots of snow on the higher elevations, and we hope to go skiing while we're here. Skiing involves going downhill on slippery boards. Teddy says that we've been going downhill for years, so skiing should be easy. I'm not sure how to turn on skis yet, so I hope that the trees will jump out of the way.

I will write more when time permits. My hands are still sore from changing flat tires. Love to the family,

Your Son,
Woodrow

***

Sadie selected one more letter to read before turning in for the night:

January 19, 1920
San Francisco, California

Dear Mother and Father,

We finally reached California after about 7,500 miles of driving and riding, 13 flat tires, two accidents (one was not our fault—more on that later), and $3,261.49 of Father's money—quite a college graduation present!

When we looked out over the San Francisco Bay, Teddy said he could picture a bridge across its mouth someday. I can't see that ever happening—the mouth is way too wide.

People here are still talking about the 1906 earthquake and fire. Now I understand why Father's 1905 investment in an earthquake insurance company here did not work out so well.

We were at a seaside amusement park when another quake occurred. Calvin thought that it was just one of the rides. I had just gotten off the boardwalk when it collapsed from the shaking. I felt relieved until the tsunami carried me about 500 yards inland. I managed to dodge the shark that was swept along with us; it bit Calvin instead. A moray eel got me; I think. We plan on eating seafood here before it eats us.

Father had asked me to bring him back a redwood tree for a souvenir if we ever made it to California. I've now seen them; I'm not sure that it's possible. Would he accept a photograph of one instead? Our camera got drowned in the wave, but would he pay for another?

This may be my last letter for a while as the ground is now shaking again, and we are afraid that California may fall into the sea. Father may want to scoop up oceanfront land in Nevada while it's available. Please convey my love to all the family.

Your loving Son,
Woodrow

p.s. Please thank Uncle Sean and Aunt Eloise, and Father for all the Christmas gifts. The life preservers, snake-bite kit, new tires, first aid supplies, parachutes, and bail coupons may come in handy.

About the car accident mentioned earlier: Calvin was driving. He successfully dodged a deer running across the road from right to left. He hit the one running the other way.

***

The last letter she read that night left Sadie wondering about Woodrow's trip back home, as well as the prospects for his future—some things to ponder until she could unearth more letters, perhaps.

Everyone Loves a Parade

Have you heard the one about Jacques and André?

Jacques and Andre, veteran logging truck drivers, were being interviewed for a new job. The interviewing foreman asked Andre a question:

"Say you're driving a full load of logs, going down a long, steep grade. Down at the bottom there is a railroad crossing, and a long train is passing through. You touch your brakes, and the brakes fail completely. What would you do?"

Andre thought for a few moments, then replied, "I'd reach over and wake up Jacques."

The foreman was incredulous. "With a full load, no brakes, and a train at the bottom of the steep grade, why would you take the time to wake up Jacques?"

Andre's simple response: "Jacques, he's never seen an accident zis beeg!" Until August 13th, 1949, that is…

***

The coastal village of Smithport was in high gear to celebrate its bicentennial on the 13th of August 1949. The hamlet was founded officially in 1749 by Cyrus and Bogus Smith, two brothers who, history says, never got along and started a feud of sorts which had been perpetuated to this day—the town equally divided among the C Smith and B Smith progeny and supporters.

As the town historian and local stringer (reporter) for the *Bangor Daily News,* it was my task to put together an updated history of the town, as well as to cover the bicentennial festivities for the press. The recorded town history to date is replete with anecdotes about the C Smith versus B Smith shenanigans. For example:

July 28, 1766—Cyrus finds dead skunk in his cider processing vat.

December 10, 1771—Bogus's musket barrel full of tree sap.

May 30, 1778—Cyrus was signed up for colonist brigade without his knowledge.

April 4, 1842—Clyde (C Smith side) discovers bear in his locked outhouse.

December 12, 1898—Harmon (B Smith side) receives letter reportedly nominating him for president. Later elected town dump attendant by write-in votes.

November 26, 1932—Bryce (C Smith side) encounters porcupine in his maple syrup tank, clearly a sticky situation.

November 30, 1932—Melvin (B Smith side) discovers that his skis have been coated with some kind of sticky substance.

March 3, 1948—Derwin (C Smith side) has his lobster boat fastened to a piling with two long bolts; the boat sinks when the bolts are removed.

This is just a light sampling among the village's less noteworthy historical events.

"One Must Be Organized"

Inna Quagmyre was an imposing woman of robust construction and forceful demeanor, who had been imposing her will on the good citizens of Smithport for the previous five years. She swept into town in her brand-new Cadillac from parts south and west (Philadelphia or some other silly-named place, some said), newly widowed and with ample means to support her ample frame. Some local wags suggested that her husband may have passed on in self-defense.

Smithport townsfolk didn't really like Inna, but they were sufficiently intimidated by her to not protest openly when Inna anointed herself chair-woman of the town's Bicentennial Committee. They had to grudgingly admit that she was a good organizer and had a way of getting things done, even if she had to pay for them herself. She was not a force to be taken lightly!

Among her many self-appointed responsibilities, Inna determined the events to be held, culminating in a grand parade through the town center, advertised far and wide. She specified the route and the order of march, after soliciting volunteers to participate. No person or organization dared to object. Inna even quelled the Smith feud for a time, almost.

Once committed, many did develop some enthusiasm for their individual efforts. Four groups volunteered to build floats: the area 4-H Club, the Odd Fellows Lodge, the Grange, and the combined VFW/American Legion posts. The high school marching band would do their very best to entertain (they did). The fire department's new (1936) pumper truck would lead the parade, followed by the Grange float, then marchers from the various social groups, the Smithport High band, then the town officials in an open vehicle (read farm wagon), then the Odd Fellows float, then Inna's Cadillac carrying 1949's Miss Mudflats and her court, the VFW float, a visiting fife and drum corps, clowns, and bringing up the rear, the 4-H float. It would be another triumph of superb planning, Inna convinced herself unashamedly.

The parade route would start at the baseball field northeast of the cen-

105

tral village. It would circle past Tillie and Mac's animal pens (goats, rabbits, llamas, and sheep), ease onto Main Street, and continue through the entire downtown (all eight blocks of it), until turning onto Smith Avenue to file past the reviewing stand where out-of-town celebrities would be seated (two out of the 38 invited actually showed up). The parade would finish up at the old airfield southwest of town...if it wasn't finished before.

Floatsam and Jetsam

Given that most folks had never before had to construct a parade float, genuine attempts were made by the four groups to emulate the works of others. The Macy's Thanksgiving and Rose Bowl parades provided inspiration, if not actual details.

For example, since no flowers were in sufficient supply to decorate the Grange float, it was decided to use a variety of vegetables, straw, pumpkins, corn stalks, and other produce to carry out the agricultural theme. The 4-H float would carry prized animals to display the members' accomplishments. The Odd Fellows used chicken wire for the rough form of their patriotic float, stuffing the wire with dyed paper napkins, until they ran out. They then resorted to bits of cloth, cardboard, and anything else they could muster to complete the task.

The veterans' float proved to be the epitome of ingenuity. The members chose to build it in the shape of a WWII tank. Lacking replica parts, they substituted an inverted watering tub for the turret, stovepipe for the turret cannon, pie tins for the tread's wheels, and draped fish nets stuffed with twigs and leaves along parts to represent camouflage. They figured that a hefty coat of olive drab paint would set the proper mood.

How to make the floats mobile was a concern for all four groups, and each came up with its own solution. The Odd Fellows resorted to an often recalcitrant dump truck, with a mechanic aboard just in case. The VFW/American Legion tank was constructed over a Ford flatbed farm truck. Two distinguished veterans, 92-year-old Angus MacDuff and 81-year-old Colonel Korne, would sit on upright kitchen chairs toward the rear of the tank, looking like combat observers peeking out of open hatches.

The Grange float, being on the weighty side, would be towed by Cedric "Dill" Pickle's ancient Farmall tractor, the only vehicle they could find with the moxie to pull such a load. The 4-H group put together a 4-mule team, figuring that an agrarian animal theme should be drawn by "animules," and four would be the most appropriate number.

Event-ualities

Inna's grandiosity knew no bounds. In addition to the culminating parade, there should be a parade of boats in the harbor (two volunteered; the rest were lobsterboats that couldn't be risked), a community tug-of-war (some suggested Smiths against Smiths), a traditional baked bean supper, and fireworks the night before (rained out). Given the underwhelming response (and weather) for the preliminaries, Inna threw all of her ponderous charisma into the parade itself.

"Let's go see the parade, children"

Amazing even the most diehard local skeptics, the day of the parade dawned bright and fair—a prototypical Maine summer day. The cool mist of morning gave way to an 82-degree, sunny day, with puffy clouds and a warm southwesterly breeze. Even more amazing, people came. They came from Portland, Lewiston, and Bangor. They came from Fairfield, Palermo, and Presque Isle. Even Denmark, Mexico, and Norway (Maine, of course) were represented. It was a good day to watch a parade—and witness they did!

Getting the fire truck ready took some doing. Despite the rain, the truck had seen action the night before the parade. The small fire at the VFW hall may have been started by an errant firecracker, but no one would admit to being involved. On the way back to the firehouse/Beano hall, the hoses were hung up to dry as usual from the windmill tower alongside the lane just off of Main Street. The hoseless truck had then returned to its quarters to be spiffed up for the next day's festivities.

At precisely 1:00 p.m., the town hall's tower bell chimed to signal the start of the parade. The pumper pulled out on schedule, Inna being on hand to wave it along, furiously. Shortly after, the Grange's mobile produce stand (as many viewed it), tractor in the lead, got its start. Various groups straggled along behind—Elks, Girl and Boy Scouts, Rainbow Girls, local sewing and quilting circle, dump patrol, etc. Then came the high school's marching band. The high school band had never before looked or sounded so in tune as it did that day, each teen meticulous in preparation, intense concentration etched on each bandperson's face, every step carefully placed to synchronize with all others—truly poetry in motion. Each instrument carried a small clip with miniature score so a note would not be missed, each teen's focus totally on the music and tempo of the march.

The town officials followed the band, resplendent in their best Sunday-go-to-meeting togs. Then came the Odd Fellows' float with its riders in colonial regalia, dump truck sputtering and misfiring irregularly.

Inna's Cadillac then fell in line with its load of queen and attendants, the teens squealing with anticipation and delight...sounding like "stuck pigs," according to one of the trailing bicyclists.

The VFW/American Legion float-cum-tank made quite an impression with its camouflage livery, turret, cannon, and elderly costumed observers. Wary bicyclists glanced over their shoulders from time to time, seeming to gauge the military's advance. The clowns were a hit with the young spectators, although recruited from out of town—Philadelphia maybe, or worse: Boston.

The 4-H mules may have been bothered by the din of the music ahead—they refused to budge at first. They abruptly resumed motion, though, when an infuriated Inna strode up to assess their reluctance, loudly. Once the float was moving, Inna lumbered up the road to catch up with the Miss Mudflats court in her Caddy.

The leading fire apparatus reached the downtown area at approximately 1:20 p.m. At 1:46 p.m. sharp, two unrelated events occurred nearly simultaneously: the dump truck hauling the Odd Fellows backfired loudly, "back fire" being very literal, and a prankster ran by the tank and tossed a large firecracker inside the stovepipe cannon barrel, apparently trying to make the cannon seem more realistic and dramatic. That it did!

The immediate impression of the gathered throng was that the tank must have fired and scored a direct hit on the Odd Fellows' float setting it on fire, which the truck's backfire actually had accomplished. As flames crept up the rear of the float, the Odd Fellows patriotic colonists hastily abandoned ship. No one present could remember ever seeing 88-year-old Conrad Carstens move so fast, walker and all.

The stove-pipe barrel didn't fare so well. The forwardmost section blew off completely, narrowly missing two bike riders. The second section splayed outward to look for all the world like a smoking metallic flower.

While the high school band strode on, still in step, still focused on its version of "The Midnight Fire Alarm," somehow the fire crew on the pumper became aware of the growing conflagration to its rear. Hoseless, the pumper was of no use—quick action was needed. The driver took off down Main Street, turned onto Smith Avenue, and took the next right onto Lois Lane (named for Otis Lois, beloved deceased Smithport school principal, not what you were thinking), and accelerated toward Tillie and Mac's farm where the hoses had been hung to dry. The Grange float sped up, too, but the tractor was no match for the firetruck. Totally oblivious to actions ahead and behind, the band played on, all in step.

The town's dignitaries turned to discover an apparent bonfire behind them, smack dab in the middle of Main Street. Inna's Cadillac stopped suddenly and tried to reverse, scattering bicycles and riders as it crept backwards, headed toward the combat-wounded tank.

Within minutes, the pumper reached the windmill, the volunteer firemen on the rear leaping off to grab the ends of the hanging hoses. Haste was critical, so as soon as the men had snagged the hoses, the driver hit the gas, unaware that neither hose had as yet been detached from the hoisting tackle. The momentum of the engine's abrupt departure brought down the windmill tower, neatly crushing the fences surrounding the farm's goat, sheep, and rabbit pens.

Freedom! Probably terrified by the combination of siren and toppling timber sounds, critters took off in all available directions, a large mass taking the route of least resistance—straight down Main Street. Ahead was the 4-H float with its prized herd of its own, which quickly bailed out despite the 4-H personnel's attempts at restraining them, and the enhanced stampede was on!

The city-bred clowns were the first human barrier, easily overcome in the ensuing confusion. Onlookers scrambled from Smithport's unplanned tribute to Spain's "running of the bulls." Later count suggested that 11 sheep, 16 goats, one Guernsey cow, one bull, seven rabbits, and one bedraggled rooster sprinted the length of the street about the time that the band achieved its own finale.

The high school marching band had been admirably schooled—drilled to exhaustion might be more accurate—and each of the 84 members (half of the school) was determined not to miss a single note or step.

With grand solemnity they marched up Main Street, all in step, drum major Roland "Dyslexia" LaPierre in the lead. Instructed to turn right onto Smith Avenue to follow the organizations, Roland had nearly reached the critical junction when the line holding the above-street bicentennial banner was burned through by errant sparks. The banner floated down and wrapped itself firmly around Roland's head and upper torso. Thoroughly flummoxed and disoriented, he turned left while trying to fight off the encasing banner.

On he marched, struggling mightily to extricate himself while not missing a step. The first line of four in the band dutifully followed Roland's lead, intent on keeping in step and precisely following the music—and oblivious to the implication of the wrong turn.

One direction of Smith Avenue leads out of town as State Route 56. The other direction leads directly onto the town wharf, which leads directly into the town's harbor…into which Roland plunged, fully in step, followed like lemmings by each row of the oncoming Smithport High School Galloping Scallops Marching Band, the last notes of "Stars and Stripes Forever" being swallowed up by the frigid harbor waters. At least they were safe from the fire, which now was gaining momentum while the pumper had to forge its way through the melee of livestock, clowns, fife players and drummers, a dead-in-the-street tank, abandoned bicycles, and a reversing Cadillac (until it collided with the tank) to try to reach the now-spreading fire.

The Caddy/tank collision had two noticeable consequences. The two elderly veteran observers were propelled out of their chairs, into slow-motion slide/rolls down the sloping back of the makeshift tank, landing in a heap on the pavement, bruised but not beaten. Inna, riding with the teens in her precious car, became hysterical and leapt out of the Caddy, only to be trampled by a succession of goats and sheep, plus one panicked rooster.

The parade's spectators tended to split into two distinct factions. One group, the smaller of the two, made a run for it down the village's side streets, many bound for home. The second contingent sought strategic locations from which to view developments with morbid fascination. They were not to be disappointed—the fat lady hadn't yet sung.

The breeze had gained some momentum during the early afternoon, and flaming napkins, pieces of cloth, and cardboard were aloft and spreading fire throughout a downwind fan. The flying flames tended to excite the thundering herd even more as they barreled down Main Street, then scattered into detours down side roads and alleys. The prize bull, not to disappoint his trailing 4-H owner, exhibited his proud lineage by charging through the window of Carrie's China & Knickknack Emporium and thoroughly trashing the place.

The noise from Main Street's pandemonium reached the Smith Avenue viewing stand just before the Grange tractor, its driver having turned to look back toward the racket, plowed blindly into it, sending the two invited celebrities into low orbit, however briefly.

Back on Main Street, the spreading fire had reached epidemic proportions. Four buildings were aflame, two other roofs smoldered, and the erstwhile tank had erupted into a stationary torch, only the turret tub providing a donut hole of inflammability. The downtown was in mass confusion, and many of the parade's participants and spectators had hightailed it away for at least a few blocks.

It took the better part of a week to sort out the sequence of events, the B Smith crowd vociferously blaming the C Smith supporters and vice versa. The initial instigating firecracker tosser was never definitively identified as being from either camp, and the brief fistfight between the two senior citizen, tank-riding observers (one from each family) solved nothing. Inna soon recovered her dignity and panache—her trample wounds took longer—and her Caddy never again rode quite the same.

No one in the high school band drowned, but grappling hooks retrieved soggy instruments for weeks afterwards. The town lost four buildings to the fire, which finally was doused by assistance from two nearby communities. The *Bangor Daily News* ran a front-page story the next day describing the "hot time at Smithport's bicentennial parade," "tank you for the memories," and the Smithport band's brave "march to the sea."

At last contact, Inna had appointed herself chairwoman of the town's Recovery Committee.

Some Days...

Many thanks to the island worker whose real-life experience over 50 years ago provided the inspiration for this story.

Mosiah Ethridge Halbury absolutely loved his new title: First Assistant Maintenance Engineer for the island's one and only school.

"Mosey," as he was known to the other islanders, was a shining product of that school, although he officially dropped out after his fourth year in fifth grade. He hung around afterward, though, and became an unpaid helper to the sole janitor, who also was the Superintendent of Schools, cousin Elmer Halbury. Supt. Halbury also was the bus (using that term loosely) driver and lunch monitor. The one teacher had to take a break sometime!

Taking care of the school building was a true undertaking, however. Built during 1920–21, its capacity during the windswept island's heyday was 120 students. Due to dwindling island population, however, it now had only 16 students, spanning grades 1–12. The one teacher had a part-time assistant who was more of a volunteer than a paid employee.

The island school was built partly of brick, partly of wood, and now sported a patchwork of sheet metal as well. Several nor'easters had not been kind to the island, and the school building displayed many hastily repaired scars. The most recent winter onslaught reduced the brick top of the chimney to roof-top rubble, leading to the following exchange between the Superintendent and Mosey:

"You wanted to see me, Mr. Cousin Elmer?"

"Yes, Mosey. I have an important job for you to do," replied Supt. Halbury.

"Yessir! You know I can do most anything around here, except I can't drive, or cook, or do numbers, or fix cars, or do plumbing, or wiring, or..."

Supt. Halbury cut Mosey off, saying, "I know, Mosey, but I think you can do this okay. The storm knocked the top of the school's chimney down. It needs to be fixed. Some bricks are on the roof, some may be broken or on the ground, but we're getting some from Gus Halbury's old fireplace and chimney to replace the broken ones. Gus said he'd whip up some fresh mortar for you when you're ready."

"Okay, boss. I'll get right on it!"

Mosey headed right over to Gus's house, figuring to find out about mortar and bricks.

"Hi, Mosey," Gus started. "Elmer said you needed some of them old bricks 'n' fresh cee-ment. You'se gonna fix the school chimley, he said. You done work like that afore?"

"Naw, but cousin Elmer said he knew I could do it. Just get the whole bricks from you and the roof, and you'd make me some mortar for them," Mosey responded.

"You laid bricks at all?" Gus countered.

"I dunno how 'xactly, but I'll just follow the pattern of the rest of the bricks in the chimney. I'm good at patterns!" Mosey asserted enthusiastically.

"How're you gonna get these bricks up there, Mosey?"

"I got that all figgered out. There's an old pulley still stuck on the beam at the end of the roof. I'll go up the stairs to the roof and run a rope through the pulley, then haul up loads of bricks to the edge of the roof, tie

115

off the rope to the stair rail, then go up to the roof to unload the bricks. That should do the trick."

"Sounds good, Mosey, but be careful—bricks can get mighty heavy when piled up."

Those who knew Mosey best were sure that he was long on imagination, but short on details. He was, as some islanders put it, "at least one canvas short of full sail".

The next day, Gus brought a load of bricks over to the school and dropped them off. Mosey, meanwhile, had rigged up a long piece of rope through the roof-edge pulley, long enough to reach both ends to the ground. He'd also located a wooden keg in which to load some bricks for their trip to the roof. He figured to lift a few bricks at a time, heeding Gus's warning, and considering the height—three stories to the roof. Mosey also had gone up to the roof to separate the whole bricks from the broken ones, being careful to keep them from the edge so they wouldn't fall and hurt someone. He planned to be very cautious and safe.

Mosey decided to tackle the repair on the coming Saturday when no one would be at school—another of his safety measures. He would let Gus know when Mosey was ready for the mortar, after getting all of the bricks to the roof.

Saturday morning dawned bright and a bit hazy, with a light southwest breeze, perfect conditions for Mosey's endeavor. He arose early, cleaned up himself and the breakfast dishes and rode down to the school on his trusty (read that "rusty") bicycle. He wasn't allowed to drive on the island as his one foray into motor vehicle pilotage ended up in an embarrassing plunge into the harbor. Supt. Halbury's truck was retrieved eventually but never ran again.

Mosey arrived at the school as planned and immediately set to work. He hummed to himself as he placed 12 or so bricks in his elevator/keg and hoisted them up to the pulley. He tied off the rope to the rail and bounded up the steps to the roof to unload the keg, stacking the "new" bricks neatly along side the "old" whole bricks. He then retreated to the ground, lowered the empty keg, and repeated the loading and hoisting process.

By the fourth trip up the stairs, Mosey was no longer bounding; trudging would be a more apt description, accompanied by a fair amount of huffing and puffing. Although slightly built, Mosey was generally not fond of protracted vigorous exercise.

After ground-to-roof trip number four, Mosey reasoned that he had sufficient bricks to accomplish the task. He then sat down astride the peak of the gently sloping roof to study the lay of the remaining bricks upon which he would have to build.

"This should be easy," he thought. "Just pile them up with some mortar in between. Too many broken bricks up here, though. Got to clean up to make room to work."

The now-empty barrel was still aloft at the hoisting pulley, so Mosey started to gather the broken bricks and load them into the barrel, not fully aware of how many fragments were piling up. When he had finished tidying up, Mosey trekked wearily down the stairs to retrieve the full barrel.

When Mosey reached the schoolyard, he went to the rail and untied the rope, ready to guide his keg-load to the ground.

There are moments in life when events happen so quickly that immediate reactions are not well thought out. Often these moments are occasions for an "uh oh!" response (some might up the ante with "oh sh_t!").

Mosey abruptly experienced one of those moments as soon as he released the rope's grip on the railing. Expecting to have to hold the rope tightly to lower the keg, now heavy with its burden of partial bricks, Mosey hung on for dear life as he suddenly realized that the full keg outweighed him substantially, and gravity was about to dictate the outcome.

Some Days…

Up Mosey went as the keg plummeted down.

"Uh oh," passed through Mosey's thoughts while he was drawn upward as the keg rapidly descended. "Uh oh," repeated itself more insistently as Mosey fearfully watched the falling keg approaching, the idea of letting go of the rope never entering his mind. At the halfway point Mosey and the keg met, with the slight swinging of Mosey's end of the rope keeping him clear of the full force of the keg's glancing blow to his shoulder.

Onwards and upwards Mosey sailed as the keg accelerated its plunge, reaching earth precisely as Mosey's head encountered the overhead pulley beam. Mosey's brow had minimal protection from the blow—his canvas sunhat providing the sole intervention—while the laden keg grounded with enough force to crack open and disgorge most of its contents…at which point Mosey's weight exceeded that of the splintered keg.

The results were instantaneous and predictable. Mosey descended, maintaining his death grip on the rope. The remains of the keg ascended, striking a flailing leg and arm as it went by. Mosey contacted ground at some velocity, and immediately became stunned by the force of his sudden grounding, losing all focus as well as his hold on the rope.

His dazed mind had barely entertained another "uh oh," when the fractured keg, rope and all, landed post haste on Mosey's prone body. Only the accumulated pile of rope on his chest prevented more serious injury. As it was, Mosey lay in a tangled heap for some time, slowly collecting his wits and dimly trying to analyze what had just transpired…and why.

"The stars are awfully pretty tonight," slipped across his mind until Mosey gradually grew aware of the bright mid-morning sunshine.

"I don't think I can finish the chimney today, boss," Mosey much later told Supt. Halbury. "I'm sore all over, and I never did get the mortar from Gus. I'm kinda thinkin' that some days just don't go 'cording to plan! Do I get any sick days?"

Dulcinea's First (and worst) Cruise

"Spit not ever to windward, for such behavior shall return to plague thee." This 10th Commandment of Sailing was posted conspicuously on the wall of the yacht club of which my grandfather was a founding member. Given the opportunity to join, I politely declined becoming associated with "a bunch of old fuddy-duddies," as I viewed the aging throng from my lofty 18-year-old perch. If my grandfather was disappointed, I didn't have a clue until a growing realization months later.

It's not that I didn't like boats or enjoy sailing; I just knew way too much to be hampered by stodginess and late-night cigars. I was determined, in fact, to go cruising on my own proud vessel, dragging along my best friend, Axel, a non-sailor of some repute in our coastal village. Axel had distinguished himself in the local scene by various pranks—putting a "we give S&H Green Stamps" sign in the town office window, for example, and who could forget the pig's head mounted on the hood of the police chief's car? What Axel lacked in nautical savvy, I was certain could be made up for by sheer bravado.

Only one minor impediment stood in the way of my summer sailing plans—lack of a suitable vessel. I had means—four years of newspaper delivery savings, plus two more years of grocery bagging proceeds. I just needed to acquire my well-found ship, my palatial cruising yacht to convey myself and Axel beyond the visible horizon. Enter the *Soggy Sal*, stage left.

Grandpa put me on to her. He knew a club member who had a broth-er-in-law whose best friend's coworker's cousin had an old ketch from which he was desperately trying to extricate himself. How much did he want for her? How much did I have...?

The hasty transaction took place the day after the discovery, the now ex-owner bounding away with unrestrained ecstasy, $121.58 richer for the experience. I held the scribbled and foreboding Bill of Sale, and water-stained insurance and registration papers, with unbridled passion—never mind that *Soggy Sal* was last insured in 1932 (it was now 1979). Her records noted that she was designed and built in 1898, with unspecified rebuildings in 1932 and 1968. Her engine was a trustworthy (actually rust-worthy) Palmer 4-cylinder gas guzzler.

Of course, no survey was arranged or completed, the purchase allowance being depleted, saving only $54 for any necessary repairs or upgrades. The fact that she was afloat and in a season-paid slip was a con-vincing and convenient selling point. There was no time for a survey any-way. I would get to see her the next day, after work.

Most everyone is aware that first impressions are important, but can be misleading. There was no mistaking *Soggy Sal, ex-Phoenix, ex-Wunsunk, ex-Hopeless, ex-Promise*—she looked like she hadn't exited her slip in 20 years (23 actually). Topsides were peeling dark green paint, revealing layers of gray, yellow, light blue, and white. Decks were dusty, strewn with bits and pieces of line, rusty chain, dirty sails, ancient varnish, and a split main hatch. I was in love!

Obviously (to me), she just needed a thorough cleaning and some new paint, and she'd be ready to sail off to Shangri-La. Oh, she also needed a new moniker—*Soggy Sal* would just not do. After viewing and inspecting her for his first time, Axel suggested *Revolting Wreck* as appropriate, but the deciding vote for *Dulcinea* lay with me, so *Dulcinea* she became.

In order to facilitate bonding with my new vessel, I resolved to sleep aboard that night, conning Axel into joining me with a lobster dinner as incentive. I was feeling deliriously magnanimous that afternoon.

Some particulars about my purchase would be helpful, I think. They may enhance understanding of future events. *Soggy Sal,* now *Dulcinea*, as I noted above, first saw the water in 1898. She was a 32-foot gaff-rigged ketch of an old model, with only two bunks, 5'8" headroom, an old-model head (toilet), two dried out solid wooden masts, stained and dirty sails (no sail covers), a rusty hand anchor windlass, planked decks with desiccated caulking, low bulwarks, no lifelines, an outboard rudder, bowsprit with bobstay and whisker shrouds, and a canvased coachroof (cabin top)—she was undeniably beautiful! Passion can encourage one to overlook a few miniscule faults...

Axel's six-foot-two frame filled one bunk that night while I, at five-foot-eight, occupied the other. The next day would see our clean-up and refurbishing work start in earnest. I slept like a baby, Axel not so much. When his bladder forced his attention at 1:00 a.m., he cautiously put his feet down over the side of his berth into six inches of very cold water. The resultant shock propelled him upright, driving his head into and through the rotten boards and canvas of the coachroof! The sound of splintering wood awakened me, at which point I, too, went cabin wading.

Since we knew that the head was not functional, we both needed to go ashore for relief, but I stayed behind to man the pump while Axel made the bathroom run. We then took turns with the bilge pump and were making gains on the incoming water, and then the rains came—in buckets!

The new hole in the cabin overhead allowed a lot of rainwater to enter, exceeded only by the dozen or so other deck leaks which quickly threatened to undo our pumping exertions. Fortune smiled, however, as the deluge was short-lived.

The next morning's inspection revealed a temporary mystery. Once *Dulcinea*'s bilges were reasonably devoid of water, both fresh and salt, we noticed a waterline of sorts along the cabin furniture. Further investigation and observations of the tide solved the riddle. *Dulcinea* drew 5'6" of water. At low tide, *Dulcinea*'s slip contained a depth of water of about 5'2". Therefore, my proud ketch sat softly in the mud at low tide, limiting the level of ingressing seawater. The transition to being aground was so slow and gentle that it was barely noticeable, but it certainly was fortuitous. She could only sink at high tide. How lucky!

Hourly pumping slowed the interior flooding while clean-up proceeded apace, despite Axel's comments about my "tilting at windmills" inspiring *Dulcinea*'s name. After several hours she was beginning to take on the guise of a true little ship, and then Axel's cousin "Chucker" showed up. Reputedly a whiz kid with things automotive and mechanical, he was recruited by Axel to tackle the aging Palmer to see if it could be rescued from rust and oblivion. One characteristic of Chucker became as clear as his nickname when he went below to address the engine—his sensitive stomach. Mal-de-mer (mal-de-slip?) overcame him within minutes despite very little motion on *Dulcinea*'s part. Chucker chucked...all over the Palmer, not sparing much of its surface in the process.

A green Chucker abruptly emerged from the cabin, apparently in an agitated state. One grand leap put him onto the abeam floating pier with sufficient inertia to propel him overboard into the adjacent empty slip. His sputtering and gasping masked his expletive-laced expression of his true feelings, but the air over his head seemed to take on a noticeable blue tinge. One good mechanic down; *Dulcinea*'s iron beast would have to wait.

Duct tape took care of the coach roof cavity for the time being (another of the 1,001 uses for duct tape), but would not be sufficient for the next hole. When Chucker made his fateful dash, he must have provided the critical force to weaken the cockpit sole (floor), which Axel's right foot soon discovered, much to his consternation. That breach would require skilled carpentry to close, but mine would have to do instead.

The dingy sails responded well to a good hand scrubbing, delivered with a floor brush while the sails were laid out on the dock. Hosed down for a rinse, they almost looked white. One seam on the mizzen came adrift but could be repaired cheaply (duct tape) or by a sailmaker. Duct tape won the budget battle.

The final verdict on the Palmer was a postmortem—it would never run again and so was rusty ballast. We left the propeller and shaft in place, but carefully (not really) disassembled what we could and managed to haul the pieces out, including the heavy (very heavy) block and transmission. We were sailors—we didn't need an expensive, fuel-guzzling, noisy, smelly, gas-dangerous form of propulsion—no sir! We'd also live to regret that decision...

Over the next few dry days we found that about ten minutes of energetic pumping each hour near high tide could keep the bilge water at bay (pun intended)—we figured that we could live with that...but we didn't figure on the effects of sailing. Duct tape solved several issues of mild concern—holes overhead, mast splits, sail holes and decayed stitching, etc.—and a piece of scrap plywood would serve for the cockpit sole repair. More permanent solutions would have to be postponed until after this summer's all-important cruise, and until my budget would permit.

Crawling around the hull and occasional swims allowed us to scrape the peeling topsides, but no paint was available for an in-the-water coating. *Dulcinea*, therefore, sailed looking like a cross between random mosaic art and calico cat. Weather checks (cracks) in the solid masts were filled with a spur-of-the-moment concoction of sawdust and wax—which we came to regret on our first 100-degree day.

A traditional cedar bucket would stand in for the dysfunctional head—the budget wouldn't cover the rebuilding kit. The cast iron galley stove, wood-fired, would have to serve for cooking. Surprisingly, the water tank seemed clean, almost unused—we would later discover why.

No matter how much preparation takes place, the day eventually arrives for a voyage to start. Last minute gifts from our parents and my grandfather included new lifejackets to replace the old kapok and cork/canvas ones; new emergency flares and day signals; loan of a wooden dinghy with a 2-hp outboard motor, and a copy of Farley Mowat's classic true tale, *The Boat Who Wouldn't Float.*

I'd like to say that there was a brass band and an admiring throng present to see us off, but that would be a slight exaggeration. The two dock boys in distant attendance displayed disconcerting grins as they whispered to each other. I thought I overheard one say, "Good sailing," but he also could have said, "Good riddance."

It is part of mariners' folklore that it is bad luck to begin a voyage on a Friday. That day also happened to be the 13th of June, so we chose the safe course and resolved to set off on the Saturday, on a rising tide. The fact that Friday's weather included heavy rain and gale force winds didn't affect our decision in the slightest. Well, it may have just a little.

Saturday morning yielded clearing skies and a light southeast breeze, no fog in sight. Low water was at 10:35 a.m., so we figured on enough water under *Dulcinea*'s keel to be able to pull her out of her slip by 11:00. We figured wrong.

Axel volunteered (by process of elimination) to use the dinghy to tow *Dulcinea* out of the slip and into open water, where we could set sail. I, of course, would man the helm for this maiden voyage. The inability to start

124

the outboard was a minor inconvenience; Axel picked up the oars, never having rowed before in his life, jammed the tow line between his knees, and for the next ten minutes did his best imitation of a demented octopus on a hotplate, arms flailing and oars thrashing to produce no discernable movement. *Dulcinea* was still stuck fast, a most reluctant maiden.

After 15 minutes of pumping and 30 minutes more of tide rise, *Dulcinea* gave up her grim self-preservation hold on the ocean bottom and finally condescended to ease out of her longtime home to face the unknown, proud captain at the wheel. A gentle wind shift aided progress, swinging to the southwest as we made way to more obstruction-free water.

Axel's attempt to re-board *Dulcinea* met with only one tiny mishap— he capsized the dink and ended up in the drink. Our unscheduled man overboard drill did not go swimmingly. I hastily and mistakenly tossed him one of the old life preservers that we had retained for a seat cushion. It promptly sank. The next item immediately available was a coil of line near the helm. I flipped it to Axel without a second thought. As he started to haul it in to lift himself up, the mizzen gaff started to slide up the mast. I had thrown Axel the throat halyard. He went nowhere; the gaff went up, peak downward.

Eventually, Axel was able to clamber to the deck, using a heroic lunge at the aft bulwark and firm grip on a stern cleat, not to mention my hauling on the shoulders of his shirt. Retrieval was ultimately successful, despite the crude methodology. Dinghy retrieval was another challenge entirely, but the capsized skiff acted as an effective sea anchor, temporarily slowing *Dulcinea*'s drift toward a rocky lee shore. A cranial hurricane burst into my consciousness: drop anchor to stop our drift, allowing more time to deal with a dinghy awash.

To the foredeck I strode, confident in my master plan for anchoring and dinghy dewatering. Confronting my trusty (read *rusty*) windlass. I released the pawl to free the chain—and nothing happened. I quickly discovered that kicking the blasted thing did not accomplish my intent, nor did two minutes of my best invectives. Soggy Axel came to the rescue with one of the tools we'd secreted aboard for emergencies—an eight-pound sledgehammer. One good whack from the port side did the trick—anchor, chain, and windlass whipped over the side, leaving a gaping hole in the deck and an airborne trail of rust/dust as additional chain paid out from below.

If fortune doesn't outright smile once in a while, it is capable of an occasional smirk. The bitter end of the anchor chain was shackled to an eyebolt turned into the keel, and it held. The chain's gleeful departure was summarily halted, the abruptness of its stop serving to shake *Dulcinea* and knock both of her crew off their respective feet. *Dulcinea* was now anchored, firmly, with about 250 pounds of steel, iron, and rust resting on the bay's bottom.

"First things first," the captain (me) said with profound conviction. "Let's get the dinghy secure and then tackle the anchor tackle."

We probably set no record for dinghy wrestling, but between skipper and mate, we did manage to turn the skiff right-side up and lift her enough to dump out some of the water. The rest succumbed to the cedar bucket, and empty can, and a sponge.

Even with the whole crew (of two) lifting and hauling together, we were not going to force chain, windlass, and anchor back onto the deck. While we pondered the logistics of the situation, *Dulcinea* was celebrating her new freedom from her berth and return to the sea by taking in a huge gulp of clear bay waters. Maybe she thought that by lowering her foredeck closer to the surface she could help us regain the anchor? Thanks, dear *Dulcinea*, but no thanks!

Back to the pump for 15 minutes of vigorous exercise designed to strengthen us for the weighty task ahead. While determinedly yanking on the pump handle, the solution for hoisting the anchor load aboard came to me in a flash: using the main halyard tackles, both throat and peak, we could together get enough mechanical advantage to bring up the load with comparative ease—thanks, physics class! That's when the pump handle broke.

We hadn't left the protection of the larger harbor area yet, and we already had had our share of crises. Axel came to the rescue of the pump by sacrificing the sledgehammer's handle—good thing the handle was dried out and easy to draw out of the hammer's head. Taking stock of our situation, we decided to stay anchored for the night, being clear of the navigation channel, and make a fresh start in the morning. A fire for cooking would have been nice, but we'd forgotten matches. Sigh. Sleep was only interrupted by pumping episodes. It was a good night—*Dulcinea* didn't sink.

Morning brought an easterly breeze with thick fog, but the rain eventually drove that off. Overnight, during one of the bilge-draining interludes, I realized that the motion of the boat seemed different somehow. Plumbing the depths around *Dulcinea* with a makeshift sounding lead (sledgehammer head on quarter-inch line) revealed the reason: she must have settled her keel into the mud again at low ebb to take a rest from the exertion of keeping herself afloat. At least we weren't on the rocks...yet.

If we could retrieve anchor, chain, and windlass before going aground again, we might actually be able to sail and start on our cruise! Alas, it was not to be. The east wind would blow us toward shore once the anchor was off the sea floor. Staying put seemed to be the wisest course for that day. Axel decided to go for a row instead, hopefully to bring back matches, a new pump handle, some plywood or plastic to cover up the windlass hole, and two more rolls of duct tape "just in case."

Axel's rowing technique hadn't improved with disuse. He managed to ease himself into the dinghy (he named it *Sancho* for the trip) without flipping it again, set one oar in an oarlock, and lost it overboard while reaching for the other, then paddled furiously with the second oar to catch up with the first, all the while being blown toward the marina. Good thing. Finally getting both oars in gear, Axel splashed his way to the dinghy dock, tied off *Sancho*, then trotted up the ramp and out of sight.

Two hours later, having procured the necessary items and scribbled a hasty will, he thrashed *Sancho* back to *Dulcinea*, making two 360-degree rotations on the way. Another night of pumping and grounding kept *Dulcinea* above water, and dawn thankfully brought a clear sky and gentle northwest wind—thankfully, because if worse came to worst, we would get blown out to sea instead of onto the rocks.

Surprisingly, getting the anchor-chain-windlass conglomeration aboard went according to plan. What didn't go according to plan was the next event in *Dulcinea*'s saga. A curious observer out in his skiff rowed over to closely examine this possibly derelict vessel. *Dulcinea* must have taken offense, for as soon as the anchor was free of the bottom muck, she spun on her heel and sideswiped the skiff, knocking her oarsman overboard. We were much more efficient with our second man overboard drill, while the whole of us drifted slowly seaward. Would this qualify as our first sail?

I apologized to our uninvited guest, Elmer, for *Dulcinea*'s attack on his boat, and he apologized for being so close while Axel and I struggled with hauling anchor via halyards. While Elmer and I were occupied with our mutual niceties, Axel happened to peer ahead along the course of our wind-and-current-driven drift.

There's another mariner's expression that quickly leapt to my mind when Axel asked, "That green thing is in our way, isn't it?" Yup – "A collision at sea can ruin your whole day," and we were sliding directly toward the large can buoy as if *Dulcinea* was a freight train on rails. Elmer's calm remark, "You might not want to hit that," was of little comfort or helpfulness. Immediate avoidance maneuvers were required. Axel, quick thinker that he can be, reacted first.

Given just a few yards separating boat and buoy, Axel dashed aft and grabbed the dinghy painter (towline) to bring *Sancho* forward to use as a buffer between *Dulcinea* and her downwind target. Interesting concept, bad idea. A wooden cockleshell of a dinghy was not a good referee between heavyweight steel buoy and old timber sailboat—*Sancho* shattered as if exploded in a vise. I do have to admit that the bewildered face on Axel was priceless as it transformed into a look of acute distress.

Dulcinea pivoted around the buoy while Axel stood dumbfounded on the foredeck. Elmer and I were in the cockpit until he stepped over the coaming to tend his skiff, probably to protect it from *Sancho*'s fate. As our drift continued, I as captain decided that it was time to make sail. We had to disembark our bemused passenger, disentangle main halyards from anchor chain, remove the sail gaskets, reshackle the halyards to the gaff, and in other ways prepare to haul away to set sail...at last! Oh, and retrieve *Sancho*'s remains as best we could.

Did fortune finally smile on *Dulcinea*? Not that readily, apparently. The cruise budget did not allow for replacing lines, and halyards on gaff-riggers tend to be on the long side. The mizzen sail went up without a hitch. *Dulcinea* meekly turned head to wind with the benefit of the mizzen. The main peak halyard, however, produced a snarl that showed itself with the gaff halfway up the mast. A firm tug didn't undo the snag, but it did serve to part the halyard, and down came the peak, the gaff end neatly bisecting the companionway hatch.

With the mains'l now out of action, we secured the sail, gaff, and boom, then hoisted the stays'l, figuring to at least sail with jib and jigger (mizzen and stays'l). About that time, the wind died. Completely. Not a breath of air left to stir the waters. In our three days total aboard *Dulcinea* we had not yet gone more than two miles from the marina.

Fate apparently had other ideas. After a short time, bearings of the shoreline suggested movement despite being becalmed. We seemed to be in the grip of a slow countercurrent tugging *Dulcinea* toward shore, shore being a small indentation in the trees. A hasty chart consultation yielded the pleasant awareness of Calamity Cove as the maw about to swallow up our *Dulcinea*. Oh joy. I didn't dare let the thought that "things could be worse" gain traction in my addled mind, but *Dulcinea* eventually accomplished what she does best, easing gently into the mud about 30 yards from the rocks—we were safe for the moment, and nearly at low tide. The anchor rested on the bottom below the bow with about 15 feet of chain, but for the moment its presence there was superfluous.

The sun was creeping toward its daily plunge into the western hills, and we were hungry, Axel and me. We hadn't had a proper meal in forever, and we had the magnificent menu of franks and canned baked beans tempting us.

Axel used the empty mouse nest in the belly of the galley stove as effective kindling, with no thought as to the whereabouts, or method of ingress or egress, of the resident mice—no thought that is until the embers falling through the rust hole in the bottom of the stove set the galley counter on fire. No reason to panic yet, though—the two inches of bilge water above the cabin sole (floor) in the windmilling hands of a terrified would-be cook extinguished the blaze in short order (hence the term, "short order cook"?)

Cold beans were not the preferred form of sustenance we'd had in mind. Was it to be considered good fortune then that we also had forgotten to pack a can opener? Upon that realization, a frenzied and desperate Axel took matters into his own hands. Take my word for it, a sledgehammer does not make an effective or efficient can opener! Cold hot dogs became the main and only course for the evening's fare.

During that night a front blew through, but *Dulcinea* didn't seem to move much. We assumed that the unusually high water in the cabin was due to the many deck leaks—it was barely brackish—but when Axel tried the galley freshwater pump to get a drink, nothing came out. The copper water tank, maybe original equipment (?), had chosen that night to disgorge its contents into the bilge—a corrosion casualty. Also, an overnight casualty was *The Boat Who Wouldn't Float*, irreparably sunk just above the cabin sole.

When we later raised sail and attempted to hoist the anchor, first by hand and then by jury-rigged tackle, we discovered why we hadn't blown away during the night. A swim at low tide disclosed a rusted two-inch cable on the bottom to which our anchor was firmly hooked. Seven dives over the next ten minutes freed the captive anchor, and then the wind died…again.

Anchored we stayed during the hottest day of that summer—so hot that our sawdust and wax mast-crack filler melted and dripped down the sides of the mast to puddle on the boom jaws and cabin top—so hot that we both went for swims to try to escape the heat and to find water on shore to fill a jug. The water tank leak had left us with only a few cans of juice and soda for drinks and nothing for washing. Thankfully, *Dulcinea* had stayed put during our sojourn ashore; the breeze remained absent all that day.

Ashore, a slow, prickly trip through balsam firs and raspberry bushes brought us to a farm shed where we found a manual well pump. Axel had just filled the water jug when the farmer's Doberman apparently took

131

exception to our presence, resulting in a much faster and even more painful retreat to the saltwater, which did not soothe our wounds in any way. We spent a hot, itchy, sore, miserable night at anchor in Calamity Cove.

Eternal optimism and youthful exuberance notwithstanding, I was beginning to get the slightest hint of discontent from my crew ("I want to go home...now!"), as well as a creeping feeling of dread about the possible outcomes of our attempts to put to sea. The water rising around my ankles had nothing to do with it, I told myself.

Day four of the cruise started at midnight when we raised anchor. Actually, we didn't raise it—the chain rusted through and broke, leaving the anchor on the bottom. *Dulcinea* drifted off, away from shore, and caught a late evening zephyr from the southeast that gently prodded her in the direction of the harbor and marina. Because of the heat, we had slept on deck and managed to sense *Dulcinea*'s movement and impatience to sink, or at least try to. More pumping, more drifting, then we raised the stays'l to try to control our progress...which would have worked fine if the steering cable from wheel to rudder yoke hadn't slipped its moorings.

As we approached the harbor entrance, the incoming tide picked up where the wind left off. Slick as a whistle, *Dulcinea* sidled up to one moored boat, drifted around it while we fended off, then encountered another, then another, very much like watching a pinball machine in ultra-slow motion. It never crossed either of our tired minds to simply tie off to one of the moored vessels for the rest of the night to await help in the morning—our progress was too mesmerizing, I guess.

Like a well-trained homing pigeon, *Dulcinea* daintily bumped her way along the end-of-dock raft, twirled, and slid along a piling to direct her course straight for her empty slip—and safety. Axel and I just stood by the bulwarks with old lifejackets for fenders in stunned disbelief. *Dulcinea* had found her way home with no assistance from us. Thus, ended the cruise—and my summer with *Dulcinea*. Axel's kissing the ground ashore was an anticlimax and entirely uncalled for.

Dulcinea and I parted company about two weeks after our return. A retired boatbuilder from down east happened to swing by the marina and noticed her subtle, neon orange four-foot by four-foot "For Sale" sign. He realized her potential right away (half sunk, shambles, duct taped holes, etc.) and put in a $50 bid on the spot. Sold! Two years later a fully restored, gorgeous *Dulcinea* happened along to our harbor, heartbreaker that she was.

Them Things

The opening scene is a meeting room in the Harvard Harbor Social Club outside of Boston, Mass. President of the group inside, Helga Toupet (pronounced "Too-PAY"), is calling the annual planning meeting to order of SPEAC (pronounced "speak"), the Society for the Preservation of English and Culture. Helga can best be described as overbearing, pretentious, and condescending—a formidable force when in high gear this time of the year (late winter).

"I now call this meeting to order," boomed Helga. "We have much to discuss today, so let us begin. Mr. Secretary, would you please read to us the minutes of last fall's summation session."

Secretary Cabot Toupet, a dashingly handsome 26-year-old blond male, preppie to a P, son of Helga, rose as the 46 members leaned forward to hear better—all but two in the back row, that is. Twin 72-year-old spinster sisters, Flora and Fauna Purington, rarely paid attention. They had joined SPEAC about 20 years previously, thinking that the club might have been a free speech organization, but they stayed on anyway out of force of habit and curiosity. They also were the wealthy heirs of a whalebone corset fortune and provided most of the financial support for SPEAC's activities.

"That Cabot's grown into quite a cutie, a real hunk," observed Flora.

"Yes, and he sure has nice buns," whispered Fauna.

Silly Seaside Stories

"Good baking on Helga's part," giggled Flora, as a stern glance from the President froze any further comebacks.

Cabot began: "The 53rd meeting of The Society..."

"We know who we are, Cabot. Get on with it," Helga frostily interjected.

"Yes, ma'am. The meeting was held on October 18, 1928, with 48 members in attendance. The primary focus of the session was a review of that summer's intervention, which took place in El Bordello, Texas. The effort to reduce or eliminate the typical Texas drawl, which represents a gross perversion of classical English pronunciation and form, was met with mixed results. Noteworthy was the observation that most Mexican-American citizens spoke better English than did some of the native Texans.

"The intervention team was shot at only once before being run out of town, a send-off in which all 1,615 residents of El Bordello apparently participated with unbridled enthusiasm."

"I remember the sheriff," Flora whispered to her sister.

"Yes, me, too. Nice buns!" being Fauna's recollection.

"The result was not unexpected, based upon SPEAC's unhappy experience the previous summer in Reluctance, Mississippi, where the goal was to stamp out "y'all" as a corruption of the proper use of the word *you*. It was noted that SPEAC member, Porky Winningham, was recovering nicely from his alligator bite, and Durwinor Luzer had had nearly all of the tar and feathers surgically removed upon his return.

"Written into the calendar for 1929 was today's meeting of the full membership to plan this summer's protest and action, with the suggestion that the site be closer to Boston and the city's excellent medical facilities 'just in case'.

"The meeting was closed at 9:35 p.m. after a brief discussion about wine selections for the next meeting. Respectfully submitted, Cabot

135

Them Things

Toupet, Secretary."

"Thank you, Mr. Secretary," Helga barked. "Old business? There being none (no one dared to bring up any), we will now entertain new business, this summer's action to refine language usage to our high and reasonable standards. Our Target Site Committee (Helga and four cowering puppets) has selected a small coastal community in Maine, Podunkport (pronounced "Po-DUNK-port"), as our focus for summer 1929. Residents there are reported to have odd language mannerisms, such as saying, "them things," rather than "those things," and "ayuh" in place of "yes" (gasps from the SPEAC membership present). They clearly need our assistance to correct these grievous errors of expression."

Over the murmurs of concern and disapproval by those present, Helga went on:

"For an effort this substantial and significant I knew that we would require experienced reinforcements. Therefore, I have taken the liberty ("What else is new?" chuckled Flora) to correspond with Constance Fitzroy, Chairwoman of People for the Accurate Teaching of English, PATE (pretentiously pronounced, "Pat-TAY"), to see if her organization would be willing to join our expedition to Podunkport. She graciously assented to my query ("At gunpoint, I bet!" quipped Fauna). Travel arrangements from Boston to Podunkport have been made by our efficient ("He'd better be!" observed Flora) Travel Manager, Porky Winningham. Mr. Winningham, if you please."

"Uh, yes, Madam President," Porky began. "I have booked passage for 45 members on a steamer out of Boston for Wednesday, June 12, 1929. To save costs, I chose not to select a through boat. Our little ship, the *Miss Anthrope,* named after some Greek goddess I presume, will make stops at Provincetown, Gloucester, Newburyport, Portsmouth, Portland, Popham, Boothbay Harbor, Rockland, East Overshoe, and Mooseport. From there

136

we will be aboard a chartered launch to take us directly to Podunkport, where we will be met by the PATE party." This itinerary being met by uneasy silence among those present, Helga leaped in to pick up the slack, so to speak.

"Sounds delightful, Mr. Winningham," Helga icily responded. "Is there any further new business?"

"What if we *all* miss the boat—Helga did a long time ago." Flora chuckled as she whispered to her sister.

"Be on time if you wish to participate," was Helga's cold retort. "We shan't wait for slackers. There being no further business for this evening's session, I will entertain a motion for adjournment at this time."

"Oh, please let us out of here," whispered Flora.

"I wonder if our ship captain will have nice buns," countered Fauna.

"I move that we adjourn," came out of the crowd.

"Second," quickly followed.

"I could use a drink," the sisters uttered in unison.

Helga quickly closed, with the admonition for all expedition participants to be on the dock on time on the 12th of June. A flyer with necessary details would be mailed to members prior to that date.

The Voyage

The morning of June 12 promised to be a good one, on shore at least. Helga stood outside the gate to Pier D, Cabot in tow, and gazed ahead at the splendid steamship alongside the wharf.

"Why, she must be at least 200 feet long," Helga chirped to the morning air. "What a pleasant excursion this will be!"

As she worked her way through the people, crates, and luggage littering the dock (as Helga viewed it), she was able to read the nameboard prominent on the pilot house of the lovely steamship: S.S. *Rosemont*. Helga's heart sank into a morass of consternation and confusion.

"Where…" Helga's voice trailed off as Cabot pointed toward a sooty black stack showing above the end of the pier some 50 yards away. A small cluster of familiar faces was gathered close by.

As she crept up on the SPEAC group, Helga gradually saw more of the nautical apparition now visible over the end of the wharf, below the edge due to the low tide. Her name on the bow confirmed Helga's worst fear: *Miss Anthrope.*

"Good heavens!" was all Helga could gasp. Cabot looked away, not wanting to witness any growing rage on his mother's countenance.

Miss Anthrope appeared to be a mélange of peeling paint, rust, soot, and general untidiness—an antiquated sidewheeler long past her prime, if she ever had one.

"There must be some mistake," Helga softly wailed as Porky Winningham strode over to her side.

"Isn't she a beauty?" Porky opined hopefully. Helga only groaned and did her best (and famous) 13-year-old eye roll.

"We only have 21 members here, Mrs. Toupet," Porky quickly changed the subject. "We'll have to pay for the additional 23 reservations, but Captain Woodrott said that he might be able to sell them for us. He has another party waiting inside the pier warehouse building. Should I let him know?"

Helga glumly nodded assent, and Porky hurried off to see the captain before Helga could recover from her obvious state of shock.

After about 15 minutes, Porky returned. "Good news, Mrs. Toupet. The other party has offered to purchase the remaining 23 tickets." As soon as he delivered the message, Porky hustled off to get out of range in case Helga should erupt.

While Helga contemplated the imminent voyage on (as she saw it) S.S. *Scow Princess*, she wondered to herself, "What more could go wrong?" It only took another five minutes to find out.

Captain Woodrott staggered up to Helga, reeking heavily of alcohol, and said that he would be happy to "introdush" her to the leader of the other party who would be "sharin' the boyash." Uncharacteristically, Helga had no immediate response— "Still in shock, I suppose," thought Cabot. "Just wait..."

"This ish Mr. Borish Holesaw. Heesh the President of thish organiza-tion, Mishush Toupet. Heesh bought yer ticketsh," Captain Woodrott gushed.

Helga felt (and looked) bewildered. Her perfect voyage was on the rocks before leaving the dock. And who was this Mr. Holesaw? None other than the President of the Society for Conserving Old Local Dialects (SCOLD, pronounced *scold*), SPEAC's rival effort dedicated to maintain-ing "bizarre" (as Helga felt) language forms, usages, and pronunciations. Helga sunk to her knees before rallying to weakly protest to Captain Woodrott, who had already turned away and started reeling toward his command post.

"Charmed, I'm sure," Boris reached for Helga's hand just before it was suddenly whisked away. Helga apparently knew who Boris was, but he as yet did not recognize her by name, face, or reputation. Just as well.

Flora and Fauna stood nearby, amused witnesses to the proceedings.

"Nice ship, sister," Flora mused aloud. "This trip ought to be really something—worth the price of admission!"

"I can hardly wait. Boris has nice buns, Captain Woodrott not so much," Fauna observed.

Helga's usual overbearing manner seemed paralyzed as Cabot hustled his mother aboard before she could regain her poise and bluster. All of the other members of both groups eased aboard also and stowed luggage in their respective quarters. Captain Woodrott made it to the pilothouse, somehow, and signaled his crew to cast off lines. The clang to the engine room resulted in the wheels starting to churn the waters, and *Miss Anthrope* edged along and away from the wharf. A still stunned, grieving Helga stood at the stern rail, staring longingly at the S.S. *Rosemont* as *Miss Anthrope* crept past. All she could muster was a deep sigh.

Pride and arrogance would not allow Helga to admit that she would rather have traveled by train, or bus, or stagecoach, or even on foot. She had regretfully discovered at an early age, on a coastal voyage, that her stomach and the sea did not agree with one another. Helga remained at the stern rail as *Miss Anthrope* plodded toward Provincetown, passing through various shades of green, her ego vying for prominence with her insides in revolt. The mere mention of "lunch stop" at Gloucester prompted full-scale gastrointestinal rebellion as Helga made an unpleasant offering to Poseidon upon arrival.

While Helga was doing her best to hold onto her breakfast and dignity, Cabot was chatting up his new acquaintance, Boris Holesaw, and Boris's companion (and vice-president of SCOLD), Kummin Gettmy.

"And where might you be bound, young Mr. Toupet?" Boris queried.

"Our club is headed for Podunkport, Maine, to rally to a worthy cause—correcting the gross perversions of the King's English that are rampant among the resident population—or so Mother says," replied Cabot.

"Is that so?" Boris cagily responded. "You really feel that the citizens of that community have a unique form of verbal expression?"

"Oh yes, for sure. We have researched the issue extensively," Cabot defensively asserted, knowing that that was a likely falsehood.

"Very well. That may effect a change in our destination," Kummin broke in. "The situation there indeed sounds challenging. Boris, we need to discuss this later."

"Ah yes, my good man. So we shall. Mr. Toupet, I bid you adieu for the time being. I must see the captain shortly, if you will excuse us."

What he did not say to Cabot was that SCOLD was on its way to a conference in Portland, but now Boris perceived a more impactful opportunity. SPEAC's goals and methods were well known to SCOLD, and as such they needed to be countered with reason and discretion. Little did Podunkport know that it would soon become a linguistic battleground and, as events would prove, little would most residents care.

Miss Anthrope departed Gloucester a bit behind schedule and proceeded to fall farther behind with each subsequent stop. Helga managed to hang onto the rail after blessing the deeps several more times, and watched longingly as three large, elegant coastal steamers passed by—as did two coal schooners and a tugboat with barge. As *Miss Anthrope* plodded up the Piscataqua River into Portsmouth on an incoming tide, she was also passed by tandem 12-year-old boys in a wherry (rowboat). As darkness was descending and *Miss Anthrope* needed fuel and water, as well as some quick repairs, Captain Woodrott decided to layover in Portsmouth for the night and get an early start the next day. The fact that two of her running lights were out of commission did not affect his decision; rum deficit did, however.

Boris took advantage of the unanticipated delay to make alternative travel arrangements to Podunkport for his group. Helga collapsed into a cabin berth out of exhaustion and frustration. Flora and Fauna decided that, after a short nap ("beauty sleep"), a spot of tea or sherry would be nice, whichever they could find first. Cabot usually sought out attractive young women during his travels, but was persuaded (by her insistence) to attend to his mother overnight—food, water, support to the toilet, etc. He gave no thought to Boris or Boris's activities, conversation, or whereabouts; Helga was far too demanding and self-absorbed.

The next morning dawned auspiciously, Helga thought. Her stomach had settled some, her ego was in rare form, and there was no breeze but calm seas. *Miss Anthrope* got an early start and made her first two stops nearly on time, dodging patches of fog along her route. Things continued to go well until *Miss Anthrope* departed Rockland, when the east wind returned, and the thick fog closed in.

Given the conditions, Helga's anxiety returned as the fog became even thicker—one could not even see the bow from the pilothouse. A woman of action, Helga tiptoed out to the bow to peer into the murk alongside the lookout.

"Fog's thick," Helga astutely observed.

"Ayuh," was the only response, to which Helga cringed.

During the ensuing 20 minutes or so, Helga could swear that she heard cows mooing, a donkey braying, children laughing, and engines whirring. As any experienced mariner knows, fog can distort sounds and sometimes even muffle them completely. No one aboard *Miss Anthrope* that day heard any of the usual fog signals from ship or shore.

Nervous and frustrated, Helga made her way through the clinging dampness up to the pilothouse to find Captain Woodrott poring over a chart. Helga peeked over the captain's shoulder but quickly noted that she could not distinguish between pieces of land and multiple coffee stains on the wrinkled chart. The captain seemed to be having the same problem.

During his more lucid moments, Captain Woodrott might acknowledge that ded reckoning (navigating by means of direction, speed, distance, and time) was not one of his strengths. He did fine during good visibility and occasional inclement weather, but a "thick o' fog" often left him baffled, and his usual second-in-command, an excellent navigator, had taken this trip off to attend a wedding—his own.

"Well, we ain't hit nuthin' yet," the skipper mused aloud, once aware of Helga's overarching presence.

"Where are we, Captain?" Helga nervously queried.

"Now, I reckon we're right here," Captain Woodrott mumbled in return.

"I mean, how do you know where to go in this fog?" Helga demanded.

"Well, in this kind o' muck I jest heads nor'west, and I ain't never missed North America yet!" a bemused (and besotted) captain asserted, doing little to quell Helga's worst fears.

Seasoned seamen seem to have a sixth sense when it comes to navigation successfully under these conditions. Pickled seamen, on the other hand, such as our current captain, depend more upon fate or the grace of God. It apparently was one or the other that guided *Miss Anthrope* to safety that day, but not to either East Overshoe or Mooseport. She somehow managed to avoid the many ledges guarding the cove and came to a wheezing stop ten feet from a sheer rock cliff in a deep cul-de-sac known as "Redcoat's Revenge."

Only a few old charts label this indentation in Maine's rugged coast, named for a lightly recorded 1777 naval engagement between a fresh water-seeking longboat from H.M.S. *Improbable* and a large skiff carrying three patriot farmers to market. The Redcoats came under attack first, dodging a fusillade of insults and potatoes. They returned fire with muskets, and only the combination of waves and woozy aims prevented serious casualties, although the produce skiff did suffer a waterline hit and eventually sank, lacking any means of bailing.

Given *Miss Anthrope*'s stationary pose, Boris was the first to seize the initiative, requesting permission to take a small boat to the lobsterman's stage (dock) barely visible in the enveloping mist. Under the circumstances (and the captain evidently under the weather), permission was granted. Boris eventually located a working telephone and was able to coordinate a fair-weather escape as soon as circumstances would permit.

When Boris returned, Helga made her own move, but not with as much success. Dragging a reluctant Porky along with her, the two learned that the launch could no longer await the SPEAC group in Mooseport, but a stand-in could be arranged to fetch them from Redcoat's Revenge once the weather cleared, such stand-in vessel(s) not disclosed. Helga vociferously fumed on the row back to *Miss Anthrope*, a cowering Porky slumped in the soggy stern seat. Things were *not* going according to plan!

Miss Anthrope remained socked in for the remainder of that day but was able to make a ticklish escape from Redcoat's Revenge the next morning under a steady offshore breeze. She had gained a mile or so of offing when she broke down completely and was towed back into Rockland by a fortuitously passing tugboat.

Boris's rescue craft made its appearance that afternoon—an 82' diesel-powered yacht commandeered from its annual coastal cruise with the blessings of its SCOLD-sympathetic owner. Helga's new Podunkport-bound transport showed up hours later—a 74' sardine buyboat flagrantly fragrant after dropping off its most recent haul in Rockland. Helga was furious, Porky resigned to a stressful continuation of this now much-delayed expedition. Cabot hid behind the carrier's wheelhouse the whole way. Flora and Fauna booked a local taxi to carry them to the receiving wharf in distant Podunkport. Despite the poor roads, and ins and outs of the coastline, they arrived first. It seems that Boris's yacht made a leisurely pleasure cruise of the journey, while the M.V. *Gardenia*, sardine carrier, was stopped enroute to take on a partial load of herring. Helga was not pleased.

Podunkport

Like those of many Maine coastal villages, the population of Podunkport tended to swell during the summer months, but less so in Podunkport than elsewhere. In fact, the gradual arrival of the combined memberships of SPEAC, PATE, and SCOLD boosted the numbers in Podunkport by almost 15 percent, taxing the lodging resources that needed to absorb them.

Having experience with descending upon unsuspecting populaces previously, Helga swung into action soon after arrival. Her two earliest targets were the town's part-time manager, Caleb Carter, and the head schoolteacher (there were only three teachers for the eight grades), Mary Golightly. Cabot tagged along, unwillingly at first, but very enthusiastically after meeting Mary, a 25-year-old, bright-eyed, bright-minded, bright-haired, bright beauty of woman who Cabot quickly confirmed was as yet unmarried. "This trip may not be a total waste after all," drifted into Cabot's hormone-infused mind.

As impressed as Cabot was with schoolmarm Mary, Helga was the opposite with Caleb Carter, part-time town official and part-time dump attendant, whose primary claim to fame was dead-eye rat shooting at the town dump.

"You shoot rats at Podunkport's rubbish disposal site?" Helga asked with an edge of disdain, which Caleb missed completely.

"Ayuh," Caleb proudly replied. "Them is some of the dumbest critters around. Easy pickin's for a crack shot the likes o' me!"

"We really have our work cut out for us *this* time," Helga silently surmised. "Correcting 'y'all' was child's play compared with this!"

Boris meanwhile toured on foot around the village, dropping in on shops and encountering several of the local fishermen and lobstermen. He found their accents to be "intriguing" and "quaint." For example, one lobstermen's car was a "cah," his quarry a "lobstah." Helga was horrified by those same pronunciations. She determined to address the linguistic crisis head-on; Helga was not one to tread lightly (nor could she, given her bulk and usual demeanor).

"This town is in crisis, Mr. Carter," Helga energetically proclaimed. "People are in grave jeopardy here—you need to call a town meeting!"

"We ain't never had no jeopardies afore," Caleb protested. "You sure this is important?"

"I assure you that this crisis needs to be met directly, Mr. Carter. We must take action immediately, if not sooner!"

"Well, I guess I could get folks together some, if things 'er that jeopardizin'," Caleb wailed. Truth was, he had no clue what crisis Helga was jabbering about, but he imagined maybe earthquake or forest fire, or flood, or atomic attack...his imagination ran wild.

Helga also needed Miss Golightly's assistance, a recruitment process for which Cabot eagerly volunteered. Helga was certain that Mary, as a teacher, would support the effort to reform Podunkport's grammar and diction. "Such a wasteland of culture," Helga mused.

Cabot was not the only man who eyed Mary Golightly with a likely suitor's favor. Local lobsterman, Tom Piper, was already "sweet on Mary," as the locals would attest. Tom was shy, though, and had a "lithp." He'd smile in Mary's direction, but hadn't yet worked up the courage to actually talk with her. He also hadn't anticipated a prospective rival for her attention, especially not one "from away".

With Helga as the prime motivator, Caleb had the word spread person to person, and had posters printed and circulated:

Saturday, June 29, 1929, 5 p.m.
Beanhole Bean Supper
At Podunkport Grange Hall
& Opera House
Important Disaster Preparedness
Meeting Afterward
All citizens invited

Caleb rightly figured that folks were more likely to show up if food was involved. He didn't, however, figure on reporters from the *Bangor Daily News* and *Portland Press Herald* attending, mostly out of curiosity.

Despite Mary's misgivings, Helga prevailed; Mary came to support her town. Caleb, dressed in his best and only shirt and tie, called the meeting to order after everyone seemed satiated with delicious beans. Attendance at the supper was 268, the subsequent meeting drew 17 townsfolk, 45 SPEAC and PATE members, and eight SCOLD representatives.

Caleb had barely started to speak when questions began to fly:

"What's this disastah, Caleb?"

"When's them bombs gonna drop?"

"How's this gonna 'fect the lobstahs?"

"Who's in the bathroom now!"

Caleb was making his best effort to call for order when the nature of beans began to make itself known. "God knows that them beans was excellent," entered Caleb's mind, "but this is not a good time..." His thoughts trailed away as his internal machinations became more insistent.

"Folks, if you'll jest settle yourselfs down," loudly pleaded a distressed Caleb.

To his utter amazement, the room quieted suddenly, just as nature abruptly asserted itself despite Caleb's best efforts at intestinal restraint.

The echo seemed to last for seconds, the only sound in the otherwise silent space.

"That the disastah, Caleb? I wa'nt prepared for *that!*" someone shouted.

The tension broke in a deluge of laughter, catcalls, and rapid conversations. Caleb retreated to stand in line outside the one bathroom, leaving Helga near the makeshift podium (two upended lobster traps).

During their pre-town-meeting deliberations, the executives of the two action organizations (SPEAC and PATE) argued contrasting styles. PATE's Constance preferred a "contagion" approach: change the language habits of a few, and the changes will be picked up by others. Helga, SPEAC's Mistress of Subtlety (not!), pushed the "frontal assault" method: hit the population all at once with both barrels. Constance was no match for Helga's tour de force, so...

Having gained the podium by default, Helga bellowed her audience into an uneasy hush—quiet enough to hear the gaseous eruptions here and there around the otherwise silent hall. Even Flora and Fauna, seated in the back as usual, had to admit that Helga had a certain amount of persuasive charm—that of a sledgehammer in full swing.

Helga pressed her advantage during the silence. "Good people of Podunkport," she intoned. "We have come to your fair community in defense of the purity of the mother tongue. To put it bluntly, your English is atrocious!"

A voice from the back of the room, in mid-belch, spoke up. "I don't know what a '*troshus*' is, but I don't think I got one o' them things."

Helga did her determined best to ignore the unsolicited comment, while gradually becoming alarmingly aware of her own increasing internal pressure. She continued, however: "Many of your wayward vocabulary and expressions clearly are anachronisms."

Another voice piped up. "Ma'am, no clue what an 'Akronism' is, but I ain't never been to Ohio no how. We don't know how they talk in Akron."

Helga's ire was elevating by the moment, as was her intestinal pressure. It was a short-term mystery as to which might blow first. Even Helga did not expect a simultaneous explosion, but as her face reddened and the assembled throng observed in fascinated horror, Helga had barely launched into her fuming tirade on the "horrendous" language of Podunkport when the sphincter dam was breached at her nether end. Only one voice dared to speak up after the devastating report:

"Ain't no whore strong 'nough to end *us*!" The subsequent cheers and applause could have been for the defiant remark, or for Helga's monumental "gastration," as someone later labeled it.

Even single-minded Helga could tell that her spell over the assemblage was trashed—time to consider Plan B, although Helga wasn't yet sure what that plan would be.

Plan B

After the legume-fueled debacle at the town meeting, Helga temporarily at least was willing to consider the approach favored by PATE's Constance.

"We'll talk with Miss Golightly at the school to see if we can recruit at least one of her brightest students, who may have some beneficial influence on his or her peers, and perhaps even on some adults," offered Constance.

Boris, meanwhile, had elected to remain in the background for a time, as an observer and tourist poser.

At the meeting with Mary Golightly, the name of one particular student was tendered, that of Peter "Pudge" Piper, 8th grader and younger brother to lobsterman Tom Piper. Although on the rotund side, Pudge was seen as very sharp, and was well-liked and respected by the other students. Pudge worked with his older brother after school hours, on weekends, and during the summer. To seek out Pudge, then, Constance and Helga needed to go to Tom's home, but found the two brothers repairing traps on their stage.

[A lobsterman's "stage" is a pier on pilings, often 15 feet or more above the low tide line. Many stages during the early 1900's had two functions, lobstering support being one. At the seaward end of the stage might be the family's outhouse, situated so that its receipts could fall into the water and be carried out by the tide. Tom's stage still had such an accommodation. —Ed.)

Constance chose to take the circuitous route to Tom's place via dusty roads. Helga, in her usual blunt fashion, chose to take the straight-line course by water, despite her tender tummy. She hired a skiff; Cabot was drafted to man the oars.

Given the shortness of the distance, Helga arrived first. At the end of the stage, below the pier's surface, was a small float, Tom's lobsterboat being secured along the harbor side. Needing a place to tie off the skiff, Cabot rowed around to the other side of the float, passing directly under the little outbuilding as Pudge happened to be relieving himself. The light breeze scattered the stream somewhat.

"I wasn't expecting showers today, Cabot. We must go back to get my umbrella," insisted Helga.

Dutifully, Cabot quickly reversed direction and retreated toward town, hoping thereby to avoid any unpleasant harangue on his mother's part. The most direct route passed close by the small sardine packing plant, from which fish gurry was piped into the harbor at periodic intervals. Helga's timing could not have been more impeccable—just as her skiff passed by the pipe, an avalanche of effluent burst forth, nearly swamping the row-boat. It was an offal scene—yes, truly awful! Helga's sputtering tirade reached more than Cabot's ears.

Constance, meanwhile, reached Tom's home and found the brothers, none of the three being aware of Helga's and Cabot's misadventures. With Helga's absence, Constance was free to explain her mission in more tactful terms: could Pudge and Tom please say "yes" instead of the local vernacular's "ayuh"?

Tom's answer: "Yup."

Pudge's response: "Ayuh."

Constance could immediately sense that more than a simple request would be necessary; practice would perfect the usage, she honestly believed.

Pudge seemed to notice that Constance cringed at his and Tom's acknowledgements.

"You don't want us to use them words no more?" Pudge asked.

"About 'them,' Pudge, you are not using that term correctly either. You should be using 'those' for 'them'."

"We can't say those thems?" Pudge clearly was befuddled. "We got to use them thoses?"

"R-r-right," Constance stammered, becoming a bit confused herself.

"Thith ith gonna be tough," Tom chimed in. "We jutht don't talk that way here," he pleaded.

"I'll address this issue with Miss Golightly at the school. Maybe she can help," Constance offered with sincere hope in her voice.

At that point Constance effected a strategic retreat to try to get her thoughts together. While she had been visiting Tom and Pudge, and Cabot and Helga were furiously showering to attempt to remove layers of fetid fish smell, Boris had been sharing a coffee break with Mary Golightly at

Podunkport's only eatery, Louise's Lobster Lunch ("L's").

"You see, Miss Golightly, these people from Boston mean well—they're passionate about their cause, most of them anyway. They truly believe that the world would be a better place if everyone spoke totally correct English...the way *they* do, of course," Boris explained.

"What do *you* think, Mr. Holesaw?" Mary responded. "What is SCOLD's position?"

"We appreciate and support the diversity of local language mannerisms and usages that reflect each region's uniqueness and heritage," spouted Boris. "As long as the people can understand each other, we see no reason to change a thing."

"Goodness knows that I try to instill good grammar in my students, but their parents and other elders have developed their language habits over many generations. That Helga Toupet seems to think that I'm not doing my job well," Mary protested meekly.

"Helga is the driving force behind that SPEAC group. Without her they would drift apart, I think," Boris observed.

"What about that Constance Fitzroy and her PATE organization?" Mary was beginning to accept Boris's confidence and insights.

"Harmless, I should say," Boris opined. "They mean well, too, but do not have the Toupet intimidation value and forcefulness. Helga Toupet, to my thinking, is a blind force of nature driven by arrogance and lack of empathy. Unfortunately, she easily influences less self-confident individuals such as Caleb Carter, for example."

"Yes, I can see how Caleb is no match for Mrs. Toupet. What about her son, Cabot? He seems very friendly and less intense," Mary noted.

"Ah, yes. Cabot—friendly to anyone young, attractive, and wearing a skirt, I'd say. His mother's pawn."

"That explains a lot," chuckled Mary. "I'll be on guard!"

"He's harmless—just overly impressed with himself," added Boris, at the very moment that Helga and Cabot strolled in, several seagulls assuming positions just outside the L's front door.

Much as Helga often turned up her nose, figuratively speaking, among local throngs, she became aware of people in the restaurant turning their noses away from herself and Cabot as they moved toward a booth. The impression heightened her unease, considering the view that Podunkport already had of her after the ill-fated town meeting.

A voice rose just enough above the general buzz. "Somethin' fishy in heah. Somebody feedin' beans to the herring?"

Helga didn't even sit down. She spun on her heel, eyes (and nose) uplooking, and stalked out with a fawning Cabot in tow. As they hit the street, a waiting flock of seagulls became suddenly alert and interested; some quickly took flight and circled overhead. As the SPEAC execs headed down the street, the gulls followed in their frequently-following-the-fishing-boat fashion. Helga was perplexed, then shortly bombarded from above by gastrointestinal gull "gifts."

Celebration

Many fishing communities have a special ceremony at the beginning of the fishing season, a Blessing of the Fleet, sometimes accompanied by a parade of vessels. Podunkport had its own version, however, held each year on July 4th. Known as the "Blasting of the Fleet," a mock battle between the parade of fishing craft and the landbound townspeople provided an opportunity to set off fireworks as part of the fun. During that summer of 1929, some of the vessels were engine-driven, while others were still sailing craft. The parade included both.

Caleb was still smarting from the embarrassment of the town meeting,

153

and his leaving Helga Toupet holding the bag, so to speak. To try to make up for that, he offered to include her (at her insistence) among the reviewing party for the boat parade—the town dock's water-level float being the location. Helga naturally graciously accepted— "better spot than being on a boat," she speculated.

Independence Day proved to be a lovely one—warm, clear, with puffy clouds and a moderate breeze from the southwest. The parade of boats would approach from the east, change course just as the boats reached the town float, then head northeasterly with the wind from astern. The mock battle would ensue once the boats passed the float and paralleled the shore.

Helga took her place among the parade officials on the town float, glancing suspiciously upward every time a seagull flew near. The parade of fishing vessels got underway on time, and the first few boats, power-craft, passed by about 15 feet off the float and took up the battle once beyond. The concussions of firecrackers and blank-loaded mini-cannons tended to overcome any attempts at normal conversation.

The first vessel under sail to approach the reviewers was a large Friendship sloop (called such for the Maine town, not for any kind of relationship). At a length on deck of 38 feet for the sloop, the boom for the sloop's mains'l would also be about the same length. As the *Blond Bomber* made her viewing stand turn, she executed a poorly controlled gybe to bring the wind onto her starboard quarter (behind her, a bit from her right). The lengthy boom swung forward over the town float as someone there yelled over the battle din, "Hit the deck!"

Eleven of the twelve persons on the float flattened themselves to the wooden decking instantly. Having no clue what was coming, Helga did not—the swinging boom caught her amidships and propelled her over the side toward shore, directly onto the waiting mudflats. Dignity suffering more than body, Helga struggled to her knees with a clam in one hand and a starfish in the other, most of her body sporting shades of gray muck.

Helga's indignant bellow caused a momentary pause in the mock battle: "Cabot! Get me out of here!"

Flora and Fauna, seated directly above and behind the waterfront bulkhead to Helga's ample rear, had front-row seats for the action.

Affecting an exaggerated Podunkport accent, Flora remarked, "Sistah deah, our Helga seems to have parhked her cahcass in some mud."

"Ayuh," Fauna responded, at which point neither sister could contain her laughter. No one could accuse the Purington sisters of taking the proceedings much too seriously! Their mirth was shared by many in the observing crowd, truth be told.

While Helga was busy alienating many of the Podunkport citizenry, Constance and Boris had independently concluded that no good was likely to come from any further efforts on their parts, so a confab was arranged with Mary Golightly for the 5th. Cabot was invited without Helga's knowledge. Considering his interest in Mary, he was eager to attend.

At the get-together, it was Boris who suggested that perhaps Helga would be willing to leave Podunkport if she perceived that SPEAC's campaign had achieved some success.

"Maybe," Constance followed, "but she can be very tenacious."

"More like a single-minded Pitbull," Boris added. "So we need a good plan to sell success."

Cabot chimed in: "My mother went to see the Piper brothers one day but got sidetracked by a sudden shower. Maybe they could help."

"I could talk with them," Mary offered. "Caleb Carter is anxious to see Mrs. Toupet leave also. I'll talk with him, too."

Tom was shy but thrilled when Mary showed up to explain the strategy to him and Pudge. He felt that he could pull off the deception, given some coaching ahead of time and "no etheth" in what he had to say within

Helga's earshot. Pudge's "no problem" helped to put Mary and Tom more at ease. Caleb bought in also—anything to get rid of "La Formidable," as he viewed her. He was reluctantly tasked with drawing Helga into a conversation to which Mary, Tom, and Pudge would eventually become party.

Helga trudged up to Caleb's second-floor office in the Podunkport Town Hall, reportedly to receive a belated apology for her unscheduled mud bath. She also had been lured with the promise that Caleb would commit some resources of the community (he didn't say *which* resources) to the effort to stamp out the endemic errors of grammar and diction. The one-on-one session started out awkwardly as Caleb chose his words with great care. When Mary Golightly just happened to stop by, both Caleb's and Helga's spirits picked up measurably—Caleb's from sheer relief, and Helga's from reinforced hope.

"Oh yes," Mary reassured Helga, "the school will go all out come the fall session, and I'm certain that the children will be a positive influence on their parents."

On cue, Tom and Pudge happened by also, their lines well scripted and rehearsed. "Oh hello—I didn't know that you were going to be here," Tom led. "Good to meet you. I came to talk with Caleb for a moment, but I can wait."

"Yes, hello again, Miss Golightly, and to you also, Mrs. Toupet," was Pudge's first line. "We've been practicing those words that you wish for us to use in our daily exchanges. My brother and I are thrilled to be part of the endeavor; you may rest assured of that." Pudge laid it on thick, with a pre-determined glance at Tom, to trigger:

"Very true. We have been letting everyone know that our language will benefit from the improvement drive."

A relieved Tom had just finished this reassurance when a booming male voice hollered up the stairs, "Caleb—you there? Them busybody furriners from away gone yet? That SPEAC woman is a piece o' work! Sure glad I ain't hitched to that *cow*—the thought gives me the heebie-jeebies, ayuh, by gory!" The unidentified voice, gaining no immediate response from above, exited the stairwell with a loud bang of the door, which echoed within the tomblike silence on the second floor.

No one dared say a word as Helga gathered herself up to full height, avoiding eye contact with anyone present, and marched out the office door with no glimpse to the rear. Mary, Caleb, Tom, and Pudge sat in total silence until they heard all of the retreating footfalls and a slamming door, then furtive mutual glances led to barely suppressed snickers, followed by wholesale unrestrained laughter.

It was an unSPEACable pleasure for most folks of Podunkport to witness Helga Toupet's unexpected departure the next day via rented vehicle (local fishmonger's truck, sans seafood), followed by a veritable parade of other even less suitable cars and trucks, only Caleb and Mary proffering a goodbye wave, along with a deeply-felt sigh of relief.

Helga never looked back, her private thought being "Good riddance to bad rubbish." Flora and Fauna decided to stay in Podunkport for a while, Flora's mirthful comment to her sister being, "Them folks got the right idea, I think, sis!"

No argument from Fauna— "That Tom Piper's got nice buns, ayuh!"

Rails to the Island

The island's first temporary fishing settlements of the 1600's were located on Great Island, so-labeled on a 1640 chart of the coast. By 1780, after a succession of shipwrecks and castaway episodes, updated charts showed it as Misery Island. Later charts, circa 1850, displayed the appellation Misfortune Island, but by the 1880's, Misfortune had become Fortune…right up to the current 1898 date.

Fortune Island was a sizeable piece of real estate—785 acres or thereabouts. From undeveloped forest it was on the verge of developing into an impressive colony for the rich and famous. Its exclusive developers were titans of industry and bitter rivals in nearly every sphere of monetary endeavor, the Mutt and Jeff of the financial world at that time. Simoleon Greenbach ("Sim" to his few friends) was short and stocky and prided himself on his jolly, personable (he thought) nature. Lotsov Avariss, on the other hand, was tall and thin, intense and cold. Each detested the other for any number of reasons, some real, some imagined.

Fortune Island was ripe for development. On the shoreward side was a lovely sand beach, one of the few along this part of the coast. The island itself lay only one and one-half miles off the narrow, but deep, harbor of Harborside. Neither of the above-mentioned magnates was able to secure the lucrative ferry contract for the island, an astute local resident, Ferd Ferriman, having stepped in quickly when development seemed imminent—he was tipped off by the real estate agent involved in the initial sale of the divided island.

Each of the wealthy developers purchased nearly half of the island and then subdivided much of their holdings into five-acre plots for resale. Some land was set aside for power plants, club houses, recreation, and other common uses. To an outsider, the development plans of each mogul would appear to be quite similar.

One potential obstacle remained: how to get the purchasers—summer residents for the most part—to and from the island. A few would certainly arrive by yacht, but most would expect to come overland—a railroad undoubtedly would be the transportation of choice.

The nearest railhead was at the Middle Fork (known locally as Midfor) station of the Atlantic and Eastern Railroad (A&E), a full 60 miles from Harborside. What was needed, then, was a rail connection from Midfor to a dock at Harborside.

With that goal firmly in mind, two competing efforts were incorporated: the Harborside, Porcupine Gap, & Midfor Railroad (HPG&M) by Sim Greenbach, and the Midfor, Gap, & Harborside Railway (MG&H) by Lotsov Avariss. Lacking effective government oversight, the no-holds-barred race was on, stimulated by greed and one geographical fact: the only feasible route through the intervening mountains was through a narrow, one-track-only cleft—Porcupine Gap. That gap, along with all of the forest between the gap and Midfor, was owned by one Titus Canby, principal of the Beachatua Pulp & Paper Company.

Titus knew an opportunity when he saw one, and the rivalry between the proposed rail lines and their respective owners seemed ripe for exploitation. His timber interests were major shippers on the A&E and, due to Titus's influence, the A&E refused to entertain the idea of a junction with one or both new railroads until tracks were laid from Harborside to

Midfor—they had seen too many railroad proposals fall by the wayside over the years. The A&E also would not permit loads of materials to pass over their lines—all rail and equipment would have to reach Harborside by boat to begin construction at the waterfront.

To sweeten the pot, so to speak, and stoke the fires of competition, Titus purchased two lots from each of the two island developers, giving him a 20-acre parcel upon which to build a sizeable ocean-view compound someday. Having then garnered some attention from the two would-be railroad moguls, he announced that he, Titus, would donate free-of-charge the right-of-way through the gap and woods beyond, all the way to Midfor, to the party who laid rails to Porcupine Gap first, said rails needing to bring a steaming engine to the gap to demonstrate the track's viability. Titus would sit back and watch the fun—and take advantage of every chance that was presented to turn a coin.

Boatloads of material would be required, and boats need wharfs to tie to in order to unload. Harborside's harbor is narrow, but deep enough for smallish vessels, but not for large schooners or steamships. The ferry dock was occupied and not really suitable for heavy loads; new piers would be needed. The available space, though, was very tight.

The first skirmish of the Harborside Great Railroad War was fought on the water as dock-building materials, including pilings, started to arrive. Both railroad builders being financially frugal (read *cheap*), each decided to hire local labor for various tasks. Hank "Hapless" Hascal was brought on by Sim Greenbach, Pete "Petunia" Pigeon by Lotsov Avariss.

Surveyors for both railroads agreed on the general route as being the most direct and cost effective, but harbor space was at a premium. To build their waterfront facilities, they staked out claims diagonally opposite each other across the harbor. The HPG&M would build its pier on the southwest side of the harbor, the MG&H on the northeast shore.

Silly Seaside Stories

Downcoast intelligence brought word to Sim that a barge-load of pilings and lumber destined for the MG&H was on the way, pushed by a small tugboat. With mayhem in mind, Hapless ("Hap") swung into action. He commandeered a small skiff, loaded up 150 feet of one-inch line, and rowed out to meet said tug and barge. When he saw the load approaching, he started feeding the rope over the side of the skiff, directly into the path of tug and barge. As expected, the barge and tug ran over the rope, which caught up in the whirling propeller and became firmly wrapped, eventually bringing forward motion to a halt—salvo number one. What Hap didn't count on was the tangle near the end of the 150 feet of rope that caught on a thwart (seat) and resulted in the skiff's being dragged toward the stern of the tug. Hap jumped out and was rescued by the tug's crew just as the skiff was being drawn underwater and splintered by the slowly spinning wheel.

The incident bought enough delay to allow Lotsov's load to arrive first by small steamer, but too close to darkness to be off-loaded that day. Petunia used the cover of night to bring his first episode of sabotage to fruition—almost. Sim, anticipating a possible foray against his newly arrived materials, posted a guard while the steamer's crew slept ashore. The guard, a local part-time constable, was fond of the grape...in all of its various manifestations, including apple, cherry, blueberry, blackberry, and sundry other versions. Petunia's offer of a bottle of blackberry brandy "to ward off the night chill" was eagerly accepted and hoisted, while Petunia kept surreptitious watch close by.

When the guard's eyelids drooped sufficiently and he sat back on a box, leaning against the side of the steamer, Petunia happened by and offered a cigar. What happened to the lit match is still a matter of conjecture, but the fire that night was not—it toasted many of the pilings and burned the vessel to the waterline. Unanticipated by Petunia, however, was the ferocious blast occasioned by a box of dynamite that was also part of the cargo. Petunia ended up in a singed heap nearly 100 feet from the water's edge as did the guard. So ended salvo number two.

Starting from their respective locations on the harbor, each railroad had to pass through the village of Harborside, the routes being about two blocks apart. Once the courses were staked out, each side knew the projected right-of-way of its adversary. The MG&H's route would require moving two houses; the HPG&M lined up with one of the roads through town, necessitating no building moves.

The MG&H forces struck first. Preparations were made for moving the two houses. Jacking, blocking, and rigging were all done during daylight hours, under the watchful eyes of several townsfolk, including Hap Hascal. The actual moves took place between 1:00 and 4:00 a.m., however, and set both houses squarely in the center of the HPG&M right-of-way.

Undeterred for long, Hap and his HPG&M crew saw fit to lengthen and deepen the foundation holes left behind by the removal of the two houses, also working under cover of darkness.

Meanwhile, Petunia and a small crew set about to undercut, at low tide, the pilings of the newly constructed HPG&M pier. When the first load of rails arrived and were off-loaded onto said pier, it collapsed from the added weight. Recovery of the rails from the harbor mud took two more days. Security was beginning to be more of a concern than tracklaying!

Titus seized his first opportunity for profit when the MG&H's casks of rail spikes and the pallets of HPG&M tie plates and joint bars all seem to have disappeared overnight. Titus just happened to have access to more of all of those items—at inflated prices, of course.

The MG&H track crew showed up one morning to find a herd of "escaped" cattle lounging on their newly laid roadbed. The next day, swine occupied the HPG&M right-of-way, leading to a long-remembered pig chase through the downtown. Since no one stepped forward to take responsibility for the exploits, and no bragging rights were exercised, each railroad crew assumed that its rival was solely responsible for the mayhem. Titus just sat back, figuratively speaking, and smiled.

Town officials of Harborside were promised a local station in exchange for assistance in obtaining rights-of-way through the downtown area. The most suitable lot lay between the two parallel tracks—that lot obtained just weeks previously by Titus Canby. He, in turn, committed the property to each railroad, first come, first served. When two opposing construction crews showed up, the result was a monumental brawl with a Canby representative selling cold drinks and bandages, not at bargain prices. Station-building was postponed for the time being.

Once parallel rails eventually were extended from wharves through town (sans station), the crews faced their next obstacle—a marshy wetlands best characterized by mud, marshgrass, and mosquitoes, not necessarily in that order. Either fill or trestlework would be needed. The MG&H went with trestles, the HPG&M with fill.

Petunia was approached by Titus Canby about a pile-driver that he just happened to have available for lease. Usually used for forest road work, it could easily be adapted for railroad use. It would need to be brought in piecemeal and reassembled for the MG&H's purpose at the marsh-front end of track. Petunia agreed on behalf of the MG&H, so plans were made to accomplish the move and assembly. Titus then let it "slip" to the HPG&M forces what was about to happen.

It took a sizeable team to gather and transport the piledriver pieces and, along the way, the coil of cable for hoisting the gravity-propelled driver hammer took a bit of a detour where HPG&M infiltrators doctored the cable a bit. With haste being the operative principle, the piledriver was assembled and placed at the edge of the marsh. A test run was in order before the first piling would be placed. The hammer was raised to the top of the towering frame...and then the cable broke with a loud snap. With no restraint below it, the hammer plummeted deep into the mud and water below and disappeared from view.

Meanwhile, the HPG&M forces were arranging for loads of gravel to be brought in by barge and wagon, the newly laid rails to carry it to the end of track. The nearest gravel pit just happened to be property of the Beachatua Pulp & Paper Co., also owners of a fleet of freight wagons. Titus would be happy to make those resources available to the HPG&M— for a tidy sum—and he did.

The steam-powered shovel, brought to bear by the HPG&M crew and rented from Titus Canby, was steamed up one morning but soon developed serious issues: oatmeal secreted away in the boiler. It took hours to clean out the boiler, after providing an unscheduled breakfast for the work crew.

Trestlework for the MG&H finally forged ahead after retrieval of the hammer and replacement of the hoist cable. Progress was steady until mid-marsh, when parting of the tall marsh grasses revealed a sign: *Private Clam Flats, Do Not Disturb.* That notice delayed work for a day until a conference with town officials revealed the sign to be a hoax. When the MG&H crew moved it surreptitiously to the HPG&M right-of-way, that crew hastily filled in over it.

At this point, track laying advancement was about even, the two lines being parallel and about 100 feet apart. Trying to maintain security along the lengthening tracks was beginning to tax the patience, and budgets, of both parties. Resources were being stretched mighty thin. No truce was in sight, however—the incentive for speed was still too appealing. Besides, Titus was having too much fun, and profit, to intervene.

Beyond the marsh was the first patch of woods to be encountered, the terrain more hilly and rocky. A decision had to be made: blast through the ledges or circle around. Both railroads decided upon the latter. As the tracks diverged, the crews lost sight of each other for a time. MG&H tracks swung to the right, HPG&M tracks to the left, to bypass the bedrock outcrops and boulders.

Woods in this part of Maine mean wildlife (more than just mosquitoes). Titus did his best to ensure that there would be plenty available, but the first encounters were unplanned and unanticipated.

Hap was checking to see how close the HPG&M tracks could come to the ledges and still maintain sufficient clearance for trains. As he cleared away berry brambles that blocked his view, he came face to face with a black bear cub. Hap froze, realizing that bear cubs rarely were unescorted...and he was quite correct. Hap turned and ran, mama bear sprinting close behind. As he burst from the trees, his crew quickly sized up the jeopardy and scattered, some running back along the tracks toward town, some diving into the marsh grass and muck. Mama bear halted her pursuit, however, to paw through and decimate the lunch buckets that the retreating work crew had left behind. You might say that the HPG&M had "bearly" begun its trek around the ledges.

The MG&H team encountered no bears. The noise of their progress scared off the resident deer, but not the highly territorial, and thoroughly incensed, bull moose grazing with his ladies. Petunia took the lead in trying to scare off the moose. Bad idea. Yelling and waving his arms like a madman, he soon realized that Mr. Moose's pawing the ground and snorting were not signs of panic or retreat—quite the contrary, in fact. Fifteen hundred pounds of 10-foot-tall moose suddenly hurtled at Petunia at warp speed. Petunia managed to dodge the initial rush, dimly aware of his work crew also scrambling for their lives. Diving under the nearest work car saved Petunia from certain disaster, but it took a few days for his bruises, scratches, and splinters to heal enough to make it back to work.

Rails to the Island

The two railroads had divergent routes to circumvent the ledges and boulders, but they converged again just before encountering their next obstacle: a semi-dry peat bog. Beyond the bog lay the forest leading up to Porcupine Gap, the milestone goal for the competition between the two lines.

It was with a collective sigh of relief that the harborside villagers saw the rails extend beyond the town area. Sufficient disruptions had occurred to begin to sour the residents on the whole enterprise, but interest was renewed when the first locomotives arrived. They were now necessary due to the lengthening distance between the waterfront and the end-of-track work sites.

The MG&H iron horse, a diminutive 0-4-2 Porter, was delivered by barge in kit form, the pieces to be assembled on the wharf rails when unloaded. When all of the parts reached the dock surface, it became quickly apparent that one of the four necessary driving wheels had vanished—there were only three. Saboteurs had struck again, it seemed.

The HPG&M received its steam engine from the Schenectady Iron Works shortly after the MG&H Porter arrived. It was an American type—a 4-4-0 wheel arrangement—and all of the required parts seemed to be accounted for. After assembly, it was proudly steamed through town, across the marsh fill and around the ledges. At a leisurely ten miles per hour pace, it didn't slow as it crept toward the end of track at the edge of the peat bog. Despite its engineer's increasingly frantic efforts to apply the brakes, the loco proceeded to run off the rails and into the bog in stately fashion. Somehow the braking mechanism had been tampered with. Mutual recriminations between the two camps turned the Harborside air blue, but neither the original driver wheel nor the missing brake parts were ever discovered. Titus, however, was able to shortly supply both—at inflated "rush" prices, of course.

To cross the spongy bog, both railroads elected to sink pilings—to fill in a path across the peat might take too long and be too costly. Titus had supplied the pile driver used by the MG&H previously as a leased unit. He now offered it to both crews as a rental on alternate weeks—while one line drove pilings, the other could cap its newly driven pilings, place stringers and ties, and lay some rails. Of course, the piledriver would have to be moved at the end of each week, a time-consuming and difficult proposition. To ease the strain and save time, Titus would supply the moving crew each week—for a tidy sum, naturally. With this arrangement, Titus had already been compensated handsomely for his generous donation of the right-of-way through Porcupine Gap and beyond, with more to come...

While railroad-building proceeded through fits and starts, both Sim and Lotsov became preoccupied with developments on the island and with their many other holdings—too distracted to notice that Titus Canby was quietly building up influence with the Atlantic and Eastern through stock trades and gifts to directors. His infiltration into the A&E, in fact, had become strong enough to gain an exclusive right to connect any rail line from Harborside to the A&E at Midfor (or at any other point).

Once that commitment was secured, Titus sent logging crews out to the south of Midfor, ostensibly to cut pulpwood, but the area to be cut over was a straight and narrow swath through the 30 miles of forest between Midfor and Porcupine Gap—out of sight and mind of Sim Greenbach and Lotsov Avariss.

When the tracks of the MG&H and HPG&M drew close together past the ledges and just before the peat bog, they were less than 100 feet apart. Moving the one pile driver back and forth was proving to be time-consuming and exhausting. Titus stepped in to suggest that a temporary crossover—a transfer track—be laid between the two lines, which would save lots of time and effort in the long run. Despite the intensity of the inter-railroad rivalry, both Hap and Petunia reluctantly agreed, each hoping to benefit more than his rival. Titus offered to provide the switch parts and temporary trackage at cost—a generous offer, it seemed.

Once the piledriver could be brought to bear quickly, the pace of trestle-building increased, and no further incidents of sabotage occurred. The bog was finally bridged by both competitors, leaving about 15 miles of woods between their current track ends and Porcupine Gap.

With the extension of rails farther from Harborside, it became necessary to house some security personnel and workmen in tents by the temporary ends of track, opening up opportunities for various forms of skullduggery.

The first salvo in the short-lived "bee war" sent the MG&H troops flying from their canvas quarters one night when a wasp nest was tossed under a sidewall. The aggravated wasps took exception to the presence of human flesh and cleared the tent in short order.

Retaliation took place two nights later when an HPG&M worker set aside a tent flap to head for bladder relief in the woods, and a loose bag of angry honeybees hurtled through the opening, resulting in a mad midnight scramble for the shelter's occupants. To add insult to injury, sufficient honeycomb accompanied the bees to scent the evening air and attract two semi-somnambulant black bears to the scene, resulting in a thorough ransacking of the hastily abandoned tent. Both incidents demonstrated the insecurity of security, such as it existed.

A truce of sorts followed, pretty much by default, for the next few days as tracks crept into the forest and both sides nursed their wounds. Neither party admitted any responsibility for the "buzzkrieg," but tensions were rising as the tracks converged on Porcupine Gap and its narrow opening to the north.

When the rails of both roads were about five miles from the Gap, Titus had his informants circulate word to each camp that the Gap was really too narrow for a modern, standard-gauge train's clearance. The anxious concern this idea caused sent surveyors from both railways to Porcupine Gap for confirmation. Before their arrival, however, Titus had sent a crew ahead to arrange a small rockslide into the Gap, narrowing the opening just enough with loose rubble to make accurate measurements of the bedrock cliffs very difficult, if not impossible. Surveyors' return judgments to each crew suggested that some widening would be advisable "just in case."

Titus also had been busy on another front: he had incorporated the Beachatua & Midfor Southern Railway (B&MSR) to run south from the A&E in Middle Fork on a direct line for Porcupine Gap, ostensibly to transport the logs obtained along that route from the logging already in progress. However, Titus had also filed for common carrier status for the B&MSR so that it could also transport passengers and freight.

Not resting on his laurels with that step, Titus secretly tendered a lucrative offer to Ferd Ferriman for his island ferry service. Ferd reportedly was thinking it over.

Both the MG&H and HPG&M crews arrived within 200 yards of the Gap, nearly dead even, when progress came to an abrupt halt one early morning. Each crew awoke to find its encampment and work areas overrun by porcupines—hundreds of them, it seemed! The porcupines were licking and chewing anything not made of metal, and a few items that were. They were everywhere, leaving hardly a place to walk, much less to work. Both crews managed to effect strategic retreats down the tracks toward town, on foot as the locos and work cars were needle-bearer infested.

While the MG&H and HPG&M crews were safely at a distance from the Gap and out of earshot, Titus had his own workmen planting charges on the easterly side of the rocky cleft, what would be considered the MG&H side. After completing that task, they crept up to the MG&H end-of-track site and removed several lengths of rail, hiding them in the woods on the far side of the HPG&M roadbed, thus setting up that railroad to be in the lead in the race to the gap.

A few days later, Titus announced the HPG&M to be the winner. All the HPG&M crew had to do was to lay explosive charges along the westerly edge of the Gap in preparation for the Gap's widening. The MG&H's blasting materials remained in their locked wooden crates, stacked up beyond the track end.

To mark the competition's completion, Titus offered to host a celebratory bash—a cookout—to which both railroads' crews were invited. The site chosen was a small clearing about 100 yards from the entry to Porcupine Gap. The cooking grills—a chain of metal boxes about 20 feet long overall—were set up on the HPG&M tracks, between the rails, to keep them safely away from the surrounding grass, brush, and trees.

On the day of the party, Sim, Hap, and the HPG&M workers were in a jubilant mood. Lotsov chose not to attend, but Petunia and his crew reluctantly walked over to the cookout, still wary because of the many previous skirmishes. In case of HPG&M trickery, Petunia dragged with him a large roll of canvas containing a secret weapon "just in case".

The grills were well heated and meat starting to sizzle when one of the HPG&M celebrants set off a string of firecrackers, after most of those present had consumed their fair share of fire water. The sudden bursts startled most of the crowd, and positively terrified the until-then recumbent contents of Petunia's canvas package, a large and suddenly animated porcupine. The critter struggled mightily to free itself with partial success: its quills snagged the canvas fabric and dragged it along as it made a dash down the most open route, the tracks toward the Gap.

Porcupines are not especially speedy, but the creature's lurch forward scattered the nearby partygoers, one or more of whom collided with the hot grill, dumping the glowing and fatty contents into the dry grass alongside the track. The immediate flare-up caught the tail end of the porcupine's canvas train and set it ablaze. As the four-legged quillfire trundled along the track, it spread a shower of sparks in all directions, setting grass, brush, and trees alight.

The assemblage had their collective hands full (and feet busy) trying to stamp out the nearest flames. Few even noticed the porcupine-led spark show ambling down the track toward its Gap home, but everyone present took notice, and cover, when the porcupine shed the canvas precisely next to the explosives boxes of the MG&H! Whether or not the porcupine made it to safety into the woods before the eruption is a matter of lasting conjecture.

In any case, the grass and unused ties around the worksite became ablaze, the wooden crates eventually heated up and caught fire, and the explosives fulfilled their destiny, detonating with a frightful roar, quickly echoed by the charges in place in the Gap, triggered by the concussion and heat of the initial blast. The sound carried all the way to Harborside and Middle Fork. The Gap did get wider—by more than the five feet needed!

Soundly shaken by the experience, Simoleon Greenbach was only too happy (and relieved) to sell out the rail line to Titus Canby, who graciously assented to buying it at a bargain price. Lotsov Avariss, being the loser and not being able to complete his line, also sold off his MG&H properties to Titus. Both Sim and Lotsov were offered package deals for transportation on the extended Beachatua & Midfor Southern to their Fortune Island developments. The Harborside station finally was built, and Titus agreed to partner with Ferd Ferriman to maintain the island ferry service.

After all of his wheelings and dealings, Titus smugly sat back, smiled, and thought to himself, "They don't call me 'Crafty Canby' for nothing!"

Spies Among Us: The Possibly Nearly True Story

On November 29, 1944, German submarine U-1230 set ashore on a remote part of the Maine coast two spies who were trained to commit acts of espionage (and maybe sabotage and whatever other-age they could). Both were caught in New York City within weeks of their landing and remained imprisoned for the duration of the war and beyond.

Two additional spies, however, were never caught. Their (mis-)adventures have been pieced together carefully through an intense study of official German naval records, diaries, letters home, archives of the men's hometown museum, and eyewitness accounts recorded posthumously by the very persons involved. This is their story, probably.

[Editor's note: The passages in italics below have been translated as needed from the original German, English, or Pig Latin into modern American English Mainese.]

Wilhelm Wiener and Klaus von Pretzel were conscripted into the German navy (at gunpoint) during January of 1941, persuaded by patriotic fervor (of the gun bearer) to leave their tiny village of Gerschwinheimerschatseneisenunser-wurstuberdenholtzenbagendorf, population 36, minus 2. The town was so small that the destination sign on its train station overlapped the next town down the line.

Wilhelm and Klaus endured the usual basic training, and then were immediately "volunteered" for their spy training based upon their prior experiences in the U.S. Klaus had lived for a time in Massachusetts, working in an A&P grocery store as a stock boy. Wilhelm had had a term as an exchange student at the Boston Back Bay Academy for Young Women, where he had been mistakenly enrolled as Wilma Wiener—he didn't protest too much, it seems.

After many months of intense training and guided practice with American customs, slang, and mannerisms, they were pronounced ready and loaded aboard U-157 for the hazardous voyage across the stormy North Atlantic. Their country-boy constitutions did not fare well—they arrived off Maine's shores still reeling from the debilitating effects of *mal de mer.*

At precisely 1:30 a.m. on September 4, 1941, on a moonless, hazy Gulf of Maine, U-157 surfaced cautiously a mile offshore and crept to a halt to offload the two prospective spies into their little rubber boat. They were to paddle to shore, ditch their dinghy in some bushes or under some rocks, then strike out for the inland roads to hitchhike south. Good plan, questionable execution.

Their initial objective would be a landing in Clambucket Cove, just a slight indentation along a sparsely populated Maine shoreline. What the German charts didn't show, however, were the extensive mudflats that stretched seaward from that part of the shore—excellent for low-tide clamming and bloodworming, not so excellent for effecting a landing from the sea. Low tide happened to be at 1:30 a.m. that fateful night.

Wilhelm and Klaus grounded in the mud about 75 yards from shore and faced an exhausting slog through the ankle-deep muck, dragging their craft behind them. The trudge occupied all of their energy and attention for nearly 30 minutes, after which they collapsed onto the seaweed-covered, rocky shore in time to hear a cheery, "Good mornin', fellas! Need some help?"

173

Spies Among Us: The Possibly Nearly True Story

Both Klaus and Wilhelm were dumbstruck. They hadn't anticipated encountering anyone that early and along that shore—their cover story did not at all address that contingency.

Thinking fast, maybe too fast, Klaus stammered, "Guten—er, g'morning to you, sir. Yes, we are poor fishermen, and our vessel has sunk. We are castaways on this shore."

"That's a pity," responded the voice out of the darkness. "Were you boys dragging or jigging or long-lining?"

At the same time, both spy-wannabees answered:

Klaus: "Jigging."

Wilhelm: "Dragging."

"I see," observed the voice. "Lookin' fer cod, mackerel, or haddock, boys?"

Again, simultaneously:

Klaus: "Cod."

Wilhelm: "Mackerel."

"Yer vessel Eastern rigged or Western rigged?" queried the voice.

As previously:

Klaus: "Eastern."

Wilhelm: "Western?"

Neither of them had any clue what they were talking about, but their anxiety levels were rising rapidly, verging on panic.

"Well, it's too bad that you lost 'er, boys—you sound like you've had a rough go of it. C'mon up to the house, an' me an' the missus'll fix you up somethin' to warm yer bellies," offered the voice. "I'm Herbie. Who're you?"

Enough of their cover stories sprang to mind to allow coherent answers:

Klaus: "I'm Joe."

Wilhelm: "I'm Bill. What are you doing out here this time of night, Herbie?"

"Tide's out. Been clammin' some. You guys feel strong enough to carry them buckets?"

Neither Klaus nor Wilhelm could see the buckets in the dark, but they readily agreed, with sighs of relief—until they tried to heft the "buckets", that is.

"Oomph," groaned Klaus, as he stumbled forward and fell onto and over the first bucket. Wilhelm slid toward the voice and ran a leg into the second container. Both buckets contained at least 75 pounds of something—it was too dark to see the contents.

"Jest fallah me, boys. We got a ways to go up this rise, then a short walk to the house," encouraged Herbie. A few slips, falls, banged knees and elbows later, the two Germans reached the crest of the slope, panting from their exertions. Off in the distance they could make out a dim light, most likely from a window or doorway. The figure of Herbie bounded along several yards ahead, obscuring the faint illumination at times. They didn't see the brambles but definitely felt their effects, wincing at each poke as they struggled along with their loads.

After what seemed like hours the party of three reached the light.

"Jest set them buckets there by the shed, boys, an' c'mon in. Ruthie will set yous up wit' some coffee an' soup to take off yer chill from yer sinkin'." Turning to his wife, Herbie added, "Ruthie, these poor fishermen was wrecked an' cast up on our shore. They be out of work now with their boat sinkin' an' all, so I'll find 'em some work to do. The boys down at the hahbah can always use experienced help."

That last utterance by Herbie was unexpected and quite unwelcome, renewing the spies' anxieties—this decidedly was *not* part of the plan! They had to check their impulses, however, to maintain their cover—and hope that they could eventually revert to their original purposes.

"We got some spare beddin' in the attic, boys. You'll be comf'table up there. With the sinkin' an' all, you could prob'ly use some sleep."

Herbie guided "Joe" and "Bill" to a narrow staircase and up to a cob-web-infested loft where a pile of musty quilts lay. "There ye go, boys. Sleep tight—see yous in the mornin'," Herbie chirped.

"Morning?" Klaus thought. "It *is* morning already!"

"*Wilhelm, we've got to get out of here and get to the highway!*" Klaus pleaded.

"*Ja, Klaus, but we can't seem too eager—that would be too suspicious,*" Wilhelm responded.

Despite the dust and spiders, both men drifted off to sleep quickly—at least their "berths" were no longer heaving. After what seemed like minutes, though, came a pounding on the attic door.

"Up and at 'em, boys! Time's awastin'. Tides wait for no man!" crowed Herbie up the stairs.

"*Ach, Klaus. What time is it?*"

"*It looks like 5 o'clock. Can it be?*" Klaus moaned.

The two stumbled down the attic stairs to be greeted by an ebullient Herbie. "C'mon to the table, boys. Ruthie's made you a nice cod tongue an' bacon fat chowdah for breakfast. I knowed you would be grievin' your lost vessel an'd be anxious to get back on the fish, so I booked each of you on a short-haul boat for the day; fill-in work, it is. Ruthie packed you some tins of sardines for your lunches."

"You didn't have to go to all that trouble for us," Klaus protested weakly. "We should just get going and get out of your way."

"Nonsense, boys. Tweren't no trouble 'tall. You need to get back on your feet on the water, an' I aim to help! Losin' everything like that, you cain't afford to be idle," Herbie insisted.

Klaus and Wilhelm (as Joe and Bill) glumly sat down to eat, forced down their chowder amid pained mutual glances, then timidly grasped their little sacks of sardine tins as they followed Herbie toward the door.

Herbie's "Here, Fritz" startled both spies, and as they turned toward the clatter, the biggest German Shepherd they'd ever seen came bounding in from the living room, nearly knocking Wilhelm over the wood box.

"This here is Fritz, boys. He's my helper at my work. Sniffs out clams an' bloodworms real good...you'll see." Herbie's animated manner left no room for argument. The two spies trudged along the path for the one-and-one-half-mile walk to the harbor of Oddsport, dreading the day, but dreading even more the idea that they might be caught.

"Joe, this here is Hiram Foraday. He's a long-liner, an' you are gonna be his baiter for the day. He runs about 2,500 hooks all told. You do real good an' he might use you t'morry, too!" Herbie chirped.

"Bill, yer real lucky that Corky Bobber's dragger is short a deckhand today. He's a real highliner and will work you good. You boys have a good day. I'll see yous back heah 'bout 9:00 tonight!" Herbie turned away before either German could protest.

For Klaus and Wilhelm the day seemed to drag on for 100 hours of up and down motion, up and down stomachs, and periods of dejection and ejection at the rails of their respective boats. Hiram showed Joe how to cut up the bait, fix it on the interminable lengths of hooks, and feed the line into the depths *ad nauseum*. Bill struggled with the trawl rig, meekly explaining that it was so different from what he was used to (very true!). Both skippers were very patient with their temporary assistants, but neither allowed for any slack time, either. Nine p.m. mercifully arrived as both boats made their ways back into Oddsport Harbor where Herbie and Fritz were waiting.

"Good to see ya', boys. Let's get home quick-like so's we can chow down on some tendah venison stew an' chokeberry biscuits! How'd you like those yummy sardines?"

Probably just as well that shades of green and pallid countenances were not visible in the darkness. For some reason, neither spy evidenced much of an appetite, and both begged off any evening entertainment to head straight for the attic. It was an open question as to whether escape plans or dreamland would win out, but both men succumbed to sleep within minutes.

Dragging himself reluctantly out of the sleep of the dead, Klaus woke Wilhelm at about 4 a.m. *"We need to get out of here now,"* Klaus insisted. *"I'll slip down the stairs and try the door."*

Step by creaky step Klaus eased down the staircase and grasped the door handle, giving it a slight rattle. The sound was immediately greeted by a low growl on the other side of the door. Klaus let go for a moment then turned the knob a bit. Another deep growl resulted. This time Klaus kept rotating the knob until the latch clicked its opening; more growls. A slight push changed nothing—the door wouldn't budge. More push elicited a deeper, more prolonged growl, but no opening progress—Fritz apparently lay against the door and was not disposed to changing his location. Klaus briefly considered shoving hard against the door to dislodge Fritz, but fear of the possible consequences restrained his impulse. Resigned to defeat, at least temporarily, he tiptoed back up the steps and explained the dilemma to his partner. Both again resignedly hit the sheets, such as they were, until Herbie's cheery wake-up call resounded up the stairs seemingly moments later.

"Ach," groaned Wilhelm. *"How do we get out of this?"* The exhausted by resigned would-be spies descended the stairs as the attic door was opened by a distressingly buoyant Herbie.

"G'day, boys! I knowed you had a good time on the water yestr'day wit' yer fishin' duties, but I weren't able to get yous on them boats today (collective sighs of relief by the Germans), so I gotcha cushier gigs for today.

"Bill, you're needed on a coast watch patrol boat lookin' out for enemy submarines. You also get to help test out a new experimental sea-sickness remedy—the coasties've been waiting for a really rough day at sea to try it out, an' today looks like a rough one! That ol' patrol vessel ne'er was a steady one—too round in the belly. Should be a good test, an' you don't gotta do a thing but search for subs!

"Joe, you're gonna take the ferry to Rowlanrock Island to help sand and paint the bottom of a dragger hauled out there. You know the island, 'bout 15 miles offshore from Oddsport. Should be an easy day, right up your alley.

"Breakfast is waitin' on the table, boys. Ruthie's made us a tasty mackerel head an' turnip pie. Eat hearty, boys—you've got long days ahead! Oh, you 'joyed them sardines so much yestr'day we set yous up wit' some more (both men had tossed their tins overboard). Time's a wastin', boys."

Two less-than-enthused men sat down to face certain gastronomic torture, never mind the noxious fumes their repast was emitting. Barely two bites were choked down through distressed smiles when Herbie announced:

"Well, time to go, lads. Can't miss yer boats—skippers are waitin', y'know. No time to lollygag over them fine vittles. Here, Fritz!"

The two German sailors didn't know whether to feel merciful relief or anticipatory dread at the day's prospects, but they were given little time to contemplate either. Herbie led them off by force of will, back down the path to Oddsport Harbor and certain doom.

To suggest that the proposed seasickness remedy, a concoction of fish oils, didn't work well for Wilhelm would be a vast understatement. The only submarines he might have spotted that day would have had to have been directly below the patrol vessel as he spent most of the day bent over the boat's rail.

Klaus fared little better, hunched under the 75-foot fishing vessel, sanding its bottom's entire length alone, as his purported helper "took lame" at the last moment. After (and turning red from the accumulated drifting dust), Klaus was given a two-inch-wide brush with which to paint his handiwork.

"Sorry, Joe—'tis the only brush I could find. The big 'uns come up missin' this morning,' " explained the skipper. "Take yer time—y've got all day. Ferry don't come fer ya til 6:30 this evenin'."

By the time both spies returned to Oddsport and awaiting Herbie and Fritz, they were both well worn—and looked it.

"Tough day, boys? Well, t'morry we take it easy. Gonna do some clammin' an' wormin'. Gonna be too rough to go out fishin'."

"*Too rough?*" Wilhelm thought to himself. "*What was it today?*"

Klaus and Wilhelm staggered along the trail in the dark, hopefully following a barely visible Herbie, Fritz bringing up the rear. Neither man had any appetite for their dinner, Ruthie's special "fisheye porridge" with biscuits. Both cleaned up as best they could and stumbled up the attic stairs to crash and burn, any thoughts of spying being far from their minds—survival was paramount!

"*How does Herbie do it?*" wondered Wilhelm aloud.

"*I don't know—I'm drained, Will. Training was never this bad!*" commiserated Klaus. "*We've got to escape somehow!*" Trouble is, he had no clear idea of how to do so. He felt as if he was on a never-ending conveyor belt of waterborne terrors. Sleep overcame him, more like a sledgehammer than a velvet fog. Neither man made any attempt to try the attic door that night.

"Hey, boys—up an' at 'em! Them early birds catches the most worms!" crowed Herbie up the stairs, seemingly bare minutes after the spies had collapsed into profound slumber.

After a pitiable attempt at breakfast, they gloomily trailed Herbie toward the shoreline where they had landed not even three days before, but eons ago it seemed.

"Too bad about your little rubber boat, boys. Seems that the surf the past couple days done a job on it. Gotcha' a rowboat to use if we need one as the tide fills, though." Herbie seemed oblivious to their plight, irrepressibly energetic, indefatigable.

"Bill, you know Corky here. He's takin' the day off from fishin' to go clammin' with you. Joe, you an' me's gonna chase bloodworms on the flats while the tide allows. We'll meet here in a couple hours, God willin'."

Corky led Wilhelm off to the northeast, while Klaus sloshed and plodded along the mudflats trying to stay close to a magnificently mud-marching Herbie, Fritz keeping pace along the shoreline rocks and gravel beaches.

"*What's a bloodworm?*" wondered Klaus once Herbie halted his march and plunged his rake-like implement into the mud in a frenzied attack. Herbie reached down into the resulting furrow and withdrew a squirming creature nearly a foot long. Placing it in his bucket, Herbie quickly struck again and removed another worm from its lair.

"*Looks easy enough,*" thought Klaus. Several holes resulted in no squiggly captures, however, until Herbie explained what to look for—certain telltale clues in the damp mud. Klaus's next attempt yielded a glimpse of a worm that quickly disappeared. His second thrust was rewarded with a struggling bloodworm which Klaus was quick to grab—and then just as quickly regretted it. Bloodworms can bite, and this worm took out its indignant wrath on Klaus's finger, drawing blood and a gasped, "Ach du Lieber!" Herbie cast a furtive glance in Klaus's direction, then turned away to smile.

By the end of two hours the incoming tide was swirling around their feet, and it was time to meet up with Corky and Wilhelm back at the rowboat. Klaus had mastered the art of lifting bloodworms from their mucky dens, but nine of his ten fingers bore record of his *in vivo* education. Wilhelm complained that his back might be permanently bent—clamming tends to get one to feeling that way. Herbie led his charges back up the slope to the house, leaving the skiff behind on the shore. While ambling up the grade, Herbie cheerfully announced:

"No time for lunch, boys. We got a volunteer chore to help move the Widder Macon's outhouse to a new hole yer gonna dig. Shouldn't take too long—it's only a one-holer."

Klaus and Wilhelm exchanged furtive glances of distress but dutifully marched along behind their resilient leader, Fritz close on their heels. After about a half-mile trek southeast, they arrived at the Macon home. Several other men had already gathered and begun digging the new hole, barely 25 feet from the nearly full one.

"Hold off, men," Herbie intervened. "I got some fresh diggers fer ya. These boys just getting' warmed up fer diggin' this mornin'. Stand aside fer 'em, if you please."

Shovels were quickly passed to the two spies along with murmured thanks and expressions of relief. Klaus and Wilhelm gloomily bent to the task—they were pre-bent already—and began to throw aside spadefuls of soil. While they dug, the other men jacked up the outhouse a bit to place planks and pipe rollers under it to have it ready for its brief expedition to its new location.

Two hours of steady excavation yielded the desired depth, and both tired and sore diggers were then recruited to assist with the move. Planks and rollers needed to be placed ahead of the now mobile loo. When the little building was about ten feet beyond its former site, Klaus and Wilhelm started to lift the first runner planks to move them forward.

At that very moment, Herbie shouted, "Fritz...rabbit!" The until-that-instant supine Fritz abruptly leaped up and into action as if shot out of a torpedo tube. In his race past the men and into the brush he dealt Wilhelm a glancing blow, sufficient to propel him over the edge of the former, and nearly full, outhouse hole and onto his hands and knees in its odiferous contents.

Wilhelm's first impulse was to count to ten as his mother had always instructed: "Eins, zwei, drei..." His voice suddenly trailed off as he realized that he had a fascinated audience.

Herbie broke the brief tension: "Bad luck, Bill. Let's get you out of there an' hose you down afore you scare off the townsfolk, smellin' like a sewer!"

The rest of the move was incident-free, much to the relief of the German participants. Herbie was matter-of-fact about the whole procedure and remarkably upbeat as he addressed the menu for the evening meal:

"Ruthie's set to outdo herself t'night, boys. She's drudged up an ol' family recipe since I knowed you boys'll be mighty famished, skippin' yer sardine lunch an' all." Herbie didn't mention what that recipe entailed, but the odor emanating from the little kitchen was frightful. With a poorly hidden lack of enthusiasm, the two young men sat down at the table to see vacant eyes staring up at them from their soup. The biscuits were teeth-cracking, the meatloaf repugnant, the fruit pie indescribable...and largely inedible. After weak nods of appreciation, the spies dragged themselves up the attic stairs and collapsed on their ersatz beds.

"*We've got to get out of here, Klaus,*" Wilhelm pleaded. "*I didn't sign up for this—this is torture! What about the Geneva Convention?"*

"I have an idea, Wil. The sub has a repeating course that should bring it here every four days. Tomorrow is the fourth day. If we can get free by tomorrow night...."

"That's a big 'if,' Klaus. We haven't had a moment without others around us since we got here," Wilhelm noted.

"We may need some kind of ruse, a pretext to leave the house for a time at night—that is if Fritz is not blocking the door again. We must be opportunists—seize whatever small opening that comes our way...improvise."

"Ach, I'm too tired to think, Klaus. See you in the morning," Wilhelm mumbled as he sank into slumber.

The sun had barely kissed the dawning sky when Herbie swung open the attic door and hollered up the stairs, "Good mornin', boys! We gots lots to do today—up an' at 'em!"

Two nearly catatonic zombies staggered down the steps in time to hear their fate for the day: "Easy day, boys. Oddsport's got a Grand Banker in for the day to get 'er fish holds inspected. Just got to scrape out the gurry and scrub 'er down so's the ceiling can be got at. Shouldn't take but a day or so," Herbie brightly understated. "No fishin' involved, an' the gurry don't bite. Boat's at the dock—just a bit o' ocean swell to keep 'er lively. Gotcha yer favorite sardines fer lunch, too!"

As far as Wilhelm and Klaus were concerned, no more dismal words were ever spoken. Their sense of desperation was exceeded only by their fatigue. Only the thought of the probably approaching sub kept them going—the thought of how to explain their failure as spies fortunately eluding them.

Like automatons, they plodded through their assigned duties, one or more of the vessel's crew always close by. The smell was nearly intolerable—even the outhouse refuse compared favorably, Wilhelm miserably conceded. As with all bad dreams though, the workday finally drew to a close, mercifully for the spy duo.

"Good job, gents," the schooner's captain crooned. "See you tomorrow to do the other holds."

"*Tonight has to be the night*," thought both men as they trudged home behind a typically perky Herbie. When they arrived back at the house, after dark as usual, Ruthie greeted them with anxious news:

"I'm glad that you've all gotten home safe and sound. Several bears have been spotted between here and the highway. One man and his dog have been attacked; they were carrying a newly shot buck, I heard. Well, c'mon to dinner—it's just last night's leftovers, I'm afraid." Ruthie couldn't have been more afraid than Klaus and Wilhelm were.

Shortly after sitting down at the dinner table, all heard a rattling and clattering outside by the trash cans. Fritz immediately stood up, back hair erect, and uttered a low growl.

Herbie spoke up, "Sounds like them raccoons are at the garbage again, Ruthie. They must like yer cookin'," Herbie chortled. "Would you boys go out an' chase 'em off? I'll hold Fritz here so's he won't interfere. Don't worry—they weren't be bears this close to the house—they stay in the woods."

Neither Klaus nor Wilhelm objected to leaving their plates behind as they made their way outside. It would be too early to make a break for the shore, but on their wary way toward the garbage cans they discussed some possible scenarios while allowing their night vision to take hold.

They reached the source of the noises at about the same time their eyes became somewhat adjusted to the dim light. What they beheld was neither raccoon nor bear, neither fish nor fowl, but an extended family of black and white fur balls who were as startled to see humans as the humans were to see them. The skunks reacted first—it was no contest. *Eau de skunk* saturated the night air, leaving four human eyes stinging and clothing reeking as a result. Both men stumbled backwards, but far too late to have any beneficial effect. Their retreat to the house was met by a determined Herbie and Fritz at the back door.

"You boys can't come in here smellin' like that—Ruthie just won't have it! You can sleep in the hay in the shed tonight an' we'll clean yous up in the mornin' when we can see better and smell less. Sorry boys—it's just gotta be that way." Herbie sounded sincerely regretful; Klaus and Wilhelm perceived their golden opportunity and offered no objections.

Neither spy slept well—too much anticipation and excitement accompanied their fitful attempts at snoozing. At about midnight both men were awake and as alert as could be expected. The shed door creaked as they tiptoed into the night air, still fragrant from their chance encounter earlier by the trash cans.

"*I wonder if they can smell us in their sleep,*" Wilhelm whispered. The words were answered by an audible growl from within the house.

"Shh," was all Klaus could caution—they had to find the trail to the shoreline on their own, in pitch blackness. The new moon cast little light, but stars were everywhere—the Milky Way was prominent, and as they emerged from the shoreside brush, they could see that the Gulf of Maine thankfully was dead calm.

"*Perfect!*" they chimed in unison.

"*Let's drag the skiff down to the water and row straight out,*" Klaus proposed. "*The U-boat should be surfaced and recharging about two kilometers offshore. We'll watch for her.*"

After a protracted struggle, the flat-bottomed skiff made it to the water's edge, the retreating spies clambered in, Wilhelm positioned the oars and began to row—quietly at first, then more energetically when many yards out from the beach.

"*We're free, Wil—they won't catch us now!*" was just leaving Klaus's lips when the starboard oar broke in two at the oarlock, the blade drifting away into the night.

"*We're jinxed, Klaus. What rotten luck! We still have one oar—we can scull or paddle. We have to get away!*" And so, they did…while bailing the leaking skiff with gusto.

Morning came early for Herbie and Ruthie as usual, and a curiously casual inspection discovered their fishermen guests to be absent.

"Well, Ruthie," a bemused Herbie began with a twinkle in his eyes and a wink toward his wife, "I hope them German spy boys had a good time while visitin'! Go bury that leftover food an' get out the good stuff. We don't want to poison the raccoons or skunkies! After breakfast I'm goin' to bed. I'm pooped!"

Telemess

"I'm telling you, Jack, with a last name like *Baker,* you don't want to move out to that island! It's pretty and all, and the folks there are very pleasant and helpful, but as long as the phone system is as it is, living there could be a nightmare! I gave up my shoe repair business because of it."

"How so, Shomee? How could a phone system make things so bad?" Jack mused as he took another sip of his coffee. "What's the story?"

"Okay—some history for you, from the beginning:

Ile Tant Pis

"The island is one of five in the archipelago, all named by the French explorer, Gaston du Mal de Mer, around 1640 or so: treeless Ile au Naturel (Naked Island), Ile Oui-dire (Hearsay Island), Ile En Passant (Isle By the Way), Ile à Gauche (Island to the Left), and the one in question, Ile Tant Pis (So Much the Worse Island). It is the only one with a year-round population. The village, Happy Landing, is on the mainland side.

"For many years the island had no telephones at all, but the residents eventually formed a local company, subscribed shares, and in 1950 bought lock, stock, and barrel the antiquated hand-crank system being junked by the town of Green Scum Pond over in the mountains. A cable was laid out to the island, but they ran out of money as the cable reached the nearest house to the shore, the one owned by the Prater sisters, Gertrude and Gilda. The old hand switchboard was set up in their parlor, and they were recruited to answer the phone, and to take and deliver messages."

"That seems kind of awkward," Jack interrupted. "How did that work out?"

"Therein lies the problem, Jack. Not very well, it seems. The Prater sisters were hard of hearing, notorious gossips, and they often got sidetracked while performing their phone duties. Costly mistakes were made at times as a result.

"For example, well, you know that there are many capable craftsmen on the island who ship their products all over the coast and to some inland towns. As luck would have it, names were some of the reasons for the troubles.

"The rumor is that Gert and Gilda were gabbing about something or other while Gilda answered a call for "Hack" Coffin, the island's boatbuilder—he mostly builds small boats: wherries, dories, peapods, etc. The call was to be an order for six skiffs for a camp up north.

"Apparently all Gilda heard was 'Coffin,' and she wrote down the info to go to "Gloomy" Schiffe, the island undertaker and burial box builder. The order called for six 14-foot by five-foot, flat-bottomed items to be made of pine or spruce—whatever was handy. The bottoms were to be painted green, topsides white, and the insides buff—which Gilda understood to say that the occupants would be buried nude."

"She didn't catch on that the order was for boats?" Jack asked incredulously.

"No. She confused that order with a message for Gloomy for six burial boxes seven feet by 30 inches. That message went to Hack instead.

"Gloomy thought that the dimensions were very unusual, and all of his coffins had flat bottoms, but when Gilda mentioned that the caller said that they needed to hold up to three people each, Gloomy went ahead with the order, figuring that some folks just have strange burial customs.

"Hack had never built seven-foot skiffs before, but he assumed that they might be for cradles or cribs, or maybe for teaching boat skills to toddlers, so he went ahead and built them. It was weeks before that whole mess was sorted out—expensive mess, too!"

"Did the message strategy get straightened out afterward?" Jack queried.

"Never did, Jack. Take the time that someone put in an order for a custom-made grandfather clock. Gert took that message, but while yakking with her sister, all she registered was 'grandfather' and 'clock,' so the message went to Grandpa Klochsmythe, the island's wagon-builder. It called for 'six-foot-tall' and 'spring action'—Grandpa couldn't figure out the part about 'weights,' Gert's writing being so poor. Grandpa decided on a freight wagon, I guess. It looked real nice when done. Carried the seven-foot skiffs onto the ferry!

" 'Stave' Cooper, the actual clock wizard, got an order once for one of wood, round, and with four hoops. He finally concluded that that message must've been for 'Horse' Karridge, our barrel expert—a genuine cooper.

"I finally gave up on the Prater sisters' system, though, when a message for me got passed on to Doc Shoemaker, the island's veterinarian. The note asked if I could fix a brogan. Doc had never heard of that breed of dog but figured he could do it, since he'd fixed plenty of labs and spaniels. I never did get to repair that shoe.

"Then there was the day that the sisters had the weekly quilting bee and gossip fest at their house. That was the day that 'Hutch' Boudoir, our custom furniture maker, got a request for a poplar bed frame. In the confusion of babbling gossip at the Praters', Gert heard something that she interpreted as *popular, dame, bed,* and *boudoir,* all put together meaning that Hutch was having an affair! Hutch is 82—not likely, but his wife was not as amused as the other quilters were.

"Trouble is, everyone liked the Prater sisters and hated to hurt their feelings. They were apologetic and all, but the townsfolk were anxious to raise the money to extend the phone system before too much more damage could be done."

"So, what happened then?" Jack leaned forward, enthralled by what he could imagine.

"Well, there was the night when a message came for Stave Cooper. Seems that the island ferry had a breakdown and would not be able to transport a finished grandfather clock that night. A note from Gilda went to Mr. Klochsmythe saying that his fairy godfather had gone to Finland and couldn't come that night."

Jack chuckled and commented, "It sounds like things were getting worse over time. Didn't people complain?"

"Oh, they grumbled plenty to each other, but most figured that the fault was partly with the phone setup, and that confusion with names was bound to happen at times. After all, Gilda Prater was 91 and her sister was 95. Their handwriting was a bit shaky, too."

"I see what you mean about the names being confusing at times," Jack observed.

"Oh, I've only mentioned a few instances, Jack. It was really a lot worse. I haven't told you yet about 'Rusty' Steele, Otto Mattick, Dewey Doolittle, Carrie Nowate, 'Bud' Light, May Fillmore, Bertha Struck, 'Gopher' Burroughs, or 'Sporty' Carr. They all got mixed up messages at one time or another."

"So, Shomee, how did you decide to leave Happy Landing for good?" Jack's imagination was in high gear by now.

"Given all of the confusion and hard feelings over the wild gossip going around, I figured it was only a matter of time before I got victimized by it, too, my last name being Lovejoy."

***

"Chet, wake up! If you don't get moving, you'll be late for work!"

"Wha...huh? Wow, what a dream I was having! Really bizarre! What's for breakfast, Mrs. Cooke?"

The Birds and the Bees

It was early in the summer of 1930, and I was desperate for a job. The depression sparked by the stock market and banking crash had dealt my fortunes a deadly blow, not that I had had any fortune to start with.

Hanging out at the waterfront on Monk Key, just east of Islamorada, Florida, had put me in touch with a likely prospect for work— "likely" meaning a sure thing for the gullible or merely foolish. The work site in question was the battered hulk of the four-masted schooner, *Emma I. Leakey*, now sporting only three masts, since the fourth had chosen to abandon ship during her previous and only voyage in 1926.

The fact that I was not a mariner nor had ever been to sea did not dissuade me—I was young, impetuous, resilient, and immortal—thankfully ignorant of all that could go wrong.

The *Emma I. Leakey— "Emma"* we called the brute—was the brain-child of her builder, owner, and skipper—one Oddson R. Leakey. His parents' only son, he had two older sisters, after whom the two four-posters built on his own account were named.

The twin coasters were cobbled together during 1918 when materials were in short supply, but bottoms were urgently needed to transport supplies for the Great War. Oddson scavenged green lumber from neighbors' woods, metal from town dumps, cordage from purloined fishnets, and whatever else he could scavenge to advance his patriotic cause.

The Birds and the Bees

The two vessels were built side by side and launched within hours of each other. The *Emma* floated off first, after a fashion, while the *Constance M. Leakey* had the good sense to go straight to the bottom a mere two hours after her debut, a perch from which she never was persuaded to move. She had become an ersatz breakwater for the tiny Maine harbor of Hatchet Alley, although more of a long-term hindrance than help.

The *Emma*, lacking the foresight and resolve of her sister ship, remained afloat and set off in ballast for the Kennebec River to load ice for her first run to points south—Florida, to be precise. The voyage was beset with contrary winds, fouled pumps, torn sails, loss of one mast, mutiny, and decay, and inspection by a German U-boat whose captain felt sorry for the *Emma's* crew and, in a fit of perverse sadism, refused to torpedo or shell the *Emma*, reasoning that he could do more damage to the American war effort by leaving her afloat.

In due time, eight months later, the *Emma* arrived in Miami with 112 pounds of ice remaining from the 480 tons she had loaded—and that 112 pounds was refused due to fecal contamination by rodents that were never found. The *Emma* slunk off to the Keys, stubbornly refusing to sink at sea to end the misery, but instead taking up a fitful berth on the low-tide sand flats adjacent to Monk Key. There she idled in quiet repose until 1930 and her ill-timed revival.

The funds for the *Emma's* reincarnation were joyfully provided by Emma I. Cluliss (nee Leakey) herself, who inherited a sizable fortune after the alleged suicide of her wealthy husband during 1929. She was still quite taken with the honor of having a ship named after her, and fortunately she knew nothing of boats and the sea. She trusted her younger brother Oddson completely.

Oddson, on his part, was primed for one last fling at the sea—or one last fling at being lost at sea perhaps. To aid in bringing the *Emma* back to the seagoing state she never really had in the first place, he had prevailed upon his long-time first mate, one Wilberforce Synkker ("Willie" for short), and Willie's twin brother, Woodlawn Synkker ("Woody"). I've heard that, of identical twins, one is often the dominant one. Woody was one bung short of a full keg, so it wasn't hard for Willie to take the lead role. His bung wasn't too secure either.

Ever curious about names, I gleaned more about the Synkkers as we worked side by side on rescuing the *Emma*: The parent Synkkers emigrated from Estonia as a young couple. Pregnant with her first set of twins at the time, and knowing little English, the young mother took a liking to the letter W and picked names for the boys that she saw on various signs— Woodlawn Cemetery, for example. The twin girls, Wynott and Wylya, were born two years later. The last Synkker prodigy, Dewey, was an afterthought and supposedly named after the admiral. He was later noted for his ferocious bouts with seasickness and subsequent purchase of a dirt farm in Oklahoma.

The skipper, the two Synkkers, and I made up the entire crew designated to rehabilitate the aging schooner, although now I question whether the *Emma* was ever habilitated in the first place. The sands of Monk Key had been kind to her over her four-year sojourn there. Even the teredoes (shipworms) had left her alone, probably repelled by her caulking concoction of tar, spruce gum, turpentine, axle grease, arsenic powder, and niter. At high tide, the *Emma* squatted resignedly at anchor, only cycling half of the bay at a time through her gasoline-powered pumps. At low tide she squatted fast on the sand, as resistant to sinking as nature could make her.

The *Emma's* major need was a new mizzen mast. The skipper told me the labels for the four masts, starting from the bow: fore, main, mizzen, and spanker. I could never get them straight under pressure, so I just called them 1, 2, 3, and 4. We needed a new 3.

The Birds and the Bees

Now I don't know how familiar you are with the Florida Keys, but mast-size timbers just don't grow on trees there! We searched high and low, far and wide, fat and skinny, rejecting telephone poles, flag poles, a radio antenna, steel pipe, and an old railroad bridge beam. One high tide rip provided the solution, though: a storm-tossed tree from parts unknown, bark and all, branches and roots included in the bargain price—free.

I wouldn't be exaggerating one bit to say that it took the four of us all of one week to get that log ready to become a mast—stripping, cutting, planing, fitting, sanding—and it still pretty much looked like a damn tree when we were done. It was riddled with small holes, stunk to high heaven, and was shorter than the other three masts. It took another week to hoist it up using a variety of jury-rigged tackles and set it into place in the mast step on the keelson. Rigging it took three days more. We then recut the mizzen sail to fit the new spar. It was magnificent when done—well, not really.

During the next few weeks we caulked, stripped, painted, payed, greased, sanded, oiled, tarred, hefted, and toiled—well, three of us did. Oddson was out talking with agents and brokers and businessmen and shysters, trying to drum up cargo for the voyage to the north.

Two weeks of solid hustling fetched us a well-mixed load: whole logs and cut timbers of southern longleaf pine, boxes and tubs of flowering plants, wooden laths, casks of rum and molasses, pea coal in bags, bricks, barrels of turpentine, gallons of honey in glass jugs, and several boxes of bottles of perfumes and bath oils. The mix of scents below in the hold was both intriguing and frightful. Some of the cargo was to be discharged enroute, while some was to be embarked. To accomplish all the voyage's missions, we needed stops in Miami, St. Augustine, Savannah, Charleston, Ocracoke, Norfolk, Baltimore, Cape May, New York City, Norwalk (CT), Providence, Edgartown, Boston, Gloucester, Portsmouth, Portland,

Boothbay Harbor, and Rockland, Maine. The *Emma* would then join her sister in the mud at Hatchet Alley as a permanent symbol of travesty, not travel, at sea.

As the weeks toward our voyage north progressed, I got to know my fellow crewmembers, for better or for worse. The Synkker brothers, as identical twins, were cast out of the same physical mold, and at least one probably should have been left there.

Woody was a man of many talents, and none of them were particularly helpful. For example, he could contrive to cause any smoothly running piece of machinery to spasm into moribundity—it was undoubtedly a gift. For that reason, he was not allowed near the donkey engine up forward that was used to raise the sails and anchor. Since the skipper could not locate a seagoing cook until we reached Miami, Woody was drafted into that role—I had feigned ignorance of the difference between a pot and a potato, not without some accuracy. Woody's talent turned out to be making even common food items unrecognizable: potatoes that looked like mush, bread that better resembled runny flapjacks, fresh salad dressed as hog swill, etc. No cook was more warmly received than Kanga Rioux, our Miami acquisition to fill out our five-man crew. Fortunately, whatever Woody could break, Willie could fix.

Once a cargo was lined up, Oddson was anxious to pick up the rehab pace, resulting in some significant issues being neglected. While the wooden hull, crudely assembled from its beginning, did its best to survive under four years of intense tropical sun, the running rigging—lines to hoist and control the sails—withered more than the skipper had realized, or wanted to acknowledge. It was not prime cordage when the Emma was launched, and it definitely wasn't now.

Getting underway in a four-master required raising the aftermost sail first—the spanker (#4). The winch on the donkey engine fired to life at

Willie's ministrations, and the spanker sail slowly ascended. Once it was set, we hoisted the recut mizzen, only to see the spanker fall to the deck—a casualty of rotten halyards. We cleared away the spanker mess and hoisted the main as the mizzen sail collapsed. Collective sighs set the fore as the main descended with a loud crash. I'm sure that any observers on shore were greatly entertained watching our slow-motion domino effect. We didn't sail that day after all—no surprise there. Oddson turned over more of sister *Emma's* greenbacks to obtain all new cordage for the halyards, not giving a thought to the deteriorated sheets, an oversight that the perverse *Emma* was capable of ignoring for now.

Our fearless captain was typically Yankee frugal and wasn't about to turn over any of sister Emma's hard-inherited cash unnecessarily. His schooner, when first encountered after her four-year hiatus, was a mass of peeling paint and rust streaks. I'm sure that the residents of Monk Key, all eight of them, expected to see the semi-derelict *Emma* reach an ignominious conclusion on their sand flats. Their collective enthusiasm and relief were quite evident when the entire populace showed up to wave us away.

On that fateful day, the *Emma* had much the appearance of a calico cat. Oddson had raided the vessel's copious paint locker for whatever he could find. Thus, the *Emma* sported patches of dark green, yellow, white, gray, buff, and red bottom paint—the latter not necessarily on her bottom.

Getting underway did not go smoothly. Sail-setting proceeded according to plan, thanks to her new halyards, but the 250-pound anchor refused to budge. The well-rusted chain was taken up by our wheezing donkey/windlass combo, but the anchor had buried itself so deep over the four years that its flukes might have been made into a chandelier somewhere in China. The only solution was to cut the chain to lose the anchor, but thankfully it parted on cue on its own.

We were now on our way, but apparently the unfamiliar motion of the vessel stirred up its long-standing resident population into frantic activity. Rats streamed on deck from parts unknown and plunged suicidally through thronged scuppers and over the side. I had no idea that rats could swim—and many didn't. They did, however, attract the attention of several hammerhead sharks who must have had ratatouille on their menu. I'm guessing that the rats judged braving the sharks as far less risky than accompanying the *Emma* on her voyage north.

We proceeded in ballast (beach rock and sand) to Miami to fetch the first part of our cargo. Even with favorable winds, that first leg took us six days—the *Emma* was no speed demon. Our stubby mizzen mast began to display its true character during those idyllic days. I can only surmise that it must have detached itself from some windswept coast during a summer storm—it began to dry out from its immersion and untwist in remarkable fashion, developing many contorted checks (cracks) as it did so. It also was riddled with borers of undetermined genera, judging by the increasing proliferation of surface holes. Inspire confidence it did not!

Willie was at the helm one day, guiding the *Emma* through a labyrinth of bars and islets nearing Miami, when he yelped:

"Bee!"

"Be what?" nearby Woody responded.

"No—bee! Buzzer kind!" Willie exclaimed.

"Buzzard? Don't see none o' them, Willie," Woody observed brightly. "Just gulls 'n' terns."

"I been stung, dagnabit! Got me right in the belly button! Dang that smarts!"

"I don't see no bee, brother. You sure it were a bee?" Woody seemed unconvinced until, "Ow! That were a bee sure 'nough!" Woody yelled and began flailing his arms, swatting at buzzing missiles real and imagined.

As quickly as they appeared, though, they were gone. The skipper came aft to see what all the fuss was about, but only heard second-hand accounts of the attack.

"We got bees, Skipper. Hunnerds of 'em! Ferocious stingy thingies with sharp drawn swords! Me 'n' Willie both got stung! It was awful!" Woody croaked. "We fought 'em off, though."

"Where are they now, boys?" Oddson queried, looking right and left rapidly.

"I dunno, Captain. They was here just a minute afore you came. I don't see 'em," Willie added.

"Well, hold course. Maybe we seed the last of 'em," Oddson concluded. "Lemme know if any more show up."

None did—until we reached Miami, that is. That's where we loaded most of the plants and other small items. The logs and timbers we'd secure later, in Georgia and South Carolina.

The plants needed sunlight, so we kept some on deck and rotated them with those we'd stowed below. Many were in flower, and the Emma smelled much better as a result. The flowers also attracted our hidden bees—lots of them.

Going on deck and rearranging our vegetation cargo became hazardous duty. Our limited supply of medical potions became taxed severely, and wearing excess clothing to cover up resulted in broiled bodies, drowning in sweat. To sweat or be stung was the dilemma. Woody provided the possible solution while we were docked in Savannah.

Ever the scrounger, Woody met a man dockside who, for a suitable (and substantial) fee, would pass on to Woody just what was needed: four hungry woodpeckers to eat the bees. Gullible Woody returned to the *Emma* with two makeshift cages in hand, each containing a pair of likely (he thought) bee eaters. Just how he was supposed to convince the woodpeckers to remain with the ship to corral the bees was not explained, but he figured they'd stay with us once we were at sea.

Cargo embarked, we headed offshore, towed to sea by a diminutive steaming tug. As soon as the tow hawser was dropped, the *Emma* began to lift her sluggish skirts to the steady southwesterly. As we made an offing to set a course for Charleston, Woody opened the cages to allow his avian crew to do their appointed chores.

Now I don't know if land birds can become seasick, but none of the four prospective bee-eaters became airborne immediately. They sat, mostly, then staggered about a bit, one falling awkwardly to the deck. Woody was solicitous—he picked up the dazed woodpecker and placed it on the pinrail at the base of our twisted mizzen mast. For a time, the woodpecker seemed to retain a death-grip on the rail, then suddenly came to life as it must have spied something compelling on the mast itself. The bird sprang into action and attacked the spar with obvious gusto, finding lunch among the holes and checks in the *Emma's* number 3 mast.

That must have been the call to arms for the other three unwilling-at-sea guests—they joined their shipmate in a staccato rat-a-tat-tat on our forlorn mast wannabe, apparently finding plenty of fodder to spur their efforts. They worked their ways around mast hoops and halyards. Their efforts must have stirred up the nearby bees, none of whom were bothered in the least by the now preoccupied woodpeckers. We only found out much later that those birds don't generally bother with bees.

Just below the gaff saddle must have been a particularly savory feast. The woodpecker at that location defied the creaking gaff and occasionally slatting sail to drill the mast with renewed ferocity. A sizeable hole soon developed which became a nesting site—Woody had acquired both sexes, it seemed.

Our skipper was not amused. Fuming daily, he stomped around the decks, swatting at angry bees and occasionally throwing projectiles and colorful epithets at our unwelcome bug-but-not-bee eaters. That condition remained until we reached Charleston (no relief there), and then Ocracoke and Norfolk.

We rid ourselves of the logs and took on coal in Norfolk. The bees and birds remained, but a stevedore in Norfolk took Woody aside and offered him a solution for the woodpeckers: the *Emma* needed a hawk. You can guess who just happened to have a highly trained birding hawk for sale— not cheap (or cheep). Woody was hurriedly given rudimentary instructions on hawk-handling ("wear gloves") as he handed over some of Oddson's cache of sister Emma's inheritance.

Said hawk stayed caged until well at sea, at which point he (or she?) was loosed to destroy the invasive and useless not-bee-eaters. Maybe the hawk never got the instructions about eradicating the woodpeckers, and it certainly had no truck with the bees. As it flew about the rigging, though, it did present a whole new slant on the term "poop deck." Do hawks get diarrhea?

If the hawk had any passing interest on the mizzen woodpeckers, it was fleeting and unobserved. It did, however, manage to scare up the few refugee rats we'd acquired during our various port calls. The hawk would disappear below decks for hours at a time, reappearing with some poor wiggling vermin which the hawk would consume while perched in a temporary, makeshift nest in the main's gaff throat. The woodpeckers would observe with casual disinterest.

One hot and sultry day with little wind and even less patience, Oddson loudly announced that he had reached his limit—he was taking matters into his own hands, utilizing the extreme measures that the situation called for.

From somewhere in the depths of his cabin, Oddson produced an antiquated shotgun and several shells. Stomping up on deck, he loaded the first shell and aimed for the hole just below the mizzen gaff's throat. The recoil set the skipper down hard on his derrière, but the shot found its mark on the weakened mizzen top, which exploded into splinters, bringing down the remaining masthead, gaff, and sail with a loud crash. The woodpecker may have seen the writing on the wall, so to speak—it had abandoned its perch when Oddson first raised his weapon.

We now had a mess to clean up, but our valiant (and now berserk) leader was beside himself with righteous fury. A second salvo directed at the retreating woodpecker brought down the spanker-gaff and sail. All four woodpeckers then took flight as the hawk burst aloft from somewhere below and received a glancing blow from Oddson's third volley. The sudden reports must have shaken the bees' nest wherever it was down below, as the bees swarmed out in force, prepared to repel any and all boarders. Since they had no clue as to friend or foe, we were the likely targets for their ire—and irate they were!

The *Emma* was just about becalmed, fortunately, as both Willie and Woody exited expeditiously over the side, gaining some benefit from their early swimming lessons. Oddson was furious beyond reason, though, and elected to fire two more rounds, this time at the swarming bees. The casualties were the center of the mains'l and the Charley Noble (stovepipe) of the forward galley hut where Kanga had wisely hit the deck.

One more shell remained. Blind with adrenalin-fueled rage, Oddson's last shot took out the binnacle and wheel, reducing both to scrap wood, as well as eliminating our ability to steer. As one last gesture of futility, the offending shotgun was hurled overboard, narrowly missing Woody who was busy treading water. His fury at last abated, the skipper sat down on the littered deck to cry—and promptly got stung.

During the melée on deck I had managed to avoid being shot or crushed by falling spars and sails by diving below, only being stung three times wile laying low. When I came back on deck, Oddson was surveying the carnage resulting from his fusillade of fury. He wisely allowed that we should bypass our planned stops at Baltimore and Cape May—their citizens would have to obtain their rum and molasses somewhere else—and head for New York under jury rig to effect some necessary repairs…to our vessel and our pride. Willie and Woody were hoisted back aboard before becoming shark food, although both stated that their jellyfish stings were probably worse than the bee stings would have been.

The two weeks it took us to reach New York Harbor were taken up with repairs—sails, rigging, jury-rigged emergency tiller, patches, etc. The *Emma* definitely looked the worse for wear—she looked like she'd been to hell and back actually—but we did manage to sail her sans mizzen, which was beyond reasonable rescue except in the eyes of the persistent woodpeckers, who stubbornly clung to the remains of that tree.

New York City provided welcome relief from the cares of the protracted voyage. Having passed up on stops at Baltimore and Cape May, we still had the casks of rum on board, but one did not survive our port call. The source of the bees was still a mystery, but the skipper engaged a veteran beekeeper, who promised to smoke them out once and for all and take the swarm away.

For our bee exorcism, we lay alongside a rotting pier in Brooklyn—no self-respecting wharf would have us. We discharged our cargo of laths and bricks; only the plants, turpentine, coal, honey and some rum remained. The plants—those that were still intact after the shotgun purging—had to be off-loaded temporarily while the *Emma's* many hatches and deck leaks were sealed.

The bees may have taken exception to the sealing—each of us was stung at least once during the off-loading and sealing process. Kanga developed an allergic reaction to multiple piercings and swelled up like a hot air balloon. His rush to a shoreside clinic proved to be one way—he swore never to return to "that devil ship!"

On the appointed day, our savior beekeeper arrived with smudge pots in hand. Clothed in a cobbled-together netting, heavy long-sleeve red shirt, black trousers tied at the ankles, rubber boots, welder's gloves, and modified top hat, he looked for all the world like a monster from a grade D horror film. The already smoking lighter pot just enhanced the imagery.

Down below he went, and down below he stayed for the better part of an hour. Just about the time we began to fear for his safety, he emerged from the foc's'l door and closed it behind him. Within minutes smoke began to seep from every one of the *Emma's* copious pores—our sealing was only partially successful, it seemed. Soon clouds of whitish smoke encircled the *Emma's* masts and enveloped the deck.

That must have been too alarming for someone(s) not forewarned ashore as we heard loud cries of "fire!" and sirens and bells shortly thereafter. We had hardly had time to react when streams of solid water knocked us flat and swept Oddson clean off the dock into the filthy harbor water. Not a strong swimmer, he sunk like the proverbial stone to be rescued quickly by Woody, who was not to be left captainless in this foreign (to him) port.

Once dockside and still sputtering from his dunking, Oddson exasperatedly explained to the fire battalion chief that there was no fire—we were chasing bees. The beekeeper had been knocked unconscious by the blast of the water cannon wielded by the harbor's fire boat, but he recovered in time to corroborate Oddson's explanation—and just in time for the explosion in the schooner's hold that set the *Emma* on fire for real!

Fires aboard old, dried-out wooden vessels are notoriously difficult to quell, but the *Emma* took matters into her own desiccated hands and determined to sink at the dock, thwarting the attempt to haul her away to prevent the fire's spread.

For the second time in her ill-starred life the *Emma* found the comfort of the ocean's bottom to be preferable to facing the vagaries of being afloat. The blast down below must have jarred her less-than-tight planking seams to allow seawater's ingress, which she happily lapped up. What little flame that had resulted from the blast must have been extinguished by *Emma's* latest visit to Poseidon. She seemed content for the moment.

Oddson was *not*, however. With typical downeast pride and mule-headedness he was not about to allow his command to rest on her laurels on Brooklyn's bottom. He prevailed upon sister Emma to loosen her purse strings "for the last time" to recover the vessel he so proudly had named after her.

Sucker, er, *sister* Emma acquiesced, and a hasty wire brought sufficient funds for the rescue effort. Oddson reasoned that, if fire pumps could fill his schooner with water, they could take it out again, too. Enough pumps were commandeered to empty the Pacific Ocean, and the *Emma* ghostily arose from her contentment sufficiently to be towed across New York Harbor to a waiting drydock on the Jersey shore. While she sat to be repaired and recaulked, the beekeeper was allowed aboard to recover his smudge pots. Not wearing his protective gear that he had deemed "unnecessary," he was stung four times—the bees were alive and well.

Not only had the bees not succumbed or been driven away, but the hardy woodpeckers had expanded their range and taken a liking to the main topmast. Apparently, insects had moved into the dried-out spar during the trip north. The pounding of caulking mauls from below was accompanied by the rat-tat-tats from above—an out-of-synch percussion symphony. The hawk was nowhere to be seen, though—unlike seagulls which were everywhere.

His budget would not allow for replacement of the *Emma's* stubby mizzen mast, so temporary rigging had to be set up to improve support of the spanker mast and main topmast. The remains of the temporary mizzen were removed, thinking that that would discourage the resident woodpecker population. Not so, we found out—apparently a second generation had come into the world before the mizzen removal. We now had seven bug-catchers circling the *Emma's* lofty heights. Our skipper could sadly read the handwriting on the wall: our topmasts were doomed.

The *Emma* was relaunched after two weeks of frantic activity. We essentially worked round the clock to ready her for the rest of the voyage. The plants, destined for Boston, were reloaded, which seemed to please the recalcitrant bees, whose queen location was still undetected. I think Oddson's mental faculties were deteriorating by this time, as he was often observed mumbling to himself and swatting at imaginary bees—and sometimes real ones. He clearly was not the same man we had embarked with from the Keys months before.

During our busy labors while in dry dock, none of the four of us had noticed that some of the shrubbery we were transporting had produced fruit—various pods, berries, seeds, or whatever. We hadn't noticed, but it soon became obvious that sharp-eyed birds had—they clustered around the *Emma's* deckload arboretum, chittering, pecking, dropping colorful splotches, and pooping prodigiously. Periodically, Oddson would run around the deck, waving a broom in a vain attempt to drive them off. Do birds laugh? I think these did.

To shave miles and hug the shore for safety, we booked a tow across the harbor and up the East River to Long Island Sound. It had been years since a four-masted schooner had passed those shores, and many people came out to watch as the three-masted four-master sailed by. The proximity to the Connecticut and Long Island shores also made it convenient for various birds to come and go. The *Emma* was the center of much attention, some of it definitely unwanted...and messy.

We didn't dare go on deck without wearing a hat to ward off avian anal missiles from above. Heavy garments were necessary both below and on deck as the bees seemed to have stepped up their activity, perhaps in preparation for the approaching winter (?). They were not friendly to us, and we detested them.

The skipper gave up on Edgartown and Providence layovers, deciding to proceed directly to Boston to free himself from those cussed plants. He had deluded himself into thinking that, once the shrubbery was gone, the bees and birds would abandon ship, and we'd just be left with the usual complement of rats.

"Ah, foolish one," crowed Mother Nature. "I'm still having fun at your expense. Why stop now?"

As the season wore on and we made some easting, the helpful south-westerly breeze was rudely interrupted by a northwesterly blast as we slipped through The Race at the eastern end of Long Island Sound. The woodpecker-weakened main topmast was the first casualty, followed by the fore topmast, which brought down the outer headsails. The shambles on deck did some violence to our living cargo, and even the various flying creatures had the good sense to lay low for a time.

As soon as order on deck returned, so did the bees and the birds.

Under much reduced sail, the *Emma* crept through Vineyard Sound and around Cape Cod, hailing a Boston pilot as the weather was cooling appreciably. "We'll be rid of those (expletives deleted) bees and birds very soon!" chimed an elated Oddson, delirious with optimism and unrestrained joy.

Birds fly south for the winter, right? Maybe the *Emma's* birds missed their flight; they hunkered down in the schooner's various nooks and crannies, perhaps too wrapped up in the drama presented at their very doorstep—or would that be *neststep*? Do bees hibernate, or should that be *hivernate*? The *Emma* did *not* shed her interlopers in Boston; they continued the voyage somewhat under cover, stowaways all.

After Boston, Oddson threw in the towel. With the advancing season and on winter's edge, he'd absorb the losses from the last of our undelivered cargo, bypass the last few ports, and plot a course direct for Hatchet Alley. He was done with the sea—but it wasn't quite done with him!

Ospreys and eagles are birds of prey, and Maine has ample quantities of both. What about the *Emma* made our schooner the focus of the avian hotline I have no idea to this day, but as we slowly worked our way downeast past Cape Elizabeth and Seguin, ospreys and eagles would swoop low to snag unwary fish, then drop them on our deck, intentionally or otherwise. Gulls would spy the fish and bomb the *Emma's* deck, squawking and feeding in attack waves reminiscent of the Great War, intent upon gobbling up said fish. This sport continued for miles until one of the eagles became entangled somehow below decks.

Holy hell broke loose! Amid an incredible racket from the nearly empty hold, rats, woodpeckers, and bees erupted from every open hatchway. Feathers flew, upset bees blindly attacked anything that moved and some that didn't, gulls wheeled about overhead surveying the carnage for likely snacks, and alert ospreys took notice of rats and birds to join the fray.

The general pandemonium on his pride and joy was too much for our captain, who clearly slipped a cog and went over the edge. Sans shotgun or broom, he dashed below to our coal bunker, loaded a bucket, and sprinted back on deck to heave chunks of black diamonds at our winged marauders, shouting and cursing all the while!

Woody, stuck in the cookshack by the foremast, had missed most of the warm-up and ducked out to see what the commotion was about. He made it to the door, pot in hand, just in time to be struck on the forehead by one of Oddson's misguided missiles. His pot went flying, dumping raw fish chowder on the poop-slick-deck, which quickly became a target for the greedy gulls.

Temporarily blinded by the blow to his cranium, Woody slid and slipped along the deck forward, trying to keep his footing among the greasy mess, finally falling forward against the pawl restraining the renewed anchor chain. His plunge was enough to release the pawl, allowing 100 fathoms of anchor chain to rumble out through its hawse hole, adding to the general din.

The sound of the retreating chain was loud enough to catch Oddson's attention, though, whose dash forward was just in time to see the bitter end of the chain zip over the bow. The event seemed to present a crushing blow to Oddson—he simply sat down in the slop and started to cry.

Our captain appearing to be incapacitated, Willie took charge of the schooner amid the continuing chaos, and although stung twice, managed to rouse out the below-decks entrapped eagle, whose sudden presence chased off the encircling gulls. In the ruckus, the woodpeckers had made themselves scarce. The bees eventually returned to their hideout, and Willie rescued Woody from the soup, leaving Oddson to his weepfest forward.

Lacking any more misadventures, the *Emma* did finally reach Hatchet Alley. She wisely settled in the harbor's mud, reconciled to her sister ship after having abandoned her earlier to go voyaging. For several years afterward, villagers could obtain some of the best honey around by raiding the makeshift hive in the starboard shelf, behind a large hanging knee, unnoticeable unless one knew where to look.

The woodpecker families didn't leave right away, either. As guano slowly encroached upon her deck, the *Emma* aviary was prominent on quiet days, a tap-tap-tap echoing from the abandoned hull.

These days the only vestiges of either the *Constance M. Leakey* or *Emma I. Leakey* are a few timbers still visible at dead low tide in Hatchet Alley. Oddson never went to sea again. In fact, he refused to ever visit the harbor or look upon the ocean again, and he displayed an exaggerated aversion to flying creatures of any kind.

As for me, I was paid off and took up farming and beekeeping. My children and grandchildren never tired of my telling them about the birds and the bees!

Harbormaster

I'm piecing this together from my copious notes gathered over the past few weeks, having spent an unusual amount of time working on a story that I had anticipated to be dull, dull, dull. My name is Joe Coffey, and I am the (only) feature writer for *The Maine Almost Weekly*, known affectionately hereabouts as "The M.A.W." My editor sent me to cover a political (read *dull*) race near the coast. Rumors suggested that it might *not* be dull, according to my boss.

I wasn't particularly intrigued until I arrived in the town of Bottomfield to cover the contested race for Harbormaster…and found that Bottomfield was not on the coast.

Some History (and –ology)

It turns out that the geography of the area is a significant factor in the story. Bottomfield is separated from the Gulf of Maine by the coastal burg of Carport, named after the floating boxes used to store live lobsters in their natural element. At the head of Carport Harbor is a glacial berm (ridge) about 50 feet above highwater and about a quarter mile wide. Several houses are perched on the loose detritus from the last glacial retreat. The town of Carport is on the next cove over from Bilgewater, significant only because the Maine legislature has forced towns to consolidate their schools. The three towns subsequently had to pool their resources to construct their new consolidated high school, named BiCarB High in honor of the three contributing villages.

The central section of Bottomfield consists of an unusually flat, low-lying plain, perfect for the town park/fairgrounds and school athletic fields. The town's buildings, businesses, and homes cluster along the surrounding hillsides and woods. So much for Geography 101. Now for the geology.

Maine can and does have occasional tectonic events—earthquakes. One memorable one occurred the very day after an article in the *Portland Press Herald* intended to reassure the public that the Maine Yankee atomic power plant (now closed) in Wiscasset would be safe during a quake; the epicenter of the 4.0 quake was about 12 miles from the plant. Talk about timing! Maine's strongest quake happened during 1904 near Eastport. A 5.1 magnitude temblor during 1997 near Quebec City was felt across much of Maine.

I garnered all of the above background and was asking myself, "What does any of this have to do with election of a harbormaster that Bottomfield doesn't seem to need?" Enter into my notes Rufus Morgue and Edgar Towne, the hamlet's only millionaires. Both men are farmers who occasionally dabble in the stock market. Years before, both had invested heavily through a broker in a new fruit orchard company they thought—Apple, Inc. They eventually sold out and pocketed tidy fortunes, none the wiser for it.

It was Rufus who first put two and two together and came up with three and a half (wit). It seems that he heard that California was due for "The Big One." Maine could be, too, he figured, and if The Big One should hit Maine, the berm between Bottomfield's flatlands and the sea would likely be vaporized. The fields of Bottomfield would become sea floor and Bottomfield a harbor town, therefore needing the services of a harbormaster, an elected position. The fact that no such position existed in landlocked Bottomfield was an inconvenience perhaps, but not a barrier. Rufus would run for that office. It would require a vote at town meeting, though, to create the position first. The absence of any major earthquakes recently only convinced Rufus all the more that The Big One was inevitable…any day now.

When word got out about a special town meeting and its sole purpose, Rufus's archrival, Edgar Towne, decided that if the harbormaster office was created, he would run, too.

Rufus and Edgar have been competitors since their year together in kindergarten. They've fought over girls, grades, sports, women, business, and money—the latter rivalry benefiting Bottomfield greatly. Rufus had donated the new town hall, the baseball diamond, the soccer field, bleachers for both, and paid for repaving Main Street. Edgar endowed the town's library, had a new fire house built, donated the new pumper, and started a local scholarship fund. The townsfolk have been very grateful and were certain to create the harbormaster position, no matter how eccentric—whacko, actually—the idea might be.

The Race

Both Rufus and Edgar had proven to be (over)anxious to impress the voters prior to the town meeting and election. The regional inter-town softball tournament was scheduled for August 10th–12th on Bottomfield's impeccably kept field. On August 9, Rufus had 50 2-ton granite mooring blocks delivered to the flatlands to be spaced about 75 feet apart, the beginnings of an organized municipal mooring field. When the ball players arrived on the morning of the 10th, they were confronted with immovable objects creating obstacles to fielding and base running. Too late to reschedule or move the tourney, the players watched batted balls carom off the granite sentinels, creating fielding havoc. Runners from second to third had to decide whether to run around a mooring block or try to vault over it. One ran smack into it while watching a pop fly. One player I interviewed said that it was like playing softball inside a pinball machine.

Edgar, on his part, hired a geologist to mark the prospective high and low tide levels should The Big One happen soon, keeping in the equation such considerations as climate change, sea level, wave action, etc. On one hillside, Edgar located a pile driver to begin a town wharf for the island ferry slip and as a link to a floating town dinghy dock.

Not to be outdone, Rufus had massive metal tanks brought to Bottomfield's hillsides to begin construction of a commercial marine fuel dock. Things were happening so fast that many townspeople felt their heads spinning and couldn't step out of the way quickly enough!

Edgar bought up the eastside rises and Rufus those to the west. Each divided up their respective holdings and started advertising "waterfront lots," trying to outprice each other on the low side to dominate sales. A few lots eventually were sold as possible house sites, but most locals were in a daze at the rapid pace of events, some in pure awe of the frenetic lunacy involved.

Matters reached a head of sorts when Rufus commenced building a fishing weir at the head of the proposed harbor, now a blackberry thicket, while Edgar had a massive dredge assembled on site to "deepen the harbor" right down the middle of the municipal fairgrounds. Both these events occurred the day before the special town meeting. How to halt the craziness without offending either generous benefactor became the quandary facing the voters and town officials. There seemed to be no easy solution, so in typical officialdom fashion, the town fathers postponed the crucial meeting for one week to ponder the possibilities...and pray for a miraculous solution.

While the ponderings proceeded, the town's contracted attorney became *in absentia*—something about a "family crisis in Bangladesh" or thereabouts. Investigation revealed that he was beholden to both Rufus and Edgar for various and sundry real estate transactions. His void resulted in an informal appeal to the state attorney general, who had a sudden gastritis attack and would be unavailable for at least ten days, maybe longer if the town meeting was postponed again. The governor arranged a last-minute fact-finding excursion to Tokyo—something about Maine lobsters substituting as an ingredient in sushi. The harbormaster issue had become the proverbial "hot potato," it seemed.

While the delay ensued, neither prospective candidate remained idle. Ever the farmers and never fishermen, each decided that a new harbor would naturally require appropriate marine life. Their zeal was hastened by news of a 4.1 magnitude quake in southern California and an eruption of a long-dormant volcano in Iceland. "The Big One could happen any day now," they foggily reasoned.

Rufus had several pilings driven into the park's little hills with small platforms affixed on top—perches for osprey nests. Edgar countered with custom floats (now on dry land) for gulls to roost and consume their foragings.

Not to be bested, Rufus had a sizeable trench dug near the park's bandstand into which saltwater was tank-truck-delivered, followed by 300 pounds of live pogies "to get a start on populating the harbor." Edgar's hasty rejoinder was a parallel digging with its own deposit of saltwater, followed by live clams, mussels, and starfish unceremoniously dumped in. Neither candidate wanted urchins near their harbor. Two days later, both artificial pools had dried up, the saltwater soaking into and polluting the adjacent ground. Befitting a hot inland August, the resultant death, decay, and stench of sea creatures became frightful well before the postponed town meeting. While gathering facts for my story, I chose to keep a healthy distance from the park out of respect for the dead.

A Solution…Maybe

With the apparent abdication of relevant legal officialdom, a possible solution was meekly proffered by an unlikely source: one Hermione Crabapple, a senior at BiCarB High School. Unlike the vast majority of her peers, Hermione forsook the pleasures of lobstering, fishing, woodcutting, and partying at Bilgewater's abandoned limestone quarries. She is a confirmed history nerd, the class pet of BiCarB's sole History/Geography/Music teacher, Ms. Sandi Doone.

It seems that Hermione had undertaken an honors project to write a history of Bottomfield; no one had bothered (or cared) to compile one previously. She spent hours immersed in the dust of the town's library and office archives (boxes of discarded documents, actually), family genealogies and albums, and at the Maine State Museum in Augusta.

From Hermione's meticulous and largely unreadable notes, I have pieced together the following synopsis:

A monarchist patron named Rocke Bottomfield was granted by the king a large tract for shipbuilding back in 1642. The grant covered the areas now identified as Carport, Bottomfield, Bilgewater, and several other villages. Over several generations, the large tract was divided into various settlements, some of which were granted municipal charters or were later incorporated as official towns. Bottomfield, as it became known, never was. No one had ever questioned Bottomfield's status as a separate entity. All its generations of local leaders, elections, meetings, etc., had been ille-

217

gitimate—no reflection on anyone's parentage.

Hermione had gone to her teacher/honors advisor, Ms. Doone, with her findings. Ms. Doone and Hermione then had gone to the town officials with the news. If it was true, any election for harbormaster, or for any other official position, would be moot; Bottomfield was actually still a legal part of Carport despite its separate name. If Bottomfield was still part of Carport, even if Carport's harbor extended into Bottomfield's flatlands because of The Big One, Carport's harbormaster, Anker Downe, would still preside.

As reported to me, the revealing conversation went something like this:

Ms. Doone to Major Minor, Town Manager of Bottomfield, who was a minor major in the military before becoming a major minor league hitter missing the majors with the Mariners (his mother had married a major miner in Mexico):

"Major, one of my students may have a way out of the harbormaster election dilemma. She's discovered that our beloved Bottomfield is not a legal entity—the town was never incorporated."

Major Minor: "Huh? What? Not a town?"

Ms. Doone: "Right—not an incorporated town, so we're actually just a part of Carport. Carport's harbormaster would be ours, too. No election is needed."

Major Minor beamed upon that realization setting in. He had to report to the First Selectman, Imin Houston, as soon as possible. That conversation, as best I could ascertain it:

Major Minor: "Houston, we have a problem." To himself: "I've always wanted to say that!"

Houston: "Oh? How so?"

Major Minor: "Ms. Doone came to me with the news that

Bottomfield never was incorporated as a town. We're legally still a part of Carport. We won't need—we can't have a legitimate election for a harbormaster!"

Houston: "My that is good...wait! If we can't have an election for harbormaster, that leaves Rufus and Edgar out, but we're *all* out of jobs, too! *None* of our elections have been valid!"

Major Minor: "Omigosh! I didn't think of that! This is terrible good news! We can't let this get out or we're all jobless!"

Houston: "I'll have to go back to working the town *not* town—dump...er, refuse transfer and recycling center! The citizens will be up in arms; Carport's local property taxes are higher than ours! We've got to think of something –this just won't do! You're the hired brains—think of something!"

Both men reportedly sat in dumfounded silence for minutes that felt like dreadful hours. Neither spoke nor smiled, both lost in confused and befuddled thought. Finally, Imin spoke up: "Maybe Carport can attack and annex Bottomfield like Russia did with Crimea?"

"I don't think Carport has an army...or a navy," Major Minor glumly responded.

While the powers-that-be, or shouldn't-be, deliberated gloomily, Rufus and Edgar kept busy. Figuring that The Big One might not totally pulverize the gravel berm, Rufus decided that the resultant shoal would be a navigational hazard. He started pestering the Rockland Coast Guard office about the need for a buoy, or at least a day beacon, if not an actual lighthouse.

Edgar, also suddenly concerned about navigational matters, began to hassle the Army Corps of Engineers about constructing a breakwater to protect the new harbor. Both parties received incredulous, negative responses. No surprise there.

All of the preceding took place by Thursday afternoon after the postponed meeting date. With matters proceeding apace, I filed my first story by Thursday night to be printed in Friday's weekly edition. Given an otherwise unremarkable week, the Bottomfield harbormaster race made the front page of The *M.A.W.* and sold out quickly near that part of the coast. No mention was included, however, of Bottomfield's incorporation predicament.

The Solution

After their secret deliberations, Imin Houston and Major Minor realized that Ms. Doone and her astute student had to be silenced somehow before word of Bottomfield's status became widespread. They hastily repaired to BiCarB High on Friday afternoon after perusing The *M.A.W.* headlines in abject horror. School had just gotten out.

"Ms. Doone, may we have a word with you? It's about your student's research," Major Minor entreated. "We seem to be in a bit of a quandary."

Each of the two men begged Ms. Doone not to let the cat out of the bag—after all, so many innocent people would be irreparably injured by the revelation of Bottomfield's illegitimacy, they argued.

Ms. Doone listened intently, smiling inwardly like the cat that had swallowed the canary. She seemed to have the men—and the town—like putty in her hands, over the proverbial barrel—and whatever other similar clichés you might entertain.

When the men ran out of gas—hot air probably—Ms. Doone coyly proposed a course of action. She would speak with Hermione that night… the rest of the plan would reveal itself in due time. The two men slunk away with great trepidation; the weekend would be fraught with anxiety and forebodings, sleep hard to come by.

In fact, the two men were so engrossed in their personal frettings that they were not in tune with the mood of their constituents. They were barely aware that the flatlands—ball field, park, and fairgrounds—had become a stinking shamble, an obstacle course best avoided at any cost. Granite blocks, pilings, holes, decaying sea creatures, earth-moving machinery, and a giant dredge littered the landscape. No one except Rufus and Edgar harbored (pun intended) any faith that The Big One would be coming anytime soon, if ever. The townsfolk were ready to take back their town, so were open to that weekend's word-of-mouth proposal.

Town Meeting

On the appointed Tuesday evening, 126 voters and a couple dozen more fascinated observers crowded into the old opera house auditorium typically used for such gatherings. First Selectman Houston/moderator called the meeting to order at precisely 7:00 p.m. Immediately, someone with a booming voice spoke up:

"Let's get this foolishness over with so's we can get our park back!"

A murmur of support and approval swept through the crowd. Imin Houston definitely agreed with that sentiment.

"Okay, folks. You all know the contestants—candidates, I mean. Since some strong feelings may be involved, it has been requested by a third party that the voting be carried out by secret ballot. Any objections?" Imin meekly offered.

The same booming voice responded, "Third party? We ain't had the first or second party yet!" Much laughter ensued.

Houston bravely carried on amid catcalls and more guffaws. "This is the ballot box, and these papers have the names Rufus Morgue and Edgar Towne on them. You can just check off one or the other, then put your paper in the box. Major Minor here will check off your names on the voters list as you come up to vote." No further remarks were bellowed out, much to Imin's relief.

All 126 voters marched one by one to the front to cast their votes for harbormaster of the non-existent harbor of Bottomfield. All 126 voters then returned to their seats to await the official count. Thirty minutes later, the tabulated results were announced to a chorus of wild cheers, hoots, and hollers:

Rufus Morgue	1
Edgar Towne	1
Hermione Crabapple, by write-in vote	124

As moderator Houston called for order, Hermione's wail rose above the din:

"But I can't even swim, and I get seasick!"

The Old Man and the *C*

He was old. He was a man. He was forgetful. He was not a fisherman. His wife's name was Caroline...or Clementine—he couldn't remember which.

He used to own and captain a coastal tugboat he had named *C Sperm*. Observers thought the name had something to do with whales. They were wrong.

Each time he came home from the sea his long-suffering wife became pregnant. The 12 resulting daughters were named Chloe, Carol, Carrie, Celeste, Charo, Celia, Cora, Curlie, Catherine, Charity, Chastity, and Cwits. After the last-named was born he changed the name of his tugboat to *C Sick*.

Some seamen hold to the belief that changing the name of a vessel midstream is bad luck. Two days after the name change his 600-foot barge tow broke loose, and the wind blew the barge into the shallows and rocks. He took *C Sick* after the barge, forgetting that his beloved tugboat drew four feet more than did the barge. Bad idea. Tugboats do not float well without their bottoms.

So, he retired, after being tired once from a long swim. He bought a small boat, a 15-foot double-ender, called a "peapod." He thought to use it as a water taxi to ferry rich folks to their island cottages. One end was rotted, so he took his chainsaw and cut off two feet of that end. He needed boards to fashion a new end—a transom—so he removed two planks from the walls of his outhouse. His wife and dozen daughters were not happy. They rightfully complained about the breeze, and about the bugs, and about the nosy neighbors watching.

He decided to go to sea again to escape the landbound C's. He decided to take his new/old peapod and go fishing. Not wanting to show favoritism for any of his women, he named his foreshortened boat *C*...just C.

He was not a fisherman. He didn't know how to fish. He knew how to tug. He knew how to row and to impregnate. He brought some water in bottles and sandwiches, bought some bait, borrowed a cod jig, and a fishing pole, and a gaff, and a net, and a much-used fish-smelling cap and loaded up his new old *C*. He promised his wife, Columbine—or was it Calamine? —that he would bring home a nice fat fish for supper that night.

His *C* was tied to the dock by a rope from the bow. *C* had drifted around stern to the dock. Being used to boarding tugboats and barges, he stepped one foot onto the transom. *C* moved away from the dock with his right foot; his left foot remained on the dock. Bystanders couldn't believe that he could do a split. He couldn't. He fell into the harbor. Swimming was tiresome, he decided, and cold.

Dried, changed, and fortified with spirits, he re-boarded more carefully. He stepped into four inches of cold water. His new/old boat leaked some. He would take care of that. He drilled a three-quarter inch hole in the bottom to let the water out. Bad idea. He'd forgotten that he was still afloat.

More water came in than went out. His feet and ankles were getting wet—again. The only round object handy was a cold hot dog off one of his sandwiches. He crammed it into the hole. The water stopped rising. He bailed the rest out, untied *C*'s painter and rowed out of the harbor into the gray dawn to go catch a fish. He tried not to break off the hot dog.

A mile from shore he stopped rowing. He untangled the cod jigging line and dropped it over the side, forgetting to retain the wooden frame on which the line was wound. It sank out of sight. "No codfish for supper tonight, I suppose," he thought. The cod were relieved.

He then took up the borrowed fishing rod. He had never baited a hook before. He reached into the bait can to take out a bloodworm. The bloodworm took exception to being rudely grasped. It bit him. He screamed and knocked over the bait can. He stepped on a worm to subdue it. That worked. The worm was not happy.

He threaded the flat worm onto the hook and dropped it overboard, remembering to keep a firm hold on the fishing rod. He let out line—lots of line—then felt water swishing around his feet. Little fish under C had been nibbling on the hot dog. He pushed the rest of the protruding frankfurter deeper into the hole. The leaking stopped...for now.

The line in the water started to vibrate, then angle away from the boat. He thought he might have a fish on the line. He was right. His line was entangled around a whale shark. He could see its broad back and white spots a few feet below the surface. The shark was at least 25 feet long, almost twice the length of his vessel, it seemed.

He watched it with fascinated horror as it slowly dragged his C farther from shore. He forgot to let go of the pole or to cut the line, so engrossed was he in watching the great fish. An hour went by as the shark continued its sedate pace seaward. The little fish kept up while nibbling at the hot dog.

He turned to look at the shore, but it was gone—he was too far at sea to see from C. He panicked and dropped the fishing rod. It sank. The whale shark kept going and disappeared from his vision. He was alone again, except for drowning bloodworms and nibbling fishies that had again rendered the hot dog plug ineffective.

225

He was so far from shore that rowing was out of the question—too far, too tiring, and he still had not caught a fish to keep. When he bought the peapod, it came with a sailing rig—he would sail back to shore. He was not a fisherman. He was not a sailor, either.

The sailing rig was rolled up along the portside rail. He pushed the hot dog down further to stem the flow, then unrolled the light canvas sail and spars. A cloud of moths ascended with copious sprays of dust. Also, three mouse nests, two dead mice and a litter of live ones tumbled out. Little mice scattered among the bloodworms, wading for their lives. The one live big mouse made a beeline for the hot dog, which it consumed in short order. Water flowed in again. He put his left foot over the hole. The inflow stopped.

He tried to catch the live mouse while keeping his foot over the hole. Each time he reached for it an agitated bloodworm bit him. This was not working well, he decided.

"Plug!" suddenly entered his addled consciousness. He chewed tobacco. He had a plug of tobacco in his jacket pocket. A few minutes to moisten and compact it were sufficient; he plugged the hole. Neither mice nor little fish liked tobacco—"safe" for now, he believed.

He untangled the mast, sail, sprit, and rigging. He knew that the small rudder would go on the back of the boat. The rudder had metal pins (pintles) to fit into mating fittings (gudgeons) on the stern. He knew something about mating, but there were no gudgeons—he had thrown them away when he'd cut off the rotten sternpost. Maybe he could steer with an oar.

He would think about that while he tried one more time to catch a fish. He had one piece of line left—heavy, with a large hook. He would have to catch a big fish. Bloodworms were too small and dangerous for bait. He would use a dead mouse.

While his line dangled over the side, he took the occasion to contemplate the meaning of life. "Could life be more than just a breakfast cereal or a board game?" he pondered. "Maybe it's just like a can of peas or a chocolate bar."

His musing brought no answers—peas or chocolate conclusions eluded him. The sudden tug on his fishing line interrupted his reverie. He knew about tugs, not so much about life—or fishing.

He started to haul in the line—something very heavy was down there. He tugged and yanked and heaved and hauled. For an hour the line cut into his hands and yielded little.

At last a large fish, a bluefin tuna, broke the surface not more than six feet from him—and spat the dead mouse back into the boat before swimming away. "Oh well. I probably wouldn't have eaten it, either," the old man thought.

Off to seaward he could see the looming fog bank creeping in with the gentle southeast breeze. "Better set sail," he said aloud to no one in particular. The live mouse, who had taken refuge under the bow seat from the flood and irritated bloodworms, nodded knowingly in agreement...or fear of imminent demise.

The old man stepped the mast through a hole for that very purpose in the forward thwart. He loosened the sail. More reminiscent of Swiss cheese than wind-catching canvas. The moths and mice had feasted well. Then the fog overcame him and the C.

Out of the fog a gull landed on top of the stem of the peapod. It promptly pooped. The old man gave it a quizzical gaze—he thought he recalled the poop deck being aft, near the stern, so he tendered the gull a stern look.

As the fog was thickening, the gull took off and snatched the fish-smelling hat from the old man's head at the precise moment that his suspenders parted company with his trousers. In that instant he couldn't decide whether to grab for hat or pants, so he did neither. Hat flew north, trousers sank south. He then realized that the tobacco plug had disappeared. "Maybe fish *do* chew tobacco," he reasoned as the rains came to wash away the fog.

The advancing water took precedence over ankle-hugging trousers, so he again stationed a foot over the inrushing stream. He concluded that bailing was not compatible with trouser raising, so he bailed while his lowered pants soaked up their own share of seawater.

He saw a dead mouse float by. Quick as a desperate 80-year-old could be, he snatched the furry carcass, moved his planted foot, and crammed the *mousedelecti* into the spouting hole. It held while he finished bailing, retrieved his errant garment, and snow replaced the rain.

"Whoever expected snow in July!" he exclaimed to the same no one he had addressed previously. He received the same answer.

The snow squall soon departed for the shore. Mustering the remaining bait, he decided to fish some more. He had made a promise to his wife, Countonine, or was it Cutapine? "No matter," he concluded. She was expecting fish for dinner.

He had no idea of the time now. His watch had packed it in upon its first of several soakings. He would head back in as soon as he'd landed a big enough fish.

The plug mouse was holding up, so he gathered up the remains of soggy bloodworms and found a smaller hook to put on his remaining line. He dropped the baited hook and line into the depths, then withdrew his lunch sack from its corner to fetch a sandwich. Five chubby baby mice fell out and not much sandwich. The other hot dog was gone, too. He laughed—he hated hot dogs. "So much for lunch," he thought. "I wasn't that hungry anyway." He eyed the scrambling mouse pups with deep fried mouseballs in mind. "Tasty treats," he surmised, with relish.

His fishing line jerked downward. He pulled in the trembling line hand over hand. His catch was a two-foot dogfish (sand shark). Its skin was sandpapery rough. The little shark bit him—he bit it back. "Dogfish is good to eat," he reflected, "but this one is too small to feed 14 of us." He dropped it into the bottom of the peapod, watching the baby mice scatter in alarm. Two beady eyes stared at him malevolently from the dark recess of the bow. "Glare at me if you will, Mr. Mouse. You may be shark food soon enough," the old man resolutely declared.

More worms, more line over the side, more waiting. The peapod slowly drifted shoreward as the sun led him westward, the light southeast breeze wafting into, and through, the tattered sail. No rudder was needed to steer—North America lay to the northwest; he knew from long experience.

His line tugged again, another bite! Retrieved by hand, a puffer fish fell over the gunnel into his boat. He took it off the hook very gingerly. It bit him anyway. He did not bite it back. The puffer fish inflated as it flopped about in the bottom of the boat, dislodging the plugmouse. Water again poured in. The old man stabbed at the hole with his right foot. He hit the puffer fish instead. "Squish" went the fish—it was not amused. It tried to bite his foot.

With one foot over the hole, he used the last of his worms to bait his hook one more time, after changing back to his biggest hook: "Big hook, big fish!" "The big fish swim deep," he reasoned, so he let out lots of line. He felt the line go slack as the baited hook struck the bottom. Crabs promptly scavenged the bait. He didn't detect the feeding. He did eventually raise the now-empty hook about six feet to lift it off the seafloor.

"Some big fish is a sucker down there," he said aloud to the seaweed drifting by.

"Some big sucker is up there in a boat," the crabs said to each other after licking the big hook clean.

After a time, the old man felt a slight tug on his line. He knew tugs, so he gently tugged back and met some resistance. He tugged again and gained little. He knew then that he must have a big fish on his hook. He looked over the side of his C and saw seaweed and gull feathers float by.

"This big fish must be pulling my boat to the northeast," he concluded aloud. "I will keep some pressure on the line, but not enough to break it." The mice listened but did not respond.

Hours passed as the old man kept one foot on the hole and one hand on the line, never yielding more than a few feet of line to his elusive quarry. The sun sank lower in the sky, then finally set altogether. Stars appeared, then the moon rose, giving him a renewed sense of direction. He forgot about supper, wife, daughters, tides, and currents as his determination to land his large fish never flagged. Each time he drifted off to sleep, his foot would leave the hole, and the rising cold water on his feet would wake him up again.

"Stubborn fish—come up!" he shouted once. The mice woke up to scamper above the flooding boat floor.

"Stubborn fisherman!" the crabs gurgled with glee.

"Ah, my fish has changed his direction," the old man noted later. "He is now hauling us southwest, I see." The flotsam was now trending the opposite way from where it was moving earlier—about six hours earlier, in fact.

He was getting hungry. He dreamed of mouseballs, mousedogs, mouse soufflé, mouse barbeque, mouseburgers. The mice noticed his drooling stares and hunkered down out of sight...and hopefully out of mind.

Light crept into the east as the old man maintained his determined grip on the line while his quarry again reversed course.

"This is one big, stubborn fish," he mused, "but I am stubborn, too. We will have him for lunch, or maybe dinner tonight...or midnight snack."

The struggle was the greatest of his life as a fisherman—actually, the *only* true struggle, short of keeping the peapod afloat. His patience eventually wore thin, however—patience does not ever seem to wear thick.

When the sun reached its zenith, large rollers started to roll in from the southeast, a sure sign of big waves. The fish seemed to be increasingly agitated, too. The line trembled and shook, tugged and released, eased and drew taut. He decided that the fish must be tiring, or getting frustrated, or maybe hungry, or having to use the outhouse. It was time to take desperate measures.

He tentatively took up tension on the line, then exerted a bit more force, bracing his left foot on the gunnel, right foot still strategically over the hole. A large swell rocked the peapod, but it did not propel him overboard. The next one did.

Sputtering and fuming, he surfaced in the cold water, still gripping the fishing line, but not the hole. The water now filling the peapod lowered the rail enough that he could climb back in, shivering and bailing furiously to empty the boat and warm himself.

"After what I've been through, my wife Cosmoline better appreciate this big fish...and forgive my being late," he huffed hopefully.

He was relieved when the water in the boat was gone... the mice were relieved, too. His foot back over the hole, he started to haul on the line with fury, heedless of the chance of its breaking.

Up it came from the depths as each wave resulted in a renewed tug on the line.

"That fish is a fighter. He's almost as good a fighter as I am," he commented aloud as he drew the heavy line up hand over hand. Forty feet, fifty feet, sixty feet—he could feel his quarry tiring as it approached the heaving surface.

As the wire leader snaked over the gunnel, the old man dared to look over the side. Firmly snagged by his largest hook was a tangle of broken lathes, netting, crab shells, and poly rope—the remains of an old round-top lobster trap. In the midst of abject disappointment and frustration, he continued to haul on the poly rope, which eventually yielded a second, intact trap with one small crab and an urchin. That was all—no big fish, and the hook was bent.

During the climax of his efforts, he forgot to keep his foot on the hole. He regained his composure as the cold ocean water once again enveloped his ankles and alarmed the surviving mice.

"Some fish!" he fumed. "My wife, Canowine, will be so disappointed...and so angry with me!" He cried as he bailed; the tears filled the boat as fast as he bailed—which wasn't very fast.

"Faster!" urged the silent mice, unwilling as yet to abandon a sinking ship.

Fishless, he resolved to head for the harbor, the shoreline now barely visible in the haze to the west.

"Too far to row," he felt. "Sail is in tatters, but the onshore breeze may yet rescue me," he said as a warm wind slowly filled in from the northeast.

Just as he was about to despair, a vessel appeared to seaward, just outside the ever-present fog bank. It was heading in toward land. Did it see him? Did it recognize his distress from observing his tattered sail and distance from shore? Did it sense a fellow mariner in need of assistance?

Actually, no. Through binoculars, the mate of the FV (fishing vessel) *Charity* saw six little pairs of mouse paws waving frantically from the bow rail of a decrepit, truncated peapod. The *Charity* offered a tow; the old man gratefully, and graciously, accepted. Six tiny creatures tightroped unobserved along the towline. The old man kept his foot over the hole.

When FV *Charity* dropped its tow and the *C* drifted to its dock, the old man looked about himself at the mass of old lobster gear, the dead dogfish and smelly puffer fish, the shredded sail and warped spars, the bird poop and mouse droppings, and took his foot off the hole to step over the rail and onto the dock.

"Let the cussed thing sink!" he declared. He turned and strode defiantly up the gangway, done with the sea and the *C*. He would live out the rest of his days in company with his patient and tolerant wife, Carcassdine, and try to get his 12 daughters married off…sooner rather than later.

He stopped at the fish market on the way home and bought their largest flash-frozen whole haddock.

"I'm home—look what I caught!" he hollered as he came in the door, forgetting that the fish was still frozen. "Sorry I'm late…"

The Great Chowdah Bowl

"Well, what should we do with it?" lamented Farley Jackman, councilman of the downeast burg of Tua Point.

Farley stood at the top row of seats of the unfinished 22,000-seat stadium recently bequeathed to the town, whose officials had not been quick enough to refuse the gifting in a timely manner. Planned to be a domed seaside venue, construction was abruptly halted by the heirs of the eccentric multimillionaire, Dewitt Dewars, who had commissioned its building and inconveniently passed on before its completion. The ground facilities and field itself were largely intact; the roof remained a dream.

Dewitt's inspiration came from the movie, "Field of Dreams," and the optimistic line, "Build it and they will come." Now named after its coastal Maine location, Seagull Landing, no one had yet come to Seagull Landing Field.

Farley's fellow councilmember, "Tubby" Wales, chewed on the first ideas to come to mind: "It's steel and concrete—can't burn it. Dynamite's beyond the snow removal budget. Too big for a planter or lobster pound. Think it'd hold water?"

"Doubt it. Too many gates to be blocked up. Mebbe a college could use it?" Farley trailed off.

"Nearest college is 80 miles away. Not likely," considered Tubby.

The third member of the Tua Point council, "Bug" Light, scratched his fuzzy chin and balding head, then spoke up for the first time: "College... field...money...game. Got it!"

Farley's next question was quite justified, given Bug's well-deserved reputation for paucity of genius and speech (he was elected to the third council position with three write-in votes by persons who thought they were voting for an insect control measure): "Got what?"

Bug explained: "We need money for this imposing edifice, right? We need to get some use out of this municipal eyesore, right? Colleges get lots of money for getting to bowl games after the end of the regular season, right? We could host a bowl game right here, right? Am I right? Right?"

Neither Farley nor Tubby knew what to say—Bug's sudden animation took both by surprise—shock, actually.

Tubby's initial rejoinder was hesitant and unconvincing: "There are already lots of bowl games, aren't there?"

"Mebbe. We could make ours different, though. There's no bowl games in Maine, none in all of New England, in fact. Ours would be the first!" Bug was nearly peeing his waders with excitement. "We need a planning committee really soon!"

Gloom set in as Farley and Tubby pondered the likely scope of the effort involved. Bug, however, was as fired up as the other two had ever seen him.

Bug then blurted out, "Call it the *Chowdah Bowl!* No one's got one of those yet, I bet. Form a committee, guys—we got this!"

As far-fetched as Bug's idea sounded, the very existence of the stadium had been a far-fetched idea, too. Could this idea work? Would it validate the improbable dream of Seagull Landing Field? Sheesh...not likely!

However, the town fathers and mothers (and more gullible children) tagged on to Bug's irrepressible energy and broke themselves down into a variety of commitments for organizing the first annual Chowdah Bowl.

The Great Chowdah Bowl

The monumental effort began in July, about the time when Tua Point usually was overrun with tourists and other rusticators who tied up the small village's main (and almost only) street and owner-run shops.

This summer, though, the Point had a genuine tourist curiosity—Seagull Landing Field—to which the town's children provided guided tours for 50 cents a head (children under age 2 for half price). Most vacationers got short shrift this summer; townspeople were obsessed with Bowl preparations. A few summer regulars, though, had ideas and connections and offered to help.

The minutes of the early August Superordinate Chowdah Bowl Planning Organization are instructive and include the following highlights:

Game date: Most December and early January dates were taken by established Bowls. We could have had December 25, but many folks might be busy that day. January 5 was selected, the day after the College National Championship game. Game time will be 1:00 p.m.

Teams: The NCAA requires teams to have won at least six games to be Bowl eligible. That means that many Bowl teams are kind of mediocre. We want our game to be unique. Therefore, we propose to extend *our* Bowl invitations to two truly *awful* teams with large and wealthy alumni organizations. If two zero-win teams play, one will be guaranteed a season-ending victory...no tie allowed. When the fall season ends, we'll select our participants!

Sponsor: We've had a few rejections: L.L. Bean, Allagash Brewing, Hussey's General Store, Ace Hardware, Deet, Del Taco, several burger franchises, every seafood distributor on the coast, the Coast Guard Auxiliary, and the county Farmer's Cooperative. The good news is that we have found a confirmed sponsor: Swillaway Solid Waste and Sewage Disposal, Limited. The contract calls for our game officially to be the Swillaway Solid Waste and Sewage Disposal Chowdah Bowl. They'll settle for Swillaway Chowdah Bowl in the interest of brevity and memorability.

Publicity: Bowl games are always televised, usually for lucrative contracts. Maybe it is because of the lateness of the season and conflicts with other sports, but we have not yet secured a TV contract. We've been turned down by ABC, CBS, NBC, Fox, sports channels of each of the former named, and PBS. ESPN and its variations cited lack of interest, and NESN noted a schedule conflict with their coverage of the New England Indoor Tiddlywink Semi-finals. One positive note, however: WHOA, our local country music station, has expressed some serious interest in broadcasting the game—if we pay them $50 for doing so. We are uncommitted as yet, pending a budget review.

Food: We have had concession bids from three vendors: Rosita's Taco Food Truck, Blue's Eats, and Ethel's Chowder & Storm Door Company; Ethel's won.

Claude Bates has promised to provide Ethel with 5,000 pounds of prepared haddock, halibut, and cod. The Gates brothers of Aroostook County, Rusty and Perley, will supply 2,000 pounds of prime spuds. The Derry Creamery will bring the necessary cream and butter as Ethel needs it, and Tuesday Welders are fabricating the world's largest chowder pot *gratis*. Grita Hogg was persuaded to provide two pounds of bacon for those from far away who like their fish chowder perverted. With a stadium capacity of 22,000 hungry fans, we expect to need a lot of chowder!

Tickets: We hit it lucky. Sally Forth's Miss Printing has an overstock of lilac paper—she'll print us up all the tickets at half price, with a 10% bonus if she gets all the spelling correct. We also will print press passes and 100 complimentary tickets, although Sally thinks that we'll be hard-pressed to find 100 dignitaries to compliment.

Transportation: It's customary for Bowls to cover travel for the invited teams. Our budget doesn't allow for charter flights or air fare, or train travel, or charter buses, so we're sending our district's school buses to pick up the two teams that we invite. The volunteer drivers get free game tickets and chowder refills.

Miscellaneous: No report yet—too early to tell what miscellaneous is supposed to cover.

Planning continued apace, with nearly every town resident included. Word was starting to circulate, first throughout the county, then region, then state, eventually percolating New England and spreading to sports circles across the U.S. The advance publicity spurred heroic efforts on the gridiron by many borderline teams—no school wanted the ignominy of being invited to participate.

As the fall season wore on, however, some teams distinguished themselves by their ineptitude. With season records compiled and reported, only a few teams remained to meet the Swillaway Chowdah Bowl criteria—the Bowl now disrespectfully dubbed the "Futility Bowl" by ESPN pundits, and the "Toilet Bowl" by *Sporting News*.

Facing a difficult decision, the selection committee braced themselves with several rounds of seasonal grog, the month being December, and craftily put the six eligible team names into a bowl—which turned out to be full of drained crankcase oil.

Upon delicate retrieval of the slippery slips of paper, only two were readable. Therefore, the Bowl committee chose the Bilgewater Maritime & Mining Academy of Michigan (known as the "Rats"), BM&MA, and Southeastern Norwest State University of Missouri (aka the "Catamounts," or "Cats" for short), SNSU. The invitations were tendered and reluctantly accepted. The Ticket Committee sent 2,000 game tickets to each school to sell on campus and to enthusiastic alumni (if there were any).

Pre-game resumés of each team included the following important information:

BM&MA Rats: The Rats will be bringing 34 players. Twenty-six other members of the team are academically ineligible after finals, three are overdue on Lake Michigan, and four are lost in a salt mine somewhere under Windsor, Ontario. The offensive line averages just under 200 pounds, but is anchored by 480-pound left guard, Tiny Footer. Quarterback, Slim Jim Nasium, stands 5'2" tall, weighing 115 pounds. *Team Stats*: 0 wins, 12 losses. Points for: 3; points against: 312.

SNSU Cats: Field 42 players; three are frozen in on a pond in central Iowa. Quarterback, Fatty Greesbach, is 6'10" tall, weighing 189 pounds. The outstanding defensive player is junior college transfer Sister Maryalice McCarthy, 6'0" tall, 295 pounds, one of two scholarship players. *Team stats*: 0 wins, 12 losses (Note: They *could* have won one game by forfeit, but one of the SNSU players was obtained through a recruiting violation—he swore he was shanghaied from State A&T.). Points for: 6; points against: 408.

Late committee reports have included the following tidbits:

Budget/Sponsor: Swillaway plans to file for bankruptcy after the game.

Publicity: Bowl now listed on schedules and sportsbooks nationwide; odds of *neither* team winning running 2:1. We will have TV coverage after all; NESN reports that one tiddlywinks semi-finalist slammed his fingers in his car door and will be unable to tiddle for several weeks. Their ace broadcast team will set up on Jan. 4. ESPN promised to report game highlights (or "lowlights," they said) late the night of the game.

Food: The giant chowder kettle is done. They managed to get Rod Bender out after his last interior welds, but it took awhile with a small crane.

During the last few days before the big game, reports trickled in nearly daily:

Dec. 27: The four buses leave Tua Point, two to Michigan, two to Missouri.

Dec. 28: The two Missouri buses collide with each other on slick highway, cause 54-vehicle chain collision. SNSU team commandeers bi-level hog transport truck from Agriculture School to transport team and supporters to Maine

Dec. 29: Teams start out from their respective campuses. SNSU band instruments left behind in the rush to get started.

Dec. 30: Teams enroute in light snow.

Dec. 31: Teams still enroute. BM&MA buses lost on New York City roads for hours, beat off attempted busjacking, get to watch ball fall in Times Square.

Jan. 1: Teams arrive in Tua Point. BM&MA Rats put up in only motel in area; SNSU personnel farmed out to receptive and welcoming homes with buxom single daughters. Both teams exhausted from trip.

Jan. 2: All woke up to thick fog. Fish delivered to Ethel as promised, but frozen solid due to zero-degree outside temperature. Ethel not happy. Potatoes frozen also—anyone for spudsicles? Volunteers using blowtorches to try to thaw chowder ingredients.

Also, most Bowl games involve the participant teams in some form of community projects for good will. Both teams now shoveling turds at the regional animal shelter; two players bitten and will not be able to play. BM&MA Rats later sent to shovel snow off sidewalks downtown, throw snow onto Main Street. SNSU Cats even later shovel snow off of Main Street onto adjacent sidewalks. Effort appreciated, results not so much.

Jan. 3: Both teams sent to shovel snow and gull guano off Seagull Landing Field turf and stands in thick fog, never see each other out there.

Chowder under way, constant fire kept up to keep giant kettle from freezing up. Fifteen-year-old Amy Able rescued from pot after breaking through the surface ice.

Ticket sales uptick: 27 now sold. Hoping for huge gameday gate sales.

Jan. 4: NESN TV crew arrives after lost in fog. Still a thick o' fog, hard to see field surface from press box—seagulls barely visible. Teams have final run-throughs before game, take two hours to find their lodging again afterward. BM&MA marching band, the BM&MA "Marching Nineteen," practices National Anthem at field, draws three confused moose and one lost burro.

Chowder nearly ready; disposable bowls with Swillaway logo repossessed by paperware distributor because of bounced check. Charlie Horse sent to Bangor Costco to buy 22,000 Dixie cups, never seen again.

Weather report for Jan. 5 considered "promising"–fog will be gone, driven off by gigantic nor'easter coming up the coast—as promised.

The night of Jan. 4, the three councilmen huddled over their office woodstove, the outdoor temperature being minus 5 degrees.

"The latest storm update includes snowfall at the rate of four inches an hour, 50 mile-per-hour sustained winds with gusts up to 80-plus, and possible record storm surge of 12 feet or more. How far above high tide is the floor of the stadium?" Farley gloomily asked

"Around eight feet, I think" offered Tubby. "Think we should cancel the whole thing?"

Bug chimed in, "We can't. The teams are here, the bands are here, Ethel's got over 1,000 gallons of chowder simmering, NESN and WHOA are all set up, we've sold almost 100 tickets now, and we've confirmed that the governor is coming…if his hangnail doesn't flare up again."

Farley then intoned, "Oh, I'm glad you mentioned NESN. They called. Their production crew is all set up, but their ace broadcast duo were in a 38-car pileup on I-95 somewhere in Massachusetts due to the coming storm. They've found a pair of Greek language sportscaster from Tarpon Springs, Florida, who were vacationing in Mexico, Maine—they'll be here late tonight. Their names are Rip Eumenides and M.T. Philades. I think they speak English, maybe."

"Game on, then!" Bug gushed. "This'll put Tua Point on the sports map!"

Game Day

Maybe there was a dawn—with the heavy snow falling it was hard to tell. The wind whipped down the length of Seagull Landing Field, piling up eight-foot drifts at the southwest end. The town's Maintenance Engineer Supervisor (and sole plow operator), Art Painter, plowed the field's frozen surface at 5 a.m., 7 a.m., 9 a.m. –you get the idea. The repeated plowings managed to scrape away most of the markings applied on the 3rd. The goal posts were fingers of ice nearly obscured by Mother Nature's onslaught.

Farley checked his watch: 11 a.m. High tide expected to be at 2:15 p.m., kick-off at 1:00 p.m. "Not good," he reflected to himself. "What else could go wrong?"

Hoping to benefit from the stadium's lee end, Ethel had set up the gargantuan chowder pot just outside the south gate. By mounting an eight-foot stepladder, she was able to stir the mix using a canoe paddle. A crane truck that remained helped to support a heavy canvas boat tarp over the kettle to keep the snow out, and several local teens were feeding copious amounts of cordwood onto the fire underneath. Ethel's operation was ready for the anticipated crowd.

By 12 noon the NESN and WHOA crews realized that the playing surface was invisible from the press box due to the intensity of the snowfall. Adding to the frustration was the fact that the SNSU players as the designated "away" team (visitors) would be wearing their all-white uniforms. BM&MA would dress in their dark gray home colors. Both media outfits decided together to rely upon WHOA's experienced sideline reporter, Olive Tuete, a woman indistinguishable in bulk from most NFL linemen. They trusted that Olive at least would be able to see the field, since she would be standing on it.

At 12:30 p.m. the fan started to file in. Some others showed up, too, including a family of four who got lost looking for the county's ski area.

The two team warm-ups were truncated to five minutes of shivering followed by ten minutes of trying to locate their locker rooms amidst the swirling, driving snow.

At 12:50 p.m. the indomitable BM&MA Marching Nineteen struts onto the field, runs into the northeast goal post in the murk. Teams take the field, search for their respective benches. Lacking gas-fired jet heaters, each team huddles around a woodstove provided; most of benefit lost due to raging wind. Sister Maryalice leads SNSU players in fervent prayer.

The BM&MA Marching Nineteen composition includes two drummers, two cymbalists, one sousaphone (tuba), one piccolo, one trombone, two trumpets, three clarinets, two bagpipers, two ocarinas, one kazoo, one accordion, and one violin. Somewhere near the center of the field of white they launch into the Star Spangled Banner: cue the notes of "Oh say can you see, by the dawn's…" followed by pandemonium as a charging moose flashes into the band's midst, barely visible in swirls of snowflakes. Olive shortly reports live that the "amorous moose has the tuba player cornered in the south end zone, his lips frozen to the instrument's mouthpiece, yielding cacophonous bellows each time he exhales."

"Great reporting, Olive—thanks for that live update," WHOA's Sandy comments, then doesn't notice his microphone switch is frozen open. "Damn cold, Bud. Whose cockamamie idea was this ice bowl anyway? Can't even tell if there's a field down there. I'm f----- freezing!"

Olive dutifully reports on the coin toss: SNSU calls "heads." Teams and officials spend the next ten minutes looking for the coin lost in the snow. When found, it's on its edge. Re-toss comes up tails. BM&MA chooses to receive first; SNSU gets stadium's south end, facing the gale.

Just before the kickoff, Art plows the field one more time, wipes out team benches and stoves as players and coaches scatter. Three players disappear into stands, don't return, are later counted as spectators.

The SNSU kickoff nets five yards into the wind. BM&MA fails to gain yardage, then punts from the SNSU 40-yard line. Punt sails out of the stadium, strikes Ethel on the back, knocking her off the ladder.

SNSU takes over on its 20-yard line. Olive reports hearing, "Squish, squish, squish, splat," as Cats run three plays and punt. Kick sails back over punter's head into the south end zone.

By 1:30 p.m. the rising tide is making itself felt—saltwater is swirling around players' feet, over top of the frozen ground. Tackles result in a chilly "splash"! In the middle of a squall of snow, a BM&MA defender tackles the referee by mistake.

"I can't see a damned thing, Bud—can you?" booms over the air-waves due to Sandy's open mike. "Where's that cow Olive at anyway? We shoulda put a flashing light on her rear like a semi's hazard warning."

Less than two minutes later a hail of salty snowballs pelts the press box. "I'm right here, you moron! Shut off your damn mike!" Olive's hot enough to melt the snow before it lands on her.

At the end of the first quarter the score is still zero/zero. The officials confer about calling off the rest of the game.

"There's no lightning around—that's usually the only reason college games are postponed," the head official laments.

Just then there is a flash of yellow/orange light just outside the stadium's south end. The huge tarred canvas tarp has caught embers from the hot wood fire beneath the chowder cauldron and erupted in a mass of flames. The sudden loss of counterbalance upsets the crane truck, which overturns away from the simmering chowder—which now includes pieces of scorched tarp. Ethel quickly scoops out some unsinged chowder in case she gets a paying customer.

Lacking true lightning, the officials confer with the two teams, neither of which is willing to give up the chance for a historic Bowl win. The game will continue, much to the chagrin of most nonplayers present.

With two minutes to go in the first half, Bud calls down to Olive, still live broadcasting: "Olive, we still can't see the field from up here. The NESN people left 20 minutes ago to fetch some chowder; we haven't seen them since. Can you give us a recap for the last ten minutes or so of the action on the gridiron?"

Olive: "No problem, Bud—actually, I should rephrase that. Both teams have given up on punting. One team runs four downs, turns the ball over, and the opposition runs its four downs. The whole half is being played between the 40- and 50-yard lines at this point.

"We thought the BM&MA Rats had scored a touchdown a while ago, but the ball the running back thought he had under his arm turned out to be a frozen seagull. The game ball was lost in the snow again.

"During the last five minutes, about six inches of water has covered the field. It seems to have softened the frozen surface some. Hugo Furst, the Rats' captain, has been trying to get 480-pound Tiny Footer unstuck— Tiny sunk into the turf as the water melted the playing surface. The SNSU ball-carriers have had to try to run around him—that takes a while.

"It's nearly half-time, Bud. The officials have requested that a horn be placed in each end zone and blown every minute to help orient the players to the ends of the field. All the field markings have either been scraped or washed away. I would describe the game conditions as a bit challenging. Back to you, Bud and Sandy."

To augment the BM&MA's Marching Nineteen, the committee had arranged for a regional baton twirling exhibition at half-time. The band sloshed onto the field, followed by 22 twirlers in hip waders. Any baton tossed in the air came down at least five feet downwind. One such toss knocked out the next girl on its descent. The BM&MA's fight song, "Chew 'em up, Rats," was rendered unrecognizable by the storm, but the lovesick moose reappeared to harass the intrepid tuba player. The official paid attendance for the first Swillaway Chowdah Bowl was announced: 104; actual attendees: 12 hardy souls.

By the start of the second half, the ocean's encroachment onto the field had reached a depth of one foot. Horns sounded at irregular intervals in each end zone. Art Painter had given up trying to plow the field—his last attempt had resulted in a tsunami that nearly washed away the wooden player benches. The struggling wood stoves on the sideline meant to warm the players were raised up on concrete blocks and supplemented by life jackets and inflatable rafts. Ethel's chowder fire was in serious trouble, though—the sea level rise had snuffed out most of its warmth, and the exposed surface of the chowder was congealing. Ethel was in a state of logical contradiction: beside herself.

Football futility was evident on the field. The ball was like a chunk of ice. Dialogue among offensive players on both sides often went like: "It's cold—you take it!"

"Heck no! *You* carry the thing!"

"Is the game over yet? My feet are soaked, and I can't feel them any-more."

"I have to go to the bathroom, but I think my pee may be frozen."

"Where's the ball?"

"I dunno. I thought *you* had it!"

"Let's let them score so we can get this over with…"

Farley and his two council mates sat in the back of the VIP box trading sullen looks and head shakes. Tubby finally broke the silence: "Maybe this is why New England has no Bowl games…"

Farley glanced up, "Ya think?"

The nor'easter raged on, but thankfully the tide's ingress to the stadium peaked at one and one-half feet. The teams' enthusiasm for their Bowl game had peaked two hours earlier.

To avoid the masochism of overtime, one of the teams would have to score. After a hurried time-out late in the fourth quarter, the BM&MA quarterback deliberately fumbles the ball in front of Sister Maryalice. She pounces (read: splashes) on the ball, lets out a loud whoop, and slogs furiously at her personal hull speed for the end zone. Not wanting to lose sight of her in the swirling blizzard, the shivering officials slosh alongside her, followed close behind by the confused, lovesick young moose, attracted by Sister Maryalice's bellow of triumph!

Not being able to see what used to be the goal line, now underwater and nearly obliterated, the determined Sister forges on to run headlong into the ice-encrusted goalpost and collapses into a dazed, soggy heap, still gripping the frozen pigskin.

Celebration erupts on the BM&MA sideline as the good Sister had scored at the wrong end, having gotten disoriented in the general snow-shrouded mêlée at the line of scrimmage. The referee signals a *safety,* giving BM&MA two points.

"Well, Bud and Sandy, it looks like we have a winner. The Rats triumph over the Cats, 2-0, in the first-ever Swillaway Chowdah Bowl game, truly one for the ages," Olive solemnly intoned.

Bud thought to himself, "Anyone who survived it has definitely aged. I never saw a single play."

Just outside the south gate, as all those present—players, coaches, broadcasters, and diehard fans—were exiting the stadium, Ethel's chowder-top ice sheet had expanded enough to crack open the giant cauldron, loosing over 1,000 gallons of cooling fish chowder onto the slowly receding sea and unsuspecting homebound waders, bringing Tua Point a fitting climax to the first (and likely last) Chowdah Bowl.

Coffin Corner

His house was the biggest, most elaborate in the small hamlet of Starboardport, Maine, perched on the southern edge of a peninsula jutting into Brownhill Bay. Monopolizing the corner of Claymore Land and TNTT Town Road, it commanded a view of the harbor directly down the steep grade to the town wharf.

The house was purchased with the proceeds of its proprietor's one successful invention, a fuel additive for outboard engines that helped to prevent internal saltwater corrosion. To say that its developer, Euslis "Dimmy" Whitmore, was a bit eccentric would be a vast understatement. Ever the tinkerer since childhood, his accomplishments included 127 rejected patents—so many, in fact, that the patent office had a rubber stamp made just for his applications—it read "Hahaha!"

Among Dimmy's rejects was a bed ejection device wired to an alarm clock, designed to assist those who are reluctant to get out of bed in the morning. A push of the clock's *snooze* button would trigger the ejection feature. A test run sent the test dummy hurtling through a second-story bedroom window to land on a just-completed wedding cake below being delivered by child's wagon across the street. I can't imagine why that patent was not successful....

Another reject: a patent for a new embalming fluid (did I mention that Dimmy was the town's undertaker?) It's one flaw was its tendency to dissolve corpses after setting for 48 hours. The pool of body melt horrified the folks at one open-casket funeral.

Dimmy was not discouraged or dissuaded, though. He bounced back with another exemplary reject: a folding ladder for fire departments with small trucks. Apparently, it took over an hour using the Jaws of Life to extricate the hapless fireman who had kindly offered to try out the ladder.

Undaunted Dimmy was back weeks later with another patent attempt: a rocket fuel refined largely from fish guts and sardine gurry. The test rocket reached an impressive altitude of 20 feet before exploding into a cloud of what can best be described as "cod liver oil on steroids." The town stunk for weeks.

His most recent effort, though, should net Dimmy at least Honorable Mention in the Patent Office's Futility Hall of Fame. In a noteworthy effort to reduce the cost of burials for families of limited means, Dimmy created a simple pine (or cedar) box to fit inside a very elaborate and expensive outer casket, which would only be rented for the ceremonies. The deceased would be interred in the box only. Dimmy's new "Rent-a-Casket" sign appeared days later, in bright red and yellow, contrasting with the white banks of snow lining the hill that cold February day.

It was only days later when Dimmy's new concept would be put to the test. Starboardport's eldest citizen, Captain Courson Weighoff, had passed on at the age of 98. His widow, Carrie, now age 36, could only afford the Rent-a-Casket option. A bit of a local scandal at the time, Carrie had married the captain three years before for his money—money, it turned out, that he didn't have after all. The captain, aware that Carrie was already the widow of a wealthy Boston businessman, impulsively married Carrie for *her* money—which she already had run through with a lavish lifestyle. They were both nearly broke.

Accordingly, Dimmy arranged the good captain's remains in a standard wooden box, nestled in the fancy rental outer casing. To make removal of the pine box easier, Dimmy had installed a revamped version of his ejection mechanism in the rental coffin, as yet untested.

The captain's wake and service were held in the front rooms of Dimmy's Victorian funeral home. Since actual burials were nearly impossible undertakings in Maine's frozen ground, the least expensive and easiest option was to store the body in the town's largest freezer, that being the one at Starboardport Seafood next to the town pier. Dimmy's hearse being in the shop for repairs (after testing of his latest seat-warming device toasted the whole front of the vehicle), he managed to borrow Sal Monella's pick-up truck (with Sal) for the short trek to the freezer.

All went well as they eased the funeral casket out the door and down the icy steps toward the truck. New fallen snow covered everything in sight, including the black ice that the previous day's fog had enhanced. As the two men approached the waiting truck, Sal lost his grip on the sidewalk and casket, and grabbed a protruding lever to try to steady himself.

The widow Weighoff watched in horror and disbelief as her late husband's wooden box took advantage of Dimmy's ejection mechanism to go airborne, clear the back of the pick-up truck, and find temporary rest in the middle of the street—from where it determined to slide sled-like down the steep hill, gathering considerable momentum on its icy track.

During its headlong descent, the fleeing oblong zoomed past the post office and nearly ran down portly Hilda Hightower as she stepped out of Gus's Grocery with two arms full of food in paper bags, all of which went flying. The captain's box was followed by an out-of-control Dimmy, who was trailed at a distance by a slipping and sliding Sal.

Over halfway down the long grade the captain's vessel hit a wedge of ice and tumbled end for end in front of Clyma Crabtree, who had just staggered noisily out of Tillie's Tavern and Social Club. The blow was sufficient to loosen the coffin's lid and wrench it free, whereupon the captain's corpse flew upright for a brief second to flash before Clyma's glazed eyes. Startled and momentarily entranced, Clyma ducked, then went sprawling in the snow as the bounding coffin careened past. For the fourth time that week, he swore off booze.

The corpsic captain glided at speed past his intended freezer repose and found the iced-over town wharf, from which the coffin launched itself with gusto into the chilly harbor waters. Dimmy reached the end of the pier in time to see the weighted box sink out of sight—then bob to the surface 20 feet farther out. The captain apparently was not yet done with the sea.

It took Dimmy a few minutes to register why the oblong box looked different from that distance—the lid was missing; no, it was afloat near-by—it was the captain himself who was AWOL! As Dimmy and now Sal watched helplessly spellbound, the outgoing tide charmed the opened box, and likely the now-free captain himself, into setting a seaward course.

"What to do?" agonized Dimmy, temporarily unsure of what option to follow.

He stood staring at the cold harbor water as the grieving widow caught up with Dimmy. She spied the pine box sailing off, sans lid and corpse contents, and wailed, "Where is my husband?"

Dimmy tried to be compassionate: "I dunno—his vessel's out there. He must be out there, too."

"But he can't swim!" Carrie blurted out with obvious distress.

Sal chimed in, "He could grab the box," an instantaneous response delivered without a great deal of forethought.

Dimmy only added to Carrie's agony. "He can't grab the coffin—he's too old, and besides, he's dead as a doornail anyway."

Carrie started to sob, her tears freezing before they reached the pier's frozen planks.

"We'll fetch him back, Miz Weighoff—he can't get far without his ship," Dimmy reassured the captain's widow. "So, he can't swim; can he float?"

Carrie wailed some more. "He's wearing his best uniform, too—it'll be ruined!"

"Oh, when we bring him back, we'll change his clothes," Dimmy offered. "We can't freeze him while he's soaked in salt water anyway. What else does he have to wear?"

"I gave away all his clothes to Goodwill after he died," Carrie sniffled. "He hasn't a thing to wear!"

"Oh. Well, we'll find him something appropriate," Dimmy muttered absently as he gazed out at the floating coffin, now nearly 50 yards away. "We got to fetch him back first anyway."

Ocean currents can seem capricious at times, and while his wooden container drifted one way, his remains took on another course. Dimmy wasn't sure if an embalmed body would sink or float, so he notified Starboardport's draggers and lobstermen to be on the lookout for an aged, shipless captain on the local waters. The captain, however, stayed partially submerged until running aground at high tide, his location coincidently being Coffin Cove, nearly a mile northeast of Starboardport's harbor.

Coffin Cove's appellation had nothing to do directly with the dead. On November 29, 1852, the schooner *Fairchild B. Coffin* piled onto the unnamed cove's gravel beach during a violent autumn gale. Coffin Cove it subsequently became.

As the unusually high water receded, the captain remained grounded during that five-degree (F) night. By the time he was discovered by two teenage boys wandering the shoreline for flotsam, the corpsicle had become completely stiff and solid, more of a stiff than previously.

"Whoa! Look, a mannikin washed up on the beach!" exclaimed Teen

#1, Robby Redcrest.

"What's a 'mannikin?' " queried Teen #2, Wally Seaton.

"A dummy you put clothes on, like in the stores, dummy," Robby explained.

"It looks old—and cold. Is it worth anything?" Wally hopefully tendered.

"Mebbe. Mebbe the antique and junk shop at the corner may want it," Robby equally hopefully suggested. "Let's take it there."

"It sure looks old—old fashioned clothes, too," Wally noted as he helped to hoist the corpsic captain on both teens' shoulders. "Not too heavy, but it sure is cold!" Wally added.

Thirty minutes later the two resourceful teens set their load down on the porch of Maggie's Corner Antique & Thrift Emporium, located at the intersection of U.S. Rte. 1A and Coffin Cove Road, a.k.a. Coffin Corner.

Maggie was roused out by the clattering and "clunk" on the shop's rickety porch. "Whatcha got there, boys?" Maggie croaked, pipe in hand.

"A mannikin, Miz Maggie—frozen some, it is. Can you use it?" Robby replied, still hopefully.

"Well, I've no room in the shop, but I could prop it up outside here on the veranda to greet customers, I 'spose. How much you boys askin' for it?" Maggie asked.

"Oh, how 'bout five dollars?" Robby offered, glancing toward Wally for confirmation.

"Done!" was Maggie's instant reply. Clenching her pipe between her teeth, Maggie dug out a fiver from an apron pocket filled with various baubles and trinkets. "Help me set it up against this post—I'll tie it there so it won't fall over."

The boys stood the corpsicle captain up against a porch post while Maggie ran a tattered rope around his chest to secure him to the upright.

"There." Maggie stated, "He looks like a sea captain in that get-up. He needs a hat and pipe," she asserted as she tapped the tobacco out of her pipe and jammed it into the frozen lips of the corpse. A few minutes of noisy rummaging resulted in Maggie's retrieval of a battered captain's hat, which she unceremoniously planted firmly on the frozen head. "Now he's ready to be a greeter."

Thankfully, the temperatures remained well below freezing over the next few weeks, and the porch roof shielded the erstwhile captain from the direct rays of the sun. Meanwhile, Dimmy had prevailed upon one local lobsterman to capture the adrift coffin and its detached lid. No sign of the captain's body was reported, however—no comfort for those few in mourning.

Somehow, newspapers picked up the story, but only in part. The Rockland *Courier-Gazette* proclaimed, "Mystery Surrounds Captain's Disappearance," while the *Bangor Daily News* headline stated, "Starboardport Captain Lost at Sea." Neither paper mentioned that the missing captain was of the corpse persuasion. Minor detail?

Concern about the captain's absence did not interfere with Dimmy's experimental efforts, however. Unsatisfied with current embalming chemicals and methods, Dimmy was inspired to seek a solution in modern epoxies, plastics, and expanding foams. He was satisfied enough with one concoction to write up a patent application before taking an opportunity to put it to a practical test. Then came the fire.

It started in the very back of the store where Maggie had her living quarters. Whether from her wood stove or pipe ashes may never be determined, but the fire quickly spread through years of accumulation of wooden antiques, junk furniture, ancient paper goods, kerosene lamps, dry fabrics, and cardboard boxes. By the time the Starboardport Volunteer Fire Department arrived, the fire was intense, widespread, and very hot—hot

255

enough to thaw a frozen greeter/statue/captain and then completely dry him out. Of the large antique shop, only the porch was still standing, precariously, when the fire was finally subdued. The captain's pillar tottered menacingly but did not fall—it did catch the attention of one of the volunteers, though—one Sal Monella.

Reporting back to Dimmy late that night, Sal excitedly opened with, "I think I've found your Captain Weighoff, but I didn't know he smokes a pipe."

"He doesn't—he didn't," Dimmy asserted in reply. "Where is he?"

"At Maggie's store—what *was* Maggie's store. He works there—*worked* there, I think. He's still there—I think," Sal stammered. "You need to come see tomorrow when it's light. Bring the hearse."

Early the next morning Dimmy and Sal trucked the newly repaired hearse out to Coffin Corner. Swaying in the breeze was a porch roof post with a shriveled, desiccated captain's corpse firmly affixed to it—so firmly, in fact, that Dimmy resolved to take the whole post, captain and all—then found that the assembly would not fit inside the funerary transport. In consequence, Captain and pillar were strapped to the hearse's roof for the trip back to town.

Getting the captain into Dimmy's shop was a bit of a struggle but leverage with a crowbar did the trick to peel the corpse off the post, whereupon the captain's remains were again laid out on Dimmy's prep table. The captain looked horrible after his ordeal at sea and fireside, more like a freeze-dried prune. Dimmy hoped to keep his widow from viewing her late husband in such a state, so he resolved to quickly try his new preservation formula on the shriveled body. It needed to be injected by veterinary syringe, he thought—perhaps in several places to spread its benefits throughout the recumbent corpse. He then left it to "cure" for 24 hours. He hoped that that time interval would be long enough.

Just as Dimmy was about to go down to the shop to check on his previous day's handiwork, the widow Weighoff showed up at his door.

"I heard that you may have found my husband—or what's left of him, Mr. Whitmore. If true, I would like to see him and make arrangements for his burial. A thaw is coming soon."

"Indeed, your wandering husband—his body, that is—is in repose in my shop, benefiting greatly from my new, revolutionary preservation technique. I'm sure you'll be pleased with his condition," Dimmy crooned.

Dimmy tentatively took Carrie's elbow to escort her down the stairs to the basement mortuary lab. He opened the door and turned on the lights to reveal the captain's body lying on the prep table. He no longer appeared shrunken and dried out. The expansion foam had apparently done its job. The captain's cheeks were puffed out like a greedy chipmunk's, his eyes were open and bugged out, his tongue protruded straight out between puffy lips, his arms stuck straight out perpendicular to his body, his feet had burst his shoes and, most noticeably, a large bulge at his crotch suggested a pronounced vertical orientation for his male equipment!

After a quick scan, Carrie blurted out, "I never saw it *that* big anytime during our three years together!" As she examined her deceased husband even further, she became even more intrigued and dumfounded.

Unsure what to do or say, Dimmy tendered, "He does look a bit puffy, but his color is good!" He was sure that the chemical curing process had ended until…

The two watched with fascinated disbelief as the captain let out what sounded like a prolonged sigh, or fart, and one jacket button popped skyward as the corpse's belly appeared to rise. Carrie shrieked as a second button shot upward, followed by a third and fourth. The brass buttons were no match for the cataclysmic forces at work in Dimmy's chemical concoction.

"Perhaps we should leave him be for a while," Dimmy weakly suggested as he took the widow Weighoff by the arm to guide her back upstairs. Carrie looked back over her shoulder to notice the captain's corpse shudder and shake, arms twitching wildly as she exited the room.

Dimmy later faced an unexpected dilemma. Pressing a reluctant Sal into a helper role, Dimmy stared at the now-immobile body, which had taken on the character of a solid block of plastic, or so it seemed.

"We can't bury him like this," Dimmy lamented. "With his arms out like wings, he won't fit into his wooden burial box, and we couldn't nail down the lid with his, uh, sex equipment sticking up that high."

Sal offered, "You could chop his arms off and tuck them into the box beside him—and could cut down his...you know, his thing sticking up there." Both men cringed uncomfortably at that thought.

"The widow would never go for it," Dimmy concluded, the idea of mutilating a perfectly good corpse sending shivers down his spine.

"Maybe his arms could just stick out the sides of the box," Sal next suggested. "You could cut arm holes..." Sal's voice trailed off as Dimmy shook his head.

"We'd have to bury him on his side to allow for his wideness, and even then, the hole might not be deep enough—his hand might stick up out of the ground."

Both men sat glumly for 15 more minutes. Sal then brightened up: "He was a sea captain, right? How 'bout burying him at sea?"

Dimmy looked up with a hopeful expression. "That might work! I wonder if his wife, er, widow would go for it." Dimmy glanced over at the plasticized captain and resolved to present the concept of a proper sea burial to Carrie.

"But I already have a plot arranged for my husband," Carrie protested the next day.

"You could sell that and save money. A sea burial would be much cheaper—less expensive, that is," Dimmy intoned in his most persuasive, funeral director's voice.

"I suppose," Carrie hesitantly replied. "He really did love the sea. He might be happier there."

"Sure—that's a good thought," Dimmy added. "I bet he's smiling already," ("*and not smelling*," Dimmy thought to himself). "I can make all the necessary arrangements; don't you worry," Dimmy reassured Carrie. "It'll be warm very soon, day after tomorrow if all goes well."

True to his word, Dimmy did his best to ensure a dignified sea burial for the captain. His best had some flaws, though. First, he found out that most planned sea burials had the body sewn into a canvas sack; lacking one or the time to make one, Dimmy found a surplus parachute and rolled (using that term loosely) the body into it—or it around the corpse's out-stretched arms and other noticeable projection. A skydiver's chute, it was composed of bright yellow, green, orange, and red nylon panels.

Second, Dimmy had hoped to commandeer a cooperative lobster-man's or fisherman's boat for the occasion. All prospects had to work or begged off for some other reason (grandmother ill, hangnail, fear of possible atomic attack, boat sunk—maybe). Dimmy did finally gain the use of the town's work barge used for setting and hauling moorings; its outboard engine was known far and wide for its unreliability— "diabolical," gossip said.

The local nondenominational minister agreed to preside, despite his extreme propensity toward seasickness. The ceremony was set for the coming Friday; all arrangements were wrapped up by Thursday evening— except for the ominous weather forecast.

Friday morning showed up at the usual time, complete with thick fog and a biting onshore breeze that made piloting the mooring-cum-funeral barge a precarious endeavor at best. Volunteer pilot and navigator was Sal, never a mariner by nature. The burial party also included Dimmy, the multicolor enshrouded corpse, Mrs. Weighoff, preacher Hiram A. Sermon, and Clyma Crabtree, who staggered down the town wharf and fell onto the barge unnoticed in the cloying murk.

It took Sal several minutes to get the recalcitrant outboard started. During that interval, Clyma crawled under some sheltering fabric to sleep it off, not noticing his proximity to the plastic corpse. Once the motor came to life, Sal set course for the open ocean, dodging moored boats, floating lobster cars, buoys, driftwood, and other real or imagined obstructions. In the process, he completely lost his bearings, as imminent events would clearly demonstrate.

After a suitable passage of time and distance, Sal concluded from the motion of the water that the assemblage was sufficiently off soundings to allow the deceased to disappear below the building waves. If anything, the fog was thicker—visibility on the water might have been 25 feet or so.

Dimmy had anticipated that the corpse would not sink on its own, so he had filled the captain's pockets with old lead sinkers and a few beach rocks, no calculations required (or made). Pastor Sermon intoned some suitable passages about death, the afterlife, and commitment to the depths of the sea, after which Dimmy tried unsuccessfully to wrest the shrouded corpse overboard.

The bundle seemed a lot heavier than Dimmy had anticipated— "*should sink better*," he reasoned. As the others watched, Sal came to Dimmy's aid, and the two managed to shove the load over the side.

Within seconds of its hitting the cold water, a violent thrashing erupted under the parachute fabric. Carrie promptly fainted, Pastor Sermon crossed himself despite not being Catholic, and Dimmy and Sal jumped back in horror as the colorful cloth seemed to rise on its own. It took several minutes of frantic struggle laced with several truly blue oaths before a rapidly sobering-up Clyma emerged from under the shroud, standing in less than three feet of water, next to an equally vertical, rigid captain, anchored firmly in the mud.

"Where the devil did *you* come from?" Dimmy blurted out as a now-green preacher chose to attend to the still unconscious Carrie.

"I dunno," Clyma sputtered while reaching to try to climb back aboard. "Who's he?" he added while pointing to the captain. "He's quiet... and stiff."

"He's dead," Dimmy simply stated.

"I didn't kill him!" Clyma protested weakly. "Did I?"

"No—we're here to bury him," Sal chimed in.

"In this muck?" Clyma queried suspiciously, still not sure what he'd stumbled into.

"No—at sea," Dimmy replied.

"You missed," Clyma cleverly observed.

With impeccable timing, the fog fates chose that moment to lift enough to see the shore of the harbor barely 100 feet away—the barge was nearly dead center above the shallows extending from that part of the shoreline. Dimmy extended a hand to help Clyma aboard, but Clyma was well stuck in the muck. As a result, he pulled Dimmy overboard.

Sal had to maneuver the mooring crane to haul both Clyma and Dimmy back aboard the barge, then a hoisting rope around the captain's chest under his still-outstretched arms managed to dislodge him from the gooey harbor bottom. The captain-en-corpse was welcomed back on deck about the time that his shocked widow came to.

"Honest, your husband didn't come back to the living, Miz Weighoff. It was Clyma under the cloth, too," Dimmy cheerfully explained. "We still need to sink the captain, though...out there," Dimmy added, pointing

261

toward the now-visible open gulf.

"Oh…okay," Carrie whispered, lost in thought, maybe.

Sal ministered to the reluctant outboard for several minutes before it smokily coughed to life. The funeral party then set a course to take it at least a mile from shore, the rocking setting the pastor's stomach adrift again. By the time the barge came to an uneasy halt for the second time, the poor man had already committed his belly's contents to the briny deep not once, but twice—with gusto. His new speech of interment was mumbled between gulps and dry heaves and was largely incomprehensible. "Just do it," were his final thoughts on the subject, apparently.

The hastily rewrapped corpse, muddy legs and all, was summarily slid over the side, the parachute catching on a protruding nail during the drop. The captain created a hearty splash before disappearing out of sight—only to bob to the surface seconds later and about 20 feet away.

"*Too much foam for the weights,*" was Dimmy's first thought as he pondered his obvious miscalculation.

"Gees, that dead guy's hard to kill!" Sal exclaimed in astonishment.

Carrie accepted her late husband's re-emergence with suitable aplomb—she swooned again, this time directly into the arms of the seasick preacher, who did his best to support her while mid-retch. "*This burial at sea business was 'not for the faint of heart!'* " Dimmy drearily concluded.

The barge's outboard chose that occasion to resist Sal's efforts at a restart. "Shoulda left it running," he mumbled as the group watched the floating captain drift off in the current while the wind gently wafted the barge on a divergent course. "*Given enough distance, the solid corpse-cum-flotsam could become a navigational hazard*"—a thought that made Dimmy shudder.

Fortune smiled, though, in the form of a passing lobster boat, flagged down from a short distance off. Given a quick summary of the situation, the lobsterman went off to corral the deceased, refusing to take him on board for any amount of money or sympathy. He dropped a loop around the captain's ankle and towed him to the barge, where the crane lifted him back aboard.

There was no joy or relief as the lobsterman towed the barge back to the town dock, leaving Dimmy and the captain's widow to deal with what was becoming simply a disposal issue. Cremation? His "wingspan" would not fit into a standard crematorium. Landfill material? Against the law. Heavier weights? Possible. Burial? Only with a bigger hole and different box. Remove his arms? Propriety argued against it.

Dimmy faced all kinds of internal questions. Would the foam-filled body actually burn…or sink? Could it be melted? Who could make a coffin for his current shape? Why doesn't he smell worse? Who's going to pay for all this? Is there a more useful, albeit macabre, resolution?

Some of life's solutions present themselves in unlikely places or in unlikely ways—or both. Two days after the sea burial debacle, a knock came at Dimmy's front door. Upon its opening, a tall, distinguished-looking gentleman presented himself.

"Hello. My name is DeWinter Snowe. Some weeks past I stopped by a shop at Coffin Corner run by a woman I only knew as Maggie. The shop has since unfortunately burned, but there was a statue of a sea captain out front. I've been informed by a Mr. Monella that the item was a statue of a Captain Weighoff. I'm told that you may know the whereabouts of that piece of nautical art—I wish to purchase it for my seafood restaurant in Boston, if it still may be available."

Dimmy thought to himself, "*Statue made of Captain Weighoff? If you only knew….*"

DeWinter mused aloud, "It seemed so lifelike…."

"More like death warmed over," Dimmy muttered under his breath.

Then aloud, "I'll talk to the wid…uh, the artist and see if it might be available."

The brief conversation the next day with Carrie Weighoff concluded with her statement, "Do whatever you think will work to get rid of his remains. I've had enough!"

Given that blanket permission, Dimmy set about the challenge of making the plasticized corpse into an acceptable facsimile of a work of art, with Sal's assistance. The storefront "statue" did not have arms spread wide or a noticeable trouser bulge—both of those problems would need to be rectified.

Dimmy proposed trying heat to remold the plastics, but steam alone did not work well on a test panel. The captain's uniform was trashed, having been singed, stretched out of shape, then salt-water-and-mud soaked; it was cut away to reveal foam-stretched skin, more plastic than epidermis, however.

Sal, being the fire expert of the two, suggested that use of a plumber's propane torch might produce the heat necessary to soften the plastic and foam. He was correct in part. As he stood by with fire extinguisher in hand, "just in case," Dimmy applied the torch to one shoulder joint, and much to his horror, the torso erupted in flames! Sal was quick with the extinguisher as thick, black smoke rose from the recumbent body.

Surprisingly, there seemed to be little serious damage—the flames had been quelled within seconds. Further inspection, however, revealed that the prominent crotch projection had melted into a lump, and some of the surface plastic seemed more brittle. The captain's face hadn't been visibly altered—the tongue still protruded in a mock salute.

When the flames exploded, Dimmy jumped back, striking the arm he had proposed to attempt to bend. The arm didn't bend—it broke off with a loud crack and hung by a bit of sinew or cartilage. Epoxy would "weld" it back into a more natural pose, Dimmy figured. A forceful *whack* created a match by the other arm. Only the tongue remained a problem—to whack or not to whack? The idea of breaking off a tongue seemed sacrilegious somehow. Both men shuddered at the thought. So a totally frustrated Dimmy used a portable grinder to grind it down instead.

With a "new" surplus uniform that fit his new shape, the captain appeared resplendent as a work of art. A new hat and pipe (partly to disguise the stub of the tongue) completed the ensemble. Mr. Snowe showed up on time, was pleased with the outward appearance of his new *objet d'art* and forked over the requested $5,000 for his purchase. Dimmy saw that Carrie Weighoff received $4,000 of that for an "inheritance"; he graciously pocketed the rest as a fair fee for his extended services—Sal got a tip of $50.

If you should happen to be in Boston soon, plan on a good seafood repast at the pierside restaurant called *The Captain's Table.* Captain Weighoff will be there, just inside the front entrance, to silently greet you.

It's in the Mail

There's been a theory floating about for years in Physics or Philosophy, or some -ology or another, that the mere flutter of a butterfly's wings in one tiny part of the world could set off a chain of events of cataclysmic proportions in some other part of the planet. To do so would require an amazing set of coincidences of timing and confluences of occurrences it is thought—such as what happened one early June day on a small scale in the oceanfront outpost of Foggy Fetch, Maine. The requisite flutter came not from a butterfly, though, but by the unintended graces of a sole honeybee.

Foggy Fetch is in the geographic heart of a string of islands known as the Greater Blueberries. That appellation distinguishes them, of course (or off course?), from the Lesser Blueberries, the Greater Blueberries largely uninhabited outliers.

Several barely populated villages cling tenaciously to the rocky harbors among the Greater Blueberries, and for 23 years they have greeted the daily mail boat with notably restrained affection. That craft, an aged converted military launch, has been captained all of those years by Foggy Fetch's nautical mailman, Duwitt Wynott, whose mastery of his craft has been questionable, but reasonably reliable.

He named his stout vessel *Maid of the Mail*, inspired by Niagara Falls' *Maid of the Mist*. Local folks just called her *Maid*, if not other unprintable nomens. Duwitt did his best to live up to his long-memorized version of the United States Postal Service motto, which he often was instigated to spout: "Neither rain, nor snow, nor sleet, nor fog, nor goon of night will keep me from my pointed rounds!" He clearly had lost the thread of his credo's meaning over the years.

This particular June day, early in the morning, Duwitt had been sure to gas up the *Maid* and have her lying alongside the float immediately below the large shed used by local watermen to store nets, lines, buoys, and other fishing-related gear. The shed, in turn, had long before settled in and monopolized its place at the bottom of Water Street, the primary thoroughfare through the town and to the harbor.

The Foggy Fetch post office, in one corner of the town's only general store, occupied a prime location at the top of Water Street's significant slope. Partway down the hill, Water St. leveled out for a brief stretch, rose over a prominent ledge, and then plunged precipitously toward the waterfront where the shed lay footing the decline.

Duwitt started his rounds at the post office where several packages awaited delivery to the islands, several addressed to faculty at the Greater Blueberries Oceanographic and Marine Sciences Center (GBOMSC for short) located on Little Blueberry Island. Among the packages was a large wooden crate marked, "Live Cargo, This Side Up," which Duwitt hastily retrieved from its inverted orientation. Other crates were also heavy, and one large cardboard box was marked "Foodstuffs". All items were dutifully loaded aboard the spanking new mail truck for the short descent to the *Maid of the Mail*—a much faster descent than Duwitt ever anticipated, however.

Duwitt was deathly afraid of bees. His one sting at age eight had resulted in an emergency hospital stay at the Blueberry Regional Medical Center and Lumber Company, and a diagnosis of a severe allergy to bees.

Duwitt stepped into the mail truck, started the engine, and took the truck out of gear at the precise moment that the bee appeared front and center.

Panic ensued. Duwitt leapt out of the cab, totally forgetting to engage the emergency brake or stop the engine. The "flutter" of the bee was sufficient to propel Duwitt 20 feet from the shiny mail truck which, now unrestrained by mechanical forces, began a slow roll toward the harbor.

Once bee-free, Duwitt watched with sudden horror as his loaded charge picked up its pace seaward, outpacing his huffing attempt to overtake it and cease its momentum. Alas, capture was not to be.

Straight as an arrow, the truck tracked downhill, slowing briefly at the ledge rise, then plowing directly toward the storage shed, where Duwitt hoped it would come to rest. Alas, it too was not to be.

The tinder walls of the ancient shed were no match for the rolling mail missile that struck it amidships with great force, buckling the street-side wall, gathering gobs of lines and netting, and exploding through the opposite wall to hurdle the float and land nose down in the cockpit of the unsuspecting *Maid of the Mail*, which responded appropriately to the sudden onslaught from above by succumbing to gravity and rapidly sinking in six feet of water and harbor muck.

Considering the early hour, there were only a few onlookers who witnessed the debacle and a stressed, red-faced Duwitt, who eventually caught up with the carnage. He tiptoed through the splintered shed to view his new truck face down on the remains of his beloved Maid, wrapped in a tangle of cordage, boxes and bags floating free and threatening to head out to sea on their own.

Otis Stubblefield, a very part-time lobsterman, was first to offer his condolences and use of his skiff to retrieve the errant mail. Otis also had a barely functional lobster boat, but he currently was more than three sheets to the wind, as the saying goes—more like a full-rigged ship in his miasma of inebriation. How Otis could still navigate on foot was a mystery, Duwitt thought.

In any case, Duwitt was quick to accept the skiff offer and, lacking a second oar, sculled out into the harbor to gather the wayward packages and mailbags. The wooden crates seemed to have survived their dip; the cardboard cartons might be dried out enough to preserve their contents, Duwitt speculated. The paper envelopes in the mailbags had not fared so well—many were reduced to paper mush or were barely readable—but, the mail must go through!

There was no immediate need to attend to the mail truck, *Maid of the Mail* (now emulating a submarine), or the shed—the damage was done. Delivery of the mail, such as it was, was priority number one.

In his magnanimous, alcohol-infused state, Otis volunteered his decrepit lobster boat, aptly named *Foggy Noggin*, to take the place of the late *Maid* as the mail delivery vessel—with the provision that he would navigate, he being the captain of his "fine, hic, wessel." Duwitt reluctantly accepted, the *Foggy Noggin* appearing to be the only option immediately available. The mail items being loaded (the captain still so), the *Foggy Noggin* set out on Duwitt's "pointed rounds."

While Otis steered a meandering course toward the first Great Blueberry drop-off, Duwitt set the large, very wet and heavy cardboard box on top of the very warm engine box to dry out (hopefully). While that box sat and heated up, the wood crate marked "Live Cargo" began to live up to its billing—it began to vibrate frightfully and bounce around a bit. Otis took no notice—his navigation abilities were being whiskey-tested—but Duwitt became increasingly alarmed, fearing that some poor sea creature might be reaching its limit of dry (?) endurance. But he didn't dare to open the agitated crate…yet.

After 20 minutes or so, the cardboard box atop the engine box was clearly not drying fast enough, so Duwitt asked Otis if he could open the engine compartment and place the box directly over the hot engine. Preoccupied with trying to steer a straight course, ledges be damned, Otis mindlessly assented. The noise level picked up as soon as Duwitt uncovered the ancient Palmer to place the saturated box astride it.

Otis's wanderings through the rock-strewn waters near the Greater Blueberries resulted in some brief dings and hasty course corrections which drew Duwitt's attention away from his cargo. Out of his shifted focus, the large cardboard carton began to bulge in every dimension. Whatever "foodstuffs" were enclosed were clearly in an expansive mood—and that's exactly what the 50 lbs. of oatmeal did. The seams of the box were no match for the slowly heating oatmeal—the box split on two sides simultaneously and buried the wheezing engine in 50 lbs. of warm, sticky oatmeal. Air intake now fouled, the Palmer coughed to a stop about 100 feet from its first mail stop. The wooden box continued to rattle and shake.

A woozy Otis rotated slowly to investigate the condition of his engine troubles, while Duwitt focused on the intermittent gyrations of the wooden crate. Both men were oblivious to the slow approach of another craft from *Foggy Noggin's* port side—oblivious, that is, until five short, rapid bleats of a loud horn nearly startled the two men out of their skins!

The state ferry to Great Blueberry, the 85-foot MV *Berry Islander*, was bearing down on them in slow motion, the *Foggy Noggin* inconveniently broken down within the direct path to the ferry's landing slip. The collision occurred softly, but not soft enough for *Foggy Noggin's* spongy topsides, which sprung a multitude of leaks as the ferry, twin diesels in full reverse, brushed the now foundering lobsterboat aside and into the gravelly shallows, where she soon came to rest. For the second time that day, the U.S. mails took a dunking, but were waded ashore by a gradually sobering

Otis and a temporarily frustrated Duwitt.

What to do? The mails must continue on their "pointed rounds," but two vessels had been pulled from under the mails already. While pondering his plight, Duwitt delivered the Great Blueberry mail sack to its drop-off spot, Cabot's Store, where a pint of seawater and a mash-up of mail mush poured out upon the sack's being opened. Apparently mail sacks weren't waterproof.

Duwitt gathered up the few pieces of outgoing mail and turned to leave the store when fate stepped in and offered up Senator Lloyd Oliver Franklin London, Jr. (Lloyd O.F. London), a regular summer resident of Great Blueberry. As a dedicated public servant, he was quick to offer up the use of his family vessel to help save the mails.

That vessel, the 28-foot *Steamy Mimi,* was a wood-fired, steam-powered launch that had served the London family for three generations—since 1926, in fact. Duwitt stammered the need for some haste—he was behind schedule already—so while he and Otis loaded the boxes, bags, and wooden crate onto *Steamy Mimi*, the Senator built a fire and got up steam.

Soon enough, the entourage headed out toward Little Blueberry Island and its mail deliveries to the island's good folks and the GBOMSC. Otis insisted on passage, too, temporarily abandoning his beloved *Foggy Noggin* to the vagaries of the tides. Between mail items, three men, and the propulsion plant, the launch squatted in the water and made slow, but stately, progress.

Much to Duwitt's fascination, the wooden crate continued its occasional vibrations. When still three miles short of Little Blueberry, the Senator fed the last of his kindling sticks to the fire, and Duwitt saw the perfect excuse to sacrifice the crate to the noble cause of ensuring delivery of the U.S. Mail—the crate had been originally shipped via United Parcel anyway, he reasoned. The presence of a U.S. Senator would bear witness to Duwitt's need and professional integrity—he did not take lightly his act of opening the mail, even if out of necessity—but his curiosity was the clincher.

The crate rumbled and shook as Duwitt used a screwdriver to pry the lid off the mysterious crate. Dragging the lid aside to be split into kindling, he stood back, not at all sure what might leap out.

Nothing happened at first. After the first few seconds, the crate's movements ceased, then ever so tentatively an angular head appeared above the edge of the crate, a tongue flicking rapidly as the head rose to survey its surroundings. It was a snake!

All three men jumped back, Otis nearly flinging himself over the side. Still hazy from his extended bender, Otis pulled out a flask and took a mighty swig, while muttering, "I've *got* to stop drinking!" assuming that the snake must be a hallucination.

Senator London and Duwitt were certain that the reptile was very real. It slowly revealed itself over the next few minutes as it eased its eight-foot length and considerable bulk over the lip of the crate and onto the launch's floorboards. The three men huddled together and inched their collective way along the gunnel as the python (which turned out to be the pet of a GBOMSC researcher) seemed drawn to the heat of the steam plant's boiler. Making contact with the varnished mahogany of the boiler jacket, the snake seemed content to wrap itself around its warmth and remain there for the rest of the voyage, partially blocking access to the fire, which needed to be fed.

Duwitt's gentle entreaties, "Here snaky snaky," garnered no results. Senator London went to the far reaches of the launch's stern to reduce the rest of the crate to firebox size, but feeding the fire fell to Duwitt as the mail carrier in charge.

Duwitt warily eyed the python; the snake warily eyed Duwitt, who gingerly tugged a coil far enough above the fire door to occasionally feed the flames. Little Blueberry drew closer and closer, thankfully for the snake-stymied crew of *Steamy Mimi*. Senator London steered from forward and over the wheel to distance himself from the reptile, while Otis took up a position perched on the edge of the fantail, occasionally wobbling on edge over the stern.

Thankfully, *Steamy Mimi* retained enough momentum and pressure to limp to the dock at Little Blueberry's GBOMSC. Two clusters of activity awaited their arrival.

One was a mechanic with engine parts strewn across much of the float. The Center's sole vessel was temporarily out of commission, meaning no at-sea research or reliable shore transportation for a while.

The second cluster consisted of two anxious waiters: Punjab Punphunni, Ph.D., the Center's only herpetologist and owner of the boiler-wrapped Burmese Python, and Myer N. Muddsen, Ph.D., visiting scientist from Norway. His specialty was whales, manatees, walruses, sea lions, and other large aquatic mammals; his girth was only exceeded by those of some of his subjects.

Punjab spoke up first. "Where is the mailboat...and where is my snake?"

"Long story," Duwitt offered and then just pointed.

"What have you done to her?" Punjab excitedly burst out.

"Long story," Duwitt repeated. "Please get it...her."

Myer spoke up next. "I need a ride to shore with these boxes." He pointed to two low, rectangular boxes labeled *Live Cargo—Handle with Care*. "Our boat is not working," painfully obvious from the array of engine parts and a sweating mechanic.

The *Steamy Mimi* barely made it to Little Blueberry and clearly was not the choice to complete the mail route. Two more stops remained—Wee

It's in the Mail

Blueberry Isle, population 12 this summer, and Truly Miniscule Blueberry, the home of a reclusive writer/artist best known by his pen name, Happy Camper. That island was barely a dot on the chart, but its resident received art and writing supplies, and periodically sent out finished works.

Duwitt and Otis unloaded the mail cargo, such as it was, and passed over the soggy packages and still-dripping bag of letters. It was lunch time, Duwitt was hungry and Otis thirsty, but the mail must go through!

Senator London couldn't help further, and Duwitt was despairing when a large Friendship sloop hove into sight, close aboard the island's northwest cliff. Duwitt hollered and waved, and the sloop altered course to pass just off the end of the dock.

Unsure what to convey, Duwitt yelled, "I commandeer your vessel in the name of the United States of America mails!" Duwitt briefly considered that he might be committing piracy or a nautical version of eminent domain...or something else. But desperate times required desperate measures.

The bewildered sloop owner jibed around in a large loop and slacked sheets to ease alongside the end of the float, perpendicular to the recently arrived *Steamy Mimi*.

"We—I—the mail needs your boat," Duwitt stammered.

Hiram Greene, the portly owner and skipper of the 35-foot Friendship sloop *Utility Futility*, listened attentively while Duwitt explained his—and the U.S. Mail's—predicament.

"But my sloop is engineless," Hiram protested weakly.

"That's okay—we have wind, but there's me, boxes, bags, and two other people," Duwitt explained. "We really need your assistance—now!" he firmly assured Hiram.

"Okay...glad to help," Hiram responded.

Duwitt and a reeling Otis loaded the remaining saturated items, the

Center's outgoing mail and packages, Myer's two crates, and then Myer himself—definitely not a natural sailor. His ancestors must *not* have been Vikings…

When Myer clumsily clod aboard, the *Utility Futility* heeled about 10 degrees despite the sloop's ballast and six-foot draft. When Hiram went to assist Myer, the sloop heeled another five degrees, alarming an already unsteady Otis.

Duwitt had sailed some—Otis and Myer not at all. Hiram drew in the mainsheet as Duwitt pushed off a bit, and *Utility Futility* slowly gathered way, bound downwind for Wee Blueberry.

Once the sloop had settled into a steady groove on course for Wee Blueberry, Myer could not hold back his curiosity.

"Mr. Greene, why the name *Utility Futility*? That's an unusual boat name."

Hiram thought for a moment and then replied. "Early in May, lightning hit a big maple tree next to my cabin. The bolt split the tree from top to bottom, and one part fell onto the cabin, crushing one corner and severing the telephone and power lines, as well as the propane pipe. The sparking power line set off the gas—the explosion reduced the cottage to smithereens and flattened my outhouse. I've been living on the boat ever since.

"When I bought the boat, the previous owner had called her *Iceberg* in honor of her finishing last in every Friendship sloop race—the title matched her sailing characteristics at the time. I've tuned her up a bit since."

Hiram drifted off in reflection, pulled out his pipe, tamped in some tobacco and lit up. Along with the sloop, the smoke drifted downwind—until the breeze became fitful and then died altogether. The *Utility Futility* wallowed uneasily in a gentle swell, the long and heavy boom swung way out to the starboard side.

When loading the mail, Duwitt was in a hurry to get underway, so bags and boxes were arrayed in the cockpit and on deck, not down below. Myer sat in the cozy cockpit until the rolling of the becalmed sloop stimulated some queasiness.

Without a word, Myer crept across the cockpit, over several boxes and bags, past Otis, and placed his ponderous bulk over the port quarter bulwark. The move shifted the balance of the sloop substantially, and the boom responded accordingly.

As 35 feet of solid spar swung inward and toward the port side, an alarmed Hiram hollered, "Jibe ho!" Duwitt and Otis ducked, Hiram stayed low at the wheel, while Myer abruptly turned and stood up. The boom caught him square on his ample belly and propelled the rotund Myer N. Muddsen, Ph.D. about 10 feet into the chilly Gulf of Maine.

Otis, during his dive for cover, crushed the corner of one of Myer's "live" boxes, upsetting the container and sending its contents—25 lab mice—flying. Twenty managed to land on-board and promptly scattered. Five described parabolic arcs into the drink and swam for their lives. Three found refuge on the island of Myer's thick, curly hair. The other two crept up the drooping four-part mainsheet in which Dr. Muddsen was now entangled.

Hiram made a quick lunge for the mainsheet, ejecting the smoldering contents of his pipe as he did so. The embers lay hidden amongst the assorted mail until the breeze returned about 15 minutes later, at which point the only dry mailbag burst into open flames.

Prior to the fire, the dilemma of how to get the portly Myer N. Muddsen back aboard was presented. There was no danger of him drowning, entangled as he was, and three tiny mice had a vested interest in his staying afloat.

Silly Seaside Stories

The solution involved drawing in the mainsheet to bring Myer close to the sloop's topsides, then lowering the sail to use the throat tackle to hoist him out of the water after encircling him with a bridle rig. The hoist was complicated by Myer's discovery of the mice in his hair and consequent violent thrashing to try to dislodge them—unsuccessfully as it turned out. They abandoned their refuge when Myer's sodden corpus reached the deck, at which point they scurried to join their comrades in the darker recesses of *Utility Futility*.

Myer's retrieval was completed just before the wind's return to fan the flames resulting from Hiram's pipe embers. Myer was still sopping wet, a decided asset as he rolled over the cockpit coaming and selflessly hurled himself onto the growing conflagration. The gesture was amazingly effective on the fire, but the experience proved that the sloop's cockpit sole wasn't up to the challenge of defending itself against a heavyweight missile's impact—mail, Myer Muddsen, Otis, and Duwitt tumbled in a heap into *Utility Futility's* bilges. Several terrified mice sprinted for cover.

Duwitt had learned much earlier in life *not* to ask the question, "What else could go wrong?" As he extricated himself from the jumble of limbs, mail, and splintered sole, the reality of his plight and limited progress sunk in... but the mail must go through!

Here he was, on vessel Number 4 (an engineless sailboat), still only halfway between Little Blueberry and Wee Blueberry islands— "Neither rain, nor snow, nor fire, nor fat..." his mind drifted off as he stared into the tiny eyes of an unsympathetic mouse atop Myer's curly mane once again.

Duwitt's head finally popped up to take in the shocked stare of Hiram Greene, still unbelieving that his beloved sloop, and home, had so abruptly lost part of its sole—or should that read *soul*?

Whichever, the wind was filling in from the west, which would mean some close-winded work to fetch Wee Blueberry. The easy downwind run was over. Mains'l reset, mail retrieved, bruises assessed, *Utility Futility* came back on course for the U.S. Mail to complete its "pointed rounds." Three minutes later one or more mice finished chewing through the old seawater intake line for the long-dead engine with its frozen-open seacock.

The intrusion of more than the usual amount of saltwater into the Friendship sloop's bilge was first noticed by Otis, the last to dig his way out of the cockpit sole's collapse. He had set to work to rescue the mail items, retrieving them and placing them on deck when he paused, bent low, looked forward under the bridge deck, took a long swig from his nearly empty flask, and blurted out, "We're sinking!"

Duwitt immediately thundered in total frustration, "This tub better not *dare* sink—it's carrying the United States Mail!"

Hiram's response was a bit more practical. "We need to find the leak and plug it." He noticed several mice hustling from the bilge to the lazarette, not a good sign. He was devoted to his boat—and to remaining afloat. Before heading below, he addressed Myer:

"Dr. Muddsen, please take the wheel while I go below."

He replied hesitantly, "Er...okay. But don't you need it to steer? Should I bring it back when you're done?" He looked completely baffled.

"No...yes...no, I mean just hold us on course for a while, thank you," Hiram hastily pleaded while he ducked below.

A bewildered Myer stepped around the cockpit sole hole and grasped the wheel in a good death grip facsimile.

Otis, being a longtime lobsterman and seasoned mariner, kept his cool and adopted a pragmatic approach to the crisis: he frantically tossed all the packages and mailbags up onto the cabin top, jumped up there himself, and hugged the mast with one arm while holding his nose with the other hand. He was thus prepared for a *Titanic* moment.

Hiram and Duwitt took time to notice the slow rise of bilge water and the apparent current being generated from one source, a breach of the defunct engine's cooling water hose. As before, the related seacock resisted all efforts to budge its handle. Folding over the hose and pinning it down that way slowed the inflow to a steady trickle. Hiram and Duwitt agreed that frequent pumping while maintaining their course for Wee Blueberry would be the best solution. Initial pumping actually reduced the bilge water level, providing an opportunity for a couple of the bolder rodents to return their attentions—and little teeth—to the hose.

It was touch-and-go as to whether *Utility Futility* would make it to the Wee Blueberry wharf while still afloat. Otis stayed wedded to the mast, stoically insisting on being the last one to go down with the sloop, captain be damned. With the island in sight and soon close aboard, spirits on the sloop slowly rose, although she clearly was losing freeboard. Thirty feet from the end of the wharf, *Utility Futility* softly eased to a halt, keel nosed into the soft mud of Wee Blueberry's small basin…facing two more hours of ebbing tide.

With thoughts only that "the mail must go through," Duwitt came up with an inelegant strategy: sails down and gasketed, the main topping lift could be used to raise the main boom as needed. He would mount the spars with a package or mailbag in hand, shimmy out to the end, and then Myer would climb on deck on the starboard side (nearest the dock). The resultant shift in the sloop's posture, a decided starboard heel, would allow the boom's 35-foot length to swing Duwitt with mail over to the dock for his drop-off or pick-up—the U.S. Mail would go through!

The strategy worked well for the first two deliveries. On the third try, Myer's moveable ballast foot caught a cleat, and in one graceless motion, Dr. Muddsen tumbled over the side for his second time that day. The sloop's reaction was to shift rapidly to port. That shift brought the boom bearing Duwitt and the just-retrieved Wee Blueberry outgoing mailbag whizzing over Hiram's head to slam against the shrouds and fling the mail-man and load at least 40 feet abeam the sloop's port side! Neither Myer nor Duwitt seemed thrilled by their unexpected dunkings as suggested by several irreverent oaths from both parties.

Fortunately, Duwitt was an excellent, and highly motivated, swimmer, and the cold gulf water stimulated a quick return to the sloop, where the dangling slack mainsheet was available for Duwitt to haul himself back aboard.

As previously, Myer presented the greater challenge, especially since the sloop had settled into a noticeable list to port with the wild swing and falling tide. Once the main boom was again centered, the throat halyard tackle could again be brought into play to hoist a dripping, sputtering, indignant Myer Muddsen back on deck.

One more package remained to be delivered. It was small enough that Duwitt briefly contemplated heaving it to a person on the island's wharf, despite its being marked *Fragile*. Just as he was winding up to make the throw, a small skiff poked around a corner of the pier, heading toward *Utility Futility*.

"Ahoy there, mates! Can I be of any assistance?" rang out across the intervening water. The voice had a British accent maybe, Duwitt thought. The Aussie took only slight offense at the mistake.

Buster Carr introduced himself as he drew alongside. Duwitt quickly outlined the predicament of the U.S. Mails. Buster enthusiastically gave over control of the 16-foot flat-bottomed skiff out of probably misguided patriotic fervor. The plan was for Duwitt to embark Myer, take the remaining mail, drop off that last small package, and row the one-and-one-half miles to Truly Miniscule Blueberry Isle (TMBI on most charts), and then continue on to Foggy Fetch, hoping that daylight, seas, and weather would cooperate. Buster would stay aboard to help Hiram peel Otis off the mast and rescue the sloop.

A soggy and shivering Myer Muddsen was lowered ever so gently into the skiff, with all the remaining mail items stacked as far forward as possible. Their weight was nowhere near enough to counterbalance Myer's substantial bulk sitting on the stern thwart. The bow of the skiff cleared the surface by a good six inches, maybe more, while freeboard aft was barely four inches. Duwitt silently prayed for calm seas and divine guidance...

The waters between Wee Blueberry and the shore were strewn with rocks and ledges, and Duwitt gingerly threaded his way between some as he approached TMBI. The skiff passed East Chop, then West Chop, followed by Chop Chop.

Myer didn't dare move for fear of upsetting the delicate balance of the rowboat. TMBI presented little but cliffs, with the exception of a very small gravel beach for landing small boats. Normally, Happy Camper would paddle out in his solo kayak to meet Duwitt's mail boat, but this time he just watched the two-passenger skiff approach.

Myer could contain his discomfort no longer—he had been watching the cockroach uneasily for several minutes as it scurried along the bottom of the boat, under and out from under the thwarts.

As Duwitt paused his rowing in the shallows to drift up to the beach, Myer pounced. He rose up suddenly and slammed his foot down toward the evasive insect, missed, and drove his foot through the bottom of the skiff—which promptly filled and sank in one foot of water. Duwitt dove for the mail and barely prevented its being dowsed again.

Duwitt gloomily answered Happy's many questions, then accepted Happy's offer of the one-person kayak to complete the mail run back to Foggy Fetch. Dr. Muddsen would have to stay behind with Happy, who clearly was not.

Bungee cords or straps held much of the mail on the kayak's narrow decks, including two paintings being sent to the mainland by artist Happy. The paintings were too large to lay flat, so each was strapped in place on edge, one ahead of the small cockpit, one behind. When Duwitt pulled clear of the lee of the tiny island, the paintings became unwieldy sails that fought the kayak's shoreward progress.

Duwitt struggled past several more ledges—The Pinnacles, the Binnacles, The Spectacles, and The Wrectacles—and finally reached the last stretch of open water outside of Foggy Fetch's harbor.

Duwitt struggled to control and propel the keel-less, rudderless kayak in the building wind and waves. The vertical paintings caught the breeze and forced leeway toward the coast, but away from Foggy Fetch. As he paddled, his thoughts wandered back over the long and eventful day. "What else could possibly go wrong?" he mused. Big mistake; he would soon find out...

Now and then a wavelet would splash onto the kayak's deck, dampening the mail and Duwitt's enthusiasm for the voyage. His resolve remained strong, though—the mail must go through! The short chop and setting sun made visibility ahead very difficult. In his concentration to paddle effectively and counteract the wind and waves, Duwitt did not notice the dark shape approaching abeam, below the surface, and the tip of the dorsal fin just clearing the surface. Unnoticed, the shape dove deep, then shot toward the surface to clamp the black paddle blade firmly in its jaws and snatch the paddle swiftly out of bewildered Duwitt's hands. He sat stunned as the paddle, nearly vertical, made off for about 25 feet before disappearing beneath the waves. He watched helplessly as the buoyant paddle, minus a sizeable chunk off one end, bobbed up about 100 feet to windward.

Now minus his primary propulsion, Duwitt considered using one of the paintings as a stand-in paddle, but he didn't want to risk further water damage to his cargo. As long as the wind held, he would eventually wash ashore to the east of Foggy Fetch, somewhere with a shelving shorefront, he hoped. It was getting late, past his usual suppertime, Duwitt figured. Dismally frustrated, he watched the shore grow closer— "The mail must go through," still his number one concern.

An hour later, near sunset, the kayak approached a gravel shore, missing a ledge and steep cliffs by only a few yards. Duwitt was finally feeling optimistic about his landfall when the kayak slowly swung parallel to the shore and abruptly rolled over onto its side in the light surf.

Duwitt squirmed free of the tight cockpit and found himself in only about a foot of water. He quickly righted his craft, but not soon enough to rescue the mail strapped on deck—it all received a thorough dousing. Nevertheless, it all had to reach the Foggy Fetch post office; Duwitt was now doubly determined, almost maniacal about his goal! "Neither rain, nor surf, nor ocean, nor rocks, nor cold…" His mind drifted off as the chill of ocean water suddenly made him shiver and shake.

To cope with the chill, he stripped down to his dripping boxer shorts, wringing out his outer garments and rolling them into a ball of sorts. Duwitt picked up the paintings, packages, and mailbags—all quite soggy—and used the bungee cords and straps to bind them together and to his damp body. Overall, he looked a bit like a pack ostrich as he trundled across the barrens toward the only coastal road.

Darkness had fallen by the time Duwitt reached the narrow local road. He had only stumbled along for about a quarter mile when headlights from behind illuminated his track. The rattletrap pick-up slowed and pulled up alongside Duwitt.

"Whatchu doin' out here, Duwitt?" a raspy voice queried.

"Deliverin' the mail—what else!" came Duwitt's exasperated reply.

"Need a ride?" an amused voice, different from the first, then asked.

Duwitt pondered some smart remark, but then reason prevailed. "Yes...I'd really appreciate that."

Noting the bundle secured around Duwitt and his dripping, semi-naked condition, the second voice suggested that he'd better ride in back—the cab was too crowded ("and dry" was not voiced).

Duwitt struggled over the tailgate of the truck and plopped down among folded tarps, tools, paint buckets, and other odds and ends. The Uhwaye brothers, Homer and Ankers, were local painters and handymen, on their evening trip back to town from a job site.

"Drop me off at the post office," Duwitt managed to yell over the clatter of the truck. "Got to drop off the mail."

The brothers gave each other bemused, knowing looks, considering the sodden state of *that* mail and its bearer's apparently questionable mental condition.

Soon enough, the truck made it to the outskirts of Foggy Fetch and swung by the back-loading area of its store-corner post office. Duwitt was elated—he had seen the mail to its immediate destination! His mind again recited, "Neither rain, nor snow, nor..."

His mental litany was interrupted when he noticed that the loading area light was on, and an impatient presence awaited him.

As soon as Duwitt creakily alighted from the pick-up, the soggy load of mail still affixed, Foggy Fetch's long-time Postmaster and Duwitt's boss, Dedson Letterman, apparently ignoring Duwitt's bedraggled and partially unclothed condition, barked at Duwitt:

"Where have you been? I saw the wreck you left of our mail truck. The transfer truck to Bangor had to leave two hours ago! What took you so long?!"

"Boss, I've had a tough day fer sure. The mail's here now, though it's late, and thank goodness nothing else can go wrong," Duwitt optimistically tumbled out.

That moment is precisely when the bee swooped down to sting Duwitt's damp and vulnerable rear....

His Last Boat

She approached the weatherworn side door and knocked tentatively, then waited. Tella D. Storey, primary feature writer for the popular *Custom Boat Monthly* magazine, was there to interview the retiring dean of exquisite wooden boatbuilders, "Woody" Kraft.

The 86-year-old Woody knocked playfully on the other side of the shop door, startling the young reporter.

"C'mon in, Miss—I've been waiting for you. Care for some hot chocolate... or rum?"

"Er, no thanks," Tella stammered, a bit awed by being in the presence of one widely considered to be a boat-building genius and superb craftsman. After several compliments and background queries, Tella got down to the meat of her interview.

"Woody, you are on record as having built and launched 124 custom watercraft, from 8-foot dinghies to 65-foot schooners, all of them examples of the finest craftmanship. Most have been written up in some version of the boating press—either news sheets, magazines, and/or books. Is that an accurate summary?" Tella led.

"Yes... well, not *exactly* accurate. Now that I'm leavin' the business for good to go sailin' with my new bride, I want to set the record straight," Woody hesitantly replied.

Tella chimed in, "Oh, I didn't know you'd gotten married recently. At age 86, why'd you want to get married?" she blurted out.

"Didn't *want* to—*had* to," Woody sheepishly explained with a knowing wink, "but that's another story. I should tell you about the 125th boat to set the record clear. History is important, y'know."

Woody got up off the wooden bench and shuffled over to an ancient and worn wooden file cabinet, reached in and eventually drew out a pile of papers of various sizes, colors, folds, and crinkles. "Got to refer to my notes for the details," Woody explained. "History's got enough errors without adding more to it.

"Ah, here we go. January 22, 1964 is when the story starts," and Woody launched full speed ahead, while Tella scribbled furiously to try to keep up.

"I knew I should've brought my recorder to this interview," Tella considered to herself with profound regret already. Woody charged ahead into the following account, seemingly lost in thought:

"As I was nearly done with final touches on a lovely 24-foot catboat, a tall, white-haired man came into the shop with a large canvas sack. When he finally got my attention, he laid the sack on my design table, pulled out a roll of plans, and followed those with several banded stacks of $100 bills. I was shocked!

"'I want you to build me this boat,' he said as he unrolled the bundle of plans.

"The plans were of a very attractive 36-foot ketch, kind of like an Alden or Crocker design, but by a naval architect I'd never heard of, one Redd E. Penn. While I scanned the plans, the gentleman introduced himself, and described his history and intent thusly:

"He was 92 years old, name of Osborne Walachi Leakey, Ph.D.; his friends just called him 'OWL.' He was a self-made multimillionaire—made his fortune in chemicals, explosives, and munitions. While he talked rapid-fire, I managed to jot down quite a few details.

"Over his lifetime so far he'd owned 36 boats ranging from dinghies to a 75-foot racing schooner. All his boats, even the brand-new ones, had leaked. As a culmination of his boating career, and the boat he eventually would be buried at sea in, he wanted this gorgeous ketch to be an expensive and masterful vessel... and to leak!

"That last requirement left me thunderstruck. I'd spent my whole life in boats trying to get them *not* to leak, and now I had to *make* a boat leak!

"I'm sure my face conveyed my puzzlement, but Dr. Leakey went on to fill me in. That really didn't help. This new boat, named partly after the schooner in the old TV show, *Adventures in Paradise,* would be called *Leakey Tiki* and would be built to seep water everywhere his previous boats had done—but not enough to outright sink. Its leaks would just be reminders of all his earlier, much-loved vessels.

"For example, his 75-foot schooner, *C'est Magnifique,* leaked along her garboards when driven hard. The new ketch would have to have leaky garboards. Leakey's 35-foot Friendship sloop, built in 1906 and named *Ami Leakey*, leaked through her topside seams and around her iron fastenings. His 48-foot racing sloop, *Sea Slug*, leaked at her plank hood ends along her stem."

Woody paused to rifle through his pile of notes, then continued, Tella trying desperately to keep up.

"Leakey had bought a brand new 36-foot fiberglass sloop at one point. It leaked consistently along the hull/deck joint and around the portlights when it rained. He had named it *Optimist*—maybe not a good choice. His 28-foot ketch, *Barnacle Bill*, leaked around the mast partners.

"Trying a hopefully leakproof material, steel, he named his 32-foot metal sloop after his wife at the time, *Ice Witch*. Electrolysis started seepage around her through-hulls—the boat's, not the wife's. His next racing sloop, *Tyrant*, had a significant shaft log trickle. Leakey's 11-foot Riverside Dinghy, a 1921 build, leaked just about everywhere."

Woody slowed his pace to draw a deep breath, then continued his chronology of disaster:

"You get the general idea. A 26-foot centerboarder leaked around the trunk and pivot pin. *Patience* was her name—wishful thinking, I guess. His next boat, a 34-foot sloop he called *Pump Kin*, had planked decks and dripped over each bunk during showers— 'diabolical,' Leakey insisted.

"Then there came his 57-foot yawl, a stately craft he named *HL&S* (for *Hook, Line & Sucker*), that nearly sank when a raw water hose burst. His 48-foot motor sailor, *Constance Leakey*, had an irritating rudderpost leak, and his subsequent 43-foot schooner, *Malabar Zero*, sprung leaks along her backbone joints after a collision with an errant ledge.

"His one foray into powerboating, a 46-foot twin screw trawler maliciously named *Stinkpot,* developed irresolvable exhaust system leaks. To top it off, Leakey's most recent boat, a 37-foot yawl his new and also pregnant girlfriend christened *Whale Ho*, suffered salt water intrusion into her engine—the boat's, not the girlfriend's—and the engine became a lump of rust. The other, she apparently had acquired a semen intrusion—that's the girlfriend, not the boat, to be clear. Got that so far?"

Tella winced from writer's cramp, maybe, and weakly nodded. Woody shifted positions and then rambled on.

"So now I had to build this OWL fellow his last boat, which he would sail until his death, and then she would finally be sunk with his corpse aboard. She—the boat—would have to have many carefully controlled leaks—enough to remind Leakey of all his previous boats, but not so much as to overwhelm her pumps. Not an easy task, I figured. I thought for a long time about how to engineer this build. After all, it weren't in my nature to craft a poor joint or not properly bed a fitting. I was also thinking that this Leakey fellow had a perverse gift for naming his boats—and then he stopped by one day with his 28-year-old blond girlfriend, Chastity. 'Nuff said. She was built like—sorry, nicely constructed herself—I doubt that she ever leaked!

"Anyway, I felt stuck. The boat's design was beautiful, the money was great—Leakey spared no expense—and my work was to be flawless as usual—but to leak—leak in many places, in fact. Do I build-in leaks on purpose or just try to do a shoddy job of it? Neither approach appealed to me, and how could I calculate the amount of water leaking in versus the water being pumped out and not allow *Leakey Tiki* to sink in the process?

"Deck leaks seemed to be easy; they usually only happened when it rained. I could just leave out a bit of caulking or bedding compound here or there, especially over the four berths. Some caulking could be left out of plank seams or hood ends, but how much? Shaft logs often seeped anyway, and hoses could be given pinholes, maybe.

"In honor of *Whale Ho's* seized engine, I was to install an equivalent lump of heavy rust, despite the ketch's lead ballast shoe, bronze fastenings, and meticulous cabinetry. How much sacrilege could I tolerate? This was a test to a severe degree!

"At one point I thought I had a breakthrough idea, a veritable cranial hurricane. A local sometimes not-so-handy man—we'll just call him "Fumble-fingers Freddy" (not his real name)—had been bugging me off and on for months to hire him as an apprentice boatbuilder. I thought that if I took him on for this project, any imperfections in his work could be massaged into the required leaks. Bad idea.

"Over a period of six weeks he dropped his glasses into the molten lead we poured for *Leakey Tiki's* keel ballast. In late February he set the shop on fire while stoking the wood stove—thankfully two fire extinguisher loads took care of that: one put out the fire; the second Freddy lost control of and blinded himself temporarily with its blast.

"Days later I sent Freddy out with the trash. When he didn't return right off, I went out to rescue him—he had his tongue stuck to the steel flagpole. The next day he epoxied his hand to a couple of planks he was to edge join. I finally had to let him go in self-defense when he sat on a freshly varnished hatch and got stuck there—his pants stayed when he left. It took me awhile to peel them off the hatch.

"Despite the setbacks, the ketch took shape through the rest of that winter, spring, and summer. I had to pause at times to check on water flow for the predetermined leaks. I'm sure that occasional visitors thought I was nuts—I was beginning to think so, too! I had to allow for wood swelling, but not so much that seepage would stop. It was very stressful; I can assure you. Dr. Leakey would stop by occasionally with his equally swelling Chastity—he seemed pleased with both areas of progress.

"The ketch design was really a keel/centerboarder; her centerboard trunk was mostly below the cabin sole, making the pivot pin/leak set-up a bit tricky. I finally decided to bed the pin and trunk log joints in honey, figuring that it eventually would wash away and allow for the requisite leaks. Eventually I did the same for many other joints, but when the construction was moved outdoors for final mast stepping and rigging, the honey must have attracted a family of bears. No amount of shooing would get those brown bruins to leave until they had licked or clawed at every square inch of that ketch's hull! By the time the bears sauntered off into the woods, the *Leakey Tiki* was a sorry mess. Back into the shop she went. I spent most of the next month repairing bear damage—and trying to find a good substitute for the honey.

"By fall the ketch was back to being ready to rig, but this time I wanted the hull in the water first. Although done in private with much secrecy, I didn't want the public to know that I'd built a leaky boat, even though it was for a Leakey—the launching was noteworthy for one event. Chastity, recently married to Dr. Leakey, had had her baby girl by then and wanted to show off her restored figure at the launching, so she wore a skimpy bikini for the occasion.

"Chastity turned away as she swung the tethered champagne bottle. The bottle broke well enough, but the cord with the top part of the bottle snagged her bikini top ties somehow and tore off the top as she turned away from the boat, suggesting a new use for the term 'breasthook' maybe? That bodacious babe's boobies bounced beautifully in the building breeze…"

Woody wiped some beaded sweat from his forehead and apologized, "Oh, er, sorry…I digress…"

"Chastity didn't seem a bit fazed by her unexpected revealing, but Osborne was apoplectic. 'Cover up!' he bellowed, and all the rest of us ducked.

"We clearly were distracted by Chastity's chest unveiling, and all of us failed to notice *Leakey Tiki's* success at leaking upon reaching her intended element—she started to sink right away. Apparently, I'd done too good of a job installing water ingress points, so we quickly put extra pumps aboard to prevent her finding the harbor bottom.

"We got her rigged eventually, and she looked gorgeous with her dark blue topsides, buff decks and cabin top, and lots of shiny varnish. She did eventually swell some and leaked only moderately. Leakey was thrilled, and I was relieved, although I still didn't want anyone to know that I'd built a Leakey a leaky ketch. I got paid well, though."

At this point in the interview Woody flipped over more papers and pulled out a yellowed newspaper obituary to show to Tella and continued:

"Leakey sailed his leaky ketch for nearly three years before he passed on at age 96. As were his wishes, his family members made sure to ready the *Leakey Tiki* for his burial at sea, accompanied by a wrapped burial gift from each family member—brothers, sister, nieces and nephews, and his Chastity. The idea was kind of Egyptian-tomb-inspired, I think.

"Per his instructions, the lead ballast was removed as too valuable to waste, beach rocks being loaded below to aid the sinking. The keel bolt holes were left unfilled to allow the sea entry. Osborne himself was placed aboard in a simple—and ample—pine box—or was it cedar? Either way, the gifts, also in wooden boxes and contents undisclosed, were stuffed below with the dearly departed.

"I got to tag along on the funeral expedition on the accompanying towboat. Once the temporary bolt hole plugs were removed, *Leakey Tiki* slowly started to settle. Prayers were uttered, commitment to the deep oaths recited (we were out over a 480-foot sea trench at the time), and we waited and watched as the sea claimed Leakey and his leaky boat—almost.

"Darned if the ketch didn't stop sinking with about one and one-half feet of her topsides above water, and she didn't budge from that level! She should have had enough weight in her to taker 'er down. How could I have built a leaky boat that stubbornly refused to sink?

"No one had the courage to step aboard the supposedly foundering ketch with a dead body aboard. Superstition or not, the scenario was down-right spooky, and the occasional sounds like sighs as she rolled in the slight swell only added to the eeriness. Could she now be a haunted ship, doomed to roam the seas awash? I was perplexed…and spooked!

"At last one of the nephews took the trailing peapod and cautiously rowed over to peek through one of the cabin portlights, being careful not to put too much weight on the rolly deck. He noted that Osborne's coffin box had floated up and wedged itself athwartship under the decks at each side. That, along with the many gift boxes, was enough to prevent the ketch's plunge to the depths. The nephew wasn't about to go aboard to try to rectify (or should that be 'wrecktify') the situation, so the decision was made to wait out the sinking, figuring that she'd eventually succumb to her leaks and the waves...but she didn't.

"For three days she didn't settle any further, but she wallowed drunkenly in the ocean swells. Given her condition, unstable as she seemed, no one dared to go aboard to rearrange *Leakey Tiki's* apparent flotation aids.

"On the fourth day, the Leakey relatives mustered two boats to approach the ketch, one on each side, to pile rocks on her decks to try to force her under. Being careful to balance the load, they managed to reduce her freeboard by about six inches, but she stubbornly refused to sink.

"Later that day, the Coast Guard declared the ketch to be a navigational hazard and threatened to take unilateral action, such action unspecified at the time. Obviously, more drastic measures were called for.

"It was Osborne's brother, Eversoe, who came up with the idea of setting fire to the ketch, so she'd become something of a floating-then-sinking funeral pyre. The incendiary event was set for the next day.

"Twelve relatives and myself piled into two boats for the occasion. Six were in the brother's open launch, while the other seven, me included, were in a borrowed lobster boat. The launch drew alongside the *Leakey Tiki* to douse the cabin top with gasoline and toss aboard a flaming rag.

"It was only after kindling the fire that one of the Leakey kin mentioned that it was 'sad' that all those gift packages would be burned up— or worse. It turned out that each family member had offered up a fitting tribute to the dearly departed's career, unbeknownst to the others. The boxes, neatly gift-boxed and wrapped, contained samples of Leakey's explosives, munitions, or related chemical containers. When the realization set in, there was a mad scramble to put distance between the ketch and the burial vessels—a bit late as it turned out.

"The newspapers of the day reported a 'sonic boom,' but it was a far more dramatic episode than that. When the fire reached the contents of the ketch, all hell broke loose—*Leakey Tiki* erupted in one giant cataclysm of flame and splinters, with a roaring concussion so strong that the blast lifted the cabin roof off our lobster boat and knocked two nephews over the side! A shell must have exploded and torn through the transom of the retreating launch, which vessel promptly started to sink. All souls in the cold water were quickly retrieved from the flotsam of wood refuse and other bits and pieces. Thankfully, and miraculously, no one was seriously injured—just a bit singed!

"When the spray and smoke settled, Chastity piped up plaintively and asked, 'Where's Osborne?'

"Eversoe gazed through the remaining mist and pointed to a spot 50 feet to his left: 'There's Osborne,' then 30 feet ahead, 'there's Osborne,' then 20 more feet beyond, 'and there's Osborne...' His voice trailed off as he identified more remains of a clearly divided Osborne."

Tella gagged and came to an abrupt halt in her notetaking at that point as Woody just shook his head. "What did Mrs. Leakey do? Maybe I should come back another time to finish the interview?" she offered.

"Well, the widder Leakey just wailed. Later, she was heard to tell others that her late husband had 'just gone to pieces when his beloved boat was wrecked.' Seemed to summarize the 'casion well 'nuff.

"No need to come back, miss. I'm hungry now, an' besides, I'm done talkin' about that Leakey boat!"

The *Tortoise* and the Hair

The admiral saluted smartly, returning the captain's smart salute. He then smartly shuffled across the ship's deck, staggered over the rail, and dropped smartly into the waiting gig, which then had to be smartly dragged across the sand into the water as the ship was smartly hard aground on the sands—again. The Admiral returned to his new flagship, HMS *Inevitable*.

The Admiral's parting comment weighed heavily on the captain's mind: "You get this tub to do something noteworthy, or I'll see that you all are drummed out of His Majesty's service!"

Most of the ship's crew were hopeful, but the captain was distraught. He knew that his command had a less-than-stellar record, and he was determined to change that.

A few words should be said (as few as possible) about the vessel at the heart of this story, HMS *Tortoise* of 1770, a 28-gun picket ship captained by one Castor Oyle.

The HMS *Tortoise* actually was launched in 1764 as HMS *Speedwell*, a 62-gun lesser ship of the line, and placed under the command of Captain Erly Bedsorr, who soon stated that his new vessel should be "cut down to above the waterline and used as a slurry barge." She had turned out to be top heavy and inordinately slow. As a result, she was soon reduced by one deck and became an even lesser vessel sporting 28 cannon of various descriptions, some of which occasionally were able to be fired.

Captain Bedsorr soon was relieved of his command due to an unfortunate grounding stimulated by a profusion (or infusion?) of rum. His brief tenure was followed in rapid succession by those of Captains Courageous (Earl of Codliverpool) and Pugnacious (Duke of Ellington), both of whom begged the Admiralty to be transferred to other commands, even if just prison ship duties.

Upon receiving multiple reports of the *Tortoise's* foibles, Admiral Romeo Whistleblower came aboard while in Virginia during 1774 for an inspection sail, just after Capt. Oyle had sold the ship's copper sheathing on the black market to a colonial cookware fabricator. A soused Romeo was heard to shout, "Damn the teredoes—full speed ahead," while the ship was still fast to the dock.

Admiral Whistleblower was still aboard when the *Tortoise* collided in dense fog with the French frigate, *Juliette*. Romeo was so taken with the comely *Juliette* that he boarded her during the resulting entanglement and refused to get off her as the vessels disengaged. The French finally tossed him off her to be retrieved by the *Tortoise's* crew.

HMS *Tortoise* later distinguished herself by capturing a lightly armed Spanish privateer—she weighed only 98 pounds—and a French merchant vessel carrying a cargo of white wigs to the colonies, a hairy episode in the ship's career.

Shortly afterward, the *Tortoise* bombarded a Spanish ship thought at a distance to be a treasure carrier. It turned out to be a garbage barge ready to dump its load at sea. The *Tortoise* gallantly rescued her odiferous crew. Just before the bombardment, though, Capt. Oyle was understood to have commanded, "Don't fire until you see the flights of her flies."

In 1776, in response to the war for independence by the colonists in America, the Admiralty chose to station HMS *Tortoise* off the tiny port of

Shedagat Beach, New Jersey, as the sole blockader of that often neglected backwater harbor, a questionable bastion of five resident rebels and two loyalist Tories.

Many people today are unaware of it, but spies or informants were abundant on both sides during the Revolution. Even a lesser combatant such as Capt. Oyle had his sources of intelligence (using that term loosely). When word was received that the rebels' charismatic leader, General George Washington himself, might be in Pennsylvania, Capt. Oyle devised a plan to rescue his and his ship's reputations: he would kidnap the general!

Following a hasty review of his scheme over pudding, the clever Captain sent his second-in-command, Lieutenant Chase Rumours, to the hotbed of local gossip in southern New Jersey, Unction Junction, at the corner of which stood Honest Abe's Apothecary Shoppe. North of the Junction was an area of intense commercial activity known locally as The Strippe.

At the top of The Strippe stood the Boor's Tale Tavern, frequented by colonists, loyalists, and misogynists. Next door was Jose's Fishe & Chippes, followed south by Lafitte's Taqueau Belle. Across the dusty highway was Amador's Used Carriage & Camel Emporium, next to which lay Robin Hood's Bierhaus.

Just above the actual Junction was the eatery established by retired sea captain Hoppe Tuitt—Aye-Hoppe—specializing in flatcakes. On the diagonally opposite corner stood Klaus' Wood-fired Pizza, next to which was White's Crown Castle, where loyalists often aired their beefs.

During his reconnoitering and information-gathering expedition, Lt. Rumours felt obliged to purchase food and drink at each one of his stops in order to fit in and be inconspicuous as a mole, despite forgetting his trousers in his haste to leave the ship. Having made the rounds of all the

Junction's libation stations, Rumours staggered back to regurgitate his newly gained intelligence and other less savory things to Capt. Oyle.

"Sir, the word seems to be that General Washington will be crossing the Delaware sometime soon," Rumours belched.

"Delaware Bay, Delaware Colony, or Delaware River...or the Delaware Indians?" Oyle needed to clarify.

"Uh, sorry, sir—they didn't say," Rumours slurred. "An' I didn't think to ash...ask."

A frustrated Capt. Oyle watched impatiently as Lt. Rumours capsized and keeled over after his brief report. The captain was forced to resort to his Plan B, enlisting the aid of a Shedagat Tory, one Evers Maile. Evers agreed to send his spouse, Neva Maile, an attractive woman, to try to seduce her path to more detailed knowledge.

Maile's parting comment to the British captain was, "I only regret that I have but one wife to give for my country."

Neva took on the challenge of trying to amass more details about General Washington's current whereabouts and plans, and in the process took on several inebriated colonial sailors and settlers. One colonial spy clearly overheard Neva's cajolings and queries and made haste to report those to the colonial forces now in eastern Pennsylvania.

A much-tousled Neva reported back to Capt. Oyle, brushing aside concerns by her husband: "General Washington plans to cross the Delaware River with his colonial troops, probably on or about December 24. You haven't seen him yet, but they say he is tall, wears a white wig and long blue coat with tails, and has some wooden teeth—or a wooden leg—I forget which," at which point Neva belched loudly and suddenly sat down.

While Neva was recounting her intelligence (such as it was) to Capt. Oyle, the colonial informer elsewhere was dismounting his winded steed, forcing his icebound skiff across the river, and tumbling out his overheard information to an attentive General George Washington.

"They—the Brits—intend to intercept you and kidnap you just after you sneak across the Delaware River," the spy breathlessly reported. "They know what you look like—tall, white wig, tailored and tailed blue coat, wooden teeth…really? Anyway, that's what she—the Tory spy—was told."

The general smiled and responded, "Thank you, Thomas Brady. Someday I'm sure you'll be remembered in the history of the true Patriots." Washington quickly had a counterstrategy in mind.

Back at HMS *Tortoise,* Capt. Oyle was beginning to organize his raid upon the colonial forces: "We can't just go marching across southern New Jersey in our naval uniforms. We need to dress like the settlers here. Any ideas, Mr. Rumours?"

"Yes, well, sir, there's a William Haberdasher near The Strippe who sells lightly used clothing and is said to be kind and helpful to all. His establishment is known as the Goode Will Storre. I can try to outfit us there," Rumours replied.

"Very good, Lieutenant—see to obtaining kit for a party of twelve men, please. See Petty Officer Pence to obtain sufficient funds from petty cash—and hurry. We've no time to waste!" urged the captain.

"One more thing, Rumours. We will need transport for our raiding party. Perhaps see this Amador fellow for the necessary equipment?" the Captain suggested.

Rumours' every move in town was closely observed by a colonial spy named Ebenezer Stooge, who took copious notes on his eye-pad so he could alert General Washington to the British preparations.

Upon Lt. Rumours' return to the *Tortoise,* he reported the following to his captain:

"Sir, I have purchased suitable kit for ten men—that is all that the Goode Will Storre had. Two men will have to go dressed as women. Also, the purchase exhausted all our petty cash.

"Furthermore, Mr. Amador will trade for a freight wagon and six horses. He wants a naval cannon in return to use as a lawn ornament for his business site. I told him I would need to defer that decision to you, sir."

"Very well, Rumours. Inform Mr. Amador that we will agree to the swap—we will need the wagon to deliver the cannon to his emporium, however, if that is satisfactory to him," the captain explained.

"Aye, sir—consider it done," Lt. Rumours smartly responded.

Some hours later Rumours returned with the wagon loaded with the clothing for the twelve men, plus the six horses.

"Amador says to just leave the cannon on the shore—he will retrieve it from there later," the lieutenant reported.

"Well done, Lt. Rumours," Capt. Oyle chirped. "Saves us a tiring delivery."

Measures and Countermeasures

[In the interest of clarity for any actual reader(s), the following accounts will be identified as either "American" or "British" activities.]

American

General Washington listened as his stooge read the juicy details off his eye-pad, and then Washington spoke up:

"A wagon with twelve British seamen dressed as settler merchants making a delivery of hay, you say? And two will be dressed as women? Thank you, Ebenezer; we'll be pleased to entertain them when they arrive.

301

And we will send out a little party of our own..." The general's voice trailed off as his mind toyed with the possibilities.

British

With great effort, one large cannon was hoisted off the HMS *Tortoise* at low tide to be dragged across the drying sands to a place on the higher shore, the ship once again being high and dry. Twelve valiant men were selected for the kidnap excursion, to include the captain and his lieutenant; two of the smaller men were instructed to shave their beards before putting on their dresses and bonnets. The trip across the flat countryside would take at least two days, so stores and small arms were stashed among the load of hay in the wagon. Four horses would haul the wagon; the captain and lieutenant would be mounted; the rest of the group would walk while taking turns sharing rides occasionally on the wagon.

American

General Washington put out word that he needed at least twenty of certain items by a certain date. Local patriotic citizens were only too happy to comply, boosting Washington's spirits, some of which he sipped judiciously while sharing them with his officers.

Washington also solicited volunteers for a mission to the seacoast, to Shedagat to be specific. One hundred and two volunteered; only six were needed. The general mused, "Who was it who once said, 'loose lips sink ships'? Plato, Aristotle, Pizarro, Napoleon, Lord Nelson, me?"

British

Two days before their interception date, ten British sailors eagerly donned their colonial garb and practiced trying to minimize their royalist accents. Two others were not so thrilled. Thadeus Thigpen in particular was fighting the battle of the bulge—he didn't fit well, actually at all, into his colonial woman's clothing.

"How do women squeeze into these things?" Thad wailed. As he tugged at one side, a rip was heard from the opposite seam. "Blimey, I can't do this, mates. Let me just throw a shawl over me 'ead and shoulders. I'll scrunch down in the hay—they won't notice," Thad hopefully added.

Once suitably attired, the twelve prospective generalnappers waited until dark and high tide before swarming ashore and into swarms of Shedagat Beach's bloodthirsty mosquitoes. These vicious bugs were no ordinary bloodsuckers. Of monumental proportions, and probably colonial sympathies, they dodged all attempts to swat them away or squish them in sufficient quantities to avoid significant blood loss.

By the time the Brits reached The Strippe, they were a mass of welts and blood droplets—and squashed mosquitoes. Their first night foray ashore had not accounted for mosquito-induced delays—or torture. They decided to tarry for a while at the Boor's Tale Tavern to rest and recover, and to heft a pint or two.

American

The items that General Washington had requested trickled in over a period of two days. By the time the British force was expected to arrive, the rebels' plans were ready to be implemented. The six volunteers were ready to set out, intentionally on the same trails the redcoats were likely to take.

British

Immediately recognizing the wagon and horses outside the Boor's Tale, Amador parked his camel and went in to buy all the imbibers inside a tankard of ale apiece. Amador was always happy to accept the Crown's money, but his sympathies lay with the colonial rebels; he had perceived that his financial future might be rosier within an independent country. Besides, he knew the general intent of the British sailors, so while they drank inside, Amador's confederates were outside cutting notches into the insides of the wagon's wooden wheel spokes.

No surprise, the British force got off to a slow start the next morning, having slept off the three rounds of free drinks provided by the accommodating Amador. The wagon survived two miles of trek before one wheel collapsed, then a second. The treachery became obvious from the saw cuts part way into the spokes.

A gloomy Capt. Oyle finally realized the risk of invading enemy territory, even in disguise, as he scoured the nearby countryside for wagon wheels. A whole day passed as four wheels eventually were scavenged, each a different size than the three others. The wagon did roll but wobbled much like a drunken sailor—Capt. Oyle was reminded of Admiral Whistleblower.

American

While the British crew were entertained at the Boor's Tale, Washington's six rebels packed up and headed east toward Shedagat. Their instructions were clear, and they had been given good information about the British situation and intent. They expected—even hoped—to cross trails with the Brits; ideas abounded about possible interactions if they should meet.

British

As the British force trekked westward, they passed a series of five signs. Each of the first four in turn read one line of a rhyme:

King George is not our favorite man
He does not fit our freedom plan
So if he does not let us be
We'll drive his troops back out to sea
The fifth sign simply read *Burma Shave.*

Despite that message, the British spirits were high, mostly due to the liquid spirits hidden well in the wagonload of hay. Shortly after passing the fifth sign, the troop encountered a group of six apparent hikers headed in the opposite direction. One of the six opened the exchange—with a wink to his compatriots:

"Good day, gents...and ladies," he said, privately observing, "Wow, those women are ugly!"

Capt. Oyle returned, "Good morning, good sirs. Top of the day to you."

Another of the rebels couldn't help asking, "Where you folks headin' with that wobbly load of hay, Captain?"

Capt. Oyle gulped. "We have a load of hay for General Washington's horses, sir. Why did you address me as 'Captain?'"

"Just a figger of speech, mate," was the response.

The *Tortoise* and the Hair

"I'm *not* a mate!" Capt. Oyle burst out. "I mean, well, sorry, sir."

All six colonial troops stifled snickers, and as they passed beyond the British, they looked back with smug satisfaction. One wished that he'd been smoking his pipe so he could have tossed embers into the passing hay.

Americans

Hours later, the colonists passed a series of poetic signs facing their way:

Colonies are like a child
Whose thoughts of freedom oft go wild
So if the rebels forgo arms
We'll bless them with King George's charms

Over the fifth message, *Tory Shave*, one of the rebels chalked, "And if you believe that, we have a bridge to sell you!"

Several more hours later the colonial six reached The Strippe and surreptitiously met with Amador and several members of the local colonial militia. Plans were perfected to consider the state of the tides, daylight, and availability of local forces.

British

At about the time that the Americans completed their clandestine meetings near Shedagat Beach, as night was falling (with a thud), the British were stopped by rebel sentries at the riverbank, who were expecting the disguised British seamen.

306

"Halt! Who goes there?" one sentry barked with a stifled chuckle.

"Humble colonists bringing a load of hay for the general's horses," was Capt. Oyle's reply. He was anxious to lay eyes on the tall man with the white wig, blue jacket, etc.

"Very well," responded the sentry. "General Washington is on the other side. Two can cross to meet him, if you can get through the ice with that skiff," allowed the sentry, smiling in the darkness.

Capt. Oyle and Lt. Rumours dismounted and slid down the riverbank to a battered skiff. The river was a jumble of ice blocks, chips, and swirls as they picked their way across in the cold and dark. The captain thought about the advantage of wearing a wig during the icy winter— "My head would be wigwarm," he mused. A half hour later, the two reached the Pennsylvania shore and the colonial encampment.

As the Brits entered the light of dozens of campfires, Capt. Oyle looked around. Everywhere he looked, he saw a tall man with a white wig and long blue jacket, and at least twenty of the men were astride white horses!

Americans

As usual, HMS *Tortoise* was aground in the sand at dead low tide, her bow pointed out to sea, stern to the shore. In her current position, none of her broadside armament could be brought to bear on the shore. The crew left aboard in the captain's absence were complacent— "when the cat's away, the mice will play," was the crew's attitude. For all combatant purposes, HMS *Tortoise* was a sitting duck...er, tortoise.

Very quietly and stealthily, six colonial soldiers, plus fifteen local militiamen, crept down to the Shedagat shore, taking cover among the stubby pines and dune grass along the beach opposite the helpless, and hapless, *Tortoise*. Three managed to reposition Amador's beached cannon to face the grounded British blockader.

At the signal, the hoot of a (human) owl, the cannon roared with a hot shot at near point-blank range, about seventy-five feet, and took out the ship's mizzen mast and helm. The second heated incendiary ball set *Tortoise* afire. Her crew, taken totally by surprise, offered no resistance and dropped or leapt overboard on to the surrounding sands. Just as they did so, a rowing craft towing three other boats appeared in the bright moonlight just off the drying sand. Those sailors closest to the water were able to read the large sign affixed on poles above the lead craft:

"Amador's Rent-A-Pinnace." Just below, in slightly smaller letters, was: "We take Master Quid and Discover Coine." Any hesitation on the crew's part was demolished along with the ship when the fire reached the powder magazine. His Majesty's Ship, *Tortoise*, disintegrated into kindling and toothpicks as her crew scrambled into Amador's waiting rental fleet. Occasional musket fire over their heads encouraged their rapid exodus, stage seaward.

British

Capt. Oyle stood staring—bewildered, flummoxed, and confounded—choose any of the preceding. He looked and counted; seventy-five men in sight fit the limited description of General Washington that his spies had provided him. There couldn't possibly be seventy-five George Washingtons!

He finally stammered to a sentry, "I need to meet General Washington."

The sentry grinned and responded, "There he is—take your pick!" as his hand swept across the field of vision.

308

Capt. Oyle inwardly groaned and thought fast. "We have hay for the horses, but also we have a tooth specialist sent by Franklin himself as part of your VFW health plan (VFW = Valley Forge Winterers). We need to see which men might be eligible to exchange their wooden teeth for new, hand-carved whale-tooth ivory ones." Capt. Oyle took a deep breath, fingers crossed, and waited as his men looked toward each other with puzzled expressions.

"I see. I will circulate the word while you ready yourselves at that table," the sentry replied while indicating a nearby campsite.

Once the sentry had ambled off, Capt. Oyle barked at one of the so-called women in the wagon, "Screwluce...uh, Miss Luce, will you please come down for duty." Ceder Screwluce was the ship's carpenter who occasionally pulled teeth and at least knew something about wood. "You're going to inspect teeth, Screwluce, so look lively...and womanly."

About 30 minutes later a line of seventy-five Washington look-alikes had formed at the inspection table. Each of the seventy-five presented one or more wooden teeth while displaying significant gaps in their dentition. By the end of the "eligibility inspections," Capt. Oyle felt deep dismay.

"This just won't do," he mused to himself. "They all have bad teeth... and worse breath."

Most of the interviewees had a hard time keeping a straight face while interacting with the decidedly unattractive and gravelly voiced "Miss Luce." Capt. Oyle's conclusion? Nothing gained so far. Time to sleep; try again tomorrow.

Americans

With the *Tortoise* now in shambles, the colonial forces snuck back to Shedagat and Amador's landing to await the British tars now afloat in

The *Tortoise* and the Hair

Amador's rental fleet. Once landed, they would be taken captive for possible prisoner exchange, or at least for nonpayment of boat rental fees!

British

By the next morning, Capt. Oyle had developed a new strategy, and the spirit of amusement had spread throughout the colonists' encampment. They cheerfully anticipated the Brits' next play, not long in coming.

Capt. Oyle approached the familiar sentry. "We understand that the winning ticket for the latest drawing of the Colonies Megahundreds Jackpot was sold to someone in the camp, and we've been authorized to check the ID's of all prospective winners of the 121 pounds sterling." Capt. Oyle flashed a paper document so quickly that the sentry would not have been able to read it even if he had known how to read. The paper actually was the shopping receipt from the Goode Will Storre.

When the time came, the seventy-five or so white-wigged warriors lined up for ID and ticket checks. After the first two dozen checks, though, the captain abandoned any hope of zeroing in on his quarry—all ID's identified the bearer as "George Washington," and not one colonist had purchased a ticket for the Crown's weekly lottery.

The British captain's next strategy was to try to appeal to the general's vanity. Capt. Oyle announced the search for a face to be imprinted on eventual colonial one-dollar bills—future paper money. Lt. Rumours would be presented as the artist to do the portrait rendering, even though he protested to his captain, "But sir, I can barely draw a stick figure!" Alas, all seventy-five George Washingtons volunteered.

Capt. Oyle had run out of ready ideas. He decided to leave the colonists' camp temporarily and withdraw to a site a few miles away. Lt. Rumours would be left behind as a mole, signing up with Washington's troops as a poor dirt farmer named Farmworthy Pigge. He was to gather information to identify and locate the real General Washington and sneak off periodically to report back to Capt. Oyle.

His full report two days later revealed the following: General Washington—the real one—had just returned to camp; he had been away to requisition supplies and arrange the eventual return of seventy-five white wigs.

Also, Washington would be crossing the Delaware River soon in a Durham Boat with seating for twenty, but twenty-one soldiers were to be in the boat. Being a democratic soul, Washington had the twenty-one, which included himself, draw straws to see who would go without a seat. Washington himself drew the short straw; he would be the one standing up in the boat, sans life jacket, making him easy to spot.

Americans

Amador was in a unique position to facilitate the likely encounter between English and colonial forces—equally seemingly (dis)trusted by both sides, although his ultimate sympathies lay with the rebels.

Forty-eight of HMS *Tortoise's* sixty crew were now captive in Shedagat village, held under the watchful eyes of a dozen colonial militiamen. The rebels, with Amador's assistance, arranged for an exchange of supposedly secret messages between Capt. Oyle's party of twelve and the captive forty-eight; the *Tortoise* had been left greatly undermanned and under the weather for her insignificant duty of blockading Shedagat.

Capt. Oyle's supposed message urged his crew to come to his aid—he had been captured by Washington's troops but was lightly guarded. No awareness of the demise of his ship was evident.

The alleged message to Capt. Oyle was that his crew had escaped and was coming to help Capt. Oyle's party to capture General Washington while crossing the river. They would bring small boats and land upstream from the anticipated crossing site. The message energized the despondent crew, who were sure of support from Amador, to whom they already were in debt.

To make the crew's escape seem more convincing, Amador arranged for a binge party at the Boor's Tale, leaving only one sleepy sentry on duty that night. He also had placed three shallops on wagon frames and hitched horses or camels to each of the three wagons.

Ensign William "Willie" Hallaton had been left in charge as second mate on the *Tortoise*. He would lead the crew on its rescue expedition, guided by an experienced Delaware native, Sacapotatoes. [*OMG, Perry!!! Ha!*] The guide had been provided surreptitiously with detailed instructions couriered from General Washington himself.

The "escape" happened as expected, with the one guard dozing after downing his flask full of rum. The three wagons set out on time, on the same road that Capt. Oyle's force had taken initially. They passed the poetic signs, which now displayed a new rhyme:

The British navy had a boat
Its sailors tried to keep afloat
Some rebels fired a burning load
That made the English ship explode!
Burma Shave

The British sailors were not amused…

Miles down the road their path diverged to follow a long rough trail northwest. Sacapotatoes led the crew and wagon-boats to an area of icy calm water just below a mill dam on the upper Delaware River. From there they would drift downstream to surprise Washington's troops as they crossed the river, expected to be lightly armed and busy rowing. Maybe a good plan, questionable execution. After the shallops were launched, Sacapotatoes disappeared into the brush.

Willie split the forty-eight sailors into three groups of sixteen to a boat as they boarded and took seats to row. They all figured on a smooth, easy drift downstream, letting the current do most of the work. They did not account for how upstream they actually were, or for an ice-choked water-course.

Shortly after setting out, the English sailors heard a distant roaring ahead. As they grew closer to the sound, anxiety set in, the tars having no experience with icy river travel, but some with raging surf. Drifting around a wide bend, the source of the sound became evident—rocks, rapids, ice chunks, and swirling waters!

The first boat bounced off several boulders before spinning and cap-sizing, dumping her crew into the frigid water, hanging on to the upturned shallop for dear life. Boat 2 spun sideways and became wedged across the flow in time for Boat 3 to ram it amidships, splintering the bow of Boat 3 and demolishing the port side of Boat 2. Both groups of sailors ended up clinging to boat parts as they bounced off the rest of the rocks and dropped over a short falls to land in a calmer, very cold pool below the cataract.

The forty-eight bedraggled, nearly frozen Brits managed to drag themselves and each other out of the current onto the east shore, only to see a weathered sign nailed to a waterside tree:

Drowning of or by British soldiers strictly prohibited!
Per order of His Majesty King George

Willie immediately thought to himself, "I hope that includes sailors, too."

In a clearing just south along the riverbank the sailors encountered a much larger, newer sign:

Amador's Native Canoe Rental Livery
We take Master Quid, Discover Coine, and American Expence

Coincidently (maybe), Amador himself just happened to be present to negotiate with nearly hypothermic Ens. Willie Hallaton on behalf of the soggy and shivering sailors under his command. Yes, Amador was willing to bill the Crown for use of, and damages to, the three shallops, plus rental of a variety of canoes. Some of the craft were really intended for two, but could cram in three, while the largest were twelve-man war canoes.

Ten canoes altogether left the shore to continue the ice-dodging voyage downstream. The sailors set off optimistically but soon became misty optically as a light ground fog crept along the river's surface. The ocean-going tars were not prepared for the relative instability of their new vessels. Two capsized before reaching midstream.

Seeing the quick capsizes, one of the sailors in Willie's canoe started to curse and complain bitterly. Willie ruefully reflected, "Fine thing—I've got a tippy canoe and whiner, too."

Obscured in the moving haze was a second set of rapids, the sound also muffled by the fog. None of the rentals reached General Washington's location in an upright and dry orientation. To remain afloat, the English sailors clung to the swamped canoes as they continued to drift with the frigid current, trying to avoid ice blocks.

They Meet

General George Washington stood on a small rise in the woods overlooking the Delaware River along with two other men, recently arrived Colonial Militia Major Josiah Amador and colonial scout, Sacapotatoes. All three gazed out at the water and watched British sailor heads, ice, and swamped canoes drift by with the flow...and floes.

The general turned to Sacapotatoes and instructed, "Go ahead down to Capt. Oyle's men hidden in the trees and let them know that they'll need to rescue their rescue party as they float by. We wouldn't want any of the sailors to drown—the Crown prohibits that!" Washington smirked at that last statement.

"Major, round up your men to secure the British crew once they've thawed and dried off. They will need to help you clean up the English wreckage and litter on Shedagat Beach as prisoners of war," Washington continued. "I will try to get my crew out on the river to bop a few British heads as we cross. I'll have the men wear their wigs to help keep their heads warm. I'll stand in the bow and help bop."

Washington's nickname of "Big Bopper" was short-lived, however, but it is thought that the crossing might have inspired the modern amusement park game, Whack-a-Mole.

George Washington's crossing of the Delaware River to attack a Hessian force in Trenton, New Jersey, is well documented. Emanuel Leutze's 1851 painting, *Washington Crossing the Delaware*, is now displayed at the Metropolitan Museum of Art, but for some reason depicts only the river ice and not the bobbing British heads.

Major Amador's subsequent bill to the Crown is reproduced here:

315

Bill

Amador Enterprises
Major Josiah Amador, Proprietor
11762 Post Road
Shedagat Beach, New Jersey

Shallop rental	3 x 5 pounds	=	15 pounds
Canoe rental	10 x 2 pounds	=	20 pounds
Shallops destroyed	3 x 12 pounds	=	36 pounds
Sailor rescues	48 x 1 pound	=	48 pounds
Wagon rentals	3 x 6 pounds	=	18 pounds
Guide fee	1 x 3 pounds	=	3 pounds

Seventy-five white, powdered wigs with ponytails and ribbons

= 2 pounds

Demolition of one impediment to colonial free navigation (HMS Tortoise) = 100 pounds

Beach clean-up	=	10 pounds
Incendiary cannon balls (two)	=	6 pence
Total due	=	252 pounds, 6 pence

There is no record of the bill ever being paid. The original is currently in the Shedagat Beach Community Museum and Public Restrooms, kept for viewing under glass, next to an original colonial wig.

Stock Sail

"I'm telling you, gentlemen, this app is the wave of the future—the biggest thing on the water since pickled herring!"

The words waxed poetic off the lips of Borus Hyan Mitey Ritch as he pontificated at the bar of the Bufflehead Beach Yacht Club (BBYC). Borus, known among his acquaintances (he had no real friends) behind his back as "BM," was clearly wound up about his latest yacht and its associated electronic complexities—and his related stock purchase.

The new 85-foot yacht, a custom-build from Norway, was considered an "expedition ship", heavily constructed and capable of a 6,000-mile range at its 12-knot cruising speed. Powered with a pair of 1,350 hp MAN diesels with IPS pod drives (props facing forward), it was Borus's pride and joy, and it occupied the premier slip at the BBYC's marina in full view of visitors and harbor-gazers.

His audience collectively and inwardly groaned as Borus rambled on to impress those still present:

"This new app was developed by twin brothers, Dexter and Heesa Nurdstrom, up in Fisherman's Folly, Maine. The beta (test) version is built into the yacht and controls literally *everything* on the vessel! It's called Boatremote (BR), and the joystick helm feature is Boatremoteafloat (BRA). The software is named Strategic Operational Kinesthetic Integrated Transmission On Marine Electronics—SOKITOME. It's pure genius!

"With it, from almost anywhere, I have smartphone control of engines, steering, alarms (fire, intrusion, bilge pump, low oil or cooling water, collision, SOS, and others), anchor windlass, running and cabin lights, on/off for radios, TVs, music, and others, radar and AIS functions, dinghy crane and storage, fax machine, and searchlight controls. Twenty-four cameras and over 100 sensors monitor every function.

"It also provides stock quotes, birthday reminders, weather forecasts, telephone calls to mother, alarm clock, and it tapes Patriots, Red Sox, Bruins, and Celtics games. Oh, I almost forgot—it can start my Bentley and back it out of the garage, start the dinghy outboard and steer the tender, start the onboard coffee-maker, pour on-tap drinks at the yacht's bar, and roll down the bed covers!"

One of the reluctant audience whispered to a compatriot, "Yeah, and it'd probably satisfy his wife if he had one!"

Fellow club members had tolerated Borus's monologues many times. For all his egotistical faults, he was an excellent, if not respected, stock-broker, who had made fortunes for himself and many other BBYC members over the years.

Borus now was the controlling partner of the venerable firm Izzy, Ritch, Sumsei, & Howe, having bought out all other parties. His new yacht, *Stock Sail*, was pure powerboat, but he liked the pun.

"If any of you guys want to buy in to this new start-up, let me know—they'll be big in no time, once this new app system proves itself. Everything is controlled by this little phone," Borus enthused, holding up the thin, light, floatable, bulletproof and waterproof smartphone. "Come by when *Stock Sail* is getting ready to pull out; I'll demonstrate some features for you.

"I have so much faith in SOKITOME that I've let my captain go. I can run the whole boat! I just kept my cook, Addie Poez, and one deckhand... I forget his name. He doesn't cost much."

The last four hangers-on at the bar excused themselves one by one, leaving Borus fingering his smartphone to unlock his car doors for the short ride to his harborside 22-room "cottage" (as he called it), with a great view of the marina and the sparkling *Stock Sail*.

For several days after her delivery to her new home port, gawkers strolled by to admire the imposing yacht, blissfully unaware of her electronic complexity—and dependency. Then came July 14 and a call from Bufflehead Beach's Harbormaster, Castor Jigg.

The occasion for the call began innocently enough. Borus lived alone in his sprawling house, devoid of human companionship, but accompanied by two rambunctious cats, Bullion and Bitcoin, and one enormous and cantankerous canine, Bull Market— "Bull" for short, a fair representation of the dog's character.

On the 10 a.m. hour on July 14, Borus made a call to his main office on Wall Street in the city. Needing to check some figures from a file in his home office, he laid his smartphone down on the grand piano (which he didn't know how to play—it was just for show), neglecting in his haste to tap either the pause or lock "buttons" on the screen.

While he rummaged through the requisite file folder, the phone screen played out a colorful and light-changing screen symphony of sorts, attracting the attention of a roaming and playful Bitcoin. Leaping onto the piano and then vertically off the surface, Bitcoin pounced onto the phone with all four paws. The phone withstood the attack but slid sideways off the piano onto the floor. In the process, one paw contacted a boat-shaped icon labeled "BR."

The SOKITOME app now activated, Bullion's leap onto the skittering phone touched another icon on the newly revealed BR screen and, one-half mile away, two MAN diesels rumbled to life. Addie was the only one aboard, blissfully asleep at the time.

The muffled sounds of the yacht's engines did not disturb Addie's sleep, but the feeling of her bed covers being rolled back did. The chill on her naked, rotund form caused a mighty heave upright and out of bed, accompanied by raucous alarms causing the woodwork to tremble. Addie's only waking-fog conclusion was that the owner must have come aboard, and the yacht was about to explode!

Addie was a very recent addition to *Stock Sail's* revised crew. In a fit of competitive fervor, Borus had lured her away from Hiram Cheepe's 105-foot yacht, *Gallivanting Gourmet*, with promises of higher salary, less work, and a permanent cabin of her own. He didn't even know if she could cook. Hiram was a rival stockbroker; that's all the move needed. While being interviewed, Borus had asked Addie if she occasionally "enjoyed bouts of *mal de mer*"; not being up on the finer points of nautical life, Addie figured that it must be some kind of French dish, and she could produce it if Borus wanted.

Back at the manse, Bullion and Bitcoin were having fun with their new flat toy that kept changing colors and pictures as they batted at it. Borus was engrossed in his search, very much unaware of his cats' capers. Bull, however, was on the alert.

Hearing sounds of cat play and reasoning canine-wise, "Why should cats have all the fun?" Bull charged into the living room and, barreling over the felines, snatched the smartphone into his powerful jaws and made a beeline for the pet door to the outside world. As he scampered, he readjusted the position of the phone between his teeth several times, contacting more colorful icons and "buttons."

The unintended results one-half mile away were instantaneous and dramatic. Addie faintly heard the MANs rev up and sensed the changed motion of the boat. Anxious to leave the confinement of her restraining slip, albeit wind-and-current-free, *Stock Sail* eased into reverse at the same time SOKITOME's BRA released her breast lines and snapped her light bow and stern tethers, 24 cameras guiding *Stock Sail's* careful exit.

On his part, Bull found his newly snatched toy to be remarkably resistant to his normally effective chewing. All that happened was that the irritating screen colors kept changing. Considerably irked, Bull renewed his attack, chomping and flinging the object in his fury.

Now free of her slip, Borus's electronically controlled pride started a string of most amazing and baffling maneuvers mid-harbor. Spinning in ever-widening circles, *Stock Sail* accosted a gaggle of BBYC sailing dinghies captained by the club's junior sailors, scattering them like so many ducklings panicked by a circling hawk. Two capsized during the onslaught.

In apparent response (of victory?), raucous alarms rang out all over the invader, with lights flashing and wheelhouse-top searchlight spinning dizzily. During the din, Addie struggled up from below and made her way to where her boss/captain should have been to find the wheelhouse empty...and locked. Her station was clearly underway, but why?

Making her way to the galley, her official charge, addled Addie found the coffeemaker spewing coffee onto the counter and deck, and the microwave heating up its emptiness. Worse, the galley fire suppression system was dousing the electric cooktop with foul-smelling foam despite the stove's appearing to be off. Addie dashed for the outside deck, wondering what on earth—on water, that is—was happening!

It was when the harbor current carried *Stock Sail* among the moorage field that all hell really broke loose, and the Harbormaster became involved—not totally by choice. Castor witnessed the scattering of the junior sailing fleet and directed his outboard-powered skiff toward the offending yacht, expecting to have serious words with its owner/skipper. It was when he drew alongside the veering bow that *Stock Sail's* anchor windlass was triggered, and 150 pounds of anchor dropped down and through the bottom of Castor's skiff, followed by 600 feet of brand-new chain.

With his boat rapidly taking on harbor water, Castor grabbed hold of the dock line still dangling from the yacht's bow, complete with metal cleat and bits of dock timber still attached. With considerable effort, Harbormaster Jigg managed to haul himself to the yacht's rail and slid over it onto the deck—to be met by the raucous intrusion alarm and a blast from an anti-intruder water cannon, which pinned him to the gunnel bulwark.

Bull, of course, had no idea what havoc his antics with the smartphone/toy were creating, but by the time he reached the beach, he'd had it with the phone and ambled off to chase crabs and waves. The phone sat on a bed of seaweed courtesy of the outgoing tide while Castor, aboard *Stock Sail*, managed to crawl out from under the water cannon's barrage.

Dripping his shaky way to the bridge, Castor ran head-on into a frantic Addie. "Who are *you*?" she blurted out— "and what have you done to my ship?" Clueless Castor had no immediate reply as he wiped his eyes clear to gaze on the plump woman addressing him.

Finally, he gathered himself to speak. "Where is the captain? I'm the Harbormaster. I need to talk to him—now!"

Addie dissolved into a waterfall of tears. "I don't know! The boat's going crazy, and I can't find Mr. Ritch!"

Hoping that its soaking hadn't disabled his cell phone, Castor looked up Borus's saved number and pressed. A ring on a pile of seaweed went unanswered, but it did attract the notice of a low-flying gull. The shiny, noisy object was too good to resist—maybe a new kind of fish or clam? Off the phone flew, apparently demonstrating the lightness of its compact design.

Afloat, *Stock Sail's* 24 high-resolution cameras inexplicably shut down, leaving the circling vessel effectively blind, wheelhouse still locked. Moments later, both Castor and Addie were mystified when the yacht suddenly straightened its course after terrifying Addie and the junior fleet by its circular forays. The gull was totally unaware of its influence on the course change, of course.

Having no luck reaching Borus's portable phone, Castor next tried Borus's office; no luck there either, but Castor was given a number for a never-used (or removed) landline phone to Borus's house. The phone rang just as Borus finally found the file information he had been seeking—and just as his beloved *Stock Sail* overran a moored 26-foot 1917 Crowninshield gaff sloop.

Before Castor could speak, Borus impatiently grilled Castor, "Why are you calling me on *this* phone? I *never* use this phone!"

"There's a problem with your boat, sir," Castor meekly replied. "She's run amok, I think." A crunch emanated from the bow at that moment—scratch one 21-foot inboard launch.

Not sensing the gravity in Castor's verbal expression, Borus glanced about for his smartphone; it surely would inform him of any significant issues with his new yacht—after all, there were 24 cameras and over 100 sensors keeping watch! A cursory scan yielded no cell phone, just two indolent cats.

A glance out a water-side window was no help. The part of the harbor now occupied by his rampaging 85-footer was out of view. "What seems to be the problem, Mr. Jigg?" Borus impatiently asked.

"You'd better come down to the club and see for yourself, sir. I'm not 'zactly sure how to describe it," Castor noted apologetically. "It's a mess, sir."

The gull lost interest in its shiny find after a few minutes of burdened flight. The drop from 28 feet up did no harm, and the harbor seals on the ledge below were pleased with their new, curious distraction. Poking and prodding with moist noses did little for the seals but wonders for *Stock Sail*.

All of the noisy alarms shut down, the water cannon ceased its own deafening roar, the coffee-maker took a break, the lights went off and, most importantly, the wheelhouse doors unlocked loudly enough for Castor and Addie to hear.

Castor slid the portside door open and quickly stepped in. The bewildered look on the Harbormaster's face told the tale: there was no steering wheel, no compass, no observable gauges, or engine controls. He saw only a small vertical handle in front of three large screens filled with indecipherable data, charts, and diagrams. "Holy ravioli!" was his only printable thought.

Displaying their noteworthy senses of play and mirth, the seals butted and bandied about their newly acquired toy. It wasn't a clam, it wasn't a can, it wasn't some Spam. What was it, Sam I am? (Apologies to Dr. Seuss).

What it was was the latest in remote technology for nautical applications, the brainchild of two techno-nerds, bankrolled by the phone's –and its associated yacht's—owner, now frantically searching his home for said smartphone, still unaware of his vessel's departure from its marina slip and all rational control!

Much like one of Newton's laws, each action of the playful seals resulted in a reaction across the harbor. Almost as if on rails, the ponderous *Stock Sail*, at half throttle, mowed its way through the moored boats. In her bilge, seacocks opened and closed much like a chorus of gulping scallops, occasionally depriving the two MANs of necessary cooling water, setting off fresh alarms in the wheelhouse. Castor heard the sound and noticed the red flashes on one screen but was totally lost in trying to make sense of it all. Addie, standing behind Castor, smelled the smoke first.

Totally frustrated at being unable to locate his misplaced magic phone, Borus made his way to the BBYC to find an empty slip where his equally magic yacht should be. A sustained perusal of the harbor, however, brought his ship into focus just as *Stock Sail* ran down a 28-foot lobster boat, briefly tangling one of her forward-facing props in the unfortunate lobster boat's mooring chain—enough to change *Stock Sail's* course and send her aground on a mid-harbor spoils bank at dead low tide. Her engines continued to churn up mud as they bordered on catastrophic over-heating.

Borus frantically waved down and bellowed for the BBYC club launch to take him to his obviously distressed mega-money nautical investment. "To the *Stock Sail* out there, and step on it!" Borus shouted at the 18-year-old launch operator.

"Yes, *sir!*" shouted the hyper-aroused teen in return. The launch streaked away from the BBYC float and easily broke the "Headway Only" speed restriction in making a hasty approach to the still-churning 85-foot-er. Normally, his smartphone control would open a bulwark gate and drop down a set of steps but, lacking the phone, this clearly was no normal occasion! Standing on the launch's gunnel and hoisted from behind by its burly and highly motivated helmsman, Borus struggled over *Stock Sail's* rail and was immediately assaulted by a screaming siren and a paralyzing water cannon deluge!

Barely able to keep his mouth open, Borus shrieked, "Help!" followed by a second, barely gurgled, "Turn. It. Off!"

Looking down from a deck above, Castor shrugged helplessly and hollered, "How?"

"I (gurgle)...don't (sputter)...know!" Borus managed to gulp out.

"I…" the rest was lost in a spray of nearly bullet-speed water as Borus tried to turn to face the voice from above.

Minutes later, Borus felt an arm reach out to him amid the steady stream, grasp the ankle of one leg, and unceremoniously drag him from near drowning. Once Borus was clear of the powerful cannon current, it suddenly shut down—the silence seemed deafening.

Borus made a feeble attempt to restore some semblance of dignity while standing up, only to slip and lunge backward to bowl over the just arriving Addie.

"Good catch, miss!" Castor exclaimed as Borus rolled off his soft-bellied cook and attempted to get both upright.

"What's happening?" both Borus and Castor asked simultaneously. Just then, the *Stock Sail* lurched as she churned her way forward in the mud on the rising tide. Traces of smoke began to waft up as her engines once again exceeded heat limits, causing two events, one more welcome than the other: her MANs automatically shut down, and the yacht's fire suppression system cut loose with an exuberant display of water and foam all over the vessel. Oh, and a solitary alarm rang out from several speakers located strategically on all three decks.

Nearly a mile away, on a harbor ledge called, "Miser's Misery," two young seals had managed to flip Borus's smartphone upside down. Now lacking view of the shiny, ever-changing screen, one seal lost interest. The other snatched the glistening black phone and dove into the murky harbor waters, making no contact with any screen icons.

Four minutes after being triggered, the fire suppression and alarm systems shut down. The silence was eerie; no one dared speak, waiting for some new untoward event to occur. Without a word, Borus climbed to the wheelhouse to find that the three large touchscreens refused to respond to any touch commands; the SOKITOME system seemed frozen.

On the rising tide, it took little effort to remove Borus's dead-in-the-water yacht from its spoils bank perch and tow it to slip #1 at the BBYC. With considerable self-consciousness, a subdued Borus made his way to the club bar to harness a stiff libation—humble pie was definitely not his strong suit.

"Whatsamatter, sport?" one acquaintance at the bar queried in mock sympathy.

"Tough luck, Borus old man," chortled another.

The best Borus could muster in reply was, "Minor glitch—just working out the beta bugs. You'll see...soon, I hope," Borus muttered under his breath.

His next move was to commandeer the club telephone to place a call to Fisherman's Folly, Maine. Dexter answered the phone.

"Nurdstrom residence and shop, Dexter here," he cooed into the receiver, removing the lollipop from his sticky lips. The voice on the other end shook him.

"Dexter, this is Borus Ritch. You boys get down here pronto—even sooner!" Borus bellowed. "We've got a problem!"

"Something come up with the boat system?" Dexter innocently offered.

"Yeah, you could say that," Borus fumed. "Just get here—quick!"

Things in Fisherman's Folly rarely happened with any haste. The technowizard Nurdstrom brothers had started out with a simple quest to assist the local commercial fisherfolk. The harbor at Fisherman's Folly was well protected from the open ocean but was strewn with dangerous ledges and solitary underwater pinnacles—a labyrinth that gave rise to the harbor's original moniker of "Fisherman's Fright." The Nurdstroms simply had wanted to develop an effective harbor navigation system...and then one thing led to another in their fertile craniums. Word drifted on to

Borus, and the rest is history, as they say, with Mr. Ritch providing substantial development funds.

Considerably beholden to Borus, the twins packed up tools, spare parts, and a modicum of personal items in canvas sacks and hit Route 1 south ASAP. Three and one-half hours later, their 27-year-old Volvo pulled into the BBYC parking lot to park next to Borus's immaculate silvery-gray Bentley.

Wasting no time, Borus virtually dragged the Nurdstroms down the dock and onto the moribund *Stock Sail*. "Fix her!" was his terse directive.

The twins had only one real focus in their lives: computer electronics. They were oblivious to the usual pursuits of 20-somethings: cars, booze, sports, girls...the order hardly mattered, so...

Borus was surprised to listen to Heesa's diagnosis:

"I'm afraid that we're going to have to remove her BRA and rig up some other way to temporarily support her BOOBS."

"Her *what*?" Borus croaked.

"Her BOOBS—her Basic Onboard Operating Battery System," Dexter simply explained. "Her BRA needs to be reconfigured. It's developed what we call 'SAG,' System Accumulated Glitches, a software problem."

Somewhere toward Provincetown a young seal made a successful maneuver to dodge a feeding nine-foot mako shark, while dropping the metallic item that it had kept clenched in its teeth since leaving Bufflehead Bay. Slowly sinking, the smartphone was gobbled down by the frustrated shark, who continued to seek more satisfying quarry off the shores of Cape Cod.

Six hours passed, and the Nurdstroms reassembled the helm consoles, then reported back to an impatiently waiting Borus:

"She's done, Mr. Ritch," Dexter began. "We've uploaded some new software to give her BOOBS a lift, and her BRA's back on. There shouldn't be any SAG," Dexter reassured Borus.

Borus just shook his head and handed over a substantial check, hoping that his beloved *Stock Sail* would be problem-free in the future. He patted her varnished bulwark rail in satisfaction as a trauma-recovering Addie delivered a fresh cup of coffee courtesy of the now-tamed coffeemaker.

Far at sea, four eager fishermen aboard the 38-foot *Shark Seeker* fought and won a two-hour struggle with what turned out to be a nine-foot mako. The subdued shark would bring premium pay—mako meat is good eating.

As the shark catch was being cleaned to be ready for icing down, a small object dropped out onto the gurry-slimed deck.

"Well, would you look at that! The critter swallowed someone's cell phone—hopefully not its owner, too," one sharker remarked.

"Wouldn't it be amazing if it still worked?" a second chimed in. "Check it out."

"Screen's lit. Battery must still be good—how 'bout that!"

"It's one o' them smartphones like you see on TV," the second sharker noted. "Just touch the screen."

To the surprise of all four aboard, the screen seemed to come to life with a finger tap. Icons filled the screen; one in particular attracted the most attention, however—the one that looked like a little boat.

Tap, and many miles landward in Bufflehead Beach, two MAN diesels roared to life...

The Outcome:
An Emotionally Satisfying Short Story for Those with Little Time Available for Extensive Nautically Related Reading

Once upon a time they sailed happily ever after.

Backword

It has been suggested that a censor is a person who can find three meanings to a passage that only has two. The same may be said for some college English professors.

For those who insist on ignoring the disclaimer at the beginning of this book and keep trying to find meaning between the lines of these stories, this page is dedicated.

_____

_____

Meaning

_____

_____

About the Author

Although he prefers to deny it, citing the Fifth Amendment, these stories apparently did issue forth from his bizarre imagination and authorship, judging from the original manuscripts clearly scribbled in Perry's barely decipherable hieroglyphics, which greatly challenged his typist. He continues to assert that a keen sense of humor is an important life tool, right up there with band saws, block planes, chisels, caulking irons, sandpaper, and toilet paper.

Now well along on the seas of life, Perry is a retired clinical/school psychologist and college instructor, with additional experience as a journalist, carpenter, and sailmaker. A lifelong sailor (and occasional owner of 36 boats at last count), he also played soccer for 49 years, and still enjoys railroads (both model and real), nautical history, and geology as hobbies.